THE ICE QUEEN'S REVENGE

THE ICE QUEEN'S REVENGE

THE KYPRIAN PROPHECY BOOK 4

KYLIE FENNELL

Lorikeet
inK

Published by Lorikeet Ink, Brisbane (Yuggera and Turrbal Country), Australia. The publisher acknowledges the Aboriginal and Torres Strait Islander peoples – the Traditional Custodians of the lands on which we live and work.

www.lorikeetink.com

First published in Australia in 2022.

ISBN 978-0-6488769-9-1 (eBook)

ISBN 978-0-6454052-0-0 (paperback)

A catalogue record for this book is available from the National Library of Australia.

Cover design by Jo Edgar-Baker

Maps by Dewi Hargreaves

Author photo by Marissa Powell

Ornamental break icon by Freepik via Flaticon.com

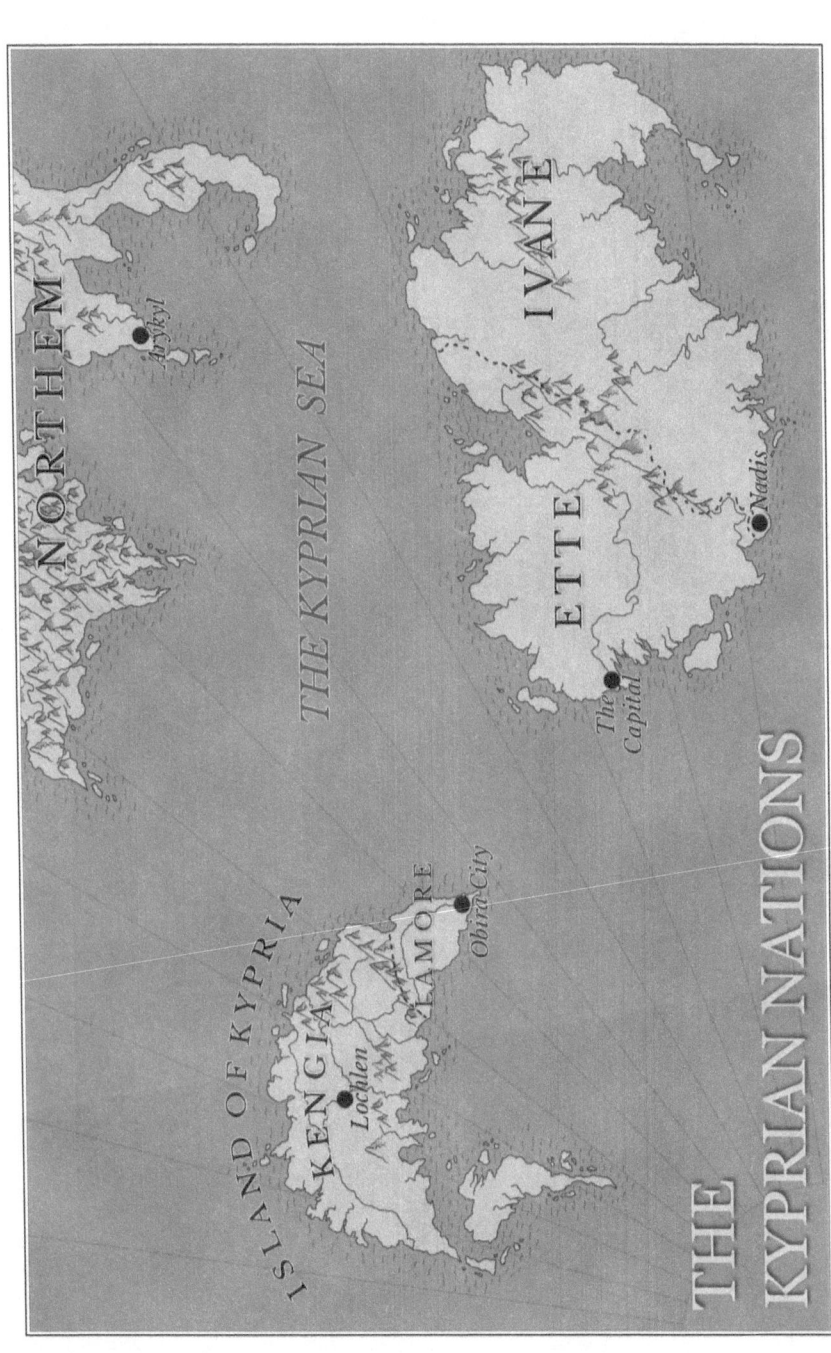

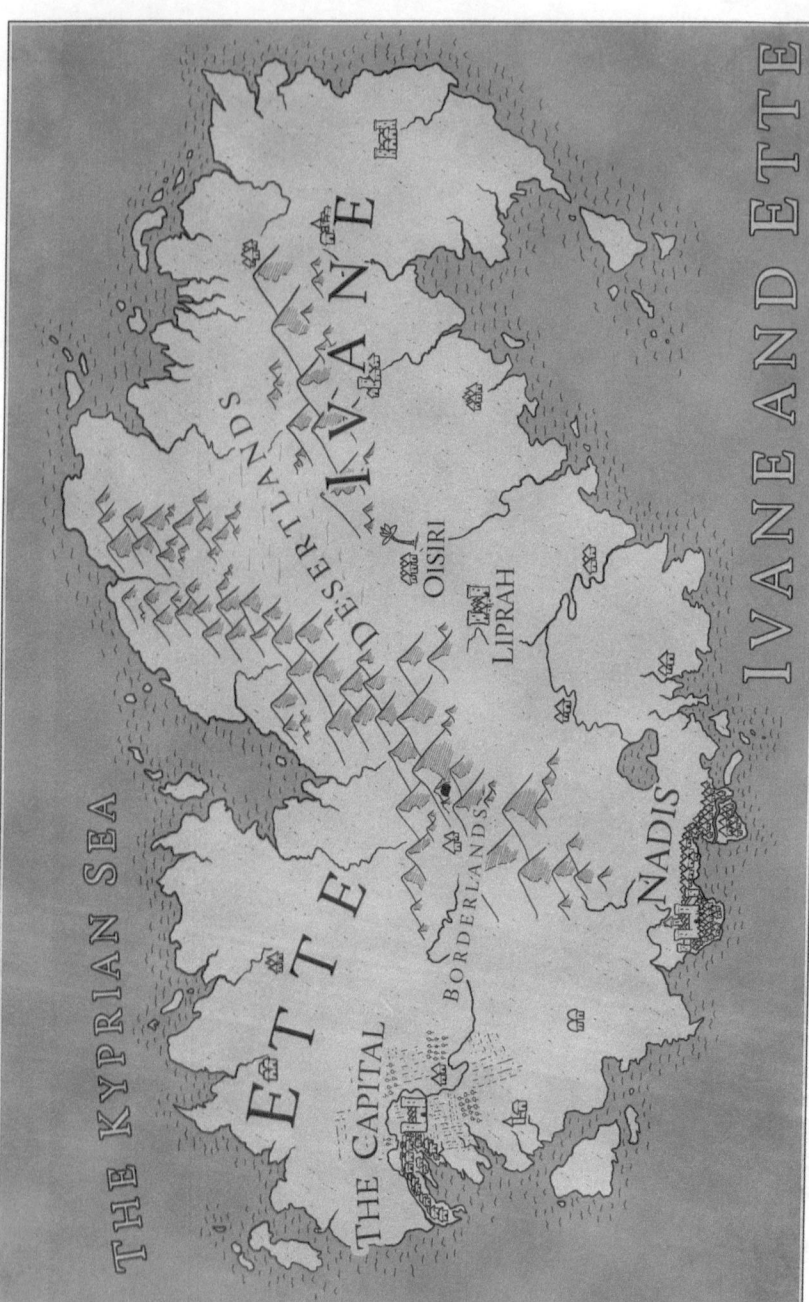

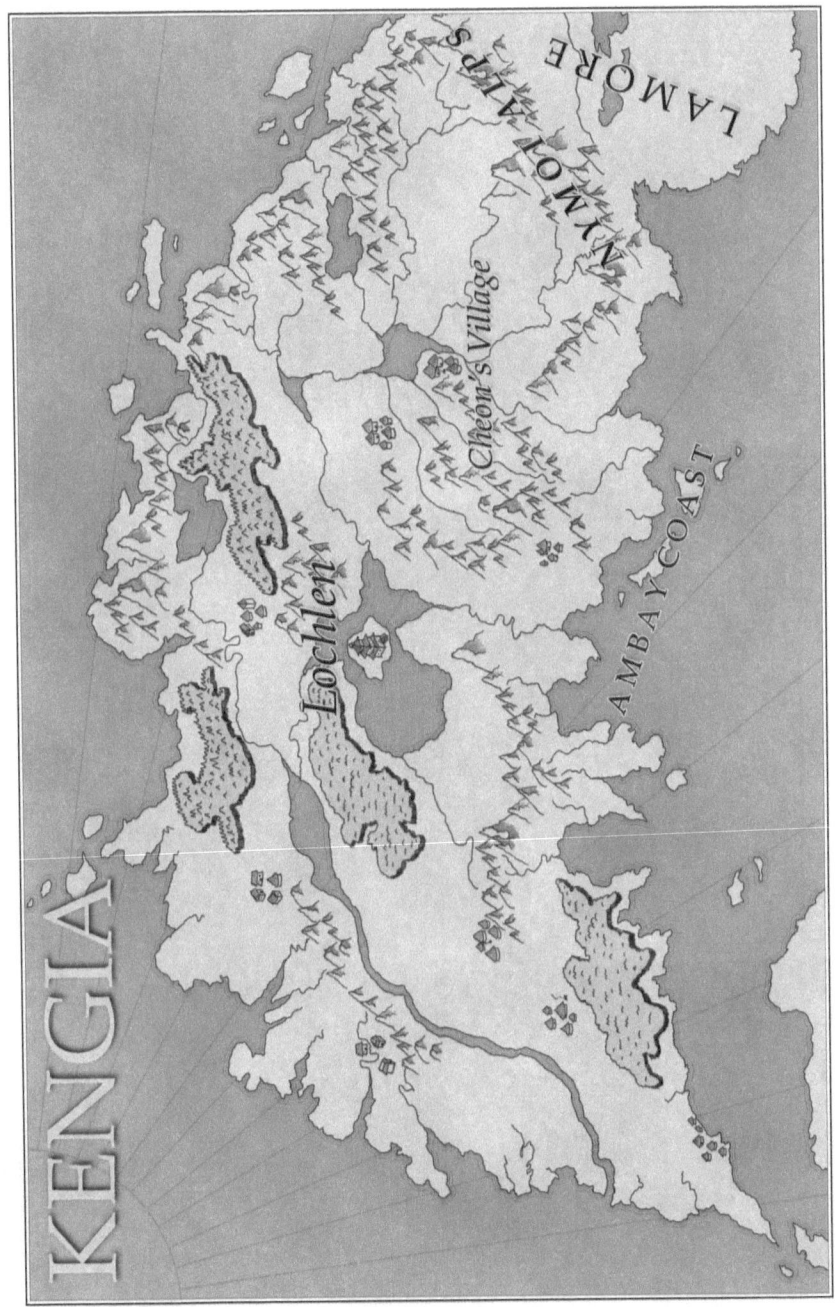

KENGIA

LAMORE

NYMOT ALPS

Cheon's Village

Lochlen

AMBAY COAST

1

*T*hose born with Northem blood in their veins viewed their country a particular way. They saw a savage beauty, a rawness in its never-ending frozen landscape. Jagged peaks and valleys forged from ice and rock; cracking, creaking glaciers – all as unforgiving and unyielding as the people who lived in the harshest of nations. It was a land wholly disinterested in supporting life, even for the people who idolised it.

A land where only the strong survived.

IT MAY HAVE BEEN spring in Northem, but it was still frigidly cold – the type of cold that burrowed its way into Theodora's bones, refusing to release her from its rimy claws. Snow still clung to the precariously rocky ground and ice hung from the hood of her cloak. Her father's narrowed gaze was on the grey clouds hanging low in the sky.

'There's a storm coming,' Horace declared. 'We should head back.'

The Huntmaster looked to Theodora for direction, but she shook her head. If she managed to hunt down the creature, she would surely rise in the estimation of all Northemers. The Huntmaster nodded and continued onward.

Theodora could almost hear her father's hackles rise. As the Lamorian King's former Chancellor, he wasn't accustomed to his orders not being followed – and was even less used to his daughter's orders being followed over his. But that was the reality for him in Northem. He was tolerated only because he was Theodora's father, kept under guard in his rooms except for the rare occasions when Theodora would take pity on him and invite him on an outing or a hunt.

Today they were hunting a rare snow leopard that had been terrorising local villages and killing stock. Malu's Huntmaster had been tracking the animal for days and was leading Horace and Theodora on horseback to a location a morning's ride from Arykyl, Northem's capital. Theodora was determined to hunt down the animal – she hoped it would help endear her to the Northem people, or at the very least prove she was worthy of their respect. *But why does it have to be so damn cold?*

Almost as if the land had read her mind, an icy gust of wind lifted a layer of snow from the ground, swirling into an eddy that blasted toward them. Theodora could barely see a foot in front of her, and the words *'Let's go back'* would have leapt from her tongue, but the Huntmaster spoke first.

'Stop here.'

He dismounted and inspected the ground, then scanned the immediate area, his eyes falling on a steep hillside to their right. Its icy surface glistened back at them. The Huntmaster grunted and collected his bow and arrow.

Theodora followed suit, but Horace shifted uncomfortably in his saddle. 'We're not climbing up that,' he asserted.

Again, the Huntmaster looked to Theodora for direction. She didn't relish the idea of negotiating the rocky incline, but she wasn't about to give up – or give in to her father's demands, for that matter.

'Lead the way,' she said to the Huntmaster in his own tongue, ignoring her father's grumbled objections.

Theodora followed the Huntmaster up the hillside, her father's panting and puffing filling the air at a distance behind her. Horace had never been a particularly fit man, but since being imprisoned in Northem he had done little but eat and drink, complaining that there was nothing else to do. The climbing was hard going, but by now Theodora was experienced in negotiating such conditions. She made it to the summit well before her father, but still doubled over to catch her breath. The Huntmaster immediately shushed her and pointed across the small valley before them to the opposite hillside.

At first, Theodora couldn't see anything amiss – but then, among the peak's snow-and-rock blanket, she caught it. A flash of white-and-black speckled fur. The snow leopard was loping across the hillside.

Theodora reached for her own bow and arrow and took up position. She tightened her gloved fingers around her bow, stretching the string back toward her. Eyes and arrow at the ready, waiting for the right shot, exactly as the Huntmaster had taught her.

The snow leopard slowed its pace, then stopped. The icy wind that had plagued them on the ground had petered out. It was silent apart from the sound of Horace's footfalls in the snow further down the hill. She wouldn't get a better opportunity. Theodora took a deep breath, but as she exhaled, the cat's head jolted upward and swung toward her, as if it had heard her breathe. Its eyes locked on her across the valley.

'Now,' the Huntmaster whispered in her ear, but she didn't move.

All she had to do was release the arrow – but the leopard's defiant gaze awoke something in her. Its blue eyes, the colour of Northem's glaciers. The colour of the Northem King's eyes. This was no ordinary creature. This was a creature that had somehow found a way not only to survive, but thrive in this place. Terrifying. Strong. Regal. Everything Theodora either was, or aspired to be.

The leopard sniffed the air but didn't drop its gaze, and in that moment they were one. A pair of survivors. Taking the creature's life would be like killing a part of herself. She willed the creature to run so she wouldn't have to go through with it, but it didn't move.

Theodora closed her eyes, reminding herself why she needed to succeed at this task. When she opened them again, something else caught her attention. Something moving near the snow leopard's back leg.

A cub. That was why it wasn't moving. The leopard was a mother protecting her child.

'Now,' the Huntmaster repeated, this time more forcefully.

Theodora bit her lip, wondering what would happen if she didn't take the shot. She scrutinised the Huntmaster's face. She sensed the frown beneath his unruly ginger beard. The disapproval in his eyes was unmistakable, but she knew he was loyal to Malu; while he may think she was weak, he wouldn't spread word of her failure if she didn't release the arrow.

The Huntmaster heaved a sigh and looked away, as if he couldn't bear to witness the shame she was bringing on them.

Her father's footsteps drew closer. Theodora knew he was brandishing one of the few firesky weapons they had managed to bring as they'd escaped Lamore; with Rea gone, they had no hope of creating new ones. Hunting was the only time Horace was allowed a weapon. Neither Theodora nor the Huntmaster feared he would use it on them to try to escape. Where would he go? But Theodora now wished she had only allowed him a bow and arrow. The leopard and her cub didn't stand a chance against the hand cannon.

She peered into the snow leopard's eyes, silently begging the creature to escape. Horace appeared by her side. His hawklike gaze immediately assessed the situation.

'What…are you…doing?' he snarled between gasps for air. 'Kill it. Kill it…now.'

Run. Theodora tried to send the desperate warning to the leopard via her thoughts, but it was no use. There was a loud bang beside her and a spray of scarlet on the opposite hillside. Theodora's ears rang and smoke from the firesky weapon caught in her throat, but her eyes were fixed on the gruesome scene across the valley.

The leopard lay motionless. The bow and arrow fell from Theodora's hands as a lone tear escaped her eye, freezing to a halt on her cheek. The Huntmaster grunted and indicated he was going to retrieve the kill.

Horace turned to Theodora, his nose and mouth screwed up like he had just eaten something sour.

'I thought I taught you better, but you are weak. You have wasted your position here and have done nothing to help me. You have brought nothing but dishonour to us.'

Something inside Theodora exploded like the hand cannon still in her father's grip. '*I* brought shame on this family?' she cried. 'What about you? You who led us into a war we could never win?'

Horace clicked his jaw from side to side. 'It would have been fine if Malu's Kengian girl had done what she was supposed to.'

'Leave Rea out of it!'

Horace raised a brow. 'There it is again. Weakness. Caring for the girl meant you couldn't see her for what she was – a duplicitous Kengian.'

Theodora's hands curled into fists by her sides. 'You wouldn't even be alive if it weren't for me. I'm the one who brought you here. I'm the one who saved you.'

'Saved me!' Horace scoffed. 'I'm a prisoner. A valuable resource wasted. The Northemers can still prevail, but Malu needs guidance. *My* guidance.'

It was quite remarkable that Horace's imprisonment hadn't affected his ego. He continually demanded that Theodora speak to Malu on his behalf and ask not only for his release, but for a place on the Northem Council made up of the country's clan leaders. Whenever he did see Malu, Horace incessantly put forward his case, claiming he could offer valuable advice and strategy for Northem's next assault – *'as there must be another campaign, for the sake of Northem's pride and future'*.

Malu always listened to Horace with a patient smile that masked his true feelings; he detested Theodora's father and would never give him a seat at the table.

'And I still have allies in Lamore who can help Malu's cause,' Horace went on now.

'Allies? Like who?'

A smirk came to his face. 'Like your mother. She is still loyal to me.'

Word had reached Theodora that Countess Datanya had left the Lamorian court to live with her friend, the Dowager Baroness of Iveness, at her manor. But Theodora hadn't heard personally from her mother, and was frankly hurt that her father had. She could only assume that Horace, a skilled manipulator, had somehow placed the blame for abandoning his wife solely on their daughter – convinced the Countess that he had left Lamore unwillingly. While Theodora had never been close to her mother, she felt the snub keenly.

'So Malu needs me,' Horace concluded.

'No one needs you,' she snapped. 'Here or in Lamore. And if you are not needed, then you must be the one who is weak.'

A muscle twitched in Horace's cheek. 'You should have been the one who died in Lamore, not your brother.'

In an instant, Theodora's anger morphed, replaced by churning bile in her stomach. Her father wanted her dead. Her mother was acting like she *was* dead. She had to look away. Instead she stared at the snow leopard's lifeless body, convinced part of her had died with the animal.

She heard her father begin his descent back down the hill,

but made no move to follow. She just sat, watched and mourned.

After some time she saw the Huntmaster make his approach on the opposite hillside. As he neared the creature, there was a hint of movement. A twitching limb. Then more movement.

She's alive.

Hope buoyed Theodora as the creature struggled to her feet. The animal held one of her back legs in the air; the limb was covered in blood, but otherwise she appeared uninjured. The cat bent down, presumably looking for her cub – but there was little left of the tiny animal. The leopard opened her mouth and emitted a heartbreaking yowl.

The Huntmaster was within striking distance, sneaking up behind the cat with his knife raised. But Theodora would not have it.

The creature was a survivor. *She* was a survivor.

Her scream echoed across the valley.

'No!'

2

_T_he snowstorm Theodora's father had predicted struck with a vengeance on their journey back to Arykyl. If it hadn't been for the Huntmaster's experience, they may not have found their way back alive. As it was, Theodora's hands and limbs were so frozen she feared they might snap right off. She had never been so pleased to see the Great Hall – which was not so great, in her experience: a large but rudimentary wooden structure, primarily used for feasting and meetings.

As the Huntmaster took Horace's hand cannon from him and escorted him back to his guarded quarters, Theodora rushed inside the dimly lit hall and headed straight for the vast open fire in the centre. She rid herself of her sodden cloak and gloves and warmed her hands over the flames, while ignoring the sidelong looks and guffaws at her dishevelled appearance. She called on a servant to fetch her a dry fur, and a clan leader seated at one of the long tables nearby remarked that if she wanted a warm coat, she should catch and kill her own trophy _'like a true Northemer'_.

Theodora had spent the best part of a year in the Northem capital, but she still couldn't understand the allure of her adopted home. Similarly, the Northem people couldn't understand why their King had chosen a Lamorian as his future wife. Theodora was promised in marriage to Malu and was, in almost every respect, his Queen, but she was also an ever-constant reminder of Northem's losses twelve months before in Kypria.

Theodora had escaped the battle at Lamore Castle with Malu and what was left of his great army of warriors. They'd fled in a handful of ships to Ette, which the Northemers had previously conquered. They had hoped to make Ette – with all of its riches and fertile lands – their own, but within weeks, a united Lamore, no longer allied with Northem, had joined forces with Kengia and mobilised against them. The new Lamorian King, Takai – the man Theodora had once thought she was destined to marry – led the combined army all the way to the Capital's gates. They outnumbered and were better equipped than the Northemers, and forced them to return to their icy lands, still licking their wounds from the earlier battles. Wounds mostly inflicted by those wielding Kengian magic.

In Lamore and Kengia, the Northemers had faced the Water Catcher, Arisa, several times, and each time she had drawn on her powers over nature, conjuring storms, tidal waves and astonishing tricks to defeat them. Then there had been Arisa's father, the Air King Alik, who had used his powers against them to equally devastating effect. Those who'd been lucky enough to survive the deadly attacks had suffered injuries so acute that many still bore them today.

Theodora laid the blame for their losses at several people's feet, including her father's, whose single-minded, selfish ambitions had blinkered him to the fact that the Water Catcher prophecy was being realised. But most of all, Theodora blamed the Water Catcher herself.

Arisa had upturned her life from the first day she'd arrived at the Lamorian court, taking everything from Theodora. Her chance of being the Lamorian Queen. Her comfortable home at Lamore Castle. And Rea...the Kengian girl with incredible powers, whom Malu had taken under his wing. Rea had been a friend of sorts to Theodora, and may have been the only one capable of killing Arisa, but had chosen to spare Arisa's life before taking the form of a phoenix and flying away. Despite this, Theodora missed Rea dreadfully and ached for news of how she fared.

But what was the point of concerning herself with Arisa or Rea? She must focus on her own survival, which relied on Malu's support outweighing the mistrust and dislike his people harboured for her. Theodora had tried to get the Northemers to thaw to her. She had learnt their language and customs, but it wasn't enough. She saw the thinly veiled hate in their strained smiles, heard the crude insults muttered under their breaths.

Theodora lifted her chin and strode to the back of the hall, past a partition that marked the beginning of Malu's quarters. She took the private hallway and entrance to the King's rooms, where she found the Northem King seated at his dining table with his brother, Hafder, and a man she had never seen before. The stranger wore a tall hat with a brightly coloured woven band and a feather sticking from it. His longcoat featured gold braided trim and was teamed with a waistcoat bearing shiny brass buttons. A gold chain with a sizeable medallion hung from his neck. His long hair was tied back in a ponytail and his clean-shaven face was scarred in a series of precise geometric patterns. Judging by the man's weather-worn skin, he was a seafarer, but too well-dressed to be a pirate. A merchant, perhaps.

None of them noticed Theodora approach, so she hung back to listen in secret to their conversation – a habit she'd developed, and perfected, back in Lamore.

The stranger was speaking in the Northem tongue, but with a heavy accent Theodora didn't recognise. He waved his hands as if acting out a great tale. She caught mention of vast faraway lands, virtually untouched arable plains, forests bursting with life and rolling, verdant hills that were home to roaming herds of beasts – 'a ready food source'. He spoke of never-ending summers and people who welcomed strangers, happily sharing the land they cared for and everything that was theirs. 'And there are giant stone pyramids, a hundred times the size of your Great Hall – temples to honour their ancestors and gods.'

Malu leant forward in his chair, his eyes shining, but Hafder's usually rock-like face twisted. He rolled his one visible eye – the other was now hidden under a patch, having been maimed during the battle at Lamore Castle. Malu's brother had been lucky to survive that day; his luck, though, was Theodora's misfortune. Hafder was the most vocal of her detractors, blaming her presence for distracting Malu from securing new territories for Northem.

'You have an active imagination, merchant,' Hafder scoffed.

The merchant lifted the gold medallion to show him. 'And is this my imagination?' Hafder reached for the coin, his gaze hungry, but the merchant snatched the medallion out of his reach. 'There is plenty more where this came from.'

Malu rubbed his chin. 'They are a peaceful people, you say?'

'Aye. There is enough to go around, so they are happy to share. If shown violence, I don't doubt they will reciprocate, but they have no need to mobilise against anyone.'

Hafder crossed his arms. 'And why would you bother telling us about this? What's in it for you?'

The merchant looked to the King. Malu nodded.

'I owe your brother a life debt,' the merchant said to Hafder, who cocked his head in question. 'I come from a long line of merchants. My father, Olix Senior, was a regular visitor to Arykyl, bringing ships of grain, flour and other food to Northem. In times of famine, what he brought on his ships was the only source of food.'

Theodora recalled Malu's stories of the great famine that had lasted nearly a decade. While Northem had never been a fertile land, in good times its people had survived on the fish they caught, the occasional deer that could be hunted, and the unappetising root vegetables and squashes that could be grown in a home plot. But all of this relied on the spring and summer months being warm and dry enough for animals and plants to thrive. Most of Malu's teenage years had passed in what was described as the 'Endless Winter'. Thousands of Northemers had perished. From what Theodora understood, Malu had been close to death several times, but it was not a subject he liked to speak on. So naturally she was curious about this *life debt* and what it had to do with the famine. She stepped back further into a shadowy corner of the room.

'Such a *hero*,' Malu sniped. 'What you fail to mention, Olix, is that your father was also the greediest of men.' The melodic tone of his voice was gone, a chilling discordance in its place. 'The prices he charged our people were criminal. He could see we were desperate and had no other choice. He could see we were all starving and he didn't care if we lived or died – only how much money could be made.'

The merchant – Olix – dropped his head in shame. Hafder's expression hardened.

Malu stood up from his chair and fixed a terrifying stare on Olix. 'Your father is why Sera died.'

Sera? Who was Sera?

Olix looked back up, his fingers clasped together, begging. 'And you saw that he paid with his life.'

'And you were spared, allowed to continue your father's business if you agreed to only ever charge our people fair prices and to repay your debt to my family.'

Hafder, too, was on his feet, his lips curled into a sneer. 'You should have told me, brother. So I could have slit his throat the moment he arrived in Arykyl.'

Malu shook his head. 'Not while he can still be useful to us.'

'But surely you don't believe this fable of a "paradise" and its people waiting to welcome us with open arms? The man will tell you anything to make good on his debt.'

Olix leapt to his feet. 'I have no reason to lie to you.' He held his hands out placatingly. 'I don't have a death wish.'

Malu stood still and silent. Theodora could almost taste the merchant's fear in the air. Eventually the King spoke. 'I will take what you have told us under consideration.'

Olix exhaled loudly.

'But you and I have other business to discuss.'

'What business?' Hafder asked.

Malu gave his brother a reassuring smile. 'Just the usual business of trade.'

Olix's expression was unreadable, but Hafder's brows bunched in suspicion. Rightly so, Theodora thought. There was nothing *usual* about any of this.

'Tomorrow, Olix. We will finish our conversation then.'

Olix nodded and took leave through the entrance used by everyone other than Malu and Theodora.

Hafder turned to Malu with a frown. 'Brother, you mustn't give any heed to this tale of venturing thousands of miles across the sea to a land that doesn't exist. The merchant is using it to be rid of you and his debt. He's hoping we'll all perish on the journey.'

Malu shrugged.

'We must focus on Ette, which is beyond the reach of Kengian magic,' Hafder went on. 'We have taken it before and can do it again, even without firesky weapons. It is no longer Lamore's territory. My spies tell me that they only have a single regiment in place to assist in the formation of a new government, and the Etteans have no forces to speak of...yet. They have never been more vulnerable. We have to strike now.' He slammed his fist into his opposite hand.

Malu frowned, his tattooed face wrinkling. 'Aren't you tired of war?'

Lately Malu's desire to conquer other lands had seemed to fade in favour of other, unknown plans. Many were curious about the King's change of heart – he was never one to back down from a fight. But Theodora knew that above all, he wanted the best future for his people. This bleak place didn't offer that. Indeed, many of the council members, including

Malu's own brother, were beginning to question their King. Theodora had tried to counsel Malu on one occasion about the matter of gaining new territories and taking revenge on the Kyprian nations, but he'd quietened her with assurances that she must trust him, kissing away any further protests. And she did trust him. Malu was the only person she *could* trust.

Hafder's eyes narrowed. 'I'll never tire of fighting for our people.'

'But at what cost? We have lost so many of our people. So much death…'

Theodora recognised the pain in his words. It was a pain she heard in his nightmares, when he would wake up drenched in sweat, crying out for all the dead Northemers he'd led into battle.

Hafder screwed up his mouth in disgust. 'I never thought I would see the day that my own brother was a coward,' he growled.

A hiss of metal cleaved the air and in an instant Malu's sword was at Hafder's neck. 'Say it again, brother.' His calm and measured tone was petrifying. 'Call me that one more time and you will see I am no coward.'

Hafder clenched his jaw, nostrils flaring. A ribbon of blood ran down his neck where the blade had broken the skin. He opened his mouth and started to form the word 'coward', but Theodora couldn't allow him. She couldn't allow Malu to follow through with his threat – not because she was concerned about Hafder's fate, but because she knew Malu would never forgive himself.

She ventured out from her hiding place. 'I'm back,' she announced with exaggerated cheer.

The men's eyes darted from each other to her and back again, no doubt wondering how long she had been there. The rise and fall of Malu's chest slowed and he lowered his sword.

'Excuse us, brother,' he said in clipped tones. 'My future Queen, the great huntress, has returned.'

Theodora expected Hafder to acknowledge her in some way, to show some form of appreciation for her saving his life, but all she saw in his unflinching gaze was hate. He bid Malu an angry farewell and left them.

Malu turned to Theodora, taking in her bedraggled appearance.

'You look frozen.' He embraced her. 'How much did you hear?'

'Pretty much all of it.'

'Mmm…'

Theodora could almost hear his mind turning over. There was much to consider, and she knew he would share his thoughts with her when he was ready. Malu rubbed her back and arms. His touch never failed to set her skin on fire.

Theodora had always admired Malu – an admiration that had only grown with her gratitude for him taking her back to Northem, despite all its shortcomings. Fleeing from Lamore, he'd offered her protection and freedom from her father's rule. In the months that had followed, he'd given her a place within his inner circle, seeking and valuing her opinion on matters of state. Hafder and the other Northem leaders begrudged her closeness to their King, but the fact that she was an outsider made it easier for Malu to confide in her, to show his vulnerable side. He shared with her his struggles to manage the clan leaders' competing demands. In those private moments, she saw the man beyond the warrior and King. A man with an extraordinary intellect and heart, unseen by anyone but her.

What started as a meeting of minds inevitably developed into a meeting of souls. And while the love between them may have grown gradually, Theodora could name the exact moment she'd known for sure that there could be no one for her but Malu.

It had been her eighteenth birthday, an occasion she'd expected to pass without notice. It wasn't as if her father was inclined or in a position to mark the day, and in absence of any other family or friends, Theodora hadn't expected any form of acknowledgement. Perhaps the lack of any expectation had made what Malu did even more touching.

Theodora had woken on her birthday to a room filled with wildflowers. Goodness knew where Malu had got them – presumably a merchant like Olix had procured them from faraway lands. There were daisies, purple bellflowers, golden clusters of lady's bedstraw, indigo-hued lupines, forget-me-nots, and bunches of exotic-looking red and pink blooms she didn't recognise. She remembered, then, having told Malu about her favourite childhood memory – one of her only happy memories from that time of her life.

On her tenth birthday, her father had gifted Theodora and her twin brother, Guthrie, a pony each. Guthrie had challenged her to a race. Neither had much riding experience, but this was no impediment to the competitive pair. They'd agreed to ride to the edge of the castle woodland and back again to the stables – the first to return would be the winner.

Guthrie's pony was larger and stronger, necessarily so to carry his hefty frame, and it didn't take long for him to secure a sizeable lead. But Theodora, it soon seemed, was a natural rider, and her lighter weight meant she was able to close the gap by the time they reached the woodland. The colour and dizzying scent of wildflowers paving the way to the forest flooded her senses as she registered the shock on her brother's face when she passed him. Guthrie whipped his pony and cursed it loudly, but it was no use; Theodora left him in her wake. It was one of the only times she'd got the better of her brother, and she would never forget the approving look her father had given her when she returned the winner. Her triumph was only soured a little by Horace berating his son for being beaten by a girl. From then on, Theodora had always associated wildflowers with the knowledge that she was capable of anything.

She couldn't believe Malu had remembered the story and the date of her birthday. It had been the perfect gift – the reminder she'd needed to push through her tribulations in Northem. Something she'd held close each time a Northemer spat on the ground where she walked or turned their back on her as she passed – an everyday occurrence when Malu wasn't near. But the wildflowers hadn't been all Malu had planned for her. He'd also gifted her the bow and arrow she had used this very day, and had seen that his Huntmaster trained her in its use.

To top it all off, Malu had his cook make Theodora a lemon syrup cake, like the ones she'd loved when she lived at Lamore Castle – and over pieces of cake served with dollops of cream, he had declared his wish for her to be his Queen.

Theodora had responded then as she had responded every day since: she would be his Queen...but only after she had proved she was worthy of his people.

It was a milestone that seemed more unattainable than ever after today.

'So, my love, did you get your trophy?' Malu murmured in her ear.

'Not exactly,' she mumbled, and he stepped back so he could see her face. Theodora explained how she had found the snow leopard but discovered she had a cub, so hadn't been able to kill her. She told Malu how her father had shot the cub and badly injured its mother, but how even then she hadn't been able to bring herself to kill the animal. How something made her want to protect the creature instead.

Theodora had expected to see disappointment in his face, but all she saw was understanding. And she supposed that he did understand. The need to look after those he cared for – the people of Northem, Rea, herself – that was what drove Malu. He was no coward. He was someone who would stop at nothing to keep others protected; it was what had driven him to invade Ette and Kengia. Yes, he was a formidable warrior, and he didn't shy away from taking a life when needed. But he didn't seek war and bloodshed for its own sake. If only Hafder and the clan leaders understood that.

Malu brushed the wet clumps of hair from her forehead. 'So where is your snow leopard now?'

'The Huntmaster has her, but she is badly injured. I'm not sure she will survive.'

Malu frowned. 'But you wish to keep it as a pet?'

Theodora shook her head. 'I want to look after her until she is well enough to be returned to the wild. If you had seen her, you would know that is where she belongs.' A sob caught in her throat. 'She shouldn't be someone's prisoner. She should be the master of her own destiny.'

This was something Theodora understood. For too long she had been her father's pawn. Malu must have read her mind, because he tightened his embrace and brought her head to rest on his chest. The steady beat of his heart calmed her.

'And so she shall,' he whispered in her ear. 'I will send for a wise woman to heal your snow leopard.'

Theodora nodded her thanks. She had so many questions for Malu. She wanted to know who Sera was. She wanted to know whether he planned on trying to find the mysterious lands Olix had told him about. She wanted to know what his other plans with Olix were. But all of her questions could wait. Right now all she wanted, all she needed, was to be exactly where she was – safe and loved in the arms of a man who truly understood her.

BY THE TIME Theodora had changed into something dry and warm, she had received word of the wise woman's arrival. She and Malu went to the Huntmaster's stables, the snow leopard's growls reaching them before they entered the timber building. The Huntmaster showed them through the door then excused himself, mumbling something about the 'madness of women'.

It was dark inside the stables except for the light from a fire in a far corner. The snow leopard hissed from a cage in the opposite corner, swatting the bars with her claws. A tall, lean woman, with long, straight, white hair that nearly reached her waist, peered intently into the cage.

'Can you heal the creature?' Malu asked.

'Perhaps,' the wise woman replied without turning. 'But only if she calms enough for me to be able to handle her.'

Theodora approached the cage with tentative steps. 'It's alright. We want to help you...'

The animal locked its gaze with hers and stopped hissing. Theodora stepped closer and reached for the door of the cage, inexplicably knowing it was safe to do so. Malu made to stop her, but the wise woman urged him to let her continue.

As Theodora's fingers made contact with the timber bars, the great cat bared her teeth, but Theodora wasn't deterred. She owed this to the creature. She must help her.

'It's alright,' she said, over and over, as she carefully unlatched the cage door, never breaking the animal's gaze.

The leopard panted with her mouth wide open, as if poised to bite at any second, but as the cage door swung open, she slowed her breath, her eyes going to the opening.

Theodora shook her head. 'You need to stay where you are, so this wise woman can fix you.' She spoke as if the creature could understand her – and perhaps the leopard did, because she didn't move or try to escape.

The wise woman, satisfied that it was safe enough to approach, waved a vial under the leopard's nose. The animal's head drooped a little and she wobbled on her feet before collapsing. Her eyes were closed, but she was still breathing.

'This will give us the time we need to fix her wound.'

With Theodora's help, the wise woman cleaned the leopard's wound and applied a poultice. She bandaged the creature's back leg and indicated for Theodora to close the cage again.

'Will she survive?' Malu asked.

The wise woman nodded. 'Yes. And she will keep her leg, but whether she can use it again, I don't know.'

'Thank you,' Theodora said, patting the leopard's speckled fur through the cage bars.

'Yes, thank you.' Malu pressed a bag of coins into the wise woman's hand, but she didn't leave. 'You can go now. Your work here is done.'

The woman's wrinkled face, like the gnarled trunk of a tree, cracked into a smile. 'My work is not quite done. I have something else for you. Another reason I was brought here.'

'Another reason?' Theodora asked.

The woman pulled a small bag from her cloak. 'A reading for you. If you wish it?'

Theodora had heard of Northem's wise women. Some were said to be talented seers. Malu compressed his lips, as if trying to decide if this woman was one who could see the future. Eventually he gave the smallest of nods.

The wise woman muttered a string of Northem words, which Theodora didn't understand. The words crescendoed, reaching a quivering pitch. And with each one, the fire in the corner pulsed and grew. It grew so large the flames filled the fireplace, threatening to burst from its confines. Theodora's concerned gaze flew to Malu, but his eyes were on the bag in the woman's hands.

With one final cry, the wise woman pulled open the bag's drawstring and threw the contents onto the dirt floor. Sticks and stones of different colours tumbled over each other and scattered across the ground. A white stone with flecks of red and gold rolled toward Theodora, coming to a stop near her foot.

The wise woman's head spun to face Theodora. Sharp eyes probed her. An expression that could have been admiration came over her face, followed by sadness. A bitterly cold shiver ran up Theodora's spine.

'The reading,' Malu prompted.

The woman muttered something inaudible and diverted her

attention to the sticks and stones on the ground. 'Mmm,' she began. 'I see a journey. I see a bright burning light in the sky. A constant sun.'

Olix had described the lands of endless summer. Could the woman be referring to the same place?

'It is a long journey by sea, then?' Malu asked. 'I will take our people to new lands?'

'It is not clear. There is old business – responsibilities to others that must be seen to first.'

Malu's shoulders slumped as if the whole weight of Northem were bearing down on him.

The wise woman consulted the sticks and stones again. 'The land I see is vast. Its reaches span from desert wastelands to prosperous cities.' This no longer sounded like the lands Olix had mentioned. 'I see metals and precious stones.' She looked at Malu. 'Promises you have made. Promises made to you.'

Malu nodded grimly, as if he understood what she meant but didn't like it. Theodora cast him a questioning look.

He took her by the arm and led her out of the wise woman's hearing. 'Ivane,' he said by way of explanation. 'It is something I have been considering. Something that will satisfy Hafder and the other councillors. Ivane is as rich as, or richer, perhaps, than Ette. Known for its mines in the east and farmlands in the south.'

Theodora bristled with excitement. If Malu succeeded, she could be Queen of a far greater land than Northem. She would have all the power she sought, far from this icy prison – but she couldn't get ahead of herself. She had been disappointed more than once. 'Isn't Ivane said to have a great army?'

'Yes, but they haven't called on it for nearly two decades. Every Ivanian may have trained as a warrior, but few have seen battle. And it will take time to gather and mobilise their forces. They will have to call on recruits from villages across the country, and by the time they are ready, we will already be on the doorstep of Nadis Palace.'

'But surely the alarm would be raised well before we manage to sail into Nadis? We would have to pass the whole Ettean or Ivanian coast.'

'Which is why we will have some forces approaching from the north via land.'

'Through the Desertlands?'

'Yes. It will be a hard journey, but will give us the element of surprise.'

'But I thought you may have favoured the idea of going to the new lands?'

Malu took her hands in his. 'I do, for you and me, and anyone else who dares to come with us into the great unknown. But many of Northem's people are like my brother – warriors, not adventurers. I owe it to the people to deliver Ivane to them, and once I have secured that, I can leave it all in Hafder's hands with an unburdened conscience. You and I can build a life together in these new lands – visit the giant pyramids.' His eyes shone. 'What do you say?'

Theodora considered everything he had said. An arduous campaign through the desert. Another war. One in which Lamore and Kengia would undoubtedly become involved. It may mean she could have her revenge on all those who had wronged her. Taking Ivane would be a slap in the face to the former Lamorian Queen, Sofia, and her companion Gwyn, who had both treated Theodora like an outsider all those years. Ivane was also Takai's ancestral land. She could get revenge on the man who'd rejected her. But this wasn't the most satisfying thought. It was that Kengia would undoubtedly come to Ivane's aid – along with Arisa, and her misplaced belief that 'good' must prevail.

But Theodora had doubts. She wasn't sure victory would be easy, or even possible, against all of Kypria's combined forces, even though they wouldn't have magic on their side so far from Kengia. And even if they did win, Malu wanted to relinquish power – something she had yearned for her whole life, and still wanted.

She gave him her most beguiling smile. 'I do miss the sun.' Malu's hopeful gaze brightened. 'But…I was wondering…Just a thought, more than anything…' He raised a brow. 'Once Northem has taken Ivane, couldn't we rule both nations from there? Hafder can rule as your regent here.'

Malu's features froze for a moment, his gaze intent on her. He took a deep breath. 'That is what you want?'

She nodded, knowing the sacrifice she was asking of Malu. 'It is.'

A veil fell over the pools of his blue eyes, a sadness, followed by a sigh of resignation. He leant toward Theodora and kissed her forehead. 'Then you shall have it, my love,' he murmured, and turned to leave.

BACK INSIDE THE HALL, everyone was feasting on great hunks of roast pig and bread washed down with mugs of mead. It was practically the same meal every night. Meat, bread and mead. And when there wasn't meat available it was fish – dried fish, pickled fish, grilled fish. The vegetable accompaniments were bland and the condiments and sauces non-existent. Starkly different to what Theodora had been accustomed to at Lamore Castle. Arykyl was where flavour went to die.

After dinner, clan leaders approached Malu one by one with petitions ranging from calls to increase taxes to adjudications over boundary lines. Malu dealt with each swiftly and decisively, and while not everyone was happy with his judgement, they accepted it with minimal complaint – at least to his face. They knew all too well what Malu was capable of when pushed. He wasn't a King who wasted his time with threats; he was a King who acted.

Theodora remembered the first time she had seen a clan leader challenge Malu's ruling. The landholder had dammed the river that ran through his property, cutting off the resource from another clan leader downstream. Malu had ordered the man to get rid of his dam and pay compensation to his neighbour, but the landholder had refused, arguing that he was able to do what he wanted on his own property. He'd gone on to publicly claim he did not recognise 'Malu the Defeated' as his King.

Malu had ended the dispute with a single sweep of his sword, which freed the man's head from his neck. As the head rolled down the hall, Malu had calmly returned to his dinner. While gnawing on a shank of lamb, he'd ordered that the fallen man's lands go to his neighbour. Everyone else in the hall had resumed their merriment and meals as if nothing had happened.

It had taken a while for Theodora to become accustomed to the brutality her betrothed was capable of. She'd developed an understanding of what it took to maintain power, and of the fact that violence was sometimes a necessary and effective tool. Even so, she still found it confronting at times.

After dinner tonight, a man dressed in farmer's attire presented himself to Malu. He was from one of Hafder's provinces in the far north. Trailing behind him was a man with similar features, his hands bound.

Hafder leant over to Malu and explained that the pair were brothers who'd come to Arykyl to sell wool from the sheep flock they both owned. The older brother was always in charge of the sales, but the younger one, through a chance meeting with their wool broker, had discovered significant discrepancies between what the broker had been paying and the share he'd been given. The older brother had been pocketing around eighty per cent instead of a half share of their profits for years.

'So the younger brother is here to ask you or Malu for a judgement?' Theodora asked Hafder.

Hafder's eye rolled in its socket. 'You've been here a year and you still don't know our customs – good-for-nothing Lamorian wench.' He muttered the last part under his breath, only to receive a sharp look from Malu.

'Family business and justice is determined by family members,' Malu explained quietly to Theodora. He nodded at the farmer. 'He has come here to inform his lord and me of his judgement, and I must respect it, whatever it is.'

Malu turned to address the younger brother.

'What have you decided?'

The Northemer's lips were set in a grim line. 'The only fitting punishment for a thief. He shall lose his hand.'

Theodora's throat constricted. 'But how is he supposed to farm and shear his sheep if he only has one hand?' she whispered to Malu, but he merely nodded his acknowledgement of the sentence.

Hafder stood up and handed his axe to the man.

Theodora's mind reeled as Hafder unbound the older brother's hands and held the right one in place on the table in front of them, while another two Northemers kept the man from escaping or thrashing about too much. The man begged his brother for mercy, tears running down the gullies in his sun-worn face. The younger brother took a deep breath and raised the axe. Malu reached for Theodora's hand under the table and squeezed it.

She looked away as the blade was brought down. A sickening scream and a thud punctured the smoky air. Theodora couldn't bring herself to look at the maimed man as he was dragged away, or at the table where his blood and severed hand remained. Instead she excused herself. Malu gave her a sympathetic smile, while Hafder shook his head at her, his lip curled in disgust, as if she were as bad as the thief – her crime: not being a Northemer.

Theodora slipped quickly from the hall, not wanting anyone else to notice her retreat or the tears threatening to spill from her eyes. She was heading toward Malu's quarters when a bony hand on her wrist stopped her. Theodora turned to see the wise woman.

'You?' She swallowed her tears. 'What do you want?'

'There is more I need to tell you,' the woman said.

'More?'

'A message for you. The bright burning light in the sky.'

'The sun?'

The woman shook her head. 'Something else. Something born of flames.'

Flames? An image flashed through Theodora's mind. An image of the red-and-gold-flecked stone that had come to a stop at her feet in the stables. The same colours of a tattoo and a creature branded in her memory.

She grasped the woman's arm. 'And that message was for me? You are sure of it?'

The woman nodded. 'The bright burning light awaits you in the land with a constant sun.'

Theodora released the wise woman and gave a triumphant laugh.

She knew exactly how she could prove her worth to all of Northem.

3

$\mathcal{T}$he moss-green waters of the Ambay Coast winked back at Arisa, oblivious to the solemn occasion of today's visit. The last time she'd been here, the craggy outline of the limestone islands that jutted out from the sea had given the appearance of an alert dragon, but today the dragon was sleeping, basking in the calm waters and the silver sun's warming afternoon rays. The sea and its sandy white shores teemed with life. Seabirds ducked and dived into the water, ascending in triumph with plump fish in their beaks. Casts of crabs scuttled across the dunes like soldiers in formation.

The landscape had recovered from the events of twelve months before, but Arisa couldn't say the same of herself.

Images flickered through her mind, as fresh as if the Lamorian and Northem forces had attacked Kengia with their devastating firesky weapons just yesterday. Arisa's eyes stung, her throat constricting at the memory of blood and smoke-filled air. Dozens upon dozens of Kengian warriors cut down. Not a single stretch of beach unmarked by death. It had been she who had put an end to the bloodshed, but it had come at a price.

She had used her Water Catcher magic to command the sea to swallow up the enemy ships, and hundreds of Lamorian soldiers and Northemers with them. She had drawn on her inner darkness; it had been key to realising her abilities. She had felt powerful – but the feeling had been quickly followed by guilt over the lives lost. The guilt had faded somewhat over time, with the knowledge that she had done what she did to protect all of Kypria, but now it was back like a tsunami.

Her remorse and sadness tinged with something else, as well. She was riddled with nerves. Every muscle and tendon in her body was tense.

Sensing her unease, Arisa's horse, Meteor, lifted her head and gave a soft whinny. On his horse beside her, Arisa's father reached for her hand.

With honour and courage, Alik planted in her mind.

Today was the anniversary of the Ambay Coast battle, and they were here to commemorate all those who had given their lives, both in Kengia and Lamore. A Lamorian contingent would be joining Arisa and Alik with the rest of their family and the other Kengian representatives.

As if on cue, a Lamorian ship peeked its bow around one of the islands. Arisa's breath hitched in her throat. She knew Takai would be on board.

When she had left him in Lamore, she had been hopeful their relationship could be rekindled. She'd thought Takai just needed time to adjust to his new role as Lamore's King, and to come to terms with the death of his father at Arisa's hands. But her hopes had been crushed.

In the beginning there had been letters – mainly filled with trivial updates and polite enquiries, friendly yet cautious, as if each of them were afraid of broaching the topic of their relationship only to learn the other party had moved on. The correspondence had become less frequent, delays explained by Takai's continual travels between Lamore and Ette. Then the letters had stopped altogether. Arisa wasn't sure who had stopped writing first, just that it was over.

There had been a small beacon of hope when she and her

family had travelled to Lamore for the opening of the hospital in Obira. The one she and Takai had planned. Together they'd overseen its foundations being laid, but the project had been scuttled by Chancellor Horace.

After becoming King, Takai had made the hospital his first priority, once he had made sure the Northemers were gone from Ette. It had been named in honour of Arisa's uncle – Prince Amund's Hospital. Arisa had been deeply touched by the gesture, seeing it as an opportunity to reconnect with Takai, but he had barely spoken to her during that visit and had thwarted any attempts she'd made to speak to him alone.

Since then there had been nothing.

Arisa's mother, Gwyn, who now lived in Kengia with Alik, had tried to rationalise Takai's behaviour, saying he was much occupied with running the kingdom, which still bore the scars of his father's cruel regime. He had also spent a great deal of time in Ette, which, after almost two hundred years of continuous Lamorian occupation, had been handed back to its people. Takai, Sar and Isla had spent many months supporting Ette in the election of its new leader and establishment of its government. Arisa understood that they had travelled the entire countryside, spreading the word of the democratic process and election, and helping rebuild the nation. Takai had volunteered a regiment of his own army and Lamorian tradespeople to assist in the reconstruction of roads, buildings and cultural sites that had been destroyed under his father's rule, and during the Northem occupation and ensuing battles.

When Takai wasn't in Lamore, he left the rule of the kingdom to his cousin, Willem, and his mother, the Dowager Queen Sofia, who served as co-regents. Elos had been appointed as Lord Commander of Lamore's forces, and the Kengian Mountain Chief, Cheon, spent part of his time at the Lamorian court as a military attaché to promote partnership and collaboration between the two nations. Arisa had also heard that the former Lamorian rebel leader, Sergei, had taken up his promised role on the King's council with relish. He had successfully lobbied for tax concessions for all Lamorians and decreased tariffs for all imports and exports passing through Obira's port. Trade with Kengia and travel between the two countries was flourishing thanks to the tunnel through the Nymoi Alps, created by Rea and her firesky cannons.

Rea…Another person who was lost to her. Despite Arisa's best efforts, she had been unable to track down her friend, but she would not give up hope. Not like she had when they were children. The same way she would not give up on Takai.

Arisa's fingers tightened around Meteor's reins as a Lamorian longboat was launched and approached the shore. Even from a distance she recognised the towering figures of Elos and Sar, Isla next to them with her unmistakable fiery red hair. Across from them sat Sofia, the Shaman Laurel, and…

The way he sat tall and erect, the set of his broad shoulders, awakened a contradiction of emotions in her. Happiness. Longing. Sadness. Anger.

From Arisa's other side, Gwyn gave her a kind smile. 'Are you ready?'

She bit her lip. Her whole body was screaming, *No. Of course I'm not ready.* But instead she nodded slowly and followed her parents on horseback down to the shore, where a platform and line of pavilions had been arranged, and her destiny awaited.

THE KENGIAN DEPUTATION formed a line in front of the platform. Alik, as King of Kengia, stood first in line, with Gwyn next to him. Arisa's grandmother, Mira, the former Kengian Queen, was next, followed by Princess Kairi, Arisa, Kairi's husband Tio, and Cheon. There was a formal greeting between the two Kings, Alik and Takai, but all forms of ceremony were quickly abandoned with the arrival of Sar, who bounded toward his adopted mother, Gwyn, wrapping her in a bear hug and lifting her off the ground. He spun around in circles until Gwyn begged for mercy. Sar then made a beeline for Arisa, performing the same dizzying display.

Arisa batted his hands, demanding he release her before she was sick. He complied, lowering her to the ground and flashing her a dimpled grin.

'Did you miss me, sister?'

'Were you gone, *brother?*' she mocked. 'I barely noticed your absence.'

He play-punched her in the arm.

'Ow!' she yelped, feigning pain, but was secretly grateful that Sar had lightened the mood.

The greetings that followed were a whir of joyful reunions mixed with tearful recollections of those who were permanently absent. Then all too soon, or far too late, Takai came to stand before Arisa.

Butterflies danced in her stomach. Her heart pounded, its racing beat thumping in her ears.

Takai's dark eyes probed her face. Darting, shifting. What was he looking for? Confirmation of her feelings – or a validation of his own, whatever they may be?

She met his gaze with a polite smile. 'Your Majesty.' She made to curtsey, but he placed his fingers gently under her chin, indicating she should rise. The hairs on her arms stood on end at his touch, her anger momentarily forgotten.

'We are beyond such formalities.' His voice was neither cold nor warm. He spoke as if stating an indisputable fact. It brought her little comfort.

'You are well?' she asked.

'I am. And you?'

'I'm well.'

Something flared in his eyes. A fleeting look of yearning. Was it yearning for *her*, or for something that could never be again? Takai opened his mouth to speak, but closed it just as quickly.

Mira appeared by his side. She gave Arisa a sympathetic smile, then turned to the King. 'Should we begin the ceremony?'

Takai held Arisa's gaze for a heart-stilling moment before nodding and excusing himself.

THE CEREMONY COMBINED both Kengian and Lamorian traditional customs. A Lamorian herald played an ode on a trumpet. Mira, as the High Shaman, performed a ritual that was similar to the ancient yew seed ceremony Arisa had witnessed on her eighteenth birthday at Lochlen. A large wreath had been made from tree branches and starling feathers, representing the elements of earth and air. The empty centre of the wreath stood for the fifth element, the aether or void. Takai tied a banner to the wreath, emblazoned with his father's peregrine falcon insignia – the flag under which the Lamorian army had once fought. It had since been replaced by a lion emblem, one favoured by Lamore two centuries before, which signalled a new future for the kingdom.

Laurel and Isla, also a trained Shaman, placed the wreath in the sea. Kairi sang a traditional folk song as the wreath drifted away from the shore, then Mira murmured some Kengian words. The wreath was enveloped in soft, glowing light, which grew and undulated like the waves around it. Mira's words crescendoed and the light crackled until there was a popping sound and sparks erupted from the water. Silver flames ringed the wreath. There was a small gasp from Sofia, who was the only one among them who had never seen the marvel of Kengian firewater before. And while Arisa had seen it previously at the ceremony in Kengia, she couldn't help but be struck by its appearance on a grander scale. The fire appeared contained, its flames almost licking the wreath but not touching it, as if protecting it, and while it drew its energy from the water's life-force – *kira* – it didn't spread. It only took what it needed to exist. Through the firewater and the wreath, the Kengian way of harmony and balance in everything was fully represented, and Lamore's old ways farewelled.

Arisa turned to watch Takai. He held his head high, but the set of his jaw and the slight rounding of his shoulders, unnoticeable to those who didn't know him as well as she did, spoke to his pain. She remembered Takai's turmoil over taking up arms against the Lamorian army and those who had served his family for so long. He had made a choice to fight with the Kengians and Lamorian rebels. He'd known it was the right thing to do for Kypria's future, but it was a hefty burden for anyone to carry.

Takai must have sensed her watching him, because he turned to meet her eyes. She nodded, willing him to know that she understood. For a moment he merely stared, and then there was a hint of a smile – strained, but enough for her to be reassured; he may not want to be with her, but he appreciated that she was there.

AFTER THE CEREMONY, Arisa sought refuge in the tent that had been set up for her. She wanted to try to collect her thoughts before having to face Takai again at dinner.

She opened her chest of belongings, selecting a clean Kengian tunic and pants in muted grey. As she lifted the clothes from the chest, her eyes fell on a red leather book and her heart lurched.

Arisa put down the clothes and picked up the Firemaster's book. She traced the outline of the phoenix and the flames, thinking of Rea. Her shaking fingers moved to the hole in the cover. A puncture mark from a crossbow bolt.

In the waning minutes of the battle at Lamore Castle, Guthrie had confronted her with his crossbow. Amund had thrown the book to her to use as a shield. It had saved her life. *Amund* had saved her life. Grief balled in her throat.

The book held so many memories for her. How she'd first

discovered it at the castle. The hours Amund had spent poring over it, searching for the secrets to firesky. How in fact it now belonged to Rea, who was a Firemaster – how she'd come to be one, no one knew, but she undoubtedly wielded the most powerful of all Kengian magic. Arisa had loaned the book to the Institute in Kengia so the Shamans and Scholars could capture all of its contents, but once they had what they needed, she had become its caretaker. Arisa took the book with her everywhere, in the hope that one day she would see Rea again and be able to give it to her. Its constant presence had been a comfort to her over the last year. Something to cling to as she came to terms with Amund's death and her new life in Kengia.

She had spent countless hours training with her grandmother and aunt, learning to balance the darkness in herself and mastering many spells her uncle would have been proud of. Even so, she used her magic sparingly – only when a Scholar or Shaman was near. After the deaths she had caused in battle, Arisa was still hesitant to unleash her full abilities. She also didn't want to bring further attention to herself. Being the prophesied Water Catcher and heir to the Kengian throne brought with it a form of hero worship that sat uncomfortably with her. The sooner everyone accepted that her duty had been fulfilled and she was no longer an object of curiosity, the better everything would be. It would give her the space she needed to heal – to heal herself, and hopefully Rea too.

'Are you alright?'

Arisa spun back toward the tent's opening to find her father watching her with a furrowed brow.

'I wanted to check on you.'

She sniffed back the tears that had been threatening to fall. 'I'm alright.'

Alik's gaze went to the book in her hands and his face softened. 'I can only imagine the thrill my brother felt when the Firemaster's book was found. He was obsessed with learning. He wanted to know everything there was to know about Kengian magic and science.'

A ghost of a smile came to Arisa's face. 'And more.'

'Yes,' Alik laughed. 'His thirst for knowledge was infinite.' He put his hand on Arisa's shoulder. 'As was his love for you.'

She nodded, not daring to speak.

Alik winced. 'I'm so grateful that he was the father to you that I couldn't be.'

Arisa put her own hand over his. 'You're here now.'

'And I'm not going anywhere.'

This time it was Arisa who winced as she gently removed her father's hand from her shoulder. Panic flared in Alik's eyes.

'What is it?'

Something had plagued her ever since she'd learnt her father was alive. She knew the story of how he had escaped Lamore Castle nearly two decades earlier, after Horace had convinced the King that Alik had bewitched him. Elos had helped Alik in his escape, but had also told him about Arisa being born. Knowing that he had a child with Gwyn, Alik had gone back to the castle only to be confronted by Chancellor Horace. Again, Alik had been lucky to escape, but was caught up in a deadly uprising in Obira City. The Lamorians had turned on all Kengians, attacking them in the streets in what became known as the blood moon massacre. Everyone thought Alik had been killed in the attacks, but he'd survived, albeit barely. He'd remained in a coma under the Shaman Laurel's care, in secret, until the most recent blood moon, when he'd regained consciousness.

Everything about his survival and escape made sense to Arisa – explaining why she had been denied a father all this time – except for one thing.

'Why didn't you use your magic?' She spoke in barely a whisper, unable to look at him.

'Sorry?'

Arisa took a deep breath and met her father's gaze. 'The

night of the blood moon massacre. Why didn't you use your magic to save yourself? To save me and my mother?'

Alik's shoulders fell. 'In hindsight, I should have. Of course I should have. But I thought…' He heaved a sigh. 'I didn't want to make things worse. People were already attacking ordinary Kengians because they thought they possessed special abilities and practised forbidden magic. I didn't want to use my powers against Lamorians and feed their beliefs. I tried to reason with my attackers instead.'

'But when that failed, you could have tried.' Arisa's voice rose. 'You could have done something.'

Alik shook his head adamantly. 'I made a promise to someone that I wouldn't use my magic in Lamore.'

'Who?'

'Your mother. She could see what was on the horizon. She was convinced that to keep the King's trust and protect Kypria in the long-term, I couldn't draw attention to my powers. And she was right. The day she told me that, I knew for sure she was the one.'

Arisa was suddenly curious. 'I assumed it was love at first sight.'

'Hardly.' A woman's voice. Arisa and Alik hadn't noticed Gwyn's arrival. 'Your father took a while to grow on me, and he was already promised…to Datanya.'

'*Datanya?*' Arisa squeaked. 'Horace's wife?'

Alik held his hands up in surrender. 'It's a long story.'

'One we don't have time for now,' Gwyn said, shooing Alik from the tent. 'Arisa needs to get ready.'

'You're going to tell me that story,' she called after her father, who waved his hand in reply as he walked away.

This was all quite a lot for Arisa to wrap her head around. 'So you were with Horace?' she asked Gwyn. 'And my father was with Horace's…' She shuddered.

'I wasn't *with* Horace. And as I said, it's time to get ready.' Only then did Arisa notice the silver dress in her mother's hands. It was a long, flowing gown, simple in design but covered in intricate silver crystals and beadwork that shimmered in the torchlight.

Arisa shook her head. 'I can't wear that. It's not a celebration.'

'But it is. It's a celebration of the lives of all those who died. They didn't give their lives so we could be miserable. They gave their lives for something they loved and believed in. The time for mourning is over. Now there is only remembering and celebrating them.'

Arisa looked uncertainly at the dress. 'I don't know.'

'Please, just try it on for me.'

Arisa nodded and slipped behind a screen to put on the dress. There was no mirror to check her appearance, but when she came back around the screen, Gwyn's hand went to her mouth. Her eyes were shining with pride. Still...it didn't seem right.

The sound of someone clearing their throat pulled Arisa's attention away from the dress.

Takai was standing inside the doorway of the tent, dressed in full Lamorian military regalia. A surge of heat flooded Arisa's body.

'Excuse me, I was just—' Takai took in her appearance, and a smile spread across his face – a smile Arisa remembered fondly.

Gwyn raised a brow at Arisa, then excused herself.

'You were just...?' Arisa prompted.

'Right...Yes...' Takai's serious look was back. 'I wanted to talk to you about something.'

Arisa's palms were instantly clammy. He must want to talk about *them* – or maybe tell her that he had moved on. Was there someone else?

He must have taken her silence for confirmation to continue. 'You know how Lamore has been supporting Ette in establishing its own government?'

This was a strange way to start a conversation about their relationship.

Takai seemed a little rattled by Arisa's continued silence. He wrung his hands. 'Well. There is to be a swearing in of the new chief of state. Quite the celebration has been planned.' He looked to her for a response, but Arisa was still trying to figure out the significance of the conversation. 'Right.' Takai rubbed the back of his neck. 'In short, I'd like you to come to the Chief Minister's inauguration.'

Something that may have been hope grew inside Arisa. '*Me?* You want me to come?'

Takai nodded. 'The Kengian royal family needs to send a representative, and who better than you? Someone who is half-Kengian, half-Ettean...' He smiled. 'And the famed Water Catcher.'

Arisa's hope deflated. 'What about Isla? She is a Kengian Princess.'

Takai shook his head. 'It would be best to have someone more senior from the firstborn line.'

'Then my mother and father are the ones who should go,' she said tonelessly. 'Gwyn was the daughter of one of the great Ettean tribal Kings, after all.'

Takai pressed on. 'I have already spoken to both your parents, and they agreed you are the best choice.'

Anger ignited inside her. 'Of course you've spoken to them already,' she sniped.

Takai's brow knitted. 'In truth...there's another reason I want...' He took a breath. 'Another reason you *should* come.'

Arisa crossed her arms. 'What is it?'

'There have been reports of a creature on the borderlands of Ette. A firebird, they're saying.'

Arisa's arms fell to her sides. 'A firebird? Is it...Could it be—?'

'We think it could be. The creature is said to have appeared in some villages. Isla saw it in the sky herself.'

Arisa paced the floor. 'It's got to be Rea. How her magic is working so far from here, I couldn't guess, but it has to be her.' She stopped in front of Takai. 'It has to be.'

Takai nodded. 'And she needs someone. A friend. Someone who can help her. She needs you, Arisa.'

She tilted her head at his last words. *Rea* needed her. Not Takai...No. Right now it didn't matter. All that mattered was helping her friend.

'I'll come to Ette,' she agreed.

'Good. We leave tomorrow.' Takai made to leave, but stopped again. He turned back and smiled. 'You look beautiful, Arisa.'

Before he could see her surprise, he had turned again and left.

Arisa watched him walk back down the beach, a thousand questions on her tongue. Her gaze went to the sea, where the firewater still burned around the wreath. A beacon in the night. A symbol of everything everyone had fought for, and of what she must fight for now.

4

Theodora visited her father in his quarters to share the news of their Ivanian campaign. His single room was in stark contrast to the opulent apartments he had occupied at Lamore Castle. There were no tapestries on the walls, no ornate furniture; just a simple stretcher, a rickety round table and two wobbly chairs. A small fire glowed in one corner, producing barely enough warmth to keep ice from forming on the window shutters.

While Horace had no one other than himself to blame for his current situation, it didn't mean Theodora didn't feel a trace of guilt at the sight of how far he had fallen. After all, with just one word in Malu's ear, she could see that her father was released – but if she was being completely honest with herself, part of her enjoyed the fact that he was beholden to her.

Another part was terrified of the hold Horace still had over her, even when imprisoned, and of how much worse it would be for her if he was unleashed.

Horace sat at the table, his head bowed over a book of Northern mythology. He looked up at her approach, his gaze as sharp as a dagger point.

'Tell Malu I want something other than this drivel to read.'

He threw the book across the table, so hard that it slid to the floor and fell at Theodora's feet. 'I'm tired of reading fantastical tales of these backward people and their great triumphs over beasts and enemies that never existed.'

'Really, Father?' Theodora crossed her arms. 'You would like me to repeat those exact words to the man who saved your life?'

Horace got to his feet. 'You expect me to be grateful for this?' He waved his hand around the tiny room.

'Yes,' she hissed. 'We should both be grateful for what Malu has done. Neither of us would have survived in Lamore. And remember, you were the one who begged me to bring you with us.'

Horace clicked his jaw. 'That was because I thought you held some sway with Malu. That you would take your position as Queen and I would be restored to power. But you have failed on both fronts. Instead you let Malu use you, treat you as his pretty little pet, a plaything. And when he is done with you, he will throw you away like a discarded toy.'

Theodora's hands clenched in anger. 'I am Malu's equal – his Queen.'

'You are not his Queen until he marries you.' A smirk came to Horace's face. 'I shouldn't be surprised that you have proven yourself inept. You have only ever succeeded in one thing, and that is in being a disappointment. In that, my dear, you're exceptional.'

Theodora's blood surged with rage but she would not be drawn into an argument with her father. This was how it always went: Horace baiting her, urging her to cement her position with Malu and gain him an adviser role. But Theodora wouldn't be pushed into either. Yes, she longed for power, but it was something she wanted to earn on her own merit, not through manipulation and trickery like her father. She had tried his way in attempting to secure Lamore's crown, and it had come to nothing. This time she would be smarter. Smarter even than her father. And if she got it right, she would have all the power she craved and much more.

Theodora forced her hands to relax. 'I have come to inform you, Father, that we will be leaving soon.'

Horace raised a brow. 'Leaving? For where?'

'Malu plans to mount an attack on Ivane.'

Horace sputtered. 'That's a fool's errand. Let me speak to him. If he wants new territories, Lamore is the best target. Their King is distracted with Ette and I have people there who will help us.'

'It is already decided.'

Horace shook his head. 'We stand a snake's chance in Northem of prevailing in Ivane.'

'You mistake me,' Theodora said with a sardonic smile. 'When I said *we*, I meant me and the Northemers, not you.'

Horace burst into laughter. 'In that case, *you* stand *no* chance of prevailing.'

Theodora's hackles began to rise again. 'And what makes you think you could make any difference?'

Horace sat down again, leaning his elbows on the table and steepling his fingers. 'I don't *think* anything. I know it. I have spent more time in Ivane than every Northemer put together. I have led an army against theirs. I know their capabilities, their tactics and their land. If Malu is determined to take this path, he will need me.'

Theodora scowled. Her father did possess knowledge that would be useful to them. More than useful – it was knowledge they would need if they were to survive. If only the price of gaining such knowledge weren't releasing a viper from its cage. Was it a price she was willing to pay?

Horace tilted his head, his keen eyes taking in her indecision. He placed his hands casually in his lap. 'You know…' he began slowly. 'It occurs to me that if Malu were to invade Ivane, others may come to its aid.'

Theodora shrugged with feigned disinterest, knowing exactly where her father was going with this.

'Yes, Takai will help defend his uncle's lands, of course, and probably Kengia too. And with them...' Horace's eyes gleamed. 'Arisa,' he said smoothly. 'You, my dear, can have all the revenge you seek...All you need to do is take me with you. It is the only way you can succeed.'

Even as Theodora's prisoner, her father knew exactly how to control her.

THE JOURNEY to Ivane was swift. A mere two days at sea before landing in the country's remote north. They sailed along the rugged northern coastline marked by craggy rock walls and cliffs, an icy wind tailing them all the way from Arykyl. It was hard to believe they would soon be entering a region known for its unforgiving deserts and soaring temperatures capable of cooking an egg on the ground.

Despite the bright silver sun overhead in the cloudless sky, the cold breeze ravaged Theodora's face. She pulled her cloak tighter, envious of the snow leopard with her thick, warm coat, staring back at her from the cage on the opposite side of the ship. Theodora had insisted they bring the animal with them, unable to entrust her care to anyone else. She had named the cat Rayl – the Northem word for *survivor* – and she and she alone checked and changed the leopard's dressing, reapplying the poultice the wise woman had given her. Theodora was the only person who could approach Rayl. The leopard growled and hissed at anyone else who came near, particularly Horace, whose presence triggered her most ferocious responses. The Northemers, of course, believed Theodora had lost her mind, and made it clear they thought the creature was good for nothing but its coat. But Malu had made it clear in turn that the animal was off-limits. Admittedly, Theodora found some plea-sure in seeing their terrified looks each time they had to pass the cage. She felt as protected and understood by Rayl as she did by Malu.

After a couple more hours' sailing, they came to a small river flanked by towering rock walls, scarred and eroded yet altogether unyielding. Here, the Northern fleet split in two. The larger longships were ordered to continue along the northern coast and then head south-east. They were to remain out of sight at a distance offshore and wait for further instructions. Meanwhile, under Malu's leadership, half a dozen smaller longships with shallow hulls were to take the river inland as far as they could go. Olix had arranged for mercenaries with horses and supplies to meet them there so they could continue their journey.

The ships inched their way along the crystal-clear river until it became so narrow that the Northemers were forced to retrieve their oars and rely solely on the wind to drive them forward. The rock walls threatened to close in on them at any moment, along with the shallow river floor, which loomed closer and closer. It was eerily silent and devoid of any signs of life, except the sound of their own echoing voices.

All too soon the river petered out and they were forced to abandon their ships. They pulled the vessels onto the rocky shore while Hafder and a handful of Northemers went in search of Olix's crew. After an hour or more they came back, scratching their heads. There was no sign of the mercenaries – or of anything else they needed to stand a chance of succeeding in their campaign.

'Too risky to continue via land,' Horace declared knowingly, and even Hafder agreed.

'We should head back and join the rest of our fleet.'

Malu's brow furrowed in consideration, and a prickle of fear ran through Theodora. The wise woman had said the bright burning light awaited them – awaited Theodora – in the land with a constant sun. That there would be a journey through that land. And Theodora was sure this *light* was key to their victory.

They had to continue inland. Only then could she secure everything she desired.

She grasped Malu's arm. 'We must take Nadis,' she whispered in his ear. 'Remember, my love – the enemy will be well-prepared for any attack via sea. Going inland gives us the element of surprise, just as you said.'

Malu nodded slowly, then flashed a triumphant grin. 'We will continue via land.'

Hafder glared at Theodora, but Horace gave her a look that may have been construed as admiration for influencing Malu, even if he didn't agree with the decision. 'I am sure our mercenaries are merely delayed and will meet us in no time,' he said.

Malu directed everyone to leave what they could behind, only carrying what was absolutely necessary. For most, this meant their weapons and a bedding roll that could be slung over the shoulder. On one of the ships they had brought a small wagon; on another, a mule. The wagon was loaded with their small amount of supplies, as well as the snow leopard's cage, which took up most of the space.

The angry looks directed at Theodora were palpable. The uncertain glances aimed at Malu were less so, but didn't escape Theodora's notice.

After a lunch of bread and dried meat, the group headed south through what was now a dry ravine, negotiating uneven terrain littered with sharp, jagged rocks capable of piercing the thickest Northemer boots. With the setting of the sun they reached the end of the canyon, and the magnitude of the task ahead became apparent.

Before them was a never-ending landscape as barren as the country they had come from. A rippling, sandy desert that went all the way to the horizon. Barefaced mountain ranges in the distance on their left and right. And if that wasn't enough to strike fear into every one of their hearts, the grisly scene at the edge of the desert was.

Under a black cloud of buzzing flies, a dozen bodies lay

splayed across the ground. Some of their throats were slit; others had gaping wounds traversing their stomachs and chests. One man had an arrow protruding from his neck. All of the men had similar features and markings to Olix.

Malu's jaw tensed.

'Help,' came a raspy cry from a figure trapped under a horse with a spear sticking from its torso.

Malu raced to the man's side, Theodora and Hafder close behind. What could be seen of the man's legs stuck out at unnatural angles.

'Free him!' Malu ordered, and the Northemers fashioned ropes to heave the animal off the man, who yelped in pain at the movement of weight. With the horse removed, it didn't take a healer to confirm the man was not much longer for this world. His flattened chest rose and fell with short, laboured breaths. Blood spilt from the corners of his parched lips.

'Water,' he wheezed. Hafder tipped a flask to his mouth.

'What happened?' Malu asked.

'Attacked…They took…everything,' he said between gasps.

'Who took everything?' Malu pressed.

The man wheezed. A shower of blood burst from his mouth.

'Who?' Malu repeated.

'…The…Dis— Discontented.' The man's eyes fluttered rapidly, and with a final gasp, his head lolled lifeless to one side.

'Discontented?' Malu directed his question to Horace, who shrugged.

Hafder shook his head and spat at Horace's feet. 'Fat lot of good you are.'

Malu advanced on Theodora's father. 'We thought you knew everything there was to know about Ivane. It is why we agreed to bring you with us.'

Horace clicked his jaw. 'I know enough to know that your plan is dead in the water, as dead as we will be if we set foot in the Ivanian Desertlands without horses and supplies. We should turn our focus to Lamore instead.'

Malu waved his hand dismissively, then addressed Theodora. 'What do you think?'

Theodora looked back and forth between her father, who did in fact know Ivane, and Malu, who was always so sure of victory. She was beginning to have doubts, but couldn't bring herself to voice them. Instead she deferred to Hafder.

'I think you should ask your brother's opinion.'

'About time he stopped taking advice from Lamorians,' Hafder grumbled.

'Brother,' Malu warned.

Hafder ground his teeth together and looked toward the ravine, then back toward the desert. Eventually he spoke.

'I figure we have come this far already…and we have supplies to last us a few more days. I say we press on – for now.'

'What!' Horace scoffed. 'You want to continue now, when hours ago you wanted to retreat?'

Hafder rounded on him. 'I never said anything about retreating. I wanted to join the rest of our fleet while we still had a chance to catch them. But we've missed that opportunity. Besides, we now have another reason to continue inland.'

'Another reason?' Theodora asked.

Malu smiled. 'The *Discontented*.'

Hafder nodded, then raised his voice so all could hear him. 'Whoever these scum may be, they have stolen from us, and we will track them down and make them pay! We will teach them what it means to make Northem your enemy!'

A collective roar of support ran through the Northemers.

'To Northem!' Hafder led a chant, on which Theodora reluctantly joined in. With each word, seeds of doubt inside her grew.

She was the one who had first convinced Malu to push on, but had she made a grave mistake? Had her quest for revenge and her pursuit of the 'burning light' signed all of their death warrants?

The answers lay before them, in the land of the constant sun

– a land that had so far shown them nothing but violence and death.

THE NORTHEMERS CAMPED the night at the edge of the ravine, seeking shelter from the biting cold among the rocky crevices and boulders. There was no place suitable for setting up Malu's tent, so like the other Northemers, he and Theodora would sleep by a fire with nothing but each other and their bedding to warm them.

She curled up against Malu, shivering. 'I thought the Desert-lands were supposed to be hot,' she moaned.

He tightened his arms around her and spoke in her ear. 'They are, by day. The mountain ranges in the east and west enclose the region, stopping the cooling rain and wind from reaching the desert. You will be begging for our Northem winters before long,' he teased.

Theodora didn't respond to his joke. Her mind was on what lay ahead.

Malu tugged on her shoulders so she would roll back to face him. 'What is it?' he asked.

'Nothing,' she lied. Even in the soft light of the fire, she could see he didn't believe her.

'You don't think we can succeed, do you?'

She bit her lip, and hurt flashed in Malu's eyes.

'I understand why some of them doubt me.' He gestured to the sleeping Northemers around them. 'They lack imagination. But you must have faith in me. My plan isn't completely lost. There is a much bigger strategy underway.'

'What is it?'

'I don't want to share the details until I am sure it can work.'

Theodora understood this. She hadn't yet shared with Malu what the wise woman had said about Rea. She wanted to be sure Rea was in Ivane first.

'Between you and me, though, I think we can succeed,'

Malu went on. 'I have been working on it with Olix for some time, and he wouldn't dare fail me.'

So that was the 'business' with the merchant he'd been referring to. The merchant Malu blamed for…

Theodora took a deep breath. 'Who's Sera?' she asked in a quiet voice.

Malu stiffened, his fingers tensing along her ribs. She immediately regretted her question, but then Malu relaxed his grip. He released her from his embrace and sat up, lifting his knees toward his chest and resting his forearms on them. His steady gaze fixed on something, nothing, straight ahead.

'She was my younger sister.' His voice was a shadow of a whisper. 'Our parents died when I was fifteen and Sera was only twelve.'

Theodora sat up and shuffled toward Malu so they were almost touching again. She wanted him to know she was here for him.

'It was the Endless Winter – the great famine. Our parents worked hard to give us the little food we had, but there was so much sickness. So much *death*.' Malu choked on the word, as if it made him physically ill. Theodora rested a hand on his arm. 'My mother was called on to help an unwell family – all of them had a bad fever. She nursed the mother and one of the children back to health but brought the sickness back to our home. Soon we were all ill. My mother was so sick she could barely stand, but she still cared for all of us. Thanks to her, my sister and I survived, but my parents…'

Malu sniffed away what may have been tears before continuing.

'By then Hafder was living in Arykyl, serving our clan leader there, so I was left to provide for my sister and myself. We had a small plot of land and a few chickens, but nothing else. We sold everything of value, even my mother's wedding ring. We travelled all the way to Arykyl, hoping to buy food, but the prices were exorbitant. I did odd jobs, any work I could get, but it was never enough. I would give whatever I earned to my sister and she would make what she could. Watery gruel. Bread made from barley and dried peas, as hard as a rock.' He gave a hollow laugh. 'At least it was something. But my sister – my beautiful sister, the kindest soul I'd ever known – was fading away before my eyes. I thought she was weakened from the fever, so I always made sure she got a bigger share of food than me, but I didn't know…' Malu's voice broke.

'Know what?'

He turned to face Theodora with tear-filled eyes, and her heart stilled. She had never seen Malu cry.

'I found out later that Sera…' His face contorted. 'Damn her – she was giving most of her food to a homeless family. She was so thin. And no matter what I did, I couldn't afford to buy the food she needed to get well.' His hands clenched on his knees. 'So when the next wave of illness came, Sera didn't stand a chance.'

One by one, the pieces fell into place in Theodora's mind. The contradictions that made up Malu. Why he had been so driven to unite all the clan leaders and build an army of warriors that could secure the resources they needed. Why he had gone after Olix's father. And even why he'd taken Rea under his wing and cared for her like a big brother. Most of all, it explained why he had to succeed in Ivane.

She took his hand and squeezed it. 'I believe in you. You *will* win Ivane for Northem, for us. You will win it for Sera.'

Malu gave a pained smile, and for a moment he looked small and vulnerable. He was no longer the King of Northem, but the scared fifteen-year-old boy who couldn't save his sister. And Theodora was the one who must save him.

5

The journey from Kengia to Ette was tortuous for Takai. While the sea was remarkably calm, the same couldn't be said for his heart.

Seeing Arisa again had brought him entirely undone. He had tried to prepare for their meeting in Kengia, telling himself too long had passed between them, that there was no chance of reconciling. He convinced himself that being apart was for the best given his responsibilities, but any form of logic had vanished the moment he saw her. Her beauty still managed to stop him in his tracks, and beneath it remained the fire, passion and strength he had come to love.

Takai knew the state of their relationship – or lack thereof – was all his fault. He cringed as he recalled how he had snubbed Arisa at the opening of the hospital in Obira. It hadn't even made sense at the time. He had named the hospital after her uncle Amund, not just to recognise what Amund had done for him and Lamore, but to show his love for Arisa. But so much had happened. Too much.

His father's death had left a traumatic legacy. On a personal level, it had taken Takai time to reconcile the fact that his father had died at Arisa's hands. Logically, he knew the King had been a flawed man, and that in that moment, when Delrik had been gripped by madness, he would have killed Takai if it hadn't been for Arisa's intervention. But there had been little logic at play in the immediate aftermath of his father's death. It was why Takai had initially pushed Arisa away – and he had regretted it every day since.

When he had needed Arisa most, when she could have helped him heal, he had chosen to shoulder his burdens alone. He'd been left in the impossible position of not being able to acknowledge his own grief and loss as so many celebrated the death of the Lamorian King. His challenges were only compounded by the fact that he'd been thrown unprepared into the role left vacant by his father. His days had become fully consumed by the business of Lamore and what he owed to Ette. He had to rebuild trust with his own people as well as the other Kyprian nations.

Working with Ette had been particularly hard. The Etteans, of course, were grateful for Lamore's assistance in defeating the Northemers and evicting them from the Capital, and recognised that they needed help re-establishing their country. But they made it clear they didn't trust Takai. Many only saw the son of the man who had oppressed them for so long. As half-Lamorian, Takai symbolised the regime that had so heartlessly occupied the country and destroyed a culture and its people. The Etteans' reaction only spurred him on to try harder, to earn their respect, to be worthy of not just Ette but Lamore...and Arisa.

How could he claim he was deserving of her when he didn't believe he was? He could have spoken to her and told her all of this, but she would only have wanted to help. She'd endear herself to Ette, the same way she had won over the hearts of Lamore, and Takai's association with her would raise everyone's estimation of him. But that wasn't what he wanted. He wanted to make amends on his own two feet – not because he was by Arisa's side; not as her shadow. Of course, he could have handled things differently. He could have told her how he really felt, how he still loved her. But what was the point now? She had a life in Kengia with her family – with people like the Custodian Jaai, who would be a better match for her.

Asking her to come to Ette now had been good politics, and Takai hoped it may provide a chance for them to become friends again. He could hope for nothing more. But his resolve had crumbled in the close confines of the ship. He couldn't stop thinking about her, wondering *what if*. The very idea of speaking to her, only to possibly learn she had moved on, tore a gaping hole inside him. And as hard as it was to avoid Arisa during the journey, he managed for the most part to do it. Their interactions were limited to civilities and Takai was careful to make sure there were others around when she was near.

Now they were on their final approach to Ette, Takai felt he could finally breathe again. He took in a lungful of salty air as he stood on the deck of his Lamorian galleon. The impossibly blue water sparkled back at him as gulls flew overhead, a sure sign land was near. Not much longer before he could get some distance between himself and Arisa. Before he could collect his thoughts and determine how to approach her.

It seemed like a sound plan, but didn't account for the fact that at that exact moment, Arisa emerged from below deck. She caught Takai's eye, but swiftly looked away before moving to the bow of the ship. Her long bronze hair billowed in the breeze, tendrils reaching out like fingers grasping his very soul. He remembered how, for a time, he'd thought she had bewitched him – used Kengian magic against him. Takai *was* bewitched, but it wasn't magic. It was an undeniable bond that only grew more impossible to fight.

'She doesn't bite.'

He jumped at the sound of Sar's booming voice beside him.

'Very funny.'

'I'm not trying to be funny, just trying to make you see sense.'

Takai crossed his arms. 'I have no idea what you're talking about.'

Sar raised a disbelieving brow. 'You two are meant for each other, and you'd be together right now if you hadn't been such a stubborn dunderhead.'

'Is that an appropriate way to speak to your King?' Takai sniped.

Sar gave his signature dimpled grin. 'I'm not speaking as your subject, I'm speaking as your best friend. And frankly, I've had enough of your hangdog looks. Just go and speak to her, misery-guts.'

Takai gritted his teeth. As always, Sar was right.

As he strode across the deck, Ette's eastern coast began to rise from the horizon, a scattering of grand stone residences nestled into leafy hillsides. His steps slowed as he got closer to Arisa. What would he say? How would he begin?

Just as he reached her, a gasp escaped her throat. The reason for her reaction became clear. The ship had just rounded the reef and peninsula that concealed the Capital. The crescent-shaped harbour was alive with dozens of trading vessels. A kaleidoscope of buildings in every shade of yellow, apricot and rose appeared to be stacked upon each other on a slope leading to a fortress that overlooked the whole city. The white stone crenellations of the fortress battlements were testament to the wealth and power of the great trading nation. In appearance, the Capital was a bright, sunny day to Obira's sprawling grey night.

'Quite magnificent, isn't it?'

Takai's words, meant for Arisa as much as the city, caught her by surprise. She spun to face him, her usually glittering silver eyes mottled with uncertainty.

'*Magnificent…*' The way she said the word was part statement, part question.

A whisper of her fragrance, the blossom-infused scent of a Kengian summer's evening, wafted toward Takai. Sweat sprung from his brow. 'It's much warmer here,' he muttered, wiping his forehead.

Arisa's eyes suddenly widened. 'You still have it?'

Takai followed her gaze to his wrist, where he wore the Kengian good fortune bracelet she had given him. He gave a weak smile.

Arisa returned it, and held up her own wrist. She was wearing the braided bracelet he had made and given her on her eighteenth birthday. They shared a stilted laugh.

'I'm glad you are here,' he said. It wasn't what he really yearned to say, but it was a start.

Her eyes flitted across his face, searching for meaning, her chest rising and falling with her breath. Then her half-smile grew for a fleeting moment before she turned her back on him to face Ette.

A moment cut short. A chance Takai feared he may never have again.

6

A lone hawk flew overhead, looping the unmarked cerulean sky, its razor-sharp eyes probing the lifeless desert for food.

'Good luck,' Theodora muttered to herself. The bird was the first living creature they'd seen since arriving in Ivane. The Desertlands were as desolate and merciless as they had feared. And blazing hot! A stifling, suffocating heat that threatened to suck the life from them.

The Northemers had stripped off their winter furs in favour of linen shirts or bare chests. Theodora had abandoned her underlayers, wearing only her lace-up suede vest and loose-fitting breeches. While it was cool, the sleeveless costume offered little protection from the elements. Her once alabaster skin had turned cherry-red, then blistered, peeling in places. Her face was already spotted with freckles. Rayl panted her way through their journey until her coat thankfully started to thin.

Acclimatising, though, wasn't their only challenge. After several days of trudging through the desert, their food and water were running dangerously low, with no hope of replenishing their supplies.

Distrust was rife among the Northemers, who no longer

bothered hiding their thoughts about 'Malu's cursed mission', forgetting their initial fervour for tracking down the Discontented. Yet Malu pressed on, exuding his usual confidence and privately insisting his plan would come together.

It didn't help that Theodora's father was constantly in her ear. 'You must convince him to abandon this lunacy,' he argued repeatedly.

On seeing Horace haranguing his daughter, Malu had offered to 'put an end to the fool's miserable existence – just one word'. But Theodora had assured Malu she could handle Horace, refusing to lower herself to his level. She might be her father's daughter in some ways, but she didn't share his special breed of cruelty.

Today, however, Horace was being particularly irritating – and unfortunately, Malu wasn't within reach to make good on his offer.

'It's not too late to attack Lamore,' Horace declared. 'Takai is so focused on helping Ette that he will be unprepared for an attack on his home soil. And I still have allies there, people loyal to me—'

'Loyal to my mother and her coin, you mean.'

Horace clicked his jaw. 'All that matters is that we can recruit Lamorians who can help us undermine any of Takai's efforts.' Her father's voice rose with excitement. 'And I can be returned to my rightful place, ruling all of Lamore.'

Theodora rolled her eyes. 'You've forgotten about the Water Catcher and the Air King, who would come to Takai's aid – with the Kengian army.'

'As they will do for Ivane,' he snapped back.

'And we welcome it,' Theodora said confidently. 'Here their magic is useless, and Arisa will be vulnerable.'

Horace tutted. 'You need to think beyond revenge if you want true power.'

'You're the last person to talk,' she scoffed. 'Your need for revenge was the only reason we challenged Kengia in the first place, and look where it got us.'

Theodora smiled to herself as a scowl formed on Horace's face. If only to spite her father, she would never doubt Malu again.

OVER THE COURSE of the day, the Northemers tracked south-west toward the mountain range that bordered Ette. By afternoon the desert plains had given way to sandstone hills, sparsely vegetated with small, spiky grey-green shrubs. They were passing along the base of one particularly rocky outcrop when an alarm was raised. Black smoke rose above the hillside.

'A village fire,' Hafder suggested.

Malu shook his head. 'A village *on* fire, judging by that.' He indicated the growing stack of smoke and frowned. 'Stay alert,' he ordered the group – but the warning came too late.

There was a cry from the Huntmaster in front of Theodora. Blood spurted from the man's throat, where an arrow was embedded.

'Shield wall!' Malu shouted, and the group began to scuttle into formation. Malu pulled Theodora behind him as the Northemers huddled together so their shields overlapped, forming a protective shell.

'The Discontented?' Hafder questioned.

'How many do you think there are?' one Northemer asked.

Another scream and a shower of blood from the back of the pack. An arrow had found its way through their defences.

'There has to be dozens,' Horace wailed, his shaking fingers reaching for the place a hand cannon would be if Malu had allowed him to be armed. 'We're doomed.' Malu glared at Horace, whose mouth slammed shut.

Hafder caught his brother's eye and nodded.

'On three,' Malu said in precise, clipped tones. 'We scramble. Everyone in different directions. I want chaos.'

There was a collective murmuring of assent, except for Horace, who squeaked, 'Have mercy. Let me have a weapon—'

Malu ignored his plea. 'Stay behind me,' he whispered in Theodora's ear. 'One...two...three!'

As ordered, the Northemers dashed in every direction. Malu stood with a hand cannon at the ready, partially shielding Theodora. He directed Jak, one of their finest warriors, to protect her as his eyes scanned the rocky hillside, trying to spot their attackers.

An arrow flew past Theodora's ear, finding a target behind her. Another Northemer fell, the arrow sticking from his leather vest. Their attackers appeared to be remarkably good shots.

Malu and the few others among them who had hand cannons fired up the hillside at random. Another Northemer yelped in pain nearby. An arrow had skimmed his ear, taking a sizeable chunk of flesh with it.

'Show yourself!' Malu challenged in his native tongue.

A scream sounded to Theodora's far right, and she turned to see one of the men by the wagon slump to the ground, an arrow in his shoulder. That arrow had only narrowly missed Rayl's cage.

Malu's jaw clenched. 'Hurry up, brother,' he muttered to himself.

Hafder? A swift glance around confirmed Hafder wasn't there. Theodora's gaze flew to the hillside, and there she caught fleeting glimpses of the Northemer scaling the slope, slipping from one boulder to another.

Malu ordered his archers to fire toward the summit, but away from Hafder's path.

An arrow whistled toward Theodora – but found her protector, Jak, instead. The arrow lodged at the base of Jak's throat. She clutched Theodora's arm. 'Help,' she gurgled through her blood-filled mouth.

Theodora lowered her to the ground. She held Jak's hand, murmuring assurances that she would be alright, that it was nearly over. But it wasn't alright. Jak died with terror in her eyes. Nothing like the honourable death in battle all Northemers purported to welcome.

These people were no different to anyone, Theodora realised. They were no different to her – they wanted to survive. She wondered if Malu had seen the same thing in his fellow countrymen and women on the battlefield. The fear. Lives cut down in their prime. No wonder he wished for a life beyond war.

A shout of surprise sounded near the top of the hillside. A string of Ivanian insults – Theodora recognised the language from spending so much time in the Lamorian Queen's rooms.

'It is safe!' Hafder's voice blasted down the slope toward them.

Confused looks and questions circulated among the Northemers. How could it be safe? Had Hafder managed to overcome all of the attackers? Had they retreated?

The answer appeared in the form of Hafder lumbering back down the hill – his knife to the throat of a teenage girl. As they neared, Theodora realised the stunning truth: there had only been one girl. She alone was their attacker.

The girl's bow and arrow were taken from her, as well as a staff topped with a blade. The whole time, she snarled at her captors, the train of Ivanian abuse continuing. From her unkempt mane of curly black hair to her flashing green eyes and dirt-smeared skin, the girl had all the appearance of a wild animal.

'Are you sure she's alone?' Malu asked.

Hafder nodded.

'Where are the others? Your people? Are you one of the Discontented?' Malu asked in Northem, but the girl didn't seem to understand. He tried again in broken Ettean, to no effect, then Lamorian. Still no response.

'Let me try,' Theodora suggested. 'I know some Ivanian.'

Malu nodded.

'Discontented?' she began in Ivanian. The girl sneered back at her. 'What's your name?' Theodora pressed, to no response. 'I'm Theodora.'

The girl gave an indifferent shrug. Theodora would have to take a different tack.

'The smoke. Was something set on fire?'

At that, the girl jutted out her chin. 'My village.'

'What did she say?' Malu asked.

'She isn't one of the Discontented. She said her village is the source of the fire.'

Malu nodded for Theodora to continue.

'What happened? Were you attacked by another village? Where are the survivors?'

The girl looked away. 'The firebird killed everyone except me. I escaped. Our village is gone.'

Firebird? Surely she was talking about Rea. Perhaps this girl could help Theodora find her. But the Northemers probably didn't *want* to find Rea. They blamed her for their defeat in Lamore. They blamed Malu for trusting her.

Theodora would have to proceed carefully.

'What did she say?' Hafder barked.

'She said they were attacked by another village and that she's the only survivor.'

Malu's mouth twitched, as if sensing her lie, but he remained silent. Horace, though, cast a questioning gaze at his daughter. He too knew some Ivanian from the time he'd spent negotiating Queen Sofia and King Delrik's marriage.

The girl seemed to catch the exchange, because she narrowed her gaze at Theodora. 'You know of this firebird?' she asked.

'Yes. And we would like to find it,' Theodora replied. 'Will you help us?'

The girl averted her gaze again and was silent.

'Enough!' Hafder grunted. 'Let's be rid of the wildcat now.'

'Please,' Theodora begged. 'You must agree to help us, or they will kill you.'

The girl turned back to face Theodora, her gaze unwavering. 'What if I wish to die?'

The fear in Jak's eyes as she was dying came back to Theodora. She wasn't convinced this girl wanted to die; there must be something she would believe was worth living for. Then it came to her.

'We want to hunt the firebird so we can kill it.' The untruth left a sour taste in Theodora's mouth, but she pressed on. 'It has wronged us and we seek revenge. Will you help us?'

The girl scrutinised the group of Northemers, as if assessing their number and abilities. 'Help invaders? You are invaders, no?'

Theodora searched her mind for a plausible explanation of their presence in Ivane. She was counting on the fact that the girl, having lived in such a remote location, may not suspect their real identity or purpose.

'We are merchants from lands far from here. But we were shipwrecked and want to go to Nadis to trade and secure a vessel.'

The girl laughed, which resulted in Hafder smacking the back of her head. 'What is she saying?' he demanded.

Theodora gestured for him to give her a moment. 'Will you help us?' she asked the Ivanian.

The girl sniffed. 'I will help you find the creature, but it must be me who takes its life.'

There was something in her manner and audacity that ironically reminded Theodora of Rea. 'Agreed. But you must also help us navigate to Nadis. And help us find food and supplies.'

The girl shrugged. 'Fine.'

Theodora flashed Malu a triumphant smile. 'If you spare her life, the girl will help us find food and get to Nadis.'

'Splendid,' Malu said in his sing-song voice. The look Hafder gave him, though, could have killed.

'She should die for what she did,' he growled.

Malu's gaze hardened. 'Do *you* want to die?' he hissed in his brother's face, then addressed the rest of the Northemers. 'Do *all* of you want to die?'

Dropped gazes, the scuffing of feet in the sand.

'Because without her' – Malu jabbed a finger at the girl – 'we will all perish. So the girl lives...*for now*.' He added the last part with a terrifyingly benign smile.

So the girl joined the Northemers. Her wrists were bound with a length of rope, its other end tied to the wagon. As soon as the Northemers' bodies were buried, they set off again.

'Are you going to tell me?' Malu asked Theodora in a low whisper as they walked ahead of the main group.

'Tell you wh—'

Malu sighed. 'You don't have to play games with me, my love. I only want the truth from you. You are the only one I can trust.'

Theodora's heart lurched. 'Alright.'

She told him about what the wise woman had said, and how the Ivanian girl's village had been destroyed by a 'firebird'. Malu listened without interruption, his face impassive.

'I didn't want to say anything until I was completely sure,' she finished.

Malu took her hand in his. 'You were right not to share any of this with the others. They don't understand Rea...But you never need to hide anything from me.' He lifted her hand to his lips. 'You and I are one.'

How had she ever doubted him? She cupped his bearded chin with her free hand. 'We are one.'

7

*A*risa disembarked into a dizzying carnival-like atmosphere. The Capital was a cacophony of colour, sights and sounds, its marketplace a sensory explosion. Stalls sold wine, olive oil, sugar and silks. There were textiles, spices, fruits and vegetables, as well as precious stones and metals in every hue of the rainbow. Coins passed hands with rapid bargaining in Ettean – the language Arisa had been learning from Gwyn during their time together in Kengia. There was also a spattering of other languages, some of which Arisa recognised, others she didn't. The streets were heaving with people who were presumably in the city for the Chief Minister's inauguration.

While some of the buildings were damaged, probably from the conflicts with the Northemers, they were in the process of being reconstructed. A sign of a nation on the rise. Isla had told Arisa that the Capital was once again the centre of banking and trade in the Kyprian region.

As their carriage snaked its way through the city up to the fortress, Arisa was unable to ignore the excited shouts: 'It's her! It's the Water Catcher!'

She sank back in her seat so she couldn't be seen. To distract herself, she let her mind wander to her interaction with Takai on the ship's deck.

He utterly confounded her. One moment it was as if he were about to declare his love for her, and the next he was formal and businesslike. Arisa was as angry as she was perplexed. Takai had played with her feelings for a year now. How long was he going to make her suffer for killing his father? He must know she had only done it to save his life. She'd had no choice.

They needed some form of resolution. One way or another, Arisa must know where she stood. But first she had to see to more pressing matters. First and foremost, she was here to represent Kengia – but just as importantly, she was here to find and help Rea.

On their arrival at the fortress, a petite young woman with an amiable smile and similar large, nut-brown eyes to Arisa's mother introduced herself as Delpha. 'Welcome to Government House,' she said.

'Government House?'

'The Chief Minister's lodgings, and the place where the new government will meet,' Delpha explained with pride.

She showed Arisa to her room. It was a simple affair. The furnishings consisted of a bed and a washbasin. The walls were bare except for a single embroidered tapestry depicting three winged women sitting among the clouds.

Delpha gestured to the tapestry. 'They are from a traditional Ettean myth.'

'I don't know that tale. You will have to tell me about it – if, of course, you're allowed to...You have the time, that is, to stay...' Arisa couldn't find the right words, unsure of Delpha's position in Ette – a place where Lamore's rule had forced both Etteans and Kengians into servitude.

Delpha must have understood Arisa's conflict, because she merely gave a kind smile before explaining, 'There are no forced servants any longer in Ette. I work here. It is my job to serve you, and I am paid to do so.'

Arisa exhaled with relief. She didn't want anyone to think the 'Water Catcher' was a bumbling dunce.

'Could I ask you something?'

'Anything.' There was something in Delpha's manner that was so much like Gwyn – an easiness in her company that Arisa immediately warmed to.

'Have you heard of a creature recently seen in Ette, said to be made of fire?'

Isla, it had transpired, knew little about the firebird and its whereabouts, having only seen it briefly in the sky over the mountains on Ette's borders. From the little she'd seen, though, she believed it was the same phoenix that had been in Lamore. Arisa was desperate for more information.

'I have,' Delpha said slowly.

Arisa indicated for her to continue.

Delpha wrung her hands. 'There are stories…It has attacked villages, razing them to the ground without mercy. Killing everyone in sight.'

Arisa swallowed hard and took a moment to compose herself before she was able to reply. 'Is that what you believe?'

A sadness appeared in Delpha's eyes. 'It doesn't matter what I believe. The creature is damned either way.'

ARISA COULDN'T GET the conversation with Delpha out of her head. She had referred to the firebird – the creature Arisa believed was Rea – as *damned*. It must be because people wanted the phoenix dead. There was even talk that the Chief Minister was putting a bounty on its head.

Dressed and ready for the inauguration celebration in the same silver gown she'd worn on the Ambay Coast, Arisa gazed out her window, toward eastern Ette. Vineyards and fields of green slipped away in the distance. The hint of a mountain range on the horizon. She wondered if they were the same mountains where Isla had seen the phoenix in the sky.

'Where are you?' she murmured.

'Right behind you,' came a familiar larger-than-life voice behind her.

Arisa turned to find Sar and Isla dressed in all their finery. Isla wore a fitted emerald-green top and wide-legged silk pants. Sar wore a doublet, also in emerald green, with gold braid trim and black breeches.

'Look at you two. What a handsome pair,' she remarked.

Sar stood up tall, blew on his closed hand and rubbed his chest, all the while making an exaggerated proud face.

Isla rolled her eyes. 'Do you see what I have to put up with?'

'You know you can't get enough of me,' he teased, kissing Isla's hand.

They were ridiculously good together. Arisa should have been happy for her cousin and friend, and she was – but seeing them together reminded her of what she'd lost with Takai.

Isla must have guessed Arisa's inner turmoil, because she batted Sar playfully on the arm and said, 'Begone with you. I wish to speak with my cousin.'

Sar gave a theatrical bow and left.

Isla sighed as she watched him go. 'He really is quite...'

'Charming. Funny. Handsome,' Arisa suggested.

'Annoying.'

But Arisa could tell by the way she said it that Isla was far from annoyed...She was clearly and deeply in love with Sar.

Isla turned back to her. 'Speaking of annoying. What are we going to do about your frustratingly foolish dunderhead of a King?'

Arisa laughed at her cousin's directness. On the journey to Ette, she and Isla had spoken at length about many topics. Having barely seen each other over the last year, they had much to catch up on. While their relationship had gotten off to a rocky start in Kengia, by the time they'd ridden alongside each other in battle, there was a mutual respect between the two of them. A friendship of sorts had followed, with the exchange of regular letters. From these, Arisa knew Isla had grown to admire Takai for his actions in Lamore and Ette – but when it came to his treatment of Arisa, she was in protective mode.

'You know he still cares for you. A lot.'

Arisa shrugged.

'It's true. You can see it in the way he looks at you. Like a pathetic, pining little puppy.' Isla shuddered. 'Do you know what his problem is?'

He can't forgive me for the death of his father, Arisa thought.

Isla didn't wait for her to respond. 'He's too righteous. All upright and honourable.' She lifted her chin, pursed her lips and pulled back her shoulders in an imitation of Takai. Arisa couldn't help but laugh. Isla relaxed her pose and took Arisa's hand in hers. 'The problem is that Takai carries so much guilt for things that weren't his doing. And until he believes he's fully atoned for his imagined sins, he will go on punishing himself.'

'What are you saying?'

'I'm saying that denying his love for you is some form of self-imposed punishment.'

Arisa pulled her hand away from her cousin's. 'I don't think that's it. I think he blames me…' But she couldn't voice her own guilt out loud to Isla. It would only make it worse somehow. She shook her head. 'Anyway, it doesn't matter. Too long has passed. Takai and I are over.'

Isla frowned. 'Don't misunderstand me. He has been a right royal fool this last year and has treated you dreadfully, but I have grown to like Takai in some ways. Besides, it isn't him I'm worried about. It's you. I know you will never be truly happy without him. You're meant for each other.'

A lump stuck in Arisa's throat. She couldn't refute the truth in Isla's words, but there was no point dwelling on something that could never be. She forced a smile and changed the subject. 'Like you and Sar. The perfect pair of lovebirds.'

Isla shoved her hands over her ears. 'La, la, la. I'm not listening.'

Arisa's strained smile transformed into a real one. 'I've missed you, cousin.'

Isla lowered her hands and gave a nonchalant shrug. 'Missed someone keeping you on your toes, more like it.'

'I might still have a few tricks up my sleeve.'

Isla linked her arm with Arisa's and led her through the door. 'And I, for one, can't wait to see them.'

THE CELEBRATORY INAUGURATION feast was taking place in the Great Room of Government House. Arisa had expected it to be similar to the Great Hall at Lamore Castle, but in reality, they were worlds apart.

The Great Room was an open-air pavilion-style space of grand proportions. White marble arches and pillars delineated the perimeter and provided support where walls would usually be in a room of the same size. Along one side was a balcony overlooking the city, harbour and sea. Vines with flowers in shades of fuchsia, peach and violet rambled up walls and along balustrades, leaving a heady scent in the air. Long wooden tables and benches ran along either side of a dance floor marked by black-and-white chequered tiles.

Musicians at the top end of the room played fast-paced melodies on steel-stringed instruments that resembled the Lamorian lute but produced an upbeat, metallic twang. There were also flutes, drums and handheld wooden percussion instruments. The music had a chaotic yet intoxicating quality, which lent itself to dancing that was free of formalities and self-consciousness. The Etteans danced with abandon. While there seemed to be some order to their steps, clapping partners danced freely with each other, moving in whatever way the music led them. Their flowing, swirling costumes in myriad colours were a symbol of pure joy. And, like their dancing, they dressed with no regard to rules, or at least no rules that Arisa was aware of.

Some women wore headdresses while others wore their hair loose. Some wore single-colour gowns with long, ballooning sleeves. Others wore sleeveless linen dresses with intricate silk embroidery: repeating floral and geometric motifs in saffron, scarlet, cobalt blue and lush green. The men's costumes were just as diverse. Isla pointed out the different styles from particular regions in Ette, as well as some from Ivane.

As Arisa wandered through the Great Room, she was greeted with admiring looks and the broadest of smiles. The words *It's the Water Catcher'* preceded and trailed her everywhere she went.

Arisa's breath quickened. It had been a long time since she'd been the focus of so much attention. In Kengia, everyone had gradually become accustomed to her – for the most part, she was no more interesting or important than anyone else. But here she was a novelty. A welcome novelty, but it was overwhelming all the same.

She scanned the room, looking for refuge. Her gaze found Takai, standing near a table at the front of the room. *Damn it.* She had been struck by his appearance in Kengia when he was dressed in full military regalia, but now, in much simpler Lamorian costume, Takai was, impossibly, even more handsome. Arisa assumed he and Sar had made a deliberate choice not to wear the uniform of the country that had oppressed Ette for so long. A wise decision, one she suspected was Takai's.

His gaze moved in her direction, as if he sensed her presence. He gave an uncertain smile. Looking as if he was excusing himself, he made to approach her.

Arisa looked around the room in desperation, not ready to speak to him. Isla, though, was occupied with Sar.

'Your Highness?' Someone behind her, speaking in Ettean. Arisa spun to face a middle-aged man with a bushy salt-and-pepper moustache and brows to match. 'We're honoured you could be here, Your Highness.' The man beamed, then hurriedly bowed.

'Ah…Thank you.' Arisa had no idea who he was. Isla thankfully came to the rescue, mouthing *the Chief Minister* from over his shoulder. 'And it is an honour to meet you, Chief Minister. Congratulations on your election.' Arisa returned his bow.

'Please call me Kris.' The Chief Minister clasped his hands in front of him, twirling his thumbs, his grin never leaving his face. 'We're a relaxed lot around here.'

'I will call you Kris, if you'll call me Arisa.'

A jolly laugh exploded from him. 'Yes. You have all the kindness and grace of your mother.'

'My mother? Did you know her?'

'Many moons ago. We were but children. She was the daughter of one tribal King and I the son of another. We were from neighbouring provinces.'

It was telling that Kris, based on his lineage, could have asserted an ancestral right to rule Ette, but had chosen to leave it to the people to decide. It made sense for a country that was forging a new future for itself.

'We saw each other often,' Kris continued, then a darkness fell over his face and his twirling thumbs stilled. 'But I never saw her again after…'

'After Lamore extended its reach to all of the tribes and put an end to any royal claims on Ette.' Arisa stated the facts as Gwyn had told them to her.

Kris nodded gravely. 'We had a choice. Fight for our birthright and die, or bend the knee to Lamore and survive. My father chose survival.' He dropped his head. 'While your grandfather fought.'

Arisa placed a comforting hand on his arm. 'Your father did what he did to protect you. My mother had a lucky escape. If the Ivanian King hadn't taken her in, she would have died too.'

Kris looked up with a hopeful smile. 'Luck we are all grateful for. Without your mother, we wouldn't have you. And if it weren't for you, none of us would be here.' He gave a caustic laugh. 'Or we *would* be here, but we'd be forced to promise fealty to Northem or—'

Kris's words came to an abrupt stop at the arrival of Takai.

'Chief Minister.' Takai bowed to him.

'Your Majesty,' Kris said with a thin smile followed by a shallow bow.

Takai had the civility not to indicate he'd taken any offence, but Arisa felt the slight keenly. She knew the burdens weighing down on Takai and everything he had done to make amends for his father's wrongdoings. He didn't deserve the contempt openly shown to him.

Kris returned his attention to Arisa. 'Please, will you come and sit with me?'

Arisa's eyes went from the Chief Minister's proffered arm to Takai's earnest gaze. She knew she was about to disappoint one of them. Her heart and mind warred within her, but a glance around the room confirmed her choice. She had a duty more important than herself. A duty to the country she represented. Takai must understand this.

She cast him an apologetic look and took Kris's arm.

The feast that followed was worthy of the momentous occasion. Sumptuous dishes showcased all of the fresh produce and fare the region was known for. Vine leaves filled with spiced fruit and rice. Grilled octopus and fish of every size and shape. Roasted vegetables marinated in herbs and oil. Flatbreads with mouth-watering dips. Pork sausage medallions with a fiery yet pleasant aftertaste. And for dessert, citrus flans, baked custards with a caramel sauce and fried balls of dough dripping with honey. All washed down with the finest of wines.

Arisa was seated between the Chief Minister and the Ivanian emissary, an amiable woman who now lived in Ette. The emissary spent most of her time in conversation with a handsome man on her other side. The man, whose name was

Kappu, was the newly appointed Commander of Ette's forces and had been working and training with Sar this past year. Sar was seated with Isla and Takai at the opposite end of the long table. Despite the distance between them, Arisa was acutely aware of Takai's weighty gaze.

After dessert, she took the opportunity to speak to the Chief Minister of the firebird, asking if a bounty was entirely necessary. Kris gave a dismissive wave, assuring her the decision had been made by the whole government at the behest of their constituents.

'But do you truly believe the creature is guilty of what it is accused?' Arisa pressed. 'I, for one, find it hard to fathom that it would attack villages indiscriminately. There must be a reason – perhaps it was provoked.'

The Chief Minister's eyes narrowed. 'You have quite an interest in the creature.' He tapped his finger on the stem of his goblet, then leant in close to Arisa. 'Tell me, do you think this is the same bird of fire that was seen at the battle in Lamore, transformed from a silver-eyed girl with magnificent powers?'

Arisa thought carefully for a moment about how much she should reveal. It certainly wouldn't aid her argument or Rea's case if the Ettean leader believed it was the same person responsible for the attacks. But what choice did she have if she wanted the man's help?

'We don't know anything for sure…but if it is the same girl, I don't believe she is dangerous, unless she is personally threatened. Putting out a bounty and encouraging people to hunt her down *will* only lead to death. For your own people's sake, I urge you to proceed carefully.'

The Chief Minister held up his hands in surrender. 'I am nothing but an instrument of the people, and this is what they've asked for.'

There was a heaviness in the way he spoke that made Arisa think perhaps part of him did wish for the autonomous powers of a sovereign King. She made to protest, but Kris had turned his back on her to speak to one of his fellow ministers. Arisa only became more determined to find Rea herself, as soon as she could be done with her duties in the Capital.

A change in music and a particular song caught her ear. It was an Ivanian waltz, a favourite of Queen Sofia's that had been played often in her rooms. Arisa had fond memories of learning to dance to it. Learning from Takai. Instinctively, she sought him out, but his place at the end of the table was empty. A hard lump of disappointment formed in her throat.

'Would you like to dance?' Takai's voice behind her.

A smile burst across her face, but she tempered herself before turning to face him. She nodded her confirmation. He reached for her hand, sending sparks through her body as he led her to the dance floor. Once there, Takai reached around her waist, holding her stiffly in the waltz pose, his jaw clenched.

They started to dance, but it was nothing like Arisa remembered. Takai moved mechanically, as if unsure of himself or wishing he were somewhere else. Perhaps it was a bit of both. She was sure he wanted to be far from the distrustful stares and whispers. After the feast he could have sat somewhere in the background of the hall or even slipped away, but he had asked her to dance. Even now she could feel the hostile looks aimed at him and the questions in the air as to why she would be with him. Arisa still hurt more than she cared to admit, but she was beginning to see the challenges Takai faced.

She smiled up at him. 'Do you remember teaching this to me? Theodora wanted to dance with you, but you chose me instead.'

His hold on her relaxed. The expression in his dark eyes softened. 'I remember. The look she gave you could have killed.'

Arisa laughed. 'Yes, she was hardly a fan of mine.'

'It was her loss,' he said with a half-smile.

'I wonder how she fares with the Northemers?'

'I think the question is how the Nothemers are faring with *her*.'

Arisa frowned. 'I don't know. Her father went with her. She must still contend with him.'

Takai cocked his head. 'You can't possibly sympathise with Theodora after everything?'

'*Sympathise?* I don't know. *Understand* why she acted the way she did, given her father's power over her…Perhaps.'

'Well, you are a better person than I.' He clenched his jaw again. 'I can never forgive her for how she treated you.'

Arisa knew Takai had meant it to sound kind toward her, but it only served to remind her that she also needed forgiveness.

'Speaking of forgiveness…' she began tentatively.

Takai stopped dancing abruptly and indicated for her to follow him from the dance floor. He wrung his hands. 'Forgiveness is something denied to me.'

Arisa reached for his arm, wanting to say it was her who sought his forgiveness, but he waved her away.

'I have no right to anything. Not until I have made amends to my people and Lamore.'

'You must stop punishing yourself for things your father did.'

Takai shook his head. 'I did things as well. I took up arms against my own people.'

'To protect all of Kypria. You sacrificed yourself for them.'

'Did I? Or did I fight with Kengia for *you* and you alone?'

Arisa froze. What was he saying? That it was her fault he felt so much guilt? She began to back away.

'That's not what I meant.' Takai made to place his hand on her arm, but she stepped further out of his reach. 'Damn it,' he admonished himself. 'I was just saying that I made choices that may have served me first and foremost, which is why now I must put others first…Or at least that's what I thought—'

Takai's words were cut short as a murmur of excitement rolled through the room. Arisa spotted a messenger making a beeline for the Ivanian emissary.

'A messenger from my uncle's court,' Takai said. He looked back and forth from the messenger to Arisa. 'I must…'

'Go. We can speak again later.' She gave what she hoped was a reassuring smile.

Takai left. But he was back a mere minute or so later, a grim look on his face.

'What is it?'

'Northemers. Their ships were sighted off the south-east coast of Ivane. An invading party was also reported in the north.'

Arisa's hand flew to her mouth. This only meant one thing. Something she'd hoped she would never have to see again.

War.

8

Theodora opened the door to Rayl's cage, knowing the snow leopard wouldn't try to attack her. The pair had an understanding. Rayl let Theodora change her dressing each day, always licking her hand in greeting. The great cat was now able to put weight on her injured leg without yowling in pain.

'You'll walk again,' Theodora said. 'I can see the determination in your eyes. And I will see that you're returned to your home.' The animal blinked as if she understood. 'In the meantime, you must build your strength.' Theodora held out a charred bird, one of the finches the Ivanian girl had caught for them.

As good as her word, the girl, whose name was Jade, had found food for the Northemers. She climbed the sides of ravines, as agile as a cat herself, finding finch nests high up the crag walls. She'd reach bare-handed into burrows and retrieve desert hedgehogs, lizards and even snakes. The best eating was a kind of rodent that had oversized ears and saucer eyes and bounded like a rabbit. Jade also found water where none of the Northemers would have thought to look. She'd shown them a type of tree called a Batu-riek – it meant *tree of life* in Ivanian, but there was little about its appearance that indicated life.

A Batu-riek consisted of a sprawling mass of lifeless, tentacle-like limbs. The thorny branches looked more like tree roots and were as dry and dead-looking as the desert itself. On first seeing the tree, one of the Northemers had set to it with an axe, remarking that it would make good firewood, but the blade ricocheted without leaving a mark. Jade had burst into uncontrollable laughter as she watched the man attempt unsuccessfully to cut the branches, again and again. Another Northemer tried, and another one, but it was no use.

Finally, Jade had explained that the Batu-riek had been forced to adapt to the desert over thousands of years, with the branches above ground impervious to fire, blade or disease. But that was not the most interesting thing about the tree. The Batu-riek had developed an ingenious way to preserve water. Beneath the ground, its branches reached for miles, tapping into water sources buried deep within the earth. It captured the water, siphoning it into gourd-shaped pods. All thirsty Ivanian travellers had to do was dig a little under the gravelly sand and retrieve one of the pods, which would give them enough water to fill several large flasks. Jade told Theodora that while most Ivanian villages had wells, Batu-riek trees were the main source of water when travelling through the Desertlands.

Now the Northemers knew what to look for, there was much talk of being rid of Jade, with Hafder the most vocal among them. Indeed, the girl's wild eyes, the colour of the stone she was named after, were unnerving. She watched her captors as if she were the hunter, not the hunted, tracking their every movement as if she would pounce on them at any moment. But Theodora needed Jade. She needed her assistance to find Rea. She just hoped Malu could keep Hafder and the others at bay long enough to find the firebird.

Theodora wanted to help Rea, to bring her back into the fold. It was just an added bonus that in doing so she could enact her final revenge on all those who'd wronged her. Then everything would be as it should be.

As Theodora waited for Rayl to finish her meal, she glanced over at Jade, who was tied to the other end of the wagon. The Ivanian sat on the ground, hands raised above her head, eyes closed. In her dozing state, she looked more like a girl than an animal. A girl who had found strength in her circumstances. A fighter. Someone who was cut from the same cloth as Rea. Someone Theodora could understand.

'Why did you lie?'

It was her father, speaking in Lamorian behind her. Rayl growled at the appearance of Horace, her fur standing on end.

'It's alright,' Theodora assured the animal. She adopted a blank look, then turned to face her father. 'I have no idea what you're referring to.'

Horace squinted down his aquiline nose at his daughter. 'You can play those imbeciles for fools' – he indicated the Northemers over his shoulder – 'but not me. You're looking for that Kengian she-wolf, but you should be careful what you wish for. Remember how she betrayed us all in Lamore.'

Theodora scowled. 'I know what I'm doing.'

'Foolish girl,' Horace sneered. 'You have let the fickle idea of friendship and your relationship with Malu cloud your judgement. Our best path forward is to take Lamore while they least expect it. It's not too late. Get that *girl* of yours to show us back to our ships.'

'Jade. Her name is Jade.'

Horace rolled his eyes. 'So now you're friends with her too? I'm telling you that Malu has planned the wrong strategy.'

Theodora squared her shoulders. 'Your opinion is neither sought nor wanted.'

Horace gave Theodora a long look before speaking. 'You are my greatest disappointment.'

Theodora clenched her hands, her fingernails digging into her palms. 'As you are to me, *Father*.'

Horace leant in so close his face was just inches from hers. 'Mark my words. You will need me. They all will need me.' He swept his arm in the direction of the Northemers. 'And you will beg me to forgive your impertinence.'

Theodora's throat constricted, remembering all the threats her father had made over the years. All the times she had 'failed' him. How he had always favoured her useless brute of a brother, even in death. She wasn't Malu's chosen Queen in this moment. She was a scared little girl unable to please her father.

'My biggest disappointment,' he repeated with a snarl.

The sound of a growl catapulted Theodora back to reality. Rayl leapt to the side of her cage, snarling at Horace, who staggered backward, almost tripping over his feet.

The Ivanian girl, now awake, exploded with laughter. Theodora had to bite her lip to stop herself from doing the same.

Horace glowered at Jade, Rayl, then Theodora. 'You're playing a dangerous game, daughter,' he hissed. 'I hope for all our sakes you know what you're doing.'

'He's delightful,' Jade said to Theodora as she got to her feet and Horace scuttled away.

A bolt of terror ran through Theodora. Had the girl understood their conversation? Did she know that Theodora actually planned on helping Rea, not capturing her?

She forced a smile. 'You understand Lamorian?'

Jade shook her head. 'I don't need to understand the words to recognise someone whose heart is as black as his. I have known men like him before. The intimidation, the threats, the undeniable hunger for power and control – it oozes from them.' She screwed up her nose. 'They reek of desperation.'

'I'm not sure I understand. I thought Ivane prided itself on equality for all – that there was no need for greed, and that everyone was at peace.'

Jade snort-laughed. 'Ivane is a big place with vast differences – there is nothing equal about it. On one hand there is the King in his comfortable palace in Nadis, who inherited his position for no other reason than being born a man...'

The girl was right. Theodora had never understood the Lamorian Queen's idolatry of her homeland. A homeland that Sofia, being the eldest child of the Ivanian King, should have ruled by right. It had always struck Theodora that Sofia's sense of Ivanian superiority was misplaced, and Jade's insights verified her view.

'…And on the other hand, there are the people who live in villages – villages like mine, if it were still here.' A darkness appeared in Jade's eyes. 'People who live simply. Their deep connection to the land means they are content with what they have despite the hardships they face. But then there are others still, who are drawn to the shiny mining cities in the south. Cities dripping with wealth, run by filthy-rich men who assure their own power by lining the royal pockets in Nadis.'

Theodora's ears had pricked at the mention of the rich mining cities, but there was something else that sparked her interest. 'So those drawn to the cities become rich?'

Jade looked into the distance, as if she could see those thriving towns. 'Perhaps *some* do, but I have seen the others – the Discontented – who have found only misery.'

'The Discontented? You know them?'

'I wish I didn't. They wander Ivane in the belief that riches are owed to them. They lie, steal and cheat. They do even worse, all in the quest for coin and power.'

'Interesting,' Theodora muttered to herself. It occurred to her that the Discontented, if properly motivated, presented an opportunity rather than a threat to Malu's plan. 'Are there many of these Discontented?'

Jade shrugged. 'Enough to employ caution in remote areas. It is why I attacked your lot, in case you were some of them. Not that I have any coin to be taken, but as I said—'

'They'll do anything to feel powerful.'

Jade grunted in confirmation. Theodora decided she would share what the girl had told her with Malu.

Jade screwed up her mouth, her sharp eyes scrutinising Theodora's face. 'What are you really doing here?'

Theodora held the girl's gaze. 'As we said, we are merchants who were shipwrecked.'

Jade laughed. 'Fine, don't tell me, then. But you should know that the Ivanian King would know of your presence here by now.'

Theodora blinked rapidly. 'How? How would he know that?'

'The people of the Desertlands – they have seen you.'

'But we haven't seen a soul other than you.'

'It doesn't mean they haven't seen you. They've probably been watching and tracking you since the moment you arrived.'

Theodora advanced on the girl. 'And how would you know this?' she snapped, but Jade merely smiled.

'There was word of it in the message stones at the last Batu-riek tree.'

'What stones?'

'You would barely notice them among the gravelly ground, unless you knew what to look for. It is one of the ways we get messages to each other out here. Everyone knows where the Batu-riek trees are and must visit them for water, so that is where messages are left.'

Theodora leant in even closer. 'And what message did you leave?'

Jade's nostrils flared. 'I didn't tell them about you – didn't need to, because as I said, they already knew you were here. But if you must know, I added to the messages about the firebird, telling how the creature attacked my village.'

Theodora stepped back to think. She needed to proceed carefully. 'What other messages were there?'

'Sightings of the creature in the sky, returning to the mountains on the Ettean border – it is believed that is where she lives.'

Theodora did a double take. 'She? You said "she".'

Jade's mouth clamped shut.

Theodora grabbed the girl's arm. 'What do you mean, *"she"*?'

'Ow!' Jade yelped as Theodora tightened her grip. 'Let go of my arm and I'll tell you.'

Theodora dropped her arm. 'Well?'

'During the attack,' she began slowly, 'the firebird landed right near my family's hut. Everyone was running and screaming, but I was stuck to the ground. I couldn't take my eyes off the creature. I noticed then that something was wrong. It was like her wings were broken.' She shook her head. 'No, broken isn't the right word for it. Her wings were made of flames, but it was like they were weighed down, or weeping. Blobs of fire were falling to the ground. The creature spat fire at me, but it was making a strained coughing sound, like it was in pain.' Jade bit her lip and looked away.

'Then what happened?'

Jade didn't answer. Theodora grabbed her shoulders and shook her. 'What happened next?' she thundered.

Jade met her steely gaze. 'The creature spoke with a girl's voice.'

Theodora gasped, releasing her. 'What did she say?'

'I couldn't understand her. She spoke in Ettean, I think.'

'She wanted your help, then?'

Jade compressed her lips. 'No. She attacked my village.'

'But you just said she was struggling. Her wings were broken. She must have wanted you to help her.'

'She attacked my village,' Jade repeated through gritted teeth.

'She wouldn't have done it for no reason. She must have been provoked.'

'Why are you defending her?' Jade's voice rose angrily. 'I thought you wanted the creature dead too.'

Theodora nodded vigorously, knowing what she said next would determine whether she could protect Rea. 'We do. She betrayed us. We lost the war in Lamore because of her. And we must have our revenge.'

Realisation dawned on Jade's face. 'So it is the same one? The one with great powers?'

Theodora nodded.

'All the more reason for us to find the creature and kill it.'

Theodora's stomach churned, but she forced another nod.

'But you will need to do something first,' Jade said. Theodora raised a suspicious brow. 'If you want even the smallest hope of not being killed, you will need to learn to defend yourself.'

Theodora's hackles rose. 'And what makes you think I don't know how to defend myself?'

Jade's eyes danced with amusement. 'Don't get me wrong – when it comes to mental ability and a proper tongue-lashing, I can see you run rings around that mob.'

She tilted her head toward a trio of Northemers passing nearby. One sliced his hand across his neck and pointed in turn to Jade, Rayl, then Theodora. They all sniggered. Jade bared her teeth at them before turning back to Theodora.

'But being able to handle yourself physically is another matter.' Her gaze returned to the Northemers. 'And I have a feeling a time will come when you will need to hold your own.'

As much as Theodora didn't want to admit it, Jade was right. Her safety among the Northemers was more than precarious, and she was tired of having to rely on others for protection. But she had also seen the capabilities of the Northemer men and women.

She gave a wry smile. 'Without Malu's protection, I am already dead. I am no match for any of them.'

'Pfft. You have many advantages over them. Your size and speed, for one. And I am going to help you.'

Theodora gave her a questioning look.

'Bring me my staff.'

And so there, in the middle of a foreign wasteland, flanked

by an injured snow leopard and an Ivanian captive, Theodora found a new resolve and the strength to be more than a survivor. She loved Malu, but she couldn't rely on him alone for protection. She would be strong enough so there would be no question of whether she was worthy of anything or anyone. She would be strong enough in mind and body to determine her own destiny.

9

'*I* don't like it.'

Takai's jaw was tense as he watched Arisa and Isla pack the saddle bags on two horses. They were heading inland toward the last reported sightings of the firebird near the Ettean mountains. Arisa ignored Takai. Nothing he said or thought could stop her from looking for Rea.

Isla, though, wasn't so inclined to be silent. 'I don't care whether you like it or not,' she snapped.

Sar crossed his arms. 'I told you. There's no point arguing with either of them.'

'But it's too dangerous. What if you encounter the Northemers?' Takai directed his question at Arisa. 'Your powers won't work here. Please, come with us to Nadis. Our ship will be ready to sail within the hour.' His voice was thick with concern.

'We'll be fine,' Arisa assured him.

Takai took her by the arm and pulled her aside. He dropped his voice to a low whisper.

'I know things haven't been good between us, but you can't put yourself in this danger.' His face contorted. 'I can't lose...'

Arisa knew his words were meant to reassure her, but they only reignited her anger. The only reason he had lost her the last time was because he'd chosen to. He had let her go back to Kengia without a fight or any promises. He'd snubbed her in Lamore.

She jutted out her chin. 'I can't lose *Rea.*'

Isla looked from Takai to Arisa and rolled her eyes. 'There'll be plenty of time for whatever unfinished business you two have when we meet you in Nadis. And the Northemers are in Ivane – no one will be looking for us in Ette. We'll find Rea and bring her back to Nadis Palace before you know it. In the meantime, you two have more important things to be worried about,' she added, referring to the very real prospect of war with the Northemers.

'We've sent for reinforcements from Lamore and Kengia,' Sar said. 'With Ivane and Ette's forces, we'll outnumber the Northemers ten to one. And once they see our new capabilities, they'll retreat before the first shot is fired.'

He was referring to the firesky weapons that Lamore and Kengia had adopted, albeit with some reluctance. They had retrieved many of the weapons from the battlefields, and with the Firemaster's book, they had been working on manufacturing more – enough to fit out their fleets and armies. The weapons – an evil necessity – were to be part of a defensive strategy and restricted to military use only. Without Rea to make more weapons for them, the Northemers would be at a significant disadvantage.

Isla frowned. Like Arisa, she was probably remembering the devastating scenes and bloodshed caused by the weapons. 'I hope you're right,' she said.

Takai placed a firm hand on Arisa's arm. 'Just be careful.'

Arisa's anger faltered. The worry in his voice and expression reminded her of someone who had loved her as much as, possibly more than, Takai. *Be careful* was something Amund used to say to her almost daily. And she had replied the same way each time.

'Aren't I always?'

Just saying the words immediately took her back to a time when her uncle was alive – a time before she knew the full extent of how her heart could break. But a smile tugged at the corner of Takai's mouth. He knew the routine.

'We'll see you in Nadis,' he said gently.

Beside them, Sar had wrapped Isla in a bear hug. She gave him a half-hearted pat on the back and made a face like she was annoyed, but it was clear from the prolonged length of their embrace and the fact Isla didn't pull away that they were besotted with each other. There was an awkward moment where Takai appeared as if he wanted to embrace Arisa, too, but she stepped out of his reach.

After their farewells, Isla and Arisa mounted their steeds and began their journey out of the Capital. They were met with smiles, shouts and waves as they passed through the city. Word that it was *the Water Catcher* spread through the streets like wildfire.

Arisa returned their greetings with a polite smile. Their attentions were heavy with expectations and weighed on her chest, pushing the air from her lungs. She prompted her horse to pick up speed, only feeling like she could breathe again once they reached the city outskirts.

Isla looked at her askance. 'They don't mean anything by it. They're just happy to see the famed "Water Catcher" in person.'

Arisa shuddered. 'But they do mean something by it. They think I'm some sort of saviour, and now with the Northemers in Ivane, they probably expect me to be able to save them somehow.'

Isla flicked a wave of long red hair back over her shoulder. 'Thankfully we won't need your powers this time. Sar's right. The Northemers will run back home the moment they realise what they're up against.'

Her cousin was right. Of course she was. So why was there a growing knot in the pit of Arisa's stomach?

They passed through the city gates, stopping as a landscape of rolling green hills, vineyards and orchards opened up before them. A river snaked to their left, the hint of a mountain range on the horizon ahead.

'Which way?' Arisa asked.

'We follow the river east, all the way to the mountains,' Isla said matter-of-factly.

'And then what?'

'We hope we find Rea...before...'

Before there was war. Before Rea was lost to them forever.

'Before it's too late.'

THEY FOLLOWED the river until nightfall, when they reached a small village that Isla said was famed for its red wine and oranges. She led the way to a tavern, where the innkeeper and several of the patrons, who seemingly recognised Arisa's cousin, received them with broad smiles. This far from the city, no one appeared to know who Arisa was, which was a welcome change.

After Isla exchanged pleasantries with several Etteans throughout the tavern, they were shown to a small courtyard and seated at a wrought iron table under a grapevine arbour. The sound of crickets and the scent of orange blossoms infused the night air. Isla chatted briefly with the innkeeper's wife in fluent Ettean before introducing Arisa as her cousin.

The woman did a double take on hearing Arisa's Lamorian accent, but recovered herself quickly. 'Any friend of Isla's is a friend of ours,' she declared, then addressed Isla. 'The usual?'

'Yes, please.'

Arisa watched the woman leave to fetch their food. 'You're quite the popular one, aren't you?'

'What? Jealous?' Isla teased.

'Quite the opposite. You must have done a lot for these people.'

Isla shrugged. 'No more than they deserved.'

'What exactly did you do?'

'I listened.'

Arisa tilted her head in question.

Isla leant forward in her chair. 'You have to understand that Lamorians aren't exactly welcome here. It doesn't matter that Takai dedicated troops to help rebuild the country's infrastructure. It doesn't matter that Sar is helping to train Ette's national guard, and that we travelled from one end of Ette to the other to support the democratic elections. None of that matters when seen through a filter of hundreds of years of Lamorian occupation.'

'That makes sense.' Arisa was beginning to see the magnitude of what Takai faced. It went some way toward explaining his behaviour.

'You see,' Isla continued, 'no one wanted to listen to Lamorians. The Etteans begrudged having to accept any help from them. It was up to me – a Kengian. Of course, Kengia has its own history with Ette and Ivane. Some can't forget how we never came to their aid against Lamore over the years, but since everything that happened with your father and the persecution of Kengians and silver-eyes, most understand that we had our own troubles. So the people here will talk to me and allow me to speak on their behalf. But more than speaking...I listen.' A dreamy look came over Isla's face. 'That's how you understand the magic of this place. You just listen.'

Magic? Did she mean actual magic, like what was found in Kengia? The question was on Arisa's lips when they were interrupted by the arrival of their food. They were served a platter of grilled and marinated vegetables alongside smoked meats, figs, soft cheeses, bread and dips.

The innkeeper's wife served them wine in blue glass tumblers, and Arisa took the tiniest of sips. She had never liked the heavily spiced wine served at the Lamorian court, but she was pleasantly surprised to find this one much lighter in body, with subtle flavours. She murmured her approval before taking another sip.

'It's good, right?' Isla beamed. 'I'll miss it when we have to go back.'

Arisa dipped a chunk of bread into a dip topped with caramelised onion. A mouthful of sweet and savoury nuttiness. It was altogether delicious. 'And where do you mean to go back to?' She had wondered more than once where Isla and Sar would settle.

Isla screwed up her nose. 'Well…we can go back to Lamore, where I am no one but Sir Sar's "lady", or we can go to Kengia, where I am a nothing member of the royal family.'

Arisa shifted in her chair, conscious of how Isla had resented her firstborn position, fearing she would never live up to the prodigal Water Catcher. 'You're not nothing. Your mother and father miss you. And our grandmother. We all miss you.'

Isla flicked her hand as if shooing a pesky fly. 'Don't worry, I'm well past any jealousy. It's just that I want to be free to be someone else. Someone who is judged by their actions, not their position. Here, I can be that person. I can be…' She sighed.

'You can be Isla.'

'Exactly!'

Arisa popped a honey-glazed fig in her mouth, relishing the moment the skin of the fruit gave way to its jelly-like interior. 'What did you mean by the magic of this place?'

Isla rolled up a wafer-thin slice of smoked meat and took a bite. 'It's not what you think,' she mumbled through her mouthful. 'You won't hear the voices of a crackling fire or the groaning of stones. It's not like how silver-eyes are taught to harness *kira*. But I suppose it's a little like our ability to hear and understand the different lifeforces in nature.'

'You can speak to nature here?' Arisa couldn't hide a hint of envy from her voice. There had been times she had wished her

Kengian magic – and its responsibilities and attention – away, but being disconnected from *kira* in Ivane felt strange. A kind of emptiness filled her, as if she were missing part of herself.

Isla gave a small shake of her head. 'Some Etteans on the borderlands speak of a connection to the natural elements that grounds them to this place. I've only experienced a hint of it. A feeling, more than anything, that there's something out there.' She cast a look over her shoulder toward the mountains. 'A tenuous thread connecting me to this place. I just can't seem to put my finger on what it is. But it gets stronger the more time you spend here, the more you listen, the more you just *be*.'

The way Isla was speaking reminded Arisa of when she'd first arrived in Lochlen with no training or knowledge of how to tap into her Kengian and silver-eyes' abilities. It was the Custodian, Jaai, who'd taught her the simplest of Kengian philosophies – to be at one with nature, without asking anything of it or yourself. It brought back bittersweet memories.

Arisa had hoped she and Jaai could remain friends, but the hurt she'd caused by choosing Takai over him ran deep. Lochlen, of course, was a small place, and inevitably they saw each other regularly, but nothing other than polite acknowledgements passed between them. It was with some relief that Arisa had recently learned that Jaai was courting a Scholar at the Institute. He seemed happy. Happier than she could ever have made him. Not when her heart had been, and still remained, with Takai.

Isla scrutinised Arisa's face. 'You're doing it wrong.'

'Huh?'

'If you want to just *be*, you can't be thinking about him.'

'How did you know—?'

Isla jutted out her chin – a mannerism the cousins shared. 'Because I know everything, including how to find Rea.'

'You do?'

'I do. I overheard someone inside mention a particular

village on the border. A village that wishes to protect the firebird and stop anyone from claiming a bounty on it.'

Arisa sat bolt upright. 'How far?'

'A couple of days' ride from here. A remote place, so I suggest you fill up on this' – she waved her hand across the table – 'because it might be the last decent meal we get for a while.'

Arisa nodded, but on looking at the mouth-watering platter before her, she couldn't eat. Not when she remembered why she was here in the first place. To save Rea from the bounty hunters. To save Rea from herself.

The further east Arisa and Isla ventured, the sparser the landscape became. The river shrank to a mere trickle. Orchards and fertile plains were replaced by scrubby hills and rocky outcrops, with villages few and far between.

Night had already fallen on the second day of their travels when they reached the border regions – the same area where Arisa's mother had spent her early years. They stopped at a small scattering of stone huts. There was no inn, no major buildings of any kind. Isla knocked at the wooden door of the closest hut, telling Arisa to let her handle the conversation.

A middle-aged man with a grizzled beard answered, cracking the door half-open. His right hand hovered over his belt, where a large knife was sheathed. After introducing them, Isla confirmed the name of the village – the place she had heard wanted to protect the phoenix.

The man looked them up and down with narrowed eyes. 'What's your business here?' he demanded.

Arisa spoke before Isla could stop her. 'We're here to help the firebird.' But the man looked at her askance the moment she started speaking – presumably he had detected her Lamorian accent.

'Help?' he scoffed. 'After a bounty, more like it.'

'We do indeed mean to help,' Isla assured him. 'We believe we know the firebird – or the girl who is the firebird.'

'Girl?' The man frowned. 'There's no girl.'

'There is,' Arisa blurted out. 'A girl taking the form of a phoenix. Her name is Rea.' Isla jabbed her in the ribs, but she wouldn't be stopped. 'And she is my friend. Please, she needs our help.'

The man shooed them away. 'Begone, the two of you. I've got no time for tale-telling.'

Isla gave Arisa a pointed look.

'Jed, stop your nonsense and invite them in.'

The door swung wide to reveal a woman wearing a food-splattered apron. Arisa's stomach growled as the smell of stewed meat wafted toward them from inside.

The woman pointed at them. 'Look at the lasses. If they're bounty hunters, they're the oddest ones I've ever seen – and they know the girl's name.'

Hope flared in Arisa. 'Rea. You know Rea?'

The woman pressed her lips together. 'We do. Or at least, we *did*. Come on inside and you can tell us more.' She gave the man – Jed – a stern look until he backed away from the door.

Isla and Arisa looked at each other. It probably wasn't wise to enter the home of an armed man who clearly didn't trust them, but what choice did they have? If they wanted to learn where Rea was, they needed these people's help.

The pair let themselves be guided inside by the woman, who said her name was Maria. She showed them to a lowset table at the centre of the main room and dusted off two threadbare cushions for them to sit on, then fetched bowls, spoons and a pot of mutton stew.

'It smells delicious,' Isla remarked, ignoring Jed's threatening gaze across the table.

'My husband is a shepherd. He keeps us in good supply of meat,' Maria said proudly. Jed managed a grunt of acknowledgement.

Over the mutton stew, which was indeed delicious, Maria asked Isla and Arisa dozens of questions. Arisa resolved to tell them everything – for Rea's sake. She told them how both she and Rea had been taken as children by the Ettean Governor at the time, a Lamorian called Sir Marcus. She explained how she had been rescued by her uncle, but Rea couldn't be saved. How, on reaching Ette, Rea had somehow escaped, but no one had known what became of her. Tears scratched Arisa's throat as she recalled how she'd been sure Rea was dead until she'd turned up with the Northern King in Lamore.

'Is that where she went? To Northern?' Maria asked.

'So she was here?' Isla jumped in. 'This is where she lived before then?'

Jed, who'd been listening in silence, puffing on a pipe, waved a hand at Arisa. 'Continue your story,' he said in a monotone voice.

Arisa went on to share what Rea had told her about the Kengian Scholar she'd lived with in Ette, and how, after the woman had died, she had ended up in Northern. How she had learned to harness her silver-eyes' magic and create firesky weapons. Arisa explained that it hadn't been until the final battle in Lamore that any of them had realised Rea could transform into a phoenix.

'You see,' she concluded, 'Rea is a Firemaster. We're not sure how, exactly, but she possesses the most powerful Kengian magic. It is the only way she could have taken on the firebird's form. But she wasn't properly trained for it and needs our help. We just need to find her.'

Maria frowned. 'But if what you say is true, Rea is responsible for many deaths in Lamore and Kengia. And if rumour here is true, she has also killed people in Ette and Ivane. Perhaps...perhaps she shouldn't be saved.'

Jed put down his pipe and rubbed his beard.

'Do you agree?' Isla asked him. 'Do you think we shouldn't help her?'

Jed turned to his wife and spoke rapidly, but Arisa was only able to recognise a smattering of words.

'It's a regional dialect,' Isla murmured. 'I only know a little, but...' Her eyes darted, following their conversation. 'They're speaking of a healer. A line of healers with Kengian blood, who lived in the mountains here. Some called them witches because they possessed some form of magic, but mostly they made medicinal cures from nature. The healers kept to themselves, but were known to help the villagers here...Rea lived with the most recent healer – it must have been the Kengian Scholar she mentioned...But they can't believe that the Rea they knew, the one who saved their—'

Isla's eyes widened.

'Rea saved their daughter's life, so they can't believe she would have done any of the things she is accused of.'

The Ettean couple stopped speaking, and Jed reached across the table and squeezed his wife's hand.

'Your daughter?' Arisa asked hesitantly. 'She is alright?'

'Our daughter caught Lamorian fever,' Maria said in a small voice.

Arisa and Amund had treated many with the same illness in Obira over the years. It had plagued Lamore for centuries, inevitably spreading to Ette and Ivane, virulent and merciless. Those who got Lamorian fever rarely survived. The only chance, albeit a small one, was catching the infection soon enough and administering Kengian medicine. Even so, many still perished.

'She was so sick,' Maria continued. 'We were sure she would die, but we sent for the healer. By then the healer was too old and frail to help, but Rea came. She brought medicine and nursed our daughter back to health.' Maria wiped a lone tear from her cheek. 'She is now married, and has a child of her own on the way.'

'So you understand why we need to help Rea?' Arisa pressed.

'We saw the firebird. It flew into our village. We were terrified at first, but it quickly became apparent the creature was injured.'

'There was something familiar about her,' Jed said. 'She spoke with Rea's voice, pleading with us to help her. But before we could do anything, the firebird flew up into the mountains. We wanted to protect her, but if she has done all these terrible—'

'Rea has only done what she needed to do to survive,' Arisa insisted. 'But there is honour in her heart. It's why she flew away from the final battle in Lamore. It's why she helped your daughter. She belongs with her people in Kengia, who can teach her how to control her powers, just like I was taught.'

Jed cocked a brow. 'You?'

Arisa nodded. 'I have told you my name, but I haven't told you that I am also the Water Catcher.'

'But that would make you the daughter of the Kengian King, Alik?'

'And my mother was Ettean. Her father was King of one of the tribes from this region.'

Maria gasped. 'You're Gwyn's daughter.' She leant across the table to look closer at Arisa. 'Other than the eyes…Yes, you have her features…as best as I can remember them.'

It was Arisa's turn to be surprised.

Jed also leant in to scrutinise her. A slow grin came to his face, and then he slammed his palm down on the table with a great laugh. 'Well, I'll be.'

'You knew my mother?'

'Of course,' Jed said. 'We grew up in the same village. But when the Lamorians came for us, the King, Gwyn's father, insisted all the children be taken to safety. Your mother – all of ten, she was – refused to go. Insisted on staying to fight.'

Arisa laughed. 'Sounds like her.'

Jed tapped his fingers on the table, surveying Arisa and Isla.

'Well?' Isla asked.

Jed's fingers stilled. 'You stay here tonight, then first thing in the morning I'll show you where you might find Rea.'

Arisa exhaled with relief.

'But you'll want to move quickly. There are reports of bounty hunters in the area.'

Arisa nodded rapidly. 'First thing in the morning.'

She just hoped they weren't too late.

10

$\mathcal{T}$akai stood fixed to the spot on the poop deck at the rear of his ship as it sailed into the Port of Nadis. It was quite a sight to behold. The port was bustling with activity. Dozens of berths, most of them occupied, loading and unloading cargo of barley, hides, fruit, nuts, spices and silks. Sailors moved with more urgency than usual, talking of storms brewing in the west. Grand stone buildings ran the length of the docks, a never-ending stream of merchants and sailors coming and going from them. Date palms sprang from the ground here and there, clumps of them on a plateau above the city. The same plateau that housed Nadis Palace: a sprawling compound of towers and ramparts made from rammed earth the colour of sand. It was equal parts a palace, a fortress and a city in its own right. But Takai barely noticed its splendour.

It was the first time he had been to his mother's homeland. His ancestral lands. Since inheriting the Lamorian crown, he had corresponded with his uncle several times on matters of state, and in his letters King Laskar had expressed a fervent wish for Takai to visit Nadis, but he'd always found a reason that he couldn't. There were his duties in Lamore. There was business to attend to in Ette.

These weren't lies, but they were a convenient means to avoid visiting the nation Takai's father had betrayed so badly. What his father had done to Ette was awful enough, but for Lamore to turn on the homeland of its Queen was unfathomable. So Takai had sent Sar instead to meet with the Ivanian King when trade or anything else needed to be discussed.

He dug his fingers into the side rail of the ship, wondering what reception he would receive.

Sar slapped him on the back. 'Relax, my friend. We are welcome here. They need us and our help against the Northemers.'

Takai's brow furrowed. 'They might need us, but it doesn't mean we're *welcome* – or at least, I might not be.'

'Rubbish. Your uncle has been pestering you to visit for ages and is disappointed every time I show up. Which is surprising, given I am a far more attractive prospect than your ugly mug.'

'Hey,' Takai cried, play-punching his friend in the arm. Sar howled like he'd been struck by hand-cannon lead. Takai's ensuing laugh drifted into a sigh filled with a thousand regrets.

'Don't tell me this is all about needing to make amends,' Sar said. 'Because you have nothing to make amends for. It was your father and those before him who wronged Ivane, not you.'

Takai shrugged.

Sar's dimpled smile fell from his face. 'I mean it, Takai. It's time to stop punishing yourself – and I'm not just talking about the business of being King. I'm talking about Arisa.'

Takai's stomach contracted at the mere mention of her name.

'It's not too late. She *will* forgive you, if you would only ask her. You're bound to each other.'

'What? Like you and Isla?'

Sar chuckled. 'Isla has never been and will never be bound to anyone or anything. She's…' A wistful look came over his face. 'She's wild. Free. Untamed. Her own person. And that is what I love—'

Takai raised a brow.

'Yes, love. That is what I love about her.'

'And she loves you too?'

Sar kicked his foot against the timber balustrade. 'I think so.'

'And you're together?'

'As long as we choose to be together...yes.'

'What does that mean?'

'It means that after we are finished in Ette, she doesn't know where she wants to go. I'm afraid she will never be content settling anywhere or with anyone.'

Takai rested a hand on his friend's arm. 'She is lucky to have you, Sar. And she's a fool if she doesn't see that.'

Sar squared his shoulders and fixed a mock-angry glare on Takai. 'If you ever call her a fool again, you'll have more to worry about than meeting your uncle.'

'Alright, alright. I'm sorry. Isla isn't a fool.'

Sar gave an approving nod. 'She is not.'

'Seriously, though. I do hope my uncle will be alright with me being here.'

'Trust me. King Laskar is not the one you need to worry about.'

An alarm sounded in Takai's head. So he *should* be worried about the reception he was about to get.

Only then did he notice the ominous black clouds in the western sky over his friend's shoulder. 'There is going to be quite the storm at sea,' he said. 'I hope our forces manage to avoid it.'

Sar's head swivelled to follow Takai's gaze. 'Ohhh...We'd better do more than hope. We need Lamore's and Kengia's forces if we want to avoid full-blown war.'

'I thought Ivanians were famed warriors. That their army rivalled any in size and skill.'

Sar shrugged. 'In King Arlo's time, that was true. And I do believe every Ivanian trains to be a warrior, but they have not had a need to fight in nearly two decades. Your uncle was not much more than a lad when Ivane last went to war. Many barely remember what it was like.'

A fresh sense of responsibility crashed down on Takai like a wave. Ivane did need them. It needed *him*. But Takai couldn't get Sar's implication out of his head – the implication that he should be concerned by someone other than his uncle.

'Who did you mean when you said the King is not the one I should be worried about?'

A half-smile twitched at the corner of Sar's mouth. 'Just that.' He nodded over Takai's shoulder.

Takai turned back toward the city, where a procession of two dozen or so mounted horses was approaching along the docks. The horses, all of them white, trotted in perfect unison, their long arching necks and tails held high. There was a gracefulness to their profiles, an athleticism Takai hadn't seen before. Then he remembered how, as a boy, he'd listened to his mother describe the magnificent horses of Ivane. They originated from the Desertlands in the country's north, where they had evolved and thrived in the harshest of conditions. Their beauty was only enhanced by the caparisons they wore: cloth in a rich shade of red, the colour of pomegranates; floral and geometric patterns embroidered in gold, blue and purple thread. The riders of the Ivanian horses wore uniforms and headwear of matching red and gold.

At the lead was a petite figure – a girl a few years younger than Takai, perhaps. She sat tall in her saddle, and there was something familiar in her straightened back, in the way she held her shoulders high.

The procession came to a stop on the dock in front of Takai's ship. Sar indicated they should move to the foredeck.

A groomsman dismounted and offered his assistance to the girl, but she swatted his hand away, dropping unaided to the ground. She scanned the ship and scowled at what she saw before striding to the end of the gangplank. She glared up at them, her stare intensified by the winged kohl around her eyes. A curved sabre hung in a scabbard at her waist, its decorative hilt glinting in the sun.

'So these are your reinforcements – a single cargo ship?' she shouted up at them in Ivanian, which, along with Ettean, Takai had taken great pains to become fluent in since becoming King.

'Greetings, Your Highness,' Sar hollered back with a beaming smile.

It dawned on Takai that this must be his cousin, Noemi. He had only ever pictured her as a young girl, a child, not a near-grown woman – and certainly not one as annoyingly arrogant as this. He could explain to her that he had made a deliberate decision not to bring any Lamorian warships to Ette, or any firesky weapons, not wishing to further inflame relations. He had instead advised Ette on building their own naval fleet, which so far consisted of only six ships. Takai could also have pointed out Ivane's lack of warships, but instead he gave a courtly smile.

'Cousin, I am glad to see you. You can be assured that both Lamore's and Kengia's forces are on their way, and the Ettean Commander isn't far behind us with his fleet.'

Noemi pulled a face like she could smell something foul in the air. 'Altogether disappointing. But not surprising.' She spun on her feet and marched back to her horse, her boots clip-clopping loudly as she went.

'What's her problem?' Takai hissed under his breath.

Sar gave him a *told you so* look.

'Are you coming or what?' Noemi yelled back up at them.

'Have you ever met anyone as arrogant or as self-important as her before?' Takai muttered under his breath.

Sar grinned. 'Do you really want me to answer that?'

'I'm not like her,' Takai protested as they made their way off the ship.

'Uh-huh,' Sar agreed with a congenial nod.

'Well, not anymore,' Takai grumbled.

Takai and Sar were given a horse each and shepherded to the rear of the procession, which weaved its way back through the port city and began the steep ascent to the palace. Beads of sweat broke out on Takai's forehead. There was a stickiness in the air, a strangling heat that was noticeably harsher than the Ettean climate. He wiped his brow, his eyes not leaving the precipitous winding path that dropped away to the harbour and city far below. His only comfort came from his sure-footed Ivanian steed, which negotiated the dizzying terrain with ease.

Eventually they reached the top of the plateau. The path led to a wide, open expanse of sandy ground, and they followed it all the way to the main gate. A dome-topped archway had been carved from the thick outer walls right below the watchhouse. An intricately carved timber gate that had more aesthetic value than function lay invitingly open.

Takai caught Sar's eye, and Sar nodded. The palace was clearly unprepared and underequipped for any form of attack.

Two guards stood at the gate, barring a man from entering. The Ivanian was barefoot and covered in dust and dirt from head to toe. Clumps of unkempt hair stuck to his forehead. His shoulder bones protruded from the top of his tunic. He held his hands out placatingly to the guards.

'Please, I must see the King. He has to know our plight. He must know how the mining overseers are destroying us.'

The guards merely pushed the man back to allow Princess Noemi and the rest of the party to continue through the gate.

'Your Highness!' the man shouted after Noemi. 'Mercy on your people.'

Noemi appeared to shift in her saddle, but continued on.

'This is how we end up Discontented!' The man stabbed his finger in the air at her back. 'You will be sorry!'

'What was all that about?' Takai asked Sar.

Sar gave a small shrug. 'No nation is immune to troubles.'

The main entrance opened up into a square courtyard lined with hedges and topiary. Beyond the courtyard was a complex of buildings that could number a hundred or more. Takai estimated it was five times the size of Lamore Castle. Paths branched off in every direction, with the procession taking the widest one straight up the hill.

Sar indicated to the left and right. 'Quarters for all those who live in the royal city.'

'So many of them,' Takai remarked.

'It's the heart and soul of the nation. The finest minds and artisans study and work here, perfecting their craft. Whether it's art, sculpture, science or cuisine, this is where an Ivanian comes to practise and master their skills.'

Takai noted the fine architecture and gardens they passed. Long rectangular ponds. Elaborate water features and fountains. Marbled breezeways and stucco buildings decorated with jewel-coloured mosaic tiles on the walls and floors.

He made a *harrumph* sound. 'I imagine there is plenty of practice to be had on the upkeep of this place.'

Sar screwed up his mouth. 'The first time I came here, I found it hard to see beyond the wealth myself. But I grew to understand the mindset of Nadis. The palace city is a centre of excellence. The people take great pride in it. Not everyone stays here to serve the King. Many come here only to complete an apprenticeship of sorts, then go back to their villages and cities to share what they've learned.'

Takai held his tongue. Sar was right, as always. Both he and Arisa had taught him the importance of having an open mind and understanding the perspectives of others.

They continued up the sloped path, passing a marketplace where craftspeople were at work making and selling their wares. The air was fragrant with the scent of incense and roasted spices. There were stalls stacked with glazed ceramics and others laden with fresh produce and fruit in every colour. The people looked up as they approached, murmurs of interest as they spotted the newcomers. Takai adopted what he hoped was an amiable expression, neither aloof nor overly confident.

The procession then took a path to the left. 'The way to the palace,' Sar explained.

The palace itself didn't appear any grander in style or size than many of the other buildings Takai had already seen. What did stand out was a glittering pool that ran the length of a tilt-yard. Its base and walls consisted of thousands of sparkling, star-shaped gold tiles.

Noemi dismounted and Takai and Sar followed suit. The Princess headed straight through a pointed archway without so much as a glance back at them. Takai looked to Sar, who shrugged.

The Lamorian King squared his shoulders and followed his cousin through a series of open galleries and courtyards. Intricately carved archways, friezes, columns and walls leapt toward him. Decorative features, geometric and symmetrical, like honeycomb, hung overhead as if reaching out to touch those who passed underneath. Dazzling mosaic walls and floors winked back at them, almost too beautiful to touch, let alone walk on.

Guards and servants bowed their heads in acknowledgement as Noemi passed. She came to a stop at a door at the end of a long hallway. The guards on either side stepped swiftly out of her way. She flung the door open and continued inside.

'King Laskar's private quarters,' Sar said in a low voice.

Takai and Sar had no sooner entered the room than a tall man with black hair and a beard, as well as Queen Sofia's eyes, came rushing toward them, his arms wide open.

'My nephew!' King Laskar cried with a face-splitting smile.

'Your Maj—' Takai's words were cut short as his uncle embraced him. Takai hugged him back, albeit not as tightly as his uncle was holding him.

After what seemed like an age, the King released Takai and stood back to appraise him.

'Yes. You are my sister's child.' His smile was, impossibly, even wider than before. Takai relaxed a little, relieved by his uncle's friendly welcome, which was in stark contrast to the Princess's. King Laskar then turned to Sar. 'And good to see you again, my friend.'

Sar bowed his head. 'And you, Your Majesty.'

King Laskar waved his hand. 'None of those fancy titles among family and friends. Speaking of which, where is Isla?'

'Isla and Arisa are coming overland from Ette,' Sar said. 'They are trying to find—'

'They will be with us shortly,' Takai interrupted. He couldn't be sure that his uncle would support anyone assisting the creature that was said to have destroyed at least one Ivanian village.

The King's brow furrowed. 'I am glad to hear I will get to meet the famed Water Catcher, but she and Isla must make haste. There are reports of Northem ships at several locations along the east and south-east coast. They have positioned themselves at the mouths of several major rivers, hovering there as if waiting for a signal.'

'And what of the Northemers reported to be in the north?' Takai asked.

Noemi made a *pfft* noise. 'They are of no concern. They are sure to perish in the Desertlands.'

Takai gritted his teeth as he tried to determine the most conciliatory response. Sar beat him to it.

'I understand the north is a dangerous place that few survive, but in my experience, it pays not to underestimate the Northemers.'

'Yes, their leader, Malu,' Takai offered, 'is quite formidable.'

Noemi crossed her arms. 'As are we Ivanians.'

'Fine points from all,' came King Laskar's diplomatic response. He turned to Takai. 'In any case, we have much to discuss.'

Discuss? If Takai's uncle knew the Northemers like he did, he would know there was little time for discussions. They had to act. And fast, if they stood a chance of defending Ivane.

But Takai had a sinking feeling that what he knew, and he himself, was not exactly welcome here.

11

*A*risa and Isla woke and dressed at dawn. Jed and Maria were waiting for them in the main room.

Maria handed each of them a small cloth bundle. 'Bread and cheese, as well as some dried fruit and nuts for the journey,' she explained.

'You can leave your horses and saddle bags here,' Jed said.

Arisa and Isla looked at each other in confusion.

'There's no path for horses where you'll be going. You'll want to pack lightly.'

Jed swung the front door open to reveal the craggy outline of the Ettean mountains, looming so close it appeared as if they would topple right onto the village.

Arisa couldn't help her sharp intake of breath. They had arrived in the dark, so she'd been unaware how near they were to the mountains. A shimmering apricot-and-lavender dawn sky, with a peppering of fluffy clouds, shrouded the jumble of sheer-faced grey peaks. Among them, one tower of rock rose hundreds of feet above the summits surrounding it.

'Rea?' Isla jabbed a finger at the mountains. 'She's up there?'

'That is where she lived with the healer.' Jed pointed to the tallest mountain. 'I haven't been there myself. The healer fiercely protected her home. We only saw her when she came down the mountain to the village store – we could leave messages for her there. But from what I understand, the cave is about three-quarters of the way up. It will take you the best part of the day to reach it.'

Isla merely nodded and prepared a blanket roll, placing her water flask and food bundle at its centre. She strapped the roll to her back with her bow and arrow. Arisa did the same, but also reached for the Firemaster's book in her satchel.

'What are you doing?' Isla asked, arms folded.

'It's Rea's. I'm returning it to her.'

Isla rolled her eyes. 'There'll be time for that later. After we've found the firebird and convinced it somehow not to kill us.'

Arisa shook her head. 'I have carried this with me everywhere waiting for this day, and I *will* return it to her.'

After giving their thanks and saying goodbye, the pair set off toward the mountains.

THEY CLIMBED the scree slope until the silver sun was high in the sky, stopping only to take water. For the first few hours of their journey the incline wasn't impossibly steep, but Arisa had to have her wits about her, negotiating the loose stones and gravel that slid underfoot. They took their lunch on a ridge that offered a bird's-eye view of much of the Ettean countryside. Beyond the sparse landscape they had just come from was a patchwork of green fields, villages, lakes and the river they'd followed from the Capital. Arisa could see how her cousin had fallen in love with this place. She should have developed her own connection, given she was half-Ettean. She wondered if the unsettled feeling gnawing away deep inside her was a sign of that connection. It was the sensation of being hauled toward something or someone, and the higher they climbed, the more pronounced the tugging became.

They continued up the mountain, using their hands in places to pull themselves up the almost-vertical rock face. Arisa stopped to wipe sweat from her brow, noticing black clouds on the western horizon.

'A storm,' she said, and Isla stopped to check the sky.

'We'll be fine.' Isla readjusted her pack. 'It's heading north-west.'

Bile rose in Arisa's throat. 'Straight toward the Lamorian and Kengian fleets.'

Isla shook her head. 'They won't set out if it's too dangerous.'

'Exactly! The Northemers will—'

'Right now we have more to worry about than the Northemers. We must be getting close, so keep your eyes peeled for any sign of the firebird.'

It was another hour or so before they came to a cave. Its entrance glowed with silver light.

'Do you feel that?' Isla whispered.

Arisa nodded rapidly. The beams of silver light were reaching out to her, wrapping around her like a rope, pulling her inside.

'Do you think the firebird is in there?'

Arisa didn't respond. She was already walking, trancelike, toward the cave entrance.

'Arisa,' Isla hissed. 'Come back.'

But Arisa couldn't have stopped even if she had wanted to.

Isla begrudgingly followed her.

The source of the light became clear once they were inside the cave. The ceiling was entirely covered in clusters of pulsating crystal. Arisa and Isla gasped simultaneously. The crystals, which glimmered silver, looked exactly like the sacred yew tree in Kengia's capital. The last Firemaster – at least, the woman who'd been thought of as the last of her line, before Rea – had crystallised the Kengian yew tree hundreds of years ago, closing a portal used by invaders from another world. The type of crystal was thought to be unique to Kengia. Only a Firemaster was capable of creating it.

'Do you think Rea made these?' Arisa asked, running her fingers along a section of crystals that was within reach. A rush of energy flooded her veins.

Isla peered closer at the crystals. 'I don't know,' she said in wonder. 'They look like they've been here for a long time.'

She was right. A film of dust had settled on Arisa's fingers as she touched the crystals. 'It doesn't make sense,' she said to herself.

Arisa and Isla moved around the empty cave, which consisted of one small room. Two timber stretchers lay in splintered pieces on the dirt floor. Niches were carved in the walls, holding vials and jars, some of which were tipped over or smashed. Arisa recognised most of the items as herbs and concoctions used in Kengian medicine. She stepped carefully to avoid a litter of shattered glass on the ground.

'Look at this.' Isla beckoned Arisa to the opposite side of the cave, where she traced charred black outlines on the wall.

Scorch marks. 'Rea has been here,' Arisa said. 'I think she was trying to heal herself.' She indicated the broken glass and stains on the ground where the medicine had dried. 'I just don't understand how these crystals came to be here, or how Rea has maintained her phoenix form so far from Kengia.'

Isla tapped her chin in thought. 'I think she draws power from the crystals. You feel it, like me – a Kengian lifeforce.'

'I do, but it's faint, like a hazy memory…'

'Not strong enough for you to access your Water Catcher powers?'

'I don't think so.'

'Well, Rea is a Firemaster. She possesses the most powerful Kengian magic.'

'Even still…' Arisa wasn't convinced there was sufficient power here for Rea to sustain her magic.

'There must be answers here somewhere.' Isla began searching the cave.

Arisa checked the furthest corners, looking for something, anything, that would shed light on how to help Rea. She was about to give up when something out of place caught her eye: an image of a monkey inscribed on a fist-sized rock, jammed into the junction between wall and floor.

Arisa's palm went instinctively to the monkey figure. The echo of a beating heart thumped under her hand. Images flashed in her mind. A silver-eyed girl etching the lines of the monkey into the rock. Her tear-stained cheeks. A woman cradling a baby in her arms. An old woman using a mortar and pestle, showing a middle-aged woman and a child what she was doing. Each of their faces different. Each of them bearing the same silver eyes.

Arisa gripped the rock, digging her fingers into the surrounding crevices, but she couldn't move it. She called for Isla to help.

Isla tried to lever the rock from its position using the tip of her knife, but it stuck firm. She folded her arms. 'That rock's not going anywhere, but it's probably not anything of importance.'

'It is important. There's something—'

An ear-piercing screech. A blast of sudden heat. The crackle of fire in the air.

They were on their feet, Isla with her knife aloft and Arisa taking in the sight she'd both hoped and feared to see: Rea, her friend, in the blazing form of a phoenix.

'It's her?' Isla asked, her eyes never leaving the firebird. Isla had only ever seen the phoenix, and Rea, from a distance on the battlefield.

'Yes,' Arisa confirmed in a thin voice. The phoenix's ragged wings of flame drooped, globules of hissing fire falling to the ground. Rea was melting before her eyes.

Arisa approached her with an outstretched hand. 'Rea, it's me. Your friend. Arisa.'

The phoenix cocked its head and Arisa ventured closer, but the bird cawed fire at her, sending her stumbling backward.

'She doesn't know who you are,' Isla said in a low voice, her grip tightening around her knife.

'You won't be able to get close enough to use that,' Arisa whispered. 'Assuming a knife would do anything to her.'

'We've got to try something,' Isla barked.

She was right. But what could they try?

Then Arisa remembered who Rea was and what belonged to her. She reached for her pack, which lay abandoned nearby on the cave floor, and retrieved the Firemaster's book. She held it up.

'Rea, I brought this for you. The Firemaster's book. It is yours. Your legacy.'

The phoenix opened its beak as if to speak, but a ball of flame burst from it, flying toward Arisa. She tried to leap out of the way to avoid it, but it caught the bottom of her wide-legged pants. Isla managed to stamp it out with her boot. The firebird's beak snapped shut and it sucked in air through its nostrils.

'It's alright, Rea.' Arisa tried to approach her friend again. 'My cousin Isla and I are here to help.'

The phoenix threw its head back and yawped as if in great pain. There was a flickering of light, a staggering of images. Then the firebird was gone, in its place a silver-eyed girl, huddled beneath a dome of flames.

Stray clumps of hair stuck to Rea's clammy forehead. '*He-l-p*,' came her strangled words. '*Al-i-a.*'

A memory came hurtling back to Arisa, from when she'd learned that Gwyn was her mother. Gwyn had told Arisa that when she was born, she'd been given an Ettean name. *Alia.* After she'd been sent into hiding in Lamore with Amund, she'd been given the name Arisa instead. But how would Rea know her birth name?

'Alia?' Isla asked. 'Is that what she said?'

'*Al-i-a*,' Rea croaked again, lifting a limp hand to point.

'*Alia*,' Isla repeated, turning the word over slowly.

'She's talking to me,' Arisa said.

Isla shook her head. 'I don't think so. She shows no sign of recognising you.'

Arisa glanced at her friend, noting her empty stare, then back at Isla. She could almost see her cousin's mind whirring over.

'It sounds like she's saying a combination of two Ettean words I've heard before…*ahha*, which means *breath*, or *life* – *breath of life*, perhaps. And *lia*, a word for rock…A life rock.' Realisation washed across Isla's face. 'She's talking about the crystals!'

Arisa's gaze went back to Rea. Her friend's shaking hand could be pointing at the crystals on the ceiling. But then Rea lowered her hand. She was indicating Arisa…No – she was pointing at the Firemaster's book Arisa clutched to her chest.

'That's why she's here – for the crystals. She thinks they can heal her.' Isla's voice was laced with wonder.

Arisa nodded, following her train of thought. 'But she needs the book – a Firemaster's spell.'

'Yes!'

Rea collapsed on the ground. Her chest was rising and falling at a dangerously slow pace.

Arisa frowned. 'But I've read every page of the book, more than once, and I would have remembered any mention of *Alia*.'

'But the book is written in—'

'Old Kengian! We only need to find a mention of *life* and *rock* together.'

The pair of them looked at the book in defeat. There were hundreds of pages of spells. It would take time to find what they needed. Time Rea didn't have.

Arisa rushed to Rea's side, getting on her hands and knees as close to the dome of fire as she dared.

'Rea,' she called. 'Here's the book. Can you find the spell you need?'

Rea raised her head a smidge, her blank gaze going to the book's red leather cover. She reached for it, but recoiled as soon as her hand made contact with the flaming dome. She took a series of shallow breaths, then began murmuring Kengian words. It was a spell Arisa hadn't heard before. A soft silver glow encased the book. Rea repeated the spell, forcing the words from cracked lips. The glow intensified until it was bright silver. Rea pushed herself onto all fours, her breath quickening as the words became louder and stronger. And, with a *whoosh*, the book cover flew open and pages flipped of their own accord, stopping after a few moments at a particular page.

Arisa scanned it. Her eyes found the words *life* and *rock*. She held the page up to show Rea. 'This is it. This is what you were looking for.'

Rea rose slowly until she was in a kneeling position. Her eyes darted across the page. She repeated the words out loud to herself several times, as though committing them to memory. Light began to return to her eyes, as if the spell had fuelled hope in her. Arisa's own spirits were buoyed. Rea would be saved. Everything was going to be alright—

The sound of running footsteps. Shouts rang through the cave. 'In here! The creature's hideout!'

'Bounty hunters,' Isla said, hurrying to the entrance.

'Rea,' Arisa pressed her friend. 'We have to get you out of here. Now!'

Isla turned back to face them, her face pale. 'Too late. They're already—'

A bolt from a crossbow whizzed past Isla, embedding itself in the cave wall.

Rea howled as her body started convulsing. Arisa reached futilely for her friend, only to burn her hand on the flames.

Isla took refuge behind the lip of the cave entrance and loaded her bow and arrow. 'We have to get out of here, Arisa.'

'Not without Rea.'

But Rea was gone. Her thrashing body had transformed back into the phoenix. The firebird stomped its way to the front of the cave, forcing Isla to fall back.

It stood at the entrance and screeched fire. Screams reverberated around the cave. More crossbows were fired, the bolts disintegrating in the phoenix's fiery form. The firebird screeched again, this time its protracted cry so loud the rock walls of the cave shuddered. The crystal ceiling overhead shook violently.

'What is she doing? She'll destroy the Alia,' Arisa yelled.

'She must be protecting them,' Isla shouted back.

The screeching continued and parts of the rock wall started to give way, dirt and egg-sized rocks showering down on them.

Isla grabbed Arisa's arm. 'We have to go. Now!'

But Arisa's gaze was fixed on the image of the monkey on the wall. The rock that had been jammed in so tight had lifted. 'I just have to...' She scrambled to yank the rock from its position as Isla grabbed their belongings.

Arisa shoved the rock one way and the other. Once. Twice. Three times...and...

'I've got it!' It only took a moment for Arisa to realise the rock itself wasn't significant. It was what lay behind it. She reached into the chamber dug out behind the rock and retrieved a fat scroll of yellowed parchments. She snatched it and shoved it into her tunic pocket.

'Come on!' Isla thrust Arisa's pack at her and they raced toward the entrance.

The firebird turned its head to look back at them. It snorted, and with one final screech, the creature beat its fiery wings and launched itself into the air.

'Rea!' Arisa cried, but the phoenix was already airborne.

Isla wrenched Arisa out of the cave just as it crumbled, the entrance vanishing in an avalanche of rubble.

12

Theodora tightened her grip on the staff in her hands, blinking back the sweat muddling her vision. She looked Jade squarely in the eyes, trying to remember everything the Ivanian girl had taught her. *Shoulders back. Balanced stance. Go forward when you strike. Sideways when you defend. Don't turn your back on your opponent. Move like the staff is an extension of your arm.*

Jade, whose hands were still bound with rope secured at one end to the wagon, lifted her chin in challenge. Theodora rushed forward to strike, but Jade, despite her restraints, ducked well clear of the weapon.

Theodora ground her teeth in frustration.

'You know this,' Jade reassured her. And Theodora did know it. She had practised under Jade's tuition every spare moment for days now. Even as they trudged through the desert, Theodora twirled and spun the staff through the air, stabbing, striking, until each movement came naturally to her. She took pride in the callouses on her palms that were testament to her many hours of training. And she paid no attention to the Northemers who scoffed at her efforts. She focused only on the endgame: never being dependent on anyone ever again.

While Malu supported her interest in staff-fighting, he had

reiterated that she would always have his protection. And she had reminded him that she chose to be with him because she loved him, not because of what he could do for her.

It had been the right thing to say. For too long Malu had shouldered the responsibility of protecting others, and she would not be a further burden to him. Malu had taken her in his arms and begged her to marry him on the spot. Theodora had given her answer between kisses. She would marry him – once they had both fulfilled their commitments. His to his people. And hers to revenge.

'Again!' Jade ordered. 'Stabbing this time.'

Theodora shook her head, the sharpened blade on the end of the staff gleaming back at her. She didn't want to hurt Jade. She needed the girl's help to find Rea – and in truth, she had grown to like her.

'Go on, do it!' a passing Northemer dared.

'She is no use to us anymore,' the Northemer's offsider growled. 'Unless she can find us something other than rodents and water that tastes like dirt.' He spat on the ground to make his point.

'Just ignore them,' Jade said. 'And stab me.'

Theodora gave a wry smile. 'That's actually what they told me to do. They're belly-aching about not having proper food to eat.'

Jade laughed. 'Weak as piss,' she said with a bright smile, addressing the Northemers. 'Without me you wouldn't have survived an hour in the Desertlands. As it is, I'm counting the hours until I get to slit your throats.'

'What did she say?' the first Northemer demanded.

'She was just saying how much she admired your hair.'

The Northemer's hand flew to his shaved head. 'Her time will come. As will yours, *Lamorian*,' he snarled.

'Careful,' his companion warned under his breath, nodding to Malu, who stood watching them with narrowed eyes a dozen feet away.

The pair of Northemers gave Theodora matching sickly sweet smiles and moved along.

Theodora lowered her staff. 'They do have a point,' she said to Jade. 'How long before we get to somewhere civilised? I'm sick and tired of smelling like month-old carrion.'

Jade leant forward and took an exaggerated whiff, before pretending to choke.

'Hey!' Theodora tapped the staff across Jade's shoulder.

Jade held up her bound hands in surrender. 'Alright, alright. You can tell your *friends* that we are less than a day's ride from a city. A city where they can replenish all of their supplies and where I hope to get word of the firebird's whereabouts.'

'Oh,' Theodora said slowly, suppressing a smile at the thought that she might be closer to finding Rea. 'That is good news.'

Jade, seemingly reading something unusual in Theodora's expression, raised a curious brow.

'Prepare yourself,' Theodora said, changing the subject. 'I'm about to stab you.'

Jade's lips curled into a smile. 'Go on, then.'

Theodora stepped back and raised the staff. She pointed it at Jade's chest and lunged.

Jade sidestepped to safety, but gave an approving nod. 'Better. A few more of those and you'll stand a chance.'

'Against the firebird?'

Jade screwed up her mouth. 'I was talking about you standing a chance against *them*.' She gestured toward the Northemers. 'Killing the firebird is going to take something special. Luckily I know exactly what's required.'

'Which is?'

Jade tilted her head one way then the other, as if considering how much to tell Theodora. She sniffed loudly and looked away. 'We're done.'

13

*A*risa and Isla passed the charred remains of the bounty hunters as they made their way back down the mountain.

'Do you think there are more of them?' Arisa asked. 'Bounty hunters?'

Isla shrugged, walking ahead of her. 'Probably.'

Tendrils of fear gripped Arisa's insides. 'What if they find her…?'

'I think she can look after herself,' Isla threw back over her shoulder.

'But we need to help her.'

Isla spun to face Arisa, eyes flashing with anger. 'Didn't you see what happened back there? What's left of those men? That creature doesn't need anyone's help.'

'What are you saying?'

'I'm saying your friend is lost forever, and her humanity with her,' she said. 'She's on her own.'

'Don't say that,' Arisa cried. 'You saw her with the Firemaster's book. There's a spell that can save her.'

Isla snorted. 'Perhaps there is. She just needs the Alia crystals to make it work.' She pointed in the direction of the collapsed cave.

'We have to do something. I can't let her down…Not again.' Arisa's last words were barely a whisper. 'If I'd saved her from Sir Marcus in the first place, none of this would have happened.'

Isla's expression softened. 'Alright. I suppose we can try.' She gave an acerbic laugh. 'I say *try*, because she may decide to obliterate us to ash as well.'

Arisa shook her head adamantly. 'She won't. I can get through to her. I know I can.'

'Two more days. That's it, and then we have to head to Nadis, whether we've found Rea again or not.'

'Two more days,' Arisa agreed.

They descended the mountain, stopping at a protected ridge to set up camp for the night. They finished off the food bundles Jed and Maria had given them and settled in.

Sleep, though, wouldn't come easily to Arisa. She woke almost every hour from dreams of Rea. The two of them playing games at school. Rea's giggling, her chestnut braids bouncing as she ran away from Arisa during a game of chasies. Arisa tried to catch her friend; at first she was laughing too, but then she realised Rea was getting further and further away, until she was a speck in the distance. There was another dream – it was of the day that Sir Marcus and Guthrie took Rea and Arisa, but instead of them being thrown into a wagon and taken to a ship, a giant firebird landed in the schoolground and incinerated Rea before Arisa's eyes. Racking sobs followed her from her dream to the real world, and she lay awake until dawn.

She glanced across at her cousin, who was sound asleep. The rising sun smouldered, signalling a hot day ahead. Arisa reached for her water flask in her pack and her eyes fell on the roll of parchments she'd found hidden in the cave. Forgetting her thirst, she carefully unrolled the scroll. It was apparent from the colour of some of the parchment, along with the faded ink and the language used, that the documents were very old, perhaps dating back to a century or more before.

Arisa went to what appeared to be the oldest parchment first. It was written in Old Kengian, and appeared to be a journal.

I am Laha. I am the daughter of Zayaka. I am a Firemaster.

Laha? Zayaka? Neither of the names were familiar to Arisa. The 'last' Firemaster – the one whose book she carried – was named Aya. She had been the governess to the Kengian Princess Mary prior to Mary's marriage to the Lamorian Prince, Alfred. Did Laha and Zayaka precede Aya? Arisa read on.

My existence and my mother's before me were wiped from the memories and history books of Kypria. Our powers were beyond their understanding. Powers born of darkness as much as light. First they took me from my mother, telling her I was dead. They exiled her across the Kyprian Sea, where her powers couldn't threaten them. They convinced her that she was a danger to Kengia, that if she cared about her country then she must leave it. She did as they bid, living a shadow of a life, until she learnt that I in fact lived. When she did return and I learnt of her, they took her from me once and for all. And I too was banished. But they will pay...<u>she</u> will pay. Emberto will see to that.

Who were 'they'? And 'she'? Whoever Laha was, she'd known the feared Lamorian King Emberto, Alfred's brother, which put her existence around the same time as Aya's. It didn't make sense.

Arisa scanned the pages, looking for more clues. She managed to glean that Aya had had a twin sister, Zayaka, who'd had a child with Kengia's Head Scholar, and that child was Laha. It explained how there could be more than one Firemaster at the time – both twins would be from the firstborn line.

And someone born to a Firemaster and Head Scholar would undoubtedly be powerful. 'They' were the Institute and the Kengian King, it seemed, and 'she' referred to Aya.

Having had her own battles with the darkness inside her, Arisa sympathised with Laha, but also understood why others were threatened by her. Yet she couldn't fathom how Aya could have been so cruel to her own sister and niece. And if Laha had been friends with Emberto, was she the reason he'd taken the throne from his brother and imprisoned Aya? Was she the reason he'd turned on Kengia and taken the rest of Kypria as his own?

As Arisa continued reading, she learned of Laha's upbringing, how she'd been ejected from the Institute and become Princess Mary's companion – allowing Aya to 'keep an eye on her'. Except for Mary, Laha had had no family or friends to speak of until they travelled to the Lamorian court. There, Laha had liberated a monkey called Chaos from the King's zoo – a *monkey*, like the image in the cave – and she'd made friends with the Lamorian Prince, Emberto.

While in Lamore, Laha had inadvertently opened a portal to another world, leaving Kypria open to attack from powerful invaders. She and Mary, using their Kengian magic, and the Lamorian Princes, with the help of Aya, had chased the invaders across Kypria, finally defeating them in Kengia.

The journal detailed their journey to Ette and the cave – it was Aya who had created the Alia ceiling to magnify the little powers they could still access here. Laha explained how Aya had used a seed crystal passed down to each Firemaster, as well as a powerful Kengian spell few could master.

Over the years I have tried the same spell myself with varying results. But the longer I am here, the weaker my powers become, fading like a slow-beating heart, surrendering to death. And if I venture far from the Alia, I am no longer myself – just an empty vessel that once was a Firemaster. The only two places where I am reminded of who I was and who I was meant to be are this miserable cave and

'Damn it!' The next words were illegible. Lost in a smudge of centuries-old dirt.

'Wha-a-at?' Isla moaned, as she woke from her sleep.

'I think I know where Rea is. Well, at least another place she might be.'

Isla rubbed her eyes. 'Where?'

'Somewhere else with Alia crystals.'

IT WAS midday when they made it back to Jed's village. By that time, Arisa had filled Isla in on everything she'd learned.

When they described the Alia crystals in the cave to Jed, he rubbed his beard and mumbled, 'You don't say.' He went on to tell them how he'd heard of Alia appearing in only one place: Oisiri. A sacred underground city below the Ivanian desert.

'That's where Rea will be heading,' Arisa said with certainty.

Jed shrugged. 'I don't know. I saw that firebird take off over the mountains into Ivane, but it wasn't in a good way. It was struggling to stay in the air. I'd be surprised if the creature made it much further than the other side of the border.'

'Then we have to hurry,' Arisa said, already packing her saddle bags.

14

'Is this a joke?' Hafder yelled as Jade brought the Northemers to a location in the desert that featured nothing but a single date palm and a pile of rocks.

'It's trickery,' another Northemer cried.

'We're going to die here for nothing,' Horace wailed.

Malu's jaw tightened. 'Where is the city she promised?' He was speaking to Theodora, but looking squarely at Jade. His ice-blue eyes had never appeared colder. Oddly, Jade's smile back to him was smug.

'This isn't a time for games,' Theodora warned her. 'You need to show us to the city.'

'It's no game,' Jade replied, her smile never leaving her face.

Malu looked to Theodora, who could only shrug.

Hafder advanced on Jade with his axe raised. Rayl roared at him from her cage. Hafder stumbled back in surprise, back-tracking toward the rocks. He tried to regain his footing, but the ground was falling away beneath him.

Theodora watched in awe as Hafder disappeared before their eyes. She and Malu raced to the edge of the rock pile and peered over to find him flat on his back on the sand, ten feet or so below them.

'Is he alright?' Theodora asked.

A string of Northern curse words confirmed he was at least alive.

'Are you injured?' Malu called to his brother.

Hafder sat up slowly, holding a hand to his head. 'I'll live, no thanks to that Ivanian wench and rotten cat—' Hafder's jaw dropped. His gaze fixed straight ahead of him. 'Whoa.'

'What is it?' Malu asked.

Hafder grinned back up at his brother. 'The Ivanian girl can live another day.'

As soon as they joined Hafder, the object of his wonder became clear. He had landed in front of a rock wall with an opening wide enough to fit two wagons side by side. From the crevice came a silver glow and the sound of running water. In the distance was an undulating hum, a collection of people's voices and industry at work.

'Oisiri,' Jade declared. 'The underground city.'

Theodora translated for Malu.

'This better not be a trap,' Hafder grumbled, but a mischievous glint appeared in Malu's eyes and he strode toward the opening.

'Tell him not so fast,' Jade urged Theodora.

'Why? Are we in danger in there?'

'Only if you don't untie me. Oisiri is a sacred city and a place of healing. Peace must be upheld there. Whatever people's differences are, they must be put aside when entering the underground city. Even foreigners like yourselves will be safe while you are in Oisiri, but not if you are seen to have an Ivanian girl as a prisoner.'

Theodora told Malu what Jade had said. After a moment's thought he nodded for the girl to be unbound.

'But we still need her to find...' Theodora whispered.

Malu gave a dismissive wave. 'Something tells me we will

find everything we need in this place.' And without another word he marched into the city.

Theodora and the Northemers followed into the silver light. It was bright enough that torches weren't required. The opening yawned wider the further they progressed, the sounds intensifying. The source of the running water and light soon became clear with the appearance of a glittering river on their right. The Northemers stared hungrily at the water, some licking their lips, but none moved. It was no ordinary river. Hanging high above the water was a ceiling covered with translucent crystals that produced a pulsing silver glow. On one side the river lapped against a rock wall, and on the bank, where they stood, four guards approached.

The guards' sharp eyes darted, undoubtedly identifying them by their appearance as foreigners – probably suspecting them as Northemers. Yet they showed no emotion.

'Welcome to Oisiri,' one guard said, formally but not impolitely. Theodora translated again.

'They don't fear us,' Hafder remarked.

'You may leave your weapons with us.' Another guard indicated an armoury off to the left.

'That is why,' Malu said, surrendering his sword. 'If we're not armed, they have nothing to fear.'

Hafder held fast to his axe and the first guard stepped closer to him. 'We are lambs to the slaughter if we do as they bid.'

'Jade said we aren't in danger here,' Theodora explained. 'That peace is upheld in the city, all quarrels put aside.'

'And you believe her?' Hafder snarled.

'What's stopping them from reporting to the King that we are here?' Horace barked.

'It doesn't matter if he does know.' Malu gave a bright smile to the guards. 'Because by the time I am done in this city, we will have already won.' He placed his hand on his brother's shoulder. 'Trust me, brother.'

Hafder scowled but handed over his axe. 'We will give up

our weapons,' he announced to the rest of the Northemers, who did as instructed but grumbled all the while. 'You'd better be right, brother,' Hafder said in a low voice.

Malu merely laughed and slapped him on the back. He then asked Theodora to enquire about whether they could drink from the river.

After some back-and-forth with Jade, Theodora imparted to Malu that the section of the river with the crystals was off-limits, but that the river also fed a series of pipes that provided running water to all of the quarters in the city. In short, Jade would take them directly to an inn where they could find accommodation and many options to quench their thirst.

As good as her word, Jade led the party up a sloping path that widened and branched out to become the underground city. She pointed out the main landmarks and amenities. Like any other city, Oisiri had a thriving marketplace, taverns, bakers, blacksmiths – every trade you could imagine. A seemingly endless network of interconnecting tunnels formed the streets and alleyways. Lamps and torches lit this part of the city, which lacked the light from the crystal ceiling at the entrance. On the roof in this part of Oisiri was something altogether stranger: what appeared to be upside-down trees. Green-tipped branches dangled toward them, familiar water-filled bulbs hanging from exposed roots.

'The Batu-riek trees are scattered throughout the city to provide oxygen for everyone here,' Jade explained.

'The Batu-riek? The ones that look like a bunch of sticks but store water underneath?'

'Exactly.'

They continued along a street that was as wide as any Theodora had seen in Obira, the thoroughfare thrumming with horse- and mule-drawn wagons. Hundreds of pedestrians dressed in all manner of costume went to and from buildings and stalls, carrying their various wares. Malu and his fellow

Northemers spread out, performing reconnaissance of sorts while satisfying their own curiosity.

'How many people live here?' Theodora asked Jade, who had snatched a bag of dates from a nearby table without the stallkeeper noticing.

She popped a plump date into her mouth. 'One hundred thousand or so residents, last I heard,' she mumbled through her food. 'At least twice that travelling through at any time.'

Three hundred thousand people. Had Theodora heard right? She could see the cogs in her father's mind ticking over.

They passed a dozen or so Ivanians dressed in maroon-and-gold uniforms. 'The King's Guards,' Jade explained. 'They have been sent to rally all the warriors. He's assembling his army at Nadis.' She spat a pit into the street and took another date from her bag.

Theodora grabbed her arm. 'His army?'

Jade held her hand up to indicate she was chewing, then spoke. 'Of course.' She spat her pit at the back of a passing woman dressed head to toe in fine silk. 'To stop you lot and the Northem ships reported along the coast from taking Ivane.'

'You knew…?'

'That you weren't merchants?' Jade scoffed. 'Obviously. I don't care what business you have with the King – this country has done nothing for me. But I do care about finding the firebird.'

'Forget the firebird,' Horace whispered in Theodora's ear. 'This may be the only chance we have to save ourselves. We leave the Northemers here in Oisiri to suffer whatever fate Ivane has planned for them. And we negotiate passage back to Lamore. I have supporters there. We can find a way back to power.'

Theodora rolled her eyes, tired of her father's ridiculous notions. Neither of them had a future in Lamore. And she would never leave Malu…Never.

She scanned the street for the Northem leader, squinting in

the dim light. 'Could use some of those light crystals here,' she said to Jade.

A shadow flitted across the girl's green eyes. 'As I said. They're off-limits. People come from all over the country just to be in their presence. They believe the crystals have healing powers dating back to a *witch* or something who created them in the first place. But they're not to be touched.' A bitter laugh escaped her mouth. 'Not unless you're prepared to be cursed.'

Theodora caught sight of Malu. He appeared to be in deep conversation with a man dressed in Ettean garb.

'Anyway, this is where I leave you,' Jade said, indicating a wooden sign above them that read *The Hawk and Mouse*. A whiff of stale alcohol and roasting meat wafted toward them from the establishment's open door. 'You'll find accommodation inside.'

'You can't leave – not yet,' Theodora insisted. 'We need to find the firebird.'

'I'll be back.' Jade moved into the path of a well-dressed Ivanian man, bumping him. 'I'm so sorry.' She apologised with a bow. The man grunted and kept walking. Jade grinned wildly at Theodora and held up a purse of coins she must have stolen from the passer-by. 'And when I return, I will hopefully have exactly what we need to succeed in our mission.' She gave a wink and skipped away down the street.

'Give up on Rea and *that* one.' Horace nodded after Jade. 'They can't be trusted.'

Theodora raised a high-arched brow. 'And you can be?'

15

*A*risa and Isla headed east from Jed's village, crossing the border into Ivane. They followed another mountain range with a plan to swing back around it and head north to Oisiri. The landscape was much the same here as where they had come from: dry and sparsely vegetated until they reached a river. From there they passed through a series of villages with barley and wheat crops dotted in between. The river widened along with the road. Signposts pointed to different quarries and mine sites, most of which were dedicated to gold mining. At no point did they spot any sign of the phoenix.

As dusk fell they reached the outskirts of a bustling town called Liprah. The town's stone buildings, each several storeys high, challenged each other in architectural style. Finely decorated friezes and façades shining with mosaic tiles and gold leaf vied for attention. Men and women dressed in richly embroidered silks and linens sauntered along the street, stopping to look in shop windows. The place radiated wealth.

They stopped outside what appeared to be the most affordable-looking inn. A well-dressed woman, dripping with gold earrings and necklaces and jade rings, appeared through an arched doorway and looked them swiftly up and down. Her lips pursed at the sight of their travel-stained tunics.

'A room…One night?' Isla asked in broken Ivanian. Neither she nor Arisa were fluent in the language.

The woman produced a booklet, which appeared to list the room options and rates. Isla whistled at the prices, bringing a smile to Arisa's face. It was something Sar did when he was surprised.

'That one,' Arisa said, pointing to the cheapest item.

The woman gave a thin smile and called for someone by the name of Rosa. No one answered the call. 'Rosa,' the woman trilled, louder this time.

After a few moments, heavy footsteps sounded from a darkened hallway and a woman – Rosa – arrived before them, wearing a muck-splotched apron over an ample bosom.

There was a rapid exchange in Ivanian and Rosa made to grab their belongings, but Arisa held firm on her satchel, not trusting anyone with the Firemaster's book. Rosa shrugged and indicated they should follow her.

She led them past an ornately decorated dining room, where a tall man with a precisely twirled moustache and a gold-cloth coat made shooing gestures at them before slamming the door. Rosa poked her tongue out at the closed door and uttered what Arisa guessed was a bunch of curse words. The woman turned back to them and rabbited on in heavily accented Ivanian.

'Not…understand…' Arisa said haltingly.

'Speak…Ettean?' Isla asked.

'I speak Ettean a little,' Rosa said. 'No one round 'ere understands me dialect. *Madam* there' – she nodded back toward the front lobby – 'she says me regional dialect is a…' Rosa stopped, her eyes rolling upward in search of the right word. 'Ah. Yes. Me Ivanian is an *em-barrass-ment!*' she said in triumph before breaking into jolly laughter.

Rosa began walking again, taking them down a narrow corridor at the rear of the building.

'The only thing embarrassing 'round 'ere is how Madam and the rest of 'em suck up to the rich folks,' she said over her shoulder. 'I only work 'ere so I can send money back to me family.'

Ivane was a curious place. From the way Queen Sofia had described her homeland, Arisa had always imagined that it was paradise. But if there was one thing she had learnt over the last couple of years, it was that nothing and no one was ever perfect or entirely what they seemed.

Rosa came to a halt outside a nondescript wooden door, which she kicked open with her boot.

''Ome sweet 'ome,' she chuckled to herself, and dumped their belongings on the floor of the windowless room. While the room wasn't luxurious, it was clean and tidy, with a large bed at its centre and a washstand against the far wall.

'You can fetch a feed out the back. Just follow ya nose to the courtyard.'

Arisa and Isla washed up and headed 'out the back' as instructed. At the centre of the courtyard was an open kitchen with three cooks scurrying back and forth between sizzling pans and simmering pots. Myriad spices permeated the air, making Arisa's stomach grumble. Wooden tables and chairs ran along a boundary wall decorated with colourful geometric tiles. Guests dressed for travel chatted, grazing on curried meat, flatbreads and rice dishes filled with dried fruit and nuts.

'This way,' Rosa bellowed at them from across the courtyard, jabbing a finger at a table where two tumblers of chilled cider were waiting for them. 'I'll be gettin' ya some food now,' she said with a broad smile. There was something about Rosa – or perhaps just the fact that she was the only kind person they'd spoken to here – that made Arisa feel like she could trust her.

'Rosa, before you go,' she said. 'Can I ask you a question?'

'Course ya can ask. Can't promise I'll knows the answer,' she chuckled.

Isla shot Arisa a warning look, but she had to try.

'I was wondering if you had seen any sign of the…firebird?'

Rosa's eyebrows shot skyward. 'Now what would you two lasses be wantin' with that creature? You can't be bounty hunters.'

'Does it matter?' Isla quipped.

Rosa took a step back and appraised them. 'Wisps of girls like you pair…You want to stay clear of that trouble, I reckon.'

Isla flicked her hair back over her shoulder. 'We'll take our chances.'

'Your funeral.' It sounded like a joke from Rosa, so why wasn't she laughing?

'The firebird,' Arisa prompted. 'Do you know where it is?'

Rosa leant in close. 'Word 'as it the firebird was seen just north of here just yesterday. Was in bad shape. Zig-zaggin' across the sky.' Rosa marked out a 'z' in the air. 'And then…' She slapped her hands together and Arisa jumped in her seat.

'Then what?' Isla asked.

'The bird just fell from the sky. Slammed into the mountains. Probably dead by now.' Rosa's smile was back. 'I'll fetch ya food now.'

Isla turned to Arisa. 'Do you think it could be true? That Rea is…'

Arisa shook her head vehemently. 'She's alive. I can feel it. Ever since the cave, I can sense something. An energy connecting me to this place, to Rea.'

'Like I told you in Ette about listening to the land?'

'I don't know. Maybe that's it.' But Arisa didn't think it was. There was something else – an energy buzzing inside her.

'You pair from Ette? Where are you from? The Capital?' A man with ruddy cheeks and a bulbous nose waved at them from an adjacent table. He spoke in Ettean and was sitting alone. 'I'm on my way back there now. I'm a wine trader,' he said, holding up a half-empty tumbler of red wine.

Arisa smiled politely, hoping he would leave them alone.

'Heard you talking in Ettean. Though *you*' – he waggled a

finger at Arisa – 'you have a Lamorian accent, if I'm not mistaken.'

'I grew up there,' she said in clipped tones. 'But I'm half-Kengian and half-Ettean.'

She had meant to put a stop to the man's chatter, but he only seemed encouraged.

'Silver eyes.' He tapped the side of his nose. 'Dead giveaway.'

'The man's a genius,' Isla muttered under her breath.

'Glad you're not a Lamorian. Cause I've got a thing or two to say about that King of theirs.' Arisa's fingers curled into fists at the mention of Takai. 'No different to his father. In fact, I think he's worse. At least King Delrik didn't pretend he wanted to help us and Ivane.'

'King Takai has devoted himself to righting his father's wrongs,' she said through gritted teeth.

'Ha!' the man cried. 'You can't tell me that he actually wanted Ette to become independent. He only freed us from the Northemers so he could take it back for Lamore. He just never counted on Ette standing up to him. There's no chance he will lift a finger to help us, or Ivane, for that matter.'

'You don't know what you're talking about,' Arisa snapped. 'His forces are on their way to Nadis as we speak to protect Ivane from the Northemers, just like they did for Ette.'

The man shuffled his chair over so he was within arm's reach of Arisa. 'So you haven't heard, then? Storms have hit the western sea. The Lamorians and Kengians are stuck at Obira Port. A convenient excuse, if you ask me. *King* Takai is showing his true colours.'

The buzzing inside Arisa's veins flared like fire being fanned to life. She forced herself to stare at her tumbler, afraid of what she might do if she looked at the man. The Ettean noticed none of this and continued undeterred.

'The Lamorian has no intention of fighting the Northemers again. And now that our country has finally wrested itself from

Lamore's grip, I wouldn't be surprised to discover that King Takai has aligned himself with the Northemers, just like his father before him.'

The buzzing spiked in Arisa's body, drumming in her head. Her fingernails dug into her palms. She stared at the cider in her tumbler with the same intensity as her surging anger. A silver glow formed on the surface, then pea-sized bubbles appeared. One. Two. Three. A dozen.

The cider was boiling, rising to the top of the glass. And she was the one making it happen.

Isla's hand flew to the glass to cover it. With her free hand she clicked her fingers so Arisa would look at her. *Stop*, she mouthed.

Arisa broke her gaze from the tumbler and the cider receded. The Ettean showed no sign of having noticed anything amiss. His attention was entirely focused on draining his glass.

'You can get back over there.' Rosa arrived with a plate of food and indicated with a nod and a filthy stare at the Ettean man for him to return to his own table. 'No one wants to 'ear y'r carry-on.'

The chastised fellow scuttled his chair back, but didn't seem inclined to be silent. 'No skin off my nose. I'll be back in Ette, safe and sound, when those Northemers march on your Nadis,' he said to Rosa. 'They'll be on your doorstep any day. They already have ships covering every major port in the east, and I hear they're already at Oisiri. You may as well dig your grave now.'

Arisa and Isla exchanged an alarmed look. Oisiri was where they thought Rea was heading. And if the Northemers were there, it was safe to assume Theodora was with them. Would Theodora bring Rea to their side before Arisa and Isla got there? And what would the Northemers do to them when they got to Oisiri?

'Well, don't be lettin' us hold ya up,' Rosa barked, yanking the man by his arm out of the chair and shooing him away. 'Go on. Begone with ya!' She nodded with approval once the Ettean was clear of the courtyard.

'Is it true?' Arisa asked. 'Are the Northemers in Oisiri?'

'That is what we've 'eard.' Rosa must have read the fear in Arisa's face, because she patted her hand. 'Don't fret, love. The King's Guards will be ready to pounce the moment those Northemers have set foot out of the city.'

'Why don't they deal with them now?' Arisa asked.

'Oisiri be a sacred city. No violence to be 'ad there. The guards take y'r weapons the moment you arrive.'

Arisa and Isla stiffened. Facing the Northemers unarmed was a frightening prospect.

Rosa gave them a motherly smile. 'There's naught to be 'fraid of. We're more than capable of dealing with the invaders and their ships without the 'elp of Lamore, Ette or anyone else. Ivanians are the finest of warriors.'

'Who haven't seen war themselves for near twenty years,' Isla muttered under her breath so only Arisa could hear.

'And what of these Northemer ships?' Arisa continued, ignoring her cousin. 'Where are they now?'

'That's the strange thing.' Rosa's thick brows converged in thought. 'Their ships 'ave anchored at river mouths along the eastern coast, not movin'. As if they be waitin' for a signal of sorts.'

'Malu has a plan, then,' Arisa said, thinking out loud.

'And what are the Ivanians doing about those ships?' Isla demanded.

'Our King is assemblin' 'is army,' Rosa said matter-of-factly. 'We not be like Ette. We'll 'ave the Northemers licked in no time.' She gave a victorious smile and excused herself.

Isla threw a piece of flatbread she'd been nibbling back onto her plate. 'Without Lamore and Kengia's fleets, Ivane is already lost.'

'Doesn't Ivane have a naval fleet of its own?'

'They've had no need for one for some time. The few ships they do have will have to stay and protect Nadis.'

'What about the ships being built in Ette?'

Isla took a large gulp of cider. 'There's only half a dozen ready to sail. And even if they had more, they don't have the trained crews to pilot them.'

'All the more reason we have to get to Oisiri and stop the Northemers from recruiting Rea. There's a chance her magic might work here, and she'll be a target.'

Isla's eyes widened. 'Speaking of which, what happened earlier with you and your drink?' Her voice rose in excitement. 'You were using your Water Catcher powers.'

'I know,' Arisa said in wonder. 'That feeling I've had ever since the cave and the Alia crystals – it just *exploded* inside me all of a sudden.'

'Do you think you can do it again?'

'Maybe,' she said hopefully. 'But it doesn't make sense. Kengian magic isn't supposed to work properly here.'

'Maybe it's because you're of the firstborn line and you're half-Ettean, so you have your own connection to this place?'

'Then what about Rea and the Firemasters before her? They're supposed to possess the most powerful Kengian magic, and if they've lived here all this time, they must be connected to the land.'

Isla clasped her hands together and rested her elbows on the table. 'Then why hasn't there been a phoenix here before? There must be something else about Rea. Another explanation for her abilities.'

Arisa sat bolt upright and stared at Isla.

'The parchments from the cave! They might have the answer.'

BACK IN THEIR WINDOWLESS ROOM, Arisa split the parchment into two piles and gave one to Isla. The pair of them read by candlelight, comparing notes as they went. It was a painstaking process, given the volume of notes and the fact that many were in Old Kengian.

A common thread appeared in all of the documents, which were written in at least six different hands. Each began with the author's name, followed by who their mother was, and their identification as a Firemaster and a descendant of the 'Lost Firemaster Laha'. Each of them spoke of a time to come when the Firemasters would take their place in a world that wasn't afraid of their power. Beyond that, the journals captured details of spells and instructions for preparing medicine – many of which Arisa recognised from the Firemaster's book or from her healer work with Amund. If only he were here with her now… If only.

'Anything about Rea?' Isla asked.

'Not yet. You?'

Isla shook her head.

Arisa stared at her parchment pile, willing the answers to jump out at her. Then an idea occurred to her. She spread out all of her documents on the bed, her eyes rapidly scanning them.

'What is it?' Isla asked.

'If there is any mention of Rea, it will be in the most recent notes. We just have to find the parchment pieces that are the least aged.'

'Of course!' Isla imitated Arisa, spreading her documents across the bed.

Arisa's fingers hovered over the parchments with the least amount of discolouration and the fewest marks on them. She selected one.

The note began as the others had.

I am Nima. I am the daughter of Ariana. I am a Firemaster, descended from the Lost Firemaster Laha.

It was what came next that grabbed Arisa's attention:

mention of the Water Catcher prophecy.

I have seen it. A vision of the one who will unite all of the Kyprian nations — if she lives.

First she must be born, and for that to happen, an Ettean Princess must be saved from the jaws of death. I can't see the how or why, just that I must intervene. I must find the Princess and take her to safety in Ivane.

Without her there won't be a Water Catcher and we'll all be doomed.

Arisa bristled with excitement. An Ettean Princess, saved and taken to Ivane…Nima was talking about Gwyn. She was talking about Arisa's mother. The next lines were faded, so Arisa could only pick up a few words here and there.

Fire
water

blood

a reckoning

Again, Nima must be referring to the Water Catcher prophecy that had predicted the coming of the Water Catcher. And as the prophecy foretold, fire had been pitted against water in the last battle at Lamore Castle. Rea, with her fire magic, had backed down, leaving Arisa to prevail. Nima must have seen it all.

Arisa picked up the next letter, written in the same hand. This one mentioned a journey to Obira.

My daughter, Daria, is to travel to Lamore.

Ette's Governor, a Lamorian by the name of Lord Ackerley…

Arisa thought back to her Lamorian history lessons. *Lord Ackerley.* There was only one she recalled ever being mentioned. The one who had ruled Ette after King Delrik retook the country, shortly after Arisa was born. He'd kept the position until his death about ten years later, when Sir Marcus had been appointed the new Governor. Rea had been born around three years after Arisa, so this certainly placed the document in the right time period.

'I think I might have something,' she told Isla. 'Look for any mentions of someone called Nima or Daria.' Isla nodded her confirmation. Arisa read on.

…Ette's Governor, a Lamorian by the name of Lord Ackerley, has heard of us and how we practise forms of Kengian medicine. He has asked for help.

It seems the invaders have succumbed to their own plague. Several Lamorian nobles, including Ackerley's wife and son, have been afflicted by the dreadful fever there is no cure for – at least no cure in this land.

Lamorian fever is beyond even my abilities, but it is said there is a healer in Obira, a master of Kengian medicine, who has developed new techniques and concoctions to successfully treat the illness.

Arisa's heart stilled. *A healer in Obira. A master of Kengian medicine.* Nima must be speaking of Amund. *It has to be him.* She took a deep breath and resumed reading.

The Lamorians are to set sail almost immediately and have asked for a healer to accompany them on the journey.

While I cannot predict the future as a Firemaster should, I have seen visions, snatches, enough for me to believe Daria must be the one who goes. In Lamore, she can harness her silver-eyes powers and perhaps even lay the foundations for our return. This could be the moment we have been waiting for, when Firemasters will take their place in the world again.

Of course, it is not without its dangers. I have heard that the Lamorian King's fear of Kengians — silver-eyes in particular — has seen them relegated to the countryside, tolerated only for their abilities to nurse the nation's barren land into fertile farmland, but this may be our only chance, so we must take it. Daria is our finest hope...I will miss her beyond words.

Arisa's eyes desperately scanned the other notes of a similar age. She stopped when her gaze landed on the name 'Erun' — the name Amund had adopted to hide his identity in Lamore. With shaking hands, Arisa picked up the parchment: a letter this time, dated sixteen years ago. She checked the last page for a name. It was signed, 'Your loving daughter always, Daria'. Arisa went back to the start and read.

Dearest Mother,

I have arrived safely in Obira, though the same cannot be said for some of the other passengers. Four souls perished on our journey here. Fortunately Ackerley's wife and child still live. I can't imagine what would have become of me if I had failed to keep them alive. On docking, Ackerley demanded a carriage be sent to convey his family and me to Lamore Castle, but his request was refused.

The Lamorian King sent guards to ensure we all stayed put on the ship to prevent the spread of fever. No appeals for mercy or arguments about the unhygienic conditions of the vessel were heeded. It was by luck more than anything that I was able to slip a note to a sympathetic guard, asking for him to send for the healer known as Erun.

Within hours Erun arrived with a well-stocked apothecary kit. The guards on duty would not allow him admittance. My hopes were dashed. I was almost out of medicine and frankly could not see any of us on board surviving, but it soon became apparent that the man was adept in the use of Kengian suggestive powers, for it was only a minute later that the same guards who'd refused entry were eagerly escorting Erun aboard.

He addressed me in Lamorian, but I could follow little of what he said. Once the guards were out of sight he switched to Kengian.

The man himself is a curious creature. He has wild hair and a dishevelled appearance. He has a nervous habit of constantly pushing his glasses up the bridge of his nose and speaks in riddles to himself, but I cannot fault his abilities, or his heart.

Arisa's chest swelled with pride. It was exactly as she remembered her uncle. Reading Daria's account of Erun – Amund – brought back a barrage of conflicting feelings, but she was drawn back to the story.

For three days, I have spent every waking minute with Erun, assisting him with calculations and the compounding of medicine. It is quite time-consuming to prepare, but one by one we are administering the medicine to the passengers. I am in awe of his scientific mind, but can tell you nothing else of the healer. He deflects any questions I ask about his family or how he came to be in Lamore. All he will say is that he has an apothecary shop in the city and a young ward who he has temporarily left in the care of a Schoolmaster. But he is generous with his knowledge and has shared his secrets for treating the fever.

Daria then outlined what Arisa recognised as the composition for her uncle's fever medicine and his typical treatment notes. It must have been how Rea had managed to save Jed's daughter from fever. Nima must have passed on Erun's cure.

There was a break after that, and a datemark for two days later.

The passengers who started the treatment first are showing positive signs of improvement. Sadly, we weren't able to save two of the sickest Lamorians.

I am quite desperate for sleep, having caught only a few minutes here and there, but I will not rest while Erun soldiers on without complaint. My admiration for him grows every day. He is as stubborn as they come, insisting I take some of the medicine to try to prevent catching fever myself, but he has met his match in me. I will not take any medicine until my charges are out of danger — they may be Lamorians, our enemy, but that is not the Kengian way. That is not our way.

Since coming to Lamore I'd hoped to feel something. A hint of growing Firemaster powers, but so far nothing. It is probably because I am tired. I am so, so tired.

There was another break in the letter, then an almost illegible scrawl — a mere few lines of scratchy words.

I should have listened to Erun. I have caught fever. And what use am I now to the others? I have failed you, Mother. I will die here in the fetid bowels of this ship, the Firemaster's legacy ending with me.

I am sorry.
Your loving daughter always,
Daria

The letter ended there.

'She *died?*' Arisa could barely believe it.

Isla looked up from her reading. 'Who died?'

'One of the Firemasters, Daria. She knew Amund, but I never remember him mentioning her. Maybe because she died.'

But something troubled Arisa. The line where Daria had said the Firemaster's legacy would end with her. If that were true, how could Rea, who was born after that, be a Firemaster?

'There must be more here. Something else. Keep looking!'

Arisa raced to find another letter with the same handwriting. She felt as if she'd checked every document twice or more and was about to give up when she found it.

Dearest Mother,

I'm happy to report that I'm recovering well, thanks to Erun and some new friends here in Lamore.

Erun has brought me to a county called Lakeford, where there is a small community of Kengians and silver-eyes. They work on farms owned by a Duke who is kind to all his tenant farmers and for the most part lets us observe our cultural practices. There is a harvest festival coming up soon called Ujej. Erun thinks I'll be well enough to attend. He visits here regularly 'to check on my progress'. I tell him it's not necessary and that there is supposed to be a Kengian healer who lives much closer, but he insists, and in truth I'm quite accustomed to his company. I'm sure there's more to his story than I'll ever know, but I too have secrets. He doesn't know I am a Firemaster, and it is best to keep it that way. Outside of Lakeford, Kengians are largely scorned and live in fear — the blood moon massacre is still fresh in everyone's minds. Silver-eyes are at the most risk, with the King himself believing they can bewitch and curse people. I can't imagine what would happen if my identity were discovered by anyone here.

It's unfair to burden Erun or anyone else with this knowledge, but when I'm by myself I try to tap into my dormant powers, just as you have told me to do. And as I regain my strength, I feel my powers growing. I can hear the babbling voices in a stream, wisps of words in the wind, the baritone uttering of the earth as it is tilled. Two nights ago, I revived a dying fire with a flick of my wrist, and images have been appearing in my sleep, too vivid to be dreams. Visions, perhaps?

In any case, I am safe and well here, but miss you terribly.

Your loving daughter always,

Daria

The parts of the letter about Amund made sense. He'd been known to travel outside of the city on occasion to see patients, and he was the kind of person who would follow up to make sure someone was healing as they should. But there seemed to be something more in Daria's words.

'They were friends,' Arisa said. 'Amund and Daria were friends.'

Isla forced her gaze from the note she was reading. A mischievous glint came to her eyes.

'I think they were more than friends.'

'Let me see.' Arisa leapt to Isla's side so she could read the same document.

'Here.' Isla pointed to a specific line in a letter written in Daria's hand: *I'm with child.*

'But that doesn't mean it's Amund's,' Arisa argued.

'There's only one way to find out.'

The pair rapidly skimmed the letter. Particular sentences and phrases jumped out at Arisa.

still weak from the fever

the last time Erun visited he was concerned

he doesn't know

the baby grows strong inside me at my expense

weaker by the day

The winter here bites cold, gnawing at my bones, but it gives me an excuse to don layers of furs and cloaks that hide my condition from Erun. He is sick with worry about my deteriorating health and would only blame himself if he knew the truth.

I saw the future – a future. Only snippets, but enough for me to know that I will die giving birth to my daughter, and that she will be one of the greatest Firemasters ever known. But she cannot be allowed to follow this path. I have seen fields of blood. Unspeakable pain. Devastating weapons. And my daughter is central to it all.

By then Arisa was hooked. Her heart beat wildly and her eyes couldn't take in the words fast enough.

It breaks my heart to say this, but maybe they were right to banish our kind. No one can control the kind of power I have seen. The kind of power that eats away at you from the inside, consuming your being and humanity if you allow it. The world is not ready for the return of the Firemasters.

I am decided. My daughter must never know she is a Firemaster. It is the only way I can protect her. This is the only legacy worth preserving. And Erun can never learn he has a daughter. I have also seen his future. He is a broken man when he learns of my death, believing it is somehow his fault. It would be so much worse if he knew I'd died giving birth to his child.

This fact aside, it's too risky for Erun to raise her. He is the smartest person I've ever met and it wouldn't take him long to figure out our daughter is a Firemaster, and then nothing could stop him and his curiosity from developing her powers. That is the kind of man he is — someone who believes we must all fulfil our destinies, and that good will always prevail. This is why I love him, but also why I must keep the greatest gift from him. That will be my biggest regret, as well as never seeing you again in this life.

I will see that my daughter is well cared for. I've spoken to a Kengian couple who live nearby who have agreed to adopt my child if anything is to happen to me. It is possible you and Erun will get to meet our precious girl — it is another thing I have seen, though the future is muddled to me. The only thing I am certain of is that no one other than you, not even my daughter herself, must discover the existence of another Firemaster.

Promise me this one thing, please, Mother, so I can depart this world with an absolved heart.

Your loving daughter always,

Daria

Isla and Arisa exhaled in unison, slumping back onto their pillows. Tears pricked Arisa's eyes.

'I can't believe it,' Isla said in a faraway voice.

'But it must be true. It's the only thing that makes sense. Rea grew up in Lakeford. She was adopted by Kengian farmers. The timeline matches.'

'But if it is true…Rea is Amund's daughter.'

Arisa couldn't name the feeling she was experiencing. It was something between shock, sadness and joy. 'And she is our cousin.'

16

Over the years, Takai had formed a picture in his mind of what Ivane was like. A picture informed by his mother's fond recollections of her homeland – a land of beauty, wisdom and formidable warriors. But he found the reality of the place differed. There was no doubt that Nadis Palace and its city were beautiful and a beacon to the finest scholars, but any military acumen the nation had once possessed was long forgotten.

Takai's uncle had offered his army at different times to help defeat the Northemers, but Lamore and Kengia hadn't called upon King Laskar. The last time Ivane had seen battle was when Laskar was a boy. Similarly, while all Ivanian children were taught fighting and martial skills, the vast majority of them had never had to put what they'd learned into practice. And this lack of experience was alarmingly evident in every conversation Takai had been privy to over the last few days. Even Ivane's lead Commander, an ageing soldier by the name of Letoi, seemed to be at a loss when it came to dealing with the Northemer threat.

With all the representatives from Ivane's major cities and regions now present in Nadis, as well as the Ettean Commander, Kappu, King Laskar had called a meeting of his Assembly to determine strategy. When Takai and Sar entered the room, the

Assembly appeared to already be at war...with itself. Leaders were on their feet, shouting at each other in rapid Ivanian. Takai could only catch a few words, mainly curses and something about 'the Discontented'. There were accusations that it was one or another's fault. What exactly they were at fault for he couldn't discern.

King Laskar was standing at one end of the table, making placating gestures with his hands, while Princess Noemi sat nearby watching the squabbling leaders, her top lip curled in disgust.

Kappu, Commander Letoi, and the King's Counsel, Ambra, stood off to the side of Laskar, heads bowed, deep in conversation. It was Ambra who looked up and noticed Takai and Sar's arrival.

'Your Majesty,' Ambra greeted Takai in a clear but not unkind voice. 'Sir Sar.' A dozen Ivanian mouths slammed shut in unison. 'Please.' Ambra indicated two vacant seats near Noemi with a smile.

From the little Takai had seen of Ambra, he seemed the kind of man who spoke rarely, but when he did speak, everyone listened. Ambra was also a healer and had been an adviser to Laskar's father. In both manner and looks, he reminded Takai of Lore – the Ivanian healer who had cared for Takai and his mother at the Lamorian court. Lore had been respected by all for his kindness and mental aptitude, but his life had come to an untimely end when he'd volunteered to be an emissary to the Northemers during peace negotiations that had ultimately failed. Malu had taken Lore's head, a cold-blooded, cowardly act Takai could neither forgive nor forget.

If Ambra was anything like Lore, he could be a pragmatic and useful ally – and Takai could use all the friends he could get right now. While the Ivanians weren't as openly hostile to him as the Etteans, there was no mistaking the wary and suspicious looks they gave him. And those were nothing compared to how his cousin regarded him.

It turned out that Noemi was second in military rank only to Letoi and wielded significant influence. Takai had sought her out on several occasions, trying to engage her in conversation about Ivane's planned strategy, but she had scorned each one of his advances. Pushing his wounded ego aside, Takai was desperate to impart his experience from fighting the Northemers, if anyone was willing to listen. This meeting was his best and only hope of helping Ivane.

Everyone took their seats again and Commander Letoi gave his latest account of the Northemers' movements. Their ships remained anchored at various river mouths, and the invaders travelling overland were reported to be in the underground city, Oisiri. Their leader, Malu, was said to be among them.

'So you will send your guards there,' Takai said. 'It should be simple enough to capture them in a city contained underground.'

Sar cringed as every other head around the table swivelled toward Takai.

'If you knew anything of our country, *cousin*,' Noemi hissed, 'you'd know that no weapons or violence are allowed in Oisiri.'

Takai's cheeks burned. This wasn't a good start.

King Laskar rested a palm on his daughter's hand and gave Takai a fatherly smile. 'My guards are there already, tracking and watching them. We plan on capturing them the moment they leave the city.'

Takai managed a small nod.

'The main concern,' Letoi continued, 'is what to do about the Northemer ships.'

'Where are the Lamorian and Kengian fleets?' asked an Ivanian representative with a long white beard.

All eyes were on Takai again, but he couldn't find his words. Sar spoke instead.

'The last we heard, they are still in Obira, waiting for the storms at sea to subside,' he said.

'A convenient excuse,' Noemi scoffed.

Laskar frowned. 'Our weather forecasters say a typhoon has formed in the western sea and conditions aren't expected to improve for several days. Isn't that the case, Ambra?'

Ambra nodded.

'Then we must send our own ships,' declared a young man with heavily bejewelled fingers.

Letoi shook his head. 'The few vessels we have must remain here to protect Nadis.'

'What of Ette's new fleet?' another Ivanian asked.

All eyes went to Commander Kappu, who shifted in his seat. 'Our government could only spare two of our ships. The others are to remain in Ette in case the Northemers set their sights on the Capital again.'

'Recreants,' Noemi said.

King Laskar's face contorted, his brow a rugged terrain of deep ridges.

Letoi sat up taller in his chair. 'We must rely on our army alone. More warriors arrive in Nadis every hour, and once our forces are fully assembled, we will outnumber the Northemers three or more to one.'

'We make our stand here in Nadis,' Noemi said with certainty.

Takai had followed the Ivanians' discussion with a growing sense of fear. None of them knew what they were up against. He found his voice again and said as carefully as possible, 'With the deepest respect, I'm not sure if numbers are enough to beat the Northemers.'

'With the *deepest respect*,' Noemi spat, 'I'm not sure we should be listening to the King of the nation that was our enemy for so long.'

There was a murmur of agreement around the table. King Laskar wrung his hands. A muscle twitched in Ambra's cheek.

Takai squared his shoulders. 'Don't listen to me, then, but think of your people. While you focus on protecting your beloved palace, all of those towns and cities out there' – he waved his hand in the direction of the city gate – 'are at the mercy of the Northem fleets.'

Noemi lifted her chin. 'As you have heard, we have no ships to send.'

'You must use everything at your disposal. Don't recall all of your warriors; ask some to stay to defend their homes. Commandeer every fishing boat and pleasure craft. Deploy them now, before the Northemers make their move – and they *will* make a move.'

Noemi crossed her arms. 'We focus on defending Nadis. It will draw the Northemers here.'

Takai could no longer conceal the frustration in his voice. 'If you knew anything of their leader, Malu – if you had faced him on the battlefield like I have – you would know he is not *drawn* to do anything. He will have a plan, something completely unexpected. Your best strategy is to meet them head-on before they have a chance to enact their plan.'

King Laskar rubbed his chin. 'Sar, what do you say? What do you think the Northemers have planned?'

Sar looked the King straight in the eye as he spoke. 'Takai and I are of one mind. Malu will have a plan that is fitting for the trickster that he is, and he is not the type of man to wait for his enemy to come to him. We must assume that if he hasn't signalled for his ships to move yet, he must be waiting for something. Right now those ships are vulnerable, but if they're not stopped, you can say goodbye to victory.'

Cries of disbelief rang around the table, but Sar was on his feet, pointing to a map of Ivane rolled out before them.

'Take a look yourself.' He jabbed a finger at each of the model ships representing the Northem vessels. 'Since the ships have been there, nothing has left those ports. No food. No metals or ore. No goods of any kind. They will take control of those ports and choke all industry. Without supplies, you will be starved into submission. So yes, the Northemers will bring the fight to Nadis.'

Noemi shook her head. 'The palace city is big enough and has enough supplies to withstand months of siege. We will have them beaten long before that.'

'And in the meantime? Malu will be strangling the rest of Ivane,' Takai cried. 'You're throwing your people to the wolves.'

Laskar slammed a fist on the table. 'Enough!'

With everyone's attention on him, he took a deep breath.

'We assemble our army here as planned. Once Malu is in custody – and he will be, as soon as he leaves Oisiri – his fleet will fall back.'

The King stood up and left the table. Evidently the meeting was over.

TAKAI AND SAR headed back to their quarters, each resigned to the fact that they would be at war again soon enough, and that Malu held all the advantages. Takai couldn't understand why his uncle couldn't see reason. And if he wouldn't listen to Takai, he should have at least listened to Sar.

'Your Majesty.' A baritone Ivanian voice behind them.

Takai turned to face Ambra. Something snagged in his throat – for a second, it was Lore looking back at him from Ambra's all-seeing eyes.

'You deserve to know that your strategy is sound,' Ambra said. 'But the King can't be sure of having the support he needs outside of Nadis to confront the Northemers. Already we are seeing fewer than we expected answer the call to arms.'

'I don't understand,' Takai said. 'Why wouldn't the Ivanians join the King's army?'

Ambra gave a resigned sigh. 'Ivane is not the place it was when your mother lived here, or when King Arlo was on the throne. Back then we had a common enemy: Lamore. We all knew what it was like to live under foreign rule. It wasn't hard to convince all Ivanians to rally against the…' Ambra appeared to be struggling to find the right word.

'Oppressors,' Takai said bluntly.

'Yes,' Ambra said. 'Ivane was united against Lamore, believing a better future lay ahead, and it *was* a better future… for many. Ivane prospered as an independent nation. Our port and mining cities thrived and the people there became richer, but that wasn't the case for those who lived at the farthest reaches, where natural resources were few. Ivane is sadly a land of those who have and those who have not.'

Takai recalled the poor Ivanian man he'd seen at the city gate on the day he arrived, begging for an audience with the King.

'And those who have not—'

'Have no wish to fight for their King,' Takai suggested.

'Worse than that,' Ambra said. 'With the right inducement, they may even take up arms against him.'

'The "Discontented",' Takai guessed. 'They are why the leaders were arguing and blaming each other in the meeting.'

Ambra nodded.

Sar clicked his fingers. 'Oisiri. Malu will use his time there to recruit supporters among the Discontented. Whatever he has planned, he will put it into play from Oisiri.'

Sar was terrifyingly right. 'Then my uncle must order the Northemers to be arrested immediately. Right there in Oisiri.'

Ambra shook his head. 'Oisiri is a sacred place. The King would never break the peace there. We must wait until Malu leaves, and we will capture him the moment he does.'

'You must hope that you do,' Takai said.

'And that the damage hasn't already been done,' Sar added.

Ambra steepled his fingers, his palms pressed firmly together. 'It is why you must help the King and Princess Noemi. You must help them fortify the city. You must advise them on the best way to withstand an attack on Nadis.'

'Didn't you see what happened back there?' Takai protested. 'They don't want to listen to anything we have to say.'

'You are a fine King, Takai, and you are your mother's son. You can make them listen.'

Sar nodded at Takai. The determined set of his jaw said that Takai could do it.

'Fine,' he conceded. 'I will try.' He expected Ambra to appear relieved, but if anything the man's expression was even graver. 'Was there something else?'

'Yes. We have received word of a silver-eyes and her companion in one of our mining towns, Liprah, asking after the firebird.'

'Arisa and Isla,' Sar said.

'Impossible,' Takai said. 'Liprah is north-east of here – they were going to head directly south from Ette to Nadis.'

'The descriptions match.' Ambra's gaze narrowed. 'Are they looking for the firebird?'

Takai and Sar exchanged a swift look.

Ambra's brow crinkled. 'That was what I feared. Then I must also inform you that the firebird was also seen in the mountains near Oisiri.'

A bolt of fear ran through Takai. This meant only one thing. Arisa and Isla were heading straight for Malu.

He grabbed the front of Ambra's robe. 'We have to warn them!'

Ambra gently prised Takai's fingers away. 'Any warning we send now won't reach them in time. We can also assume they know of the Northemers' presence and that they have decided to go to Oisiri regardless of the risk.'

'That is a safe assumption,' Sar concurred.

Ambra rested a reassuring hand on Takai's shoulder. 'And if Arisa and Isla are even half as impressive as they are said to be, I pity any Northemer who challenges them.' With a final nod, he left them.

The Counsel's words were meant well, but Takai felt little comfort. His hands clenched into fists by his side. 'We have to go after them.'

'As Ambra said, we won't reach them in time,' Sar said. 'And you have promised to help the King here.'

'You don't understand. I can't let anything happen to her. I can't fail her again.' Takai's voice broke on the last word.

'I do understand, friend.' Worry was etched across Sar's usually smiling face. 'But loving Arisa and Isla demands that we also trust them. We must trust that they can look after themselves and that they will return to us. We owe them our faith, and right now there are others who need our protection.'

A bitter laugh escaped Takai's mouth. He was duty-bound to protect a nation that didn't want his protection. Yet he couldn't protect the one he most desperately wanted to keep from harm.

17

$\mathcal{T}$heodora had found little to occupy herself with since being in Oisiri. Malu had spent the last two days in secret meetings at different locations around the city, and was yet to share with anyone the nature of those meetings. Similarly, she had seen little of Jade since they first arrived. The couple of times she had ventured out from The Hawk and Mouse, she hadn't got far before the accusatory stares and muttered threats became too much. With a good grasp of the Ivanian language, Theodora was under no illusion: the moment the Northemers left Oisiri, they would be pounced on by the King's Guards. She didn't feel safe enough to go anywhere in the city alone. Instead she spent her time in the room she shared with Malu, tending to Rayl.

The snow leopard's back leg was almost fully healed now, and Theodora had begun letting her out of the cage for exercise. Today Rayl was pacing the floor of the room, a low puffing sound coming from her mouth. Every now and then she would stop at the window and paw at the glass.

'I'm sorry,' Theodora said. 'I know it is cruel to keep you locked up, but soon we will be gone from this place and this country, and you will be free to roam your homeland again.'

She envied Rayl, in a way. At least the creature had a home to go to. Theodora didn't belong anywhere...except with Malu. The sooner he enacted his grand plan – whatever it was – the sooner they could get on with living the lives they deserved.

Rayl mewed and pawed again at the window, this time more violently.

Theodora went to the window and glanced out onto the street, trying to identify what had caught the leopard's attention. At first nothing looked amiss, but then she spotted a slight hooded figure slipping surreptitiously through the crowd. A figure she immediately recognised as Jade. *Where is she going?*

Theodora scanned the room and spied a length of gold cord used to tie back the curtains. She yanked the cord from its place and tied it around Rayl's neck.

'Enough of sitting back and watching while everyone else gets to choose their path.'

Theodora led Rayl from her room and back through the tavern. A smirk played on her face at the startled expressions of the Northemers and other patrons who leapt out of their way.

Outside they received a similar reaction, with a path cleared for them wherever they went. It made it easy to catch up with Jade, but Theodora was careful to keep her distance. They followed the Ivanian girl to a jeweller's shop. In the front window was a display of sparkling gold rings, necklaces and bracelets. Gemstones of every hue winked back at Theodora. She couldn't fathom what business Jade would have at such a place, unless she was planning on stealing the items – not an entirely far-fetched idea, given the girl's predilection for pickpocketing.

Theodora peered inside, but Jade was nowhere to be seen. The shop was a small space with a glass cabinet at one end and a door behind it, presumably leading to the jeweller's workshop. Jade must have gone back there, but why?

It was only a few moments later that Jade emerged through the doorway, slipping a large leather satchel under her cloak.

Theodora quickly searched for somewhere to hide, but it was too late.

Jade strode out of the shop and right up to her, her gaze taking in Theodora, then Rayl. An amused smile came to her face.

'Come on then,' she said, walking straight past them.

Theodora hurried to catch up. 'Come on where?'

Jade indicated a dark alleyway adjacent to the shop. Once they were in the safety of the shadows, she reached for her satchel. 'I assume you want to know what I have in here,' she said, the glint of her green eyes penetrating the darkness. She pulled out a bundle of thorned sticks that looked like they'd come from a Batu-riek tree. On closer inspection, the sticks appeared to be joined to each other via gold hinges.

Jade stepped back and, with a flick of her wrist, the sticks snapped into place to form one long staff. The thorns along its length glistened. Theodora outstretched her hand to touch them, but Jade hopped out of reach. 'You don't want to touch it. Each one of these thorns' – she pointed out the barbs with a gloved hand – 'has been infused with the venom from the desert asp – Ivane's most poisonous snake.'

Theodora gulped, imagining what it would be like to be on the receiving end of the staff. 'The wood – it looks like it came from a Batu-riek, but I thought you said the branches were impervious to damage.'

'They are,' Jade said matter-of-factly, 'from fire, axes or any ordinary tools. But no ordinary tool was used to form this weapon.' She nodded to her open satchel. There was still one item inside it. A single arrow that also appeared to have been made from a Batu-riek branch. At its head was a sharpened, glimmering crystal.

'Is that the same crystal found at the entrance to the city?' Theodora asked.

Jade nodded. 'It is Alia crystal – the only thing capable of cutting through Batu-riek timber.' Jade lowered her voice. 'But no one can know I have this.'

Theodora raised a curious brow. 'Why?'

'Because it's considered sacred...And anyone who does take an Alia crystal is cursed.'

Theodora gasped. 'You're willing to be cursed?'

Jade shrugged. 'If that's what it takes to kill the firebird, so be it.'

Theodora's heart drummed in fear for Rea. 'The firebird? You intend on using these weapons against her?'

Jade scowled. '*Her?*'

'The creature,' Theodora said hurriedly. 'You think these would actually kill it?'

'I do. Otherwise I wouldn't have spent every *hard-earned* coin I had on them.' She laughed at her own joke as she folded the staff back into her bag.

On the way back to the tavern, Jade rabbited on about the latest sighting of the firebird, saying it had been seen in the mountains nearby, but Theodora was barely listening. All she was thinking of was how she was going to stop Jade from killing her friend – and her future.

BACK AT THE HAWK and Mouse, Jade went to her room and Theodora was about to do the same, but her father beckoned her from a table in the corner. Theodora rolled her eyes, wondering if she could claim she hadn't seen him, but Horace's frenzied waving made that impossible.

She and Rayl made their way past several groups of Northemers, who shuffled their chairs and bench seats to avoid the snow leopard.

Horace pressed his chair against the wall on sighting the cat. 'Get that *thing* away from me.'

Rayl snarled in response.

'Fine,' Theodora said, turning on her heel.

'No – I need to speak with you,' Horace called after her.

Theodora smirked in triumph and took a seat opposite her father. Horace moved as far away as he could from Rayl, his sharp eyes on the snow leopard.

'Yes?' Theodora prompted.

Horace took a large swig of cider from his mug and focused his attention on Theodora. 'Have you heard what they're saying?' He nodded toward a group of Northemers huddled around a table nearby, Hafder among them.

Theodora trained her ear to their conversation, catching only snippets.

'Malu is a fool. He has no plan...'

'We'll be dead the moment we leave this place...'

'We have to leave. Forget Ivane. Forget Malu...If it was just a few of us, we could slip out unnoticed...'

'We can get to our ships...We can take Ette again...'

While Theodora wasn't surprised to hear the Northemers griping about Malu and questioning his plans, she was taken aback that Hafder wasn't defending his brother. Quite the opposite: he was nodding in agreement.

'Malu needs an ally,' Horace said. 'Someone who can advise him on a plan that has merit.'

'He already has a plan with merit,' she sniped, not adding that she had no idea what the plan was.

'Get me a meeting with him. Let me talk sense into him. I know this country. I know its people. I can get us out of this city with our lives. If we act fast enough, we can get to Obira and take Lamore – it is the last thing anyone will expect.'

'Because it's a ridiculous plan,' Theodora retorted.

Horace clicked his jaw, his dark eyes disturbingly still. 'You don't know what Malu has planned, do you? You are as much in the dark as any of us.' His lip curled into a sneer.

Theodora tightened her grip on Rayl's lead. Sensing her anger, the snow leopard emitted a low growl. 'This isn't about me,' Theodora said through gritted teeth. 'It's about the fact that you are no longer an adviser, or Chancellor. You have no power over them and you have no power over me.' She stood up from her chair and looked down her nose at her father. 'You're utterly powerless.'

Horace's face went taut, a grim smile stretching across it. 'As are you, daughter.' He inclined his head toward the Northemers. 'They will slit your throat, and mine, given the chance.'

Theodora had no response. She knew her father had spoken the truth. Instead she lifted her chin and marched from the room, Rayl matching her stride.

By THE TIME Theodora reached her room, her false bravado had vanished. She held back the flood of tears threatening to burst from her. Waiting inside was Malu, who took one look at her flushed cheeks and watering eyes and rushed to embrace her.

'It's alright,' he murmured in her ear. 'Everything will be alright.'

Then the tears came. Fat, forceful tears filled with anger, fear and an overwhelming sense of helplessness.

'They don't trust you,' she sobbed into Malu's muscular chest. 'They're going to turn against you…Hafder included. I'll be at their mercy. And Jade is going to kill Rea…and I can't do anything about it. My father is right. I'm *powerless*.'

Malu didn't interrupt her, merely drew her closer to him. Theodora lost track of time, bundled safe in his arms. She only stopped crying when Rayl licked her arm, the sandpapery sensation of the cat's tongue enough to bring her back to reality.

Malu took a step back, his piercing blue eyes probing her, falling on the masses of yellowing bruises on her arms – injuries from her training with Jade. He gently traced the largest of the bruises, hurt, then fury, flaring in his eyes.

'You don't need to do this. You don't need to carry any of these burdens. You know I'll protect you.'

'I know you will.' She blinked away the last of the tears that clung to her lashes. 'But I want to be capable of defending myself. I want to be worthy of being your Queen.'

Malu took her hand and lifted it to his lips. 'If only they could see what I see.' His voice was thick with hunger.

'What exactly do you see?' she asked tentatively.

He ran his hand through her long, dark waves of hair, stopping to caress her face. 'I see someone who has never really been *seen* before. Someone whose beauty others can't see beyond. The same beauty that weighs you down and shackles you to preconceived ideas of who you are and who you should be. It stops people from seeing the exquisite workings of your mind, your heart, your ambition, your ability to lead.'

He stopped to kiss the bruises on her arm, one by one. Prickles erupted on her skin at every touch.

'I see someone who won't shy away from something that is hard,' he purred. 'Someone who would go to the end of the world for the people she cares about. Someone who would fight to their last breath.'

He stopped kissing her arm and raised his head to face her again. His eyes glittered with tears of his own, his words landing softly as a cloud.

'That is what I see. There could be no other woman worthy of my heart. You've signed up for a task more difficult than you can imagine. You could have stayed in Lamore, but you chose to come with me.'

Theodora scoffed. 'I could have stayed and been imprisoned.'

The mischievous twinkle returned to Malu's eyes. 'Within a week, you would have had them convinced that you were innocent of everything. That you were acting on your father's orders, just another of his victims.'

Theodora gave a small laugh. 'Yes, that would very well have been my strategy. But I chose you, and right now I'm worried about you.'

Malu gave a dismissive wave. 'I have everything under control. Soon Hafder and the others will understand my plan.'

'Let *me* understand your plan.'

'On one condition.'

Theodora raised a brow.

'That you let me teach you how to use a hand cannon. If you insist on learning to protect yourself, let it be with a weapon that doesn't injure you in the process.'

'I agree.'

Malu nodded and reached for a roll of parchment on a side table. He rolled it out on the bed. It was a map of Ivane. Red crosses were marked at several locations where major rivers met the east and south-east coast.

'I have deployed our ships to Ivane's largest trading ports. They are to play a special part in my plan.'

'Do you plan on taking control of those cities and strangling all of the country's trade and supply lines?'

Malu gave an enigmatic smile, which she took as confirmation.

'Wouldn't you need more people and firepower to execute such a large campaign?'

Malu tapped the side of his nose. 'Our visit here hasn't been wasted. Thanks to what you told me about Ivane's Discontented, I have managed to recruit quite an army.'

'You have? How did you secure their support?' Ivanians who were dissatisfied with their country were one thing, but convincing them to join the Northem cause was a completely different matter. Had they been as motivated by coin as she suspected?

'You were right in your thinking, my love. All it took was enough money.' He looked over at Rayl's cage.

Initially Theodora had no idea what Malu could be referring to, but on closer inspection of the cage, she noticed that a plank of the wooden base was slightly askew. Malu, who'd been watching her with a playful grin, handed her a knife, which she used to prise open the base. The plank lifted free to reveal a compartment filled with—

'*Gold*,' she whispered.

'Not just any gold.' He beamed. 'Ivanian gold. The gold they offered to get us to leave Ette.'

Theodora recalled how the Ivanian healer, Lore, had gone to Ette with a jewelled casket filled with gold, trying to negotiate with the Northemers. Malu had taken the gold − and Lore's head, sending the latter back to Lamore in the otherwise empty casket.

'But I assumed it was all lost in Ette, or—'

'No. I've had it with me at all times. At first Rea was protecting it. Then, after the battle in Lamore, I entrusted my Huntmaster to smuggle it out. He also saw that it was concealed in Rayl's cage when we came here.'

'Who else knows about it?'

'No one.'

'Not even Hafder?'

Theodora registered a twinge of movement in Malu's cheek before he spoke. 'I love Hafder, but he is reckless and doesn't have the strength of mind of you or me.' He shook his head. 'The man got himself kidnapped by a pirate after one too many mugs of mead and too much bragging about who he was.'

Theodora shuddered.

'Yes, that's the same pirate who dared to think he could have you.' Malu stretched his neck, which made a cracking sound in protest. 'So, no. Hafder doesn't know. Your snow leopard provided the perfect ruse to bring the gold here.'

Rayl made what was almost a shrugging motion, as if she were well aware of what had been hidden in her cage.

'And now you have the means to take Ivane,' Theodora remarked. How could she ever have doubted him?

'Almost,' he said. 'First we must devise a way to escape this place, and there are other pieces of the puzzle that must come together for us to be confident of success.'

'Olix? The merchant?'

Malu took Theodora's hand in his. 'As soon as I am sure he will deliver, I will share the last of my plan with you. But you must trust me.'

'I trust you,' she said, meaning it.

'Then marry me. Right here in Oisiri. Today.'

She bit her lip. 'I don't know.'

But she did know. She knew that she wanted to marry him more than anything. She was past the idea of having to earn it. She was worthy of Malu. She was worthy of everyone. The word 'yes' danced on her tongue – but was drowned out by shouting outside the window and knocking at their door.

Malu flung the door open to reveal Jade. 'It's coming!' she cried. 'The firebird! It's on its way here.'

18

'I still can't believe it.' Isla took a drink from her flask. They had stopped to let their horses rest under the shade of a sandstone rock formation, having barely paused since leaving Liprah at dawn. She wiped spilt water from her lips. 'Rea can't be Amund's daughter…and *yet*—'

'Stranger things have happened,' Arisa finished, thinking about her own unexpected parentage, which she had only recently discovered.

'But for Amund not to know…'

'You read the letters. Daria didn't think she had a choice. She wanted to protect Rea. She saw Rea's Firemaster path and didn't want it for her. It's why she made Nima promise not to tell Rea either.'

Isla's eyes blazed with anger. 'But to keep this from Amund – she had no right.'

Arisa nodded miserably. 'I know, but I understand why she chose to keep it from him. Our uncle would have realised she was a Firemaster, and nothing would have stopped him from helping Rea embrace those powers.'

'But Rea stumbled into her abilities anyway.'

'I suppose there's no escaping your destiny,' Arisa muttered, taking a drink from her flask. It was something she had learnt firsthand.

'And look where it got Rea.' Isla swept her arm across the sandy landscape. 'Trapped between forms and worlds, hunted, alone.'

Arisa's grip clamped tighter around her flask. 'Rea's not alone. We'll find her.'

Isla jutted out her chin. 'We will.'

'How much further to Oisiri?'

Isla squinted into the distance. The silver sun was setting over the mountains in the west. The desert sparkled as if it were formed from millions of tiny diamonds. 'Not too far now. Rosa said we would reach it before nightfall.'

They got back on their horses and continued north, using the most eastern mountain as their guide. They'd been told the underground city was just beyond the range. As they passed through the craggy shadow outline of the final mountain, the buzzing Arisa had felt inside herself since the cave intensified. It was a knowing. A calling. Alia crystals were near.

'We're close,' she said.

They came over a dune to see a group of people scrambling toward a rock wall with a single date palm tree at its top.

'Where are they going?' Arisa asked.

One by one, the people disappeared through a gap in the rocks. Arisa peered closer. A silver light glowed from within the crevice. It must be the entrance to Oisiri. But why were they in such a hurry?

Wordlessly, Isla pointed to the west.

Arisa followed her cousin's gaze to catch sight of the phoenix, carving a jagged path through the sky toward them. The flailing firebird plummeted toward the ground, then rose, only to fall again. Her broken, weeping wings dripped flames. The phoenix opened her beak and released a guttural cry, which ripped through Arisa like a serrated blade in her chest. She made to head in Rea's direction, but Isla stopped her, grabbing her horse's reins.

'We have to go inside and take shelter.'

'She needs our help!'

'We have to save ourselves first.'

'It's coming!' people screamed. 'The firebird is here!'

Arisa looked back and forth between the phoenix and Oisiri. Rea was almost directly overhead. Giant blobs of fire dropped to the ground, sizzling hot and big enough to kill a person. The firebird screeched, flames erupting from her mouth, igniting the date palm tree. Arisa dug her heels into the horse's belly and she and Isla raced toward the underground city.

They reached the rock wall and dismounted before leading their horses through the crevice. Oisiri guards immediately corralled them from the entrance, directing them to take shelter further into the city, but Arisa wouldn't budge. To her right, a river gleamed silver, reflecting the light from the ceiling. Above them, a sea of pulsating Alia crystals. Every nerve in Arisa's body burst to life. A sensation that resembled *kira* hummed from her bones to her veins to her skin.

This place teemed with magic. Kengian magic.

Isla tugged her arm. 'Come on!' she shouted over the growing screams.

Arisa nodded. She needed to find a safe place to take stock of the power reigniting inside her. Given a chance, she might be strong enough to help Rea. But they'd taken no more than two steps when something – *someone* – stopped Arisa in her tracks.

Theodora strode toward them, the crowd parting as she approached. The reason for their deference was on a lead at Theodora's side. Arisa's eyes widened. *A snow leopard?*

Arisa and Theodora locked gazes, a smirk forming on the latter's face. Theodora was different from how Arisa remembered. Gone were her fine Lamorian fashions and porcelain complexion, replaced by pared-back Northern-style dress and tanned face and limbs. She had lost none of her beauty – if anything, the newfound strength and grit of her countenance made her more striking.

'Theodora?' Isla asked. She only knew Horace's daughter by reputation.

Arisa nodded.

'And a *snow leopard?*'

'A new addition,' Arisa said, her eyes never leaving Theodora.

Isla's hand went to the hilt of her longsword. In the chaos, the guards hadn't had time to take their weapons from them. 'I can take her,' she said, making to step forward, but Arisa stopped her.

'And all of them as well?'

Her eyes were on the Northemers, who had appeared behind Theodora, a grinning Malu in front. Behind him was someone Arisa had hoped she'd never see again. Horace. Albeit a shabbier version of himself, but the same man who had caused her family so much pain. As he spotted Arisa, a sneer befitting his ugly heart crept over his lips.

'Who's that?' Isla asked.

Arisa ground her teeth. 'Horace.' Again, Isla had never seen the former Chancellor in person. Horace had fled from the battlefield at Shizen Lake before the Kengian forces arrived and had never left the safety of the main keep at Lamore Castle in the final battle.

'Not him – who's the girl?'

Arisa tore her attention from Horace, locating the person who'd captured Isla's interest. An Ivanian girl with wild black hair stood at Theodora's side. There was something about the fierceness of the girl's gaze and the sly way her hand reached into the satchel slung over her shoulder that sent shivers up Arisa's spine.

'I don't know.' Why would a lone Ivanian girl have joined forces with Theodora? Arisa wasn't sure she wanted to stick around and find out. They were severely outnumbered, and within moments Theodora and the Northemers would make their way through the remaining crowd to reach them.

Arisa looked back over her shoulder, where the guards were forming a line. 'We should leave.'

Isla opened her mouth to answer, but her words were drowned out by an ear-piercing screech, the beating of wings and the thud of the firebird's approaching steps.

'Get back!' a guard screamed as the phoenix came into view. She advanced on the guards in a series of jerky movements.

'Fire!' another guard ordered his archers.

'No!' Arisa protested as a volley of arrows was released.

The phoenix cawed in anger as she watched the arrows disintegrate the moment they made contact with her fiery body. One guard ran to confront her, his sabre raised.

'Leave her be!' Arisa yelled. 'She won't hurt you unless you threaten her.'

But her warning went unheeded. The guard kept running until he was within a breath of the phoenix. The firebird opened her beak and a whoosh of flames followed, reducing the man to a pile of ashes.

The fallen guard's compatriots fell out of formation and rushed past Arisa and Isla to a safe distance directly in front of Theodora and the Northemers. Arisa noted that the Ivanian girl had a loaded bow pointed in the firebird's direction, but didn't have a clear shot. Arisa couldn't fathom how the girl thought she could succeed where the other archers had failed – but there was something different about her weapon. The sharpened arrowhead flashed silver. Not like metal, as would be expected, but like...

Alia.

Was the weapon capable of killing the firebird? Arisa had to do something – fast.

She turned her focus to the phoenix, who eyed her and Isla in return, stamping her taloned feet on the ground, snorting puffs of fire. This was their chance. Their best and perhaps *only* chance to help Rea.

Arisa took a cautious step toward the firebird, her hands held up in surrender. Then another step.

'Rea, it's me, Arisa.'

The phoenix stopped snorting fire and tilted her head. Another step.

'Your friend.'

The creature's fiery form flickered, and there was a hint of a girl. Rea. Another step.

'But I'm not just your friend, Rea. I'm your cousin.'

The fire sputtered and crackled, and the phoenix was gone, leaving Rea under a dome of flames.

'*Cousin?*' she croaked.

Another step, and Arisa was by Rea's side. 'Yes. Cousin. There's much to explain, but…you are Amund's daughter. You are of the Kengian royal line.' Arisa held her palm up to the flames, encouraging Rea to do the same. Her friend raised a shaking hand, but just as quickly recoiled and backed away.

'No. I am no one. I am nothing but damned,' she said, not meeting Arisa's gaze. 'Stay away. I don't want to hurt you like I hurt all those other people.' She looked up at Arisa with tear-filled eyes. 'I was only protecting myself.'

'I know, Rea. I know you just wanted help, and I am here to give it to you. You are my kin. The same blood runs through our veins. I'm here to help you.'

'Don't listen to her!'

It was Theodora's voice. Arisa swung around to face her, but she remained at a distance behind the guards.

'Arisa betrayed you, and now she tells lies so you will help her cause,' Theodora went on. 'It is we who are friends, Rea.'

The Ivanian girl beside Theodora lowered her bow and arrow and fixed an icy glare on her companion.

'You can trust me,' Arisa pressed. 'We're fam—'

'*No-o-o!*' Rea held her hands to her ears. Her scream

morphed into a screech, and suddenly she was the phoenix again.

The firebird turned her back on Arisa and staggered to the river. A string of muttered Kengian words fell from her beak. A spell. The healing spell Rea had found in the Firemaster's book.

The firebird lowered her beak to the river and drank. With each mouthful the phoenix's colour brightened. Her wings stopped dripping fire.

The guards, seeing their chance, snuck into position, circling her.

'No!' Theodora and Arisa yelled in unison.

The phoenix's head swivelled and she roared fire at her would-be attackers. The guards retreated, and the firebird, fully revived, stomped past Arisa and Isla, back out of Oisiri.

'Rea!' Arisa tried one more time to get through to her friend. The phoenix cocked her head, but didn't turn. And with a shake of her magnificent wings, she ran to the exit and launched herself into the air.

'Thief!' A shout from the crowd. Frantic pointing at the Ivanian girl, who had mounted a stolen horse and was thundering toward the exit.

'We have to stop her!' Arisa waved to Isla. 'She's going after Rea.'

Isla nodded and reached for her bow and arrow. In the blink of an eye she had fired, the arrow striking the girl in the shoulder.

The Ivanian fell from her horse, but got to her feet immediately and pulled the arrow from her shoulder. Scowling at Isla, she reached into her satchel, this time retrieving a bundle of thorned sticks. She flicked her wrist and the sticks assembled into a staff.

Isla smiled in challenge, stashing her bow and arrow away in favour of her Kengian swords. Arisa reached for her own swords, but Isla shook her head. 'She's mine.'

'And *you* are all mine.' Theodora's voice again, but disturbingly closer.

Arisa turned slowly. Theodora and her snow leopard stood only a few feet away. Malu was in the background, giving a series of orders to the Northemers. They seemed to be gathering weapons and horses. Theodora, though, appeared unarmed.

'If it isn't the famed Water Catcher.' Theodora's words oozed with sarcasm.

'You've missed me, then?' Arisa quipped, her hand hovering over the hilt of her longsword.

Theodora's pretty lips curled into her characteristic smirk. 'Well, I *have* been waiting for this moment.'

'But it hardly seems fair. Here I am, armed with not one but two swords, and you have…none.'

'While I can't deny taking your life with my own hands would deliver a certain satisfaction, as long as you're dead, I care not how it happens.' With that, Theodora bent down and whispered something in the snow leopard's ear, and released the animal.

Arisa was caught between her instinct to run and the will to stand her ground and fight – but before she could even unsheathe her blades, the leopard was upon her. Its massive paws slammed into her chest, throwing her to the ground. She flinched as its claws broke her skin and dug into flesh. The cat snarled in her face, its breath reeking of carrion. Theodora's laughter filled the air. Arisa tried to wriggle free, but there was no escaping the leopard's weight, the force of its paws alone pushing the oxygen from her lungs. She made to grab her short sword – and the leopard's jaws snapped around her upper arm.

Arisa tried to bite back the searing pain, but it was an impossible task. She sought out her cousin for help.

From the corner of her eye, she could see Isla fighting the Ivanian girl. Lunging, stabbing with her swords – but the girl blocked her with her staff every time. The staff itself showed no sign of damage where the blades had struck it.

'Isla!' Arisa yelled as loud as she could manage.

Isla whirled toward her. That smallest lapse of concentration was all it took for the Ivanian girl to fix on her target. She swung her thorned staff through the air, whacking Isla hard in the arm. Isla fell to the ground and in an instant the girl was gone. Mounted, and riding out of Oisiri.

Isla tried to push herself to her feet, but crumpled with every attempt. Colour drained from her face, her eyes glazing over. Something was terribly wrong, and there was nothing Arisa could do to help her cousin or herself.

The snow leopard clamped down harder on Arisa's arm, threatening to crush her bones. She was powerless…

Or was she?

She'd registered the magic of this place, its power coursing through her. All she needed to do was connect with that magic.

Arisa thought of everything she had been taught about her Water Catcher and silver-eyes abilities. She must call on the light and darkness within herself, and to do that she needed to tap into the most powerful of emotions. Anger. Fear. Love.

Arisa thought of Rea. Her parents and Firemaster inheritance kept from her. Abandoned to fight alone in this world. She thought of Amund, who'd been taken from them by Theodora's brother. Taken before he'd learned he was a father. She thought of her own mortality and the very real possibility that she may never see Takai again.

With each thought, the buzzing swelled inside her. Her hands burned hot. The energy spread up her arms. The snow leopard yelped and released its grip. Arisa's whole body was enveloped in silver light. The cat leapt off her chest and backed away from her. Theodora watched on, her dark eyes flooded with confusion, then black with fury.

Arisa sat up and got to her feet. She stood in a scarlet pool. Darkness sparked in her at the sight of her blood and of her cousin writhing in pain on the ground. She threw her arms toward the river, directing arcs of light on the water. The river bubbled and surged at her command. She made a shoving motion, and a towering wave rose from the water's surface and barrelled toward Theodora and the city.

Panicked screams and a stampede of running footsteps followed as everyone tried to outrace the wave. Theodora and the Northemers sought higher ground nearby, jumping onto rocks and wagons.

With one hand still controlling the wave, Arisa rushed to Isla's side and helped her to her feet. 'Can you ride?'

Isla gave a wobbly nod, and with Arisa's assistance she managed to get on her horse. Arisa mounted her own steed and together they rode out of Oisiri. She only recalled the wave and released her power over the river once she was sure they had put enough distance between themselves and the city.

For a moment Arisa's mind went to the people who may have been caught up in the wave, but just as quickly, she pushed the thought aside. She would have to think of them later. Right now she could only think of Isla, and of how she would live with herself if she let her own blood die.

19

*T*heodora shivered on top of the wagon, watching the deluge of rising water around her. As soon as they had heard the firebird was coming, Malu had dispatched a series of messages and orders, including the preparation of their horses and wagon, as well as Rayl's cage. Theodora was grateful for his insight – not that he could have known they would need the wagon to keep them safe from a supernatural flood. Huddled now in Malu's arms with Rayl by her side, Theodora watched in horror as three Northemer warriors clutching the wagon's timber sides were swept away. Others tried to outrun the wave, but were soon swallowed up by the surging water.

It was hard to make sense of what had happened. When Arisa had arrived with the red-haired girl – *Isla* was the name Theodora had heard her use – Theodora had been sure she would have her revenge. Arisa had been pinned to the ground, Rayl's jaws fixed tight around her arm. Given the signal, Rayl would have extinguished Arisa's life. But Theodora had been greedy. She'd wanted to prolong the gratification of watching Arisa struggle, knowing her efforts were futile. She'd wanted to see the realisation in her silver eyes that she would die and that Theodora had won. How could she have known that Arisa would be able to muster her Water Catcher powers so far from her homeland?

Theodora had not only failed in killing Arisa – she hadn't been able to bring Rea to her side, either. While she was relieved Rea had managed to escape before Jade or anyone else got to her, the Northemers' best chance to secure victory was gone with her.

'I'm sorry,' she mumbled to Malu. 'It's my fault. If I hadn't been so intent on vengeance, we and everyone else in this city wouldn't be about to drown.'

Malu shook his head. 'We're not going to die here. The water can only rise so far. Remember, the path beyond here slopes upward into the city.'

She thought back to when they'd arrived in Oisiri and remembered the incline of the path as it led into the city.

'The water won't be able to go past a certain point—'

A bolt of fear ran through Theodora. 'And then it will all rush back this way!'

'Arisa can't maintain her hold over the river from a distance. Even now you can see the water slowing.'

Theodora glanced down at the mass of water. It did appear to have lost intensity. The surface swirled and rolled more than raged. Horses snorted their way past, the water stopping at their chests.

So they would survive – but it was bittersweet comfort.

'I failed to bring Rea to us,' she said. 'We need her.'

'If all goes to plan, we won't need her.'

'We *do* need her. Now we've seen the Water Catcher has powers here.'

Malu shrugged. 'I don't know. There's something special about this place and those crystals. It must be why Rea came to heal herself here, and I suspect it's the only reason Arisa was able to summon her powers. Away from here she is vulnerable again.'

Theodora bit her lip. It wasn't just about Arisa. It was about

Rea, and the fact that Jade possessed a weapon that may very well be capable of destroying her friend.

Malu tilted his head in question. 'Is it Rea? I miss her too, but she has chosen her path and she can look after herself.'

Theodora's jaw tensed. 'That's just it. Jade has got herself these weapons – so deadly, I think she'll be able to kill Rea.'

Malu's face contorted with indecision, the expression followed by a drawn-out sigh. 'We don't have time to go after her. As soon as the water starts subsiding, we must leave for Nadis.' He gave an acerbic laugh. 'If anything, the Water Catcher has done us a favour. She has given us the perfect opportunity to make our escape. The King's Guards will be too preoccupied with the aftermath to go after us.'

'Are we ready, though? Have you got everyone you need?'

Malu gave a fiendish smile, then nodded at an Ivanian man on a boulder across from them. The man nodded back in acknowledgement. Malu directed his gaze to another Ivanian, then another and another. One by one, the Ivanians signalled that they were with Northem's King.

Hope rekindled in Theodora. The Northemers' campaign wasn't over. Nor was the chance for her to have her revenge.

20

*A*risa and Isla rode at a cracking pace from Oisiri to the mountains they had passed just an hour or so earlier. Only once they reached the alps with their rocky terrain and precipitous hiding spots did Arisa feel safe enough to stop. By then Isla was slumped forward in her saddle. Arisa pushed aside her own exhaustion and the searing pain in her arm and chest to tend to her cousin, helping her to the ground.

Isla tried to speak. Disjointed, jumbled words. 'Poison…Stop the spread…Water Catcher magic….' A delirious giggle. 'You showed them…'

Arisa winced, not wanting to think about what she'd done in Oisiri. To save herself, she had put innocent lives at risk. Perhaps some had even died in the flood of her making. Her target had been Theodora and the Northemers, but who else had she hurt? At that moment she had surrendered to the calling. The calling to harness her Water Catcher magic. But had she also given in to the darkness?

'I shouldn't have done it,' Arisa said, washing the angry-looking wounds on Isla's forearm where the weapon's barbs had punctured the skin.

Isla wobbled her head at Arisa, her green eyes shiny and

unsteady. Her freckles leapt out from her blanched face. 'You did...what you had to do,' she slurred.

'For me, yes, but what about everyone else there? How many people did I kill?'

Isla rested a clammy hand over Arisa's. 'Trust yourself... Trust your magic...You were in control the whole time...' She took a raspy breath.

Arisa grabbed a bandage from her satchel and wound it tightly above Isla's wounds. 'This will slow the spread. What do you think you were poisoned with?' But she couldn't get any further sense from her cousin, who began a mumbled rant about the 'irksome Ivanian girl' and her 'dirty trick'.

Isla needed proper medical assistance. Arisa's meagre supplies of ointments and poultices were useless against an unknown toxin. Right about now they could have used the healing water at Oisiri, but that was the last place they could go. Liprah was the next closest town. They needed to get there fast.

Arisa looked up at the twilight sky, the first stars peppering a blanket that was rapidly darkening from violet to midnight blue. They would have to travel by night. The only saving grace was a bright full moon and a lack of clouds. Arisa retrieved an amber-coloured bottle from her satchel. A tonic she had learnt to make in Kengia. A mouthful would trigger the body's adrenaline for several hours. Too much, too often, would send a person's heart into overdrive. It required careful administration and should only be used in emergency situations – but if this wasn't an emergency, Arisa didn't know what was. She helped Isla take a capful of the liquid and held her breath.

At first nothing happened. If anything, Isla looked weaker, closing her eyes, her body sagging. But then...she sat bolt upright. Her eyes opened wide.

'Do you think you can make it to Liprah?' Arisa asked.

Isla nodded with a giggle, even finding enough strength to assist with dressing Arisa's injuries.

The claw marks on her chest were mostly superficial, at least compared to the wound on her upper arm. The snow leopard's teeth had shredded Arisa's skin, exposing chunks of flesh and muscle. She cried out in agony as Isla cleaned the wound with alcohol.

'You need stitches,' Isla said, with almost her usual amount of self-assuredness.

'No time. Just bandage it.'

Isla gave a grumble of disapproval, but did as she was bid. 'At least Rea is alright.'

'Is she?' Arisa flinched as Isla wound the ribbon of linen tight around her arm. 'That girl you fought who went after Rea. She had another weapon. A bow and arrow. The arrowhead looked like it was made of sharpened Alia.'

'Alia?'

'I think so.' A sharp intake of breath as Isla reached the most damaged part of her arm. 'I wonder if it's made specifically to kill the phoenix.'

'What's her business with Rea?'

'I have no idea, but she's not all our cousin has to worry about. Theodora will go after her as well. The Northemers must mean to recruit her again.'

Isla paused to still her shaking hand. A side effect of the tonic.

'As soon as you're well enough,' Arisa said, 'we have to go after Rea.'

Isla resumed bandaging Arisa's arm, a grim set to her mouth and jaw. 'I want to help her. Truly, I do. But we don't know where she is.' She tied off the end of the linen.

Arisa tested her arm and hand, flexing her fingers. She had a full range of motion, if she didn't mind the pain that sliced through her with every movement.

'And we're needed in Nadis,' Isla added, holding one hand tight over the other to mask the trembling.

Nadis? Right now, Isla would be lucky to make it to Liprah.

THE PAIR RODE into the mining town just as the silver sun began peeking its way above the horizon. The tonic had done its job, keeping Isla alert for the journey, but the effects had nearly completely worn off. Isla could barely keep her eyes open by the time they made it to the inn they had stayed at before. There, they slipped into an alleyway by the courtyard while Arisa went in search of Rosa – the only person she thought they might be able to trust. Goodness knew who might be looking for them after what had happened in Oisiri.

She found Rosa sweeping the lobby floor. On recognising Arisa, a grin broke out on the woman's face.

'It's you. Why didn't you tell me you were the Water Catcher?'

Arisa's breath caught in her throat. Had she already heard about Oisiri? Her first instinct was to deny it. 'I'm not the—'

Rosa tapped the side of her nose. 'Sure you're not.' She dropped her voice to a whisper. 'Except you are. You were spotted 'ere by a royal messenger who asked me where you be headin'.' Her brows knitted. 'Still doesn't explain what you want with that firebird.' Rosa's gaze then fell on Arisa's bandaged arm. 'Did the creature do that to you? Are you alright?'

'I'm fine,' Arsia said, waving her injured hand, but immediately regretting it as pain shot up the limb. She took a deep breath. 'My cousin, Isla. She needs help. She's been poisoned.'

Rosa shoved her broom against the wall. 'Take me to her.'

Back outside, the Ivanian woman took in Isla's slumped form in the saddle and frowned.

'We'll take her to my room.'

They slung Isla's arms over their shoulders and half dragged, half carried her to Rosa's room, while Arisa explained how the injury had occurred. She described the thorny staff that was impervious to Isla's Kengian swords.

'The effect was immediate, then?' Rosa asked. 'As soon as

the barbs made contact?'

'Yes,' Arisa said as they laid Isla down on Rosa's bed.

Rosa made to unravel Isla's bandage and examine the wounds, but Arisa stopped her. 'The pressure bandage is keeping the poison from spreading.'

The Ivanian woman scratched her head. 'Sounds to me like the staff was made from Batu-riek branches. But any such weapon would be extremely rare. There be only one material capable of cuttin' those branches. A material only the most depraved would dare use.'

A wave of realisation rushed over Arisa. 'Alia. Someone used Alia crystals to create the staff and the…' She let her words trail away. She wasn't sure she wanted anyone to know about the weapon that may be able to kill Rea.

'A staff like that must 'ave come from the black market in Oisiri. It's a city of peace where everyone is safe, but the nature of the place means it's the perfect 'arbour for the vilest criminals.'

'So this Batu-riek tree is poisonous?'

'Not at all.' Rosa tapped her chin in thought. 'Y'know…I have heard of weapon-makers who infuse their blades with different poisons. Can you move part of the bandage so I can take a better look?'

Arisa nodded. Isla groaned as she shifted a width of linen to reveal one of the wounds underneath. It oozed yellowish pus.

'That's not right,' Arisa exclaimed. 'I cleaned it just a few hours ago – it can't be infected yet.'

Rosa took a deep breath. 'That be no infection. It's snake venom.'

'Snake?'

Rosa's mouth was a thin line. 'Ivanian desert asp. Its venom is distinct.'

'What's the cure?'

Rosa looked down at her feet. 'There isn't one.'

'But there must be.' Arisa had treated plenty of snake bites in her time in Kengia; each had its own unique treatment, but there *was* a treatment.

'The desert asp is Ivane's most poisonous snake. The only hope you've got is gettin' her to Nadis. Ivane's best minds are at the palace city.'

'Nadis! That's…' Arisa calculated in her head: it would take more than two days to get there, at top speed, but that was doubtful given Isla's condition. 'It will take too long. Isla needs help now.'

'I'm sorry, but there's no one who can help here.'

Arisa took in her cousin's sweat-soaked face. The clumps of red hair sticking to her forehead. The shadow of death discernible in her shallow breaths.

She jutted out her chin. 'I won't let her die.'

'I can help with one thing,' Rosa said.

'Yes?' Arisa said eagerly.

'You can take a barge by river and cut your travel time almost in half.'

Arisa's heart plummeted. 'I've seen the maps. The river here flows south-east, the opposite direction from Nadis, and the Northemers are said to have ships at the river mouths.'

'That is true,' Rosa said, inexplicably grinning. 'But there be a tributary only a few hours south of here that my family uses to transport grain from their farm. It be small and shallow, and if you ain't familiar with the area you'd assume it peters out to nothing, but it doesn't. Follow that waterway and it will take you south-west to a lake within a day. Cross that lake and you're half a day's ride from Nadis. Just say the word and I'll arrange the barge for you.'

It might actually work, Arisa thought. With the right amount of tonic and the chance to rest up on the barge, they could get to Nadis safely.

'What do you say?' Rosa asked.

Arisa threw her arms around the woman. 'I say you're a lifesaver.'

21

*A*s promised, Takai tried to help his uncle and Noemi. King Laskar had formed a war council with members of his Ivanian Assembly and the Ettean Commander, but neither Takai nor Sar were to have a seat at the table. Laskar had apologised for their omission, stumbling over his words as he grasped for a reason why, but no explanation was required. The Ivanians didn't trust Takai. So instead, he approached his cousin.

He found Noemi in the armoury near the palace city's main gate, taking account of their weapons. There were racks and rows of swords, bows and arrows, crossbows and blade-topped staffs as far as the eye could see. It didn't escape Takai's notice that many of the weapons were covered in a film of dust, and while he wasn't an expert in Ivanian weaponry, he suspected the arms before him dated back to the last time the country had been at war. Indeed, a flurry of guards and craftspeople appeared to be cleaning and sharpening the weapons.

Noemi took a sabre from a guard, turning it over in the light and inspecting it from each angle. She ran her finger along the curved blade, smiling as it pierced her skin, drops of blood falling to the cobalt-and-saffron mosaic-tiled floor. She glanced up at Takai's approach, her hand gripping the sword tighter.

'Impressive, isn't it?' She nodded over her shoulder at the stockpile of weapons. 'Enough for an army of ten thousand or more.'

'Yes.' Takai forced the acknowledgement from his lips. He was wondering how he could raise the fact that they may not have an army anywhere near that number without Noemi cleaving his head from his shoulders. He took a deep breath. 'I see many Ivanians continue to arrive in the city.'

He didn't add that many of them appeared to be elderly people or children with their mothers, seeking refuge. Those arriving to join the army's ranks were fewer. Based on the numbers Takai had seen training in the city, the Ivanian army would be lucky to be four thousand strong. And for every army recruit there were two or three refugees. All mouths that needed to be fed, which would put a strain on resources if there was a siege – yet little appeared to be happening in the way of boosting food supplies or fortifying the city.

'I wonder if I could assist with siege preparations? It is something I am familiar with.' Takai had learnt much under the late Duke of Lakeford, who had defended Lamore Castle against attack from rebels, and while a siege situation had never eventuated, they had been fully prepared for such a risk. Anyone who had faced battle understood that the power of pre-empting and preparing for any possibility couldn't be underestimated.

Unfortunately, Noemi wasn't 'anyone'.

'That won't be necessary,' she said tonelessly, her gaze unwavering. 'We will defeat the Northemers before there is any siege. In any case, your *assistance* isn't needed or desired.'

Takai's arms stiffened by his sides, his fingers digging into his thighs. How could he make his cousin see sense? 'I know you hope to capture Malu and his party when they leave Oisiri...' he began slowly, but stopped as Noemi blinked rapidly. What had he missed? 'That is the plan, isn't it?'

Noemi took a beat to compose herself, then her unflinching stare was back. 'The Northemers escaped Oisiri. But let them come all the way to Nadis. This way I get to meet the invaders as well as the traitors in battle myself and watch them take their last—'

'Traitors?'

Noemi's mouth slammed shut. He thought back to what Ambra had said about displaced and disenchanted Ivanians, and how, with the right inducement, they may join the Northemers.

'Malu recruited Discontented in Oisiri, didn't he?'

Noemi sniffed. 'A handful. They're of no consequence.'

'A handful it may have been in Oisiri, but there are many more who may join him. Those unhappy with the King's rule.'

A glint of silver sliced through the air. Noemi was pressing the Ivanian sabre against the base of Takai's throat. 'You have a hide to point fingers at us, after what was done to your people,' she hissed.

Takai winced as his cousin increased pressure on the blade, its razor-sharp edge biting into his skin. 'That is exactly why you must listen to me,' he whispered, his throat pulsing against the sword. 'I don't want you to make the same mistakes Lamore did. Let me help. You can trust me.'

Noemi's lip curled in disgust. 'I'm just as likely to trust you as I am to trust that Water Catcher friend of yours.'

'You know nothing of Arisa,' he said through gritted teeth.

'I know that she somehow summoned her magic in Oisiri and flooded the city, creating a distraction for Malu to make his escape. It was a miracle that no one other than a couple of Northemers died before the water subsided.'

Takai didn't understand. How could Arisa have used her powers in Ivane? And why would she have flooded the city? It didn't make sense. Unless she'd been protecting herself against the Northemers. It was the only explanation. 'Where is she now?'

'Dead, for all I care. A hawk message to Father said she was also trying to help the firebird. I told Father to issue a warrant for her arrest, but he refused on your account. But if I see her myself, I'll be sure to slit the witch's throat – if she doesn't die before then.' Noemi gave a sly smile. 'The witch and her cousin were injured pretty badly in Oisiri.'

Panic surged through Takai's body. He couldn't do anything else to help Noemi, but maybe he could do something to help Arisa and Isla. He had to at least try.

With a well-timed backward step and pivot, he wrested the sword from Noemi's hand and aimed it at her chest.

'Do it, Lamorian scum,' she challenged, and for a second Takai thought he might actually go through with it. But within moments they were surrounded by guards shouting for Takai to drop the weapon.

He released the sword, letting it clatter to the ground. The guards advanced on him.

'Let him go,' Noemi ordered. 'The Lamorian coward is no threat to me or any of us.'

Takai turned on his heel and sprinted all the way back to the palace.

IN HIS ROOM, he collected a cloak and his longbow and stuffed some bread and fruit into a bag. He was halfway out the door when Sar arrived.

'The King has had a message from Oisiri.' Sar ran his fingers through his hair and paced the room, oblivious to Takai's packing. 'The Northemers…Arisa and Isla are injured…'

Takai rested a palm on his friend's arm. 'I know. It's why I'm leaving, and you should come too.'

Sar's gaze went to Takai's bag. His face twisted in pain. 'Of course I want to go after them, but we can't. We have a duty to help Ivane.'

'My duty finished when my cousin held a sword to my neck.'

He jabbed a finger at the line of congealing blood on his throat. 'And that was just for offering help.'

Sar shook his head. 'Noemi is a difficult case, but I've had some luck with Commander Letoi. He's reinforcing the main gate with Ivanian steel and increasing the guards along the battlements. He has experienced war, and under his leadership the Ivanians *may* stand a chance.'

Takai raised a disbelieving brow.

'With the right fortification, and assuming Malu doesn't have any tricks up his sleeve…' Sar was trying to convince himself as much as Takai.

'Then they no longer need our assistance,' Takai declared.

Sar frowned. 'We have to stay. If only to prove Lamore is their ally.'

'I *am* their ally, but they don't wish to believe it – not now, perhaps not ever. And right now, Arisa and Isla need us more.'

Sar closed his eyes and took a breath before opening them again. 'Believe me, there's nothing I want more than to go after them – not that we even know where they are – but I made a Knight's oath to uphold my duties to the crown.'

'To *Lamore's* crown, not Ivane's,' Takai cried.

'But you pledged yourself to Ivane.'

'I release you, then, from your duty and my pledge.'

Sar put both of his hands on Takai's shoulders and looked him squarely in the eye. 'If you leave now, you'll regret it. I have seen how you have punished yourself for your father's misdeeds. You will never forgive yourself if you turn your back on them now.'

'And I'll never forgive myself if something happens to Arisa.' Takai stepped beyond his friend's reach and grabbed his belongings. He turned away from Sar and strode from the palace without a backward glance.

❉

TAKAI MADE his way to the stables near the main gate, where he convinced a groomsman to hand over one of the King's horses, saying his uncle was sending him to port to see if there was any news of the Lamorian and Kengian fleets. He gave the guards at the gatehouse the same story, and they let him pass with a grunt and a snide remark about 'faithless allies'.

Takai's plan didn't extend past heading north-east toward Oisiri and hoping to learn news of Arisa and Isla along the way. He clicked his tongue at the horse, expecting it to increase its pace, but it threw its head one way then the other, ears twitching, nostrils flared. The reason for the horse's distress became immediately apparent.

A whistling by Takai's ear, a whoosh of heat, a fire arrow embedding in the sandy ground directly in their path. Then another and another in rapid succession. The horse reared up in protest, throwing Takai to the ground.

Winded, he looked up at the cerulean midday sky, the sun as dazzling as Arisa's silver eyes. He had failed. He had failed the woman he loved again. Instinctively he gasped for breath, but his heart told him he shouldn't live, not if Arisa didn't.

A silhouette appeared before him, blocking out the sun. His eyes slowly adjusted until his cousin's features came into focus. Four Lamorian guards flanked her.

'I should have known you'd try to escape the first opportunity you got,' Noemi spat. 'I can't believe we share any of the same blood, you yellow-bellied miscreant.'

'Why do you care...where I go?' he panted as his breath returned. 'You don't even...want me here.'

'No, I don't, but I don't want you running off to warn our enemies, either.'

Takai pushed himself up onto all fours. 'Enemies...I'm not going to the Northemers.'

Noemi squatted so her face was only inches from Takai's. 'But you are going to the witch.' Takai clenched his jaw. 'When were you going to tell us she had powers in Ivane? Were you planning on waiting until she arrived in Nadis by Malu's side?'

Takai sat back into a kneeling position. 'Arisa is not a witch. And she is not helping the Northemers.'

Noemi narrowed her winged eyes at him. 'Liar.' She got to her feet and addressed the guards. 'Take him to his room. He is to be placed under house arrest, and if he tries to escape again…' She turned back to face Takai. 'Kill him.'

22

The Northemers travelled south-west, gathering strength with every mile. Word had spread that Malu was offering payment in gold to any Ivanian willing to join his campaign. Their numbers swelled, doubling, tripling, so much so that no one dared to challenge them at any village or town they passed. The Northemers had forgotten – or, at the very least, were pretending they had forgotten – their plans to oust Malu. Once again he was their celebrated and trusted leader, his plans unquestioned. They had even forgiven him once they'd learned Malu had known Rea was in Ivane and had planned on recruiting her. Conveniently, the Northemers had Theodora to blame.

Hafder was direct in his accusations. 'I knew you and the Ivanian wildcat were up to something from the start,' he said, riding up alongside her while Malu was distracted, speaking to an Ivanian messenger. 'The firebird destroyed the girl's village and you convinced her to help you find the creature.'

Theodora gave no response, but Malu's brother wouldn't be so easily dismissed.

Hafder huffed. 'A foolish plan. Rea is no friend of ours – she proved that in Lamore. I hope the girl finds her and kills her.'

Theodora couldn't hold her tongue a moment longer. 'Killing our chance of victory with her!'

'We need Rea as much as we need you,' Hafder sneered, 'which is to say, not at all.'

She flashed him a sickly sweet smile, picturing what it would be like to shoot him with a hand cannon like Malu had been teaching her. 'It's a shame, then, that your brother insists on keeping me around.'

Hafder shrugged. 'Malu will see sense. It might not be today. It might not be tomorrow. But it will happen, and you can be sure of one thing...' His voice went low and spiky. 'I will be there to make sure you get what you deserve.'

Theodora sat up taller in her saddle. 'We will both get what we deserve.'

As far as she was concerned, what she deserved was to be rid of Hafder and his compatriots once and for all. First they just needed to defeat Ivane, and despite what Hafder had said, they needed Rea to do it – especially now Arisa appeared to have her Water Catcher powers.

'Hafder!' Horace called, his mule trotting madly to catch up with them. 'I've been meaning to speak to you.' Hafder rolled his eyes, but Horace pressed on. 'You have to talk to Malu, get him to understand we can't prevail in Ivane. You saw what happened in Oisiri – we can't defeat the Water Catcher.'

'We have nothing to fear from the so-called Water Catcher,' Hafder scoffed. 'You saw what that snow leopard did to her. She's probably dead already.'

'And if she isn't?' Horace moved closer to Hafder to make his point. 'How do you propose stopping her?'

'I propose you get out of my face,' Hafder growled. 'But if you must know, we have consulted our Ivanian friends, who claim the magic was a temporary phenomenon only made possible by those crystals. The Kengian girl is powerless every-where else in Ivane. So Malu's strategy will prevail.'

Horace lifted his chin. 'When you have been charged with

running a kingdom like I have, identifying the winning strategy becomes second nature—'

Hafder gave a great belly laugh while Theodora bit her lip so she wouldn't do the same.

'Given your history of selecting *winning* strategies, it's a good thing you're not in charge of anything.'

Horace clicked his jaw. 'We must abandon this campaign immediately and head to Lamore.' Hafder dug his heels into his horse's belly and urged it forward to join Malu. 'We'll take Obira and Lamore Castle by surprise,' Horace called after him, to no effect.

'They won't give up this campaign,' Theodora said.

'Then they are dead already,' Horace replied matter-of-factly. 'And they are all bigger fools than I thought they were if they believe I'm going to be part of this doomed folly. I shall not perish for *them*' – his eyes shot daggers at Malu and Hafder's backs – 'or for *you*. I will have my victory and you shall have your graves.' He fell back to ride on his own.

Theodora mulled her father's words over in her head. He was adamant that he wouldn't be part of Malu's plans, that he would be victorious, but they were empty threats. Horace had no means of enacting any strategy of his own. He was utterly powerless – but in all the years Theodora's father had been charged with running a kingdom, she had learnt things, too. Including that Horace was at his most dangerous when he was denied power.

It was the final hours before dawn, when everything was at its coldest and darkest. Theodora had tossed and turned most of the night, plagued by a recurring dream. She was being chased through the Desertlands, an endless sheet of shimmering sand, but the harder she tried to run, the more her legs slowed – sluggish, as if she were running through mud. Her clothes caught on thorny bushes that gouged her limbs. She tripped over a rock, her forehead smacking the hard ground with a crack. She got back up and tried to run again, but her unseen pursuers were gaining on her. Their taunts and crazed laughter splintered the air.

Just when Theodora didn't think she could go another step, a figure of light appeared ahead of her. A phoenix. Then it was Rea – Rea beckoning her with a smile. Theodora reached deep inside herself, accessing the last of her reserves, pushing her deadweight legs until they burned. She was within arm's reach of Rea. Her fingers grasped for her friend, but found nothing. Rea was gone. The phoenix was gone. A mirage.

Then Theodora's legs gave way, her feet sinking into the ground. Not ground – quicksand!

She looked desperately around her for anything to grab hold of. There was nothing but the pounding footsteps of her pursuers. The quicksand was at her waist, her shoulders, her neck – and then they appeared: the people hunting her down. Ringing the edge of the quicksand pit were Arisa, Jade, Hafder and Horace.

'Help!' she cried, quicksand creeping into her mouth.

They didn't respond or move to help. They merely shared a satisfied smile before turning their backs and walking away.

'No! Malu! Where are—'

Theodora's words were swallowed up by the quicksand, and then she woke, dripping with sweat, Malu's name stuck in her throat.

On the nights she had woken Malu before, he had taken her in his arms, assuring her it was just a bad dream. But she could never shake the horridness of knowing that without him she was wholly alone. This morning Malu hadn't woken, so Theodora wrapped her blanket around herself and went in search of her only other comfort, Rayl. She was planning to take the snow leopard for a walk before they set off again for another long day of riding with the animal stuck in her cage.

Malu and Theodora slept at a distance from the rest of the

camp. The wagon with Rayl's cage lay between them and the others, providing a sense of protection. Protection for Theodora, but also for the Ivanian gold that was still kept in the cage's hidden compartment.

The camp was silent except for the rolling chorus of snores from the Northemers and Ivanians, who'd feasted the night before on roasted goat and mugs of cider. As Theodora approached Rayl, she expected the cat to give her usual purr or mew, but she was greeted instead by a crunching of bones. The snow leopard was eating.

Theodora froze. She was the only person who fed the cat. Before retiring for the night, she had given Rayl a bowl of shredded goat meat taken from her own plate. Who else would be feeding her at this time, and why?

Theodora rushed to the wagon, but her blood ran cold as she realised Rayl wasn't in her cage. She was on the ground several feet to the side of the wagon, gnawing on a goat shank bone, the door to her cage wide open. Theodora didn't need to ask herself why someone would have let Rayl out. The answer lay in the form of the prised-up boards at the base of the cage and the empty compartment beneath.

The Ivanian gold.

She scanned the camp in search of the thief, but could find nothing amiss. Then, from the corner of her eye: a shadow slipping among the horses. A cloaked figure packing a saddle bag; a gold bar catching in the pre-dawn light.

Theodora's first instinct was to yell and alert the others, but the thief was about to mount their horse and she didn't want to risk them getting away. She threw away her blanket and reached for the first weapon she could find – a knife that lay among the cooking utensils on the wagon.

Barefoot, Theodora padded through the sand, the horses masking her approach. She circled back around them, her eyes never leaving the thief, whose back was to her. There were only a dozen or so steps between them. With a final burst of speed, she raced up behind the cloaked figure and pressed the tip of the knife into their back.

'Turn around,' she said.

Slowly, the figure turned, a knowing smirk on the thief's face – her father's face.

Theodora jolted with surprise, but recovered quickly and tightened her grip on the knife.

'Go on, then,' Horace said in a low whisper. 'Prove to them that you're not weak. Kill me.'

'Shut your mouth,' she hissed.

Horace's smirk grew. 'That's what I thought. Then come with me. We will go to Lamore and use the gold to buy our own army. Leave the Northemers to their defeat here.'

'Be quiet,' she snapped, trying to think. She couldn't let her father go, but did she want to throw him to the Northemers' mercy?

'You'll never be one of them. You are my flesh and blood. You are smarter than this.' He screwed his nose up and nodded at the sleeping Northemers. 'You are smarter than them.'

'Put the gold back,' she said. 'And we'll pretend this never happened.'

Horace clicked his jaw. 'This is your last chance to prove you are worthy. Come with me now and I may forget what a disappointment you have been to me.'

Theodora clenched her jaw. Then she yelled at the top of her lungs.

'*Thief!*'

THE NORTHEMERS GATHERED around the kneeling Horace, his hands and ankles bound. Theodora's father met their hate-filled looks with a defiant gaze that was in stark contrast to the bloodied mess that was his face – courtesy of multiple Northemer fists and boots. Those who weren't watching Horace stared at Theodora expectantly.

'Why are they looking at me like that?' she whispered in Malu's ear.

'Because it is up to you to decide.'

'Me?'

'He is your blood, so it is your responsibility.'

Hafder strode toward Theodora with a knife in one hand and a hand cannon in the other. He held both weapons out to her. 'This is your chance,' he said, his visible eye unmoving. 'Decide once and for all whether you are worthy of being a Northemer.'

Sweat erupted from Theodora's palms. Why did she have to prove to anyone she was worthy? She had done her part, she had caught the thief, she had handed over her own father. Yet she knew this wasn't enough for the Northemers. They didn't just want Horace's hand cut off for the thief he was. They wanted him dead. But killing him would prove only one thing – that she was no different to her father.

Horace met his daughter's gaze with a sneer that was part challenge, part disdain.

Malu took her hand in his and squeezed it. In that single gesture, she knew he would support her, whatever decision she made – and it was *her* decision. Not Horace's, not Hafder's, hers.

Theodora marched straight past Hafder without accepting the proffered weapons. She stood directly in front of her father and lifted her chin before speaking, voice loud and true.

'This man has wronged you and me. He has wronged all of us, but death would be a release for him. In death he would be relieved of his incessant quest for power. A far greater punishment is for him to live, stripped of any means to secure any form of power. He shall be banished. Left here in the middle of nowhere to his own fate, be it death or otherwise.'

A collective murmur of discontent reeled through the crowd. Horace clicked his jaw.

'The man is a thief and a traitor!' Hafder shouted at his brother. 'He must die.'

Malu marched past him and stopped by Theodora's side. 'My future Queen has spoken,' he declared. 'He will be banished from us.'

Hafder threw the knife and hand cannon to the ground and stormed off. The crowd, however, didn't move.

Malu stiffened beside Theodora. 'Do any of you wish to say anything?' His voice rang impossibly loud. 'Do you dare to question me or my Queen?' Eyes went to feet. No one spoke. 'Then go! Go and pack. We have a war to win.'

Finally, the crowd dispersed.

'I'm sorry for putting you in that position with your people,' Theodora said.

Malu cupped her chin. 'You have nothing to be sorry for, and you are right. A life of exile is a far greater punishment for your father.'

A cry of 'Messenger!' interrupted them, signalling an approaching rider. Malu swiftly kissed Theodora on the cheek and left her.

'Don't expect me to thank you,' Horace spat from behind Theodora.

'I'm beyond expecting anything from you,' she said without turning, and walked away.

She joined Malu, offering to translate as the messenger didn't speak Ettean or Northem. The messenger brought news of Ivane preparing to take its stand at the palace city. Theodora asked for any word of the firebird's whereabouts, but there was none. What was of particular interest was news of two injured Kengian girls – one of whom was said to be the Water Catcher – making their way south-east by river.

'How far ahead are they?' Theodora asked.

'Half a day or so,' the messenger said. 'If you hurry, you may be able to catch them once they make land again.'

Malu didn't need any convincing to go after Arisa. They were heading in the same direction as the two women, and this may be their only chance to stop the Water Catcher while she was injured and at her weakest.

The Northemer camp was packed up in a mad flurry, with a plan for the fastest riders to track down Arisa and the wagons and slower riders to meet them at Nadis.

Theodora mounted her horse, blocking out Horace's last-ditch cries for mercy. Her father was tied to the barbed branches of a Batu-riek tree with no supplies and no means of extracting water from the tree's roots.

'Goodbye, Father,' she said, looking down at him. She was taken aback at what she saw in his eyes – something she'd only seen there once or twice before. Fear. Horace was terrified, but to his credit, he wasn't about to let on.

'You're no daughter of mine,' he said, and turned away.

23

$\mathcal{R}$eaching the other side of the lake was equally relieving and overwhelming for Arisa. It meant they were within reach of Nadis and hopefully a cure for Isla, but they would have to complete the rest of the journey on horseback. Even if Isla could make it all the way, it would be at a crawling pace. The lead they had gained on the Northemers by taking the river would rapidly evaporate back on land.

On the barge, Isla had drifted in and out of sleep. In the thick of delirium, one minute she would call for her mother; the next she'd cry out for Sar. Her chalky white face was covered in a film of sweat. The parts of her injured arm that were visible had turned black. The only thing stopping the venom from spreading through her whole body was the pressure bandage Arisa had applied. The only thing keeping her alive was Arisa's tonic – the last of which she'd tipped down Isla's throat half an hour earlier.

'Are you up to this?' she asked her cousin.

Isla fixed glazed eyes on Arisa. A shaky grin came to her face. 'Are you?'

It was late afternoon when they stopped at a town to let the horses take food and water, careful to keep their faces concealed under the hoods of their travelling cloaks. They had heard the King's Guards were searching for the Water Catcher after Oisiri. Arisa feared the reception they would get in Nadis, but they had no other choice. She had to count on Takai and Sar pleading her case. In the meantime, they couldn't risk capture, not if it could jeopardise Isla's life. They had gotten this far, and it was only another hour's ride to the palace city.

Arisa and Isla stepped behind their horses, pulling their hoods further over their faces, as a pair of Ivanian women rushed past them, carrying baskets of bread and vegetables.

'We should have gone to Nadis,' one woman puffed.

'I'd rather take my chances here,' the other panted. 'The Northemers aren't interested in us.'

'I suppose we're about to find out.'

The other woman stopped to catch her breath just ahead of Arisa and Isla's position. Her friend turned back.

'Hurry! The Town Marshal says they'll be here within a quarter of an hour.'

Arisa and Isla exchanged looks of alarm and got back on their horses. Within seconds they were galloping through the outskirts of the town. Given time, they may have taken a less travelled road, but time was one thing they didn't have. They had to take the fastest and most direct route to Nadis and hope they could get to the safety of the palace city before the Northemers caught up.

Their horses thundered down the gravel road, the landscape a blur of farmland and vineyards. Isla teetered dangerously back and forth in her saddle but pushed on without complaint.

The palace city loomed into view on the horizon at the same time as Arisa registered the pounding hooves on their tail. She snatched a glance over her shoulder. Dozens of riders. An exceedingly tall figure in the lead. A smaller figure beside him. *Malu and Theodora.*

'The Northemers,' Arisa shouted.

Isla sat up tall to take a deep, raspy breath, then nodded at Arisa. In unison, they sprang out of their saddles and pushed their weight down on their stirrups, galloping toward life – or closer to death.

Arisa didn't dare look back again, focusing only on staying on her horse and praying Isla did the same. But the growing intensity of the horses' hooves behind them told her everything she needed to know. The Northemers were gaining on them. Arisa and Isla's Ettean steeds were no match for the Ivanian horses born and bred for this stifling hot and sandy land.

Bells rang ahead throughout Nadis, where a stream of carts and Ivanians on foot were being ushered through the palace city's gate. The air was thick with the shouts and screams of the frightened, pitched against the war cries of the Northemers.

Between the gate and the Northemers, Isla lurched to the side of her saddle, her head lolling.

'Hold on,' Arisa yelled, and glanced over her shoulder, wishing immediately that she hadn't. The Northemers were so close that she could see the hate and single-minded determination in Theodora's eyes.

'Close the gate!' someone, a girl, shouted from the battlements.

Terror ripped through Arisa as she watched the timber gate swinging to a close before them.

'No! Let them through!' a familiar voice on the other side of the gate – Sar – shouted up to the battlements, pointing at Arisa and Isla.

'Sa-a-r.' Isla's broken voice.

The gate shuddered to a stop, leaving just enough room for a single rider to pass through. Arisa pulled on her horse's reins and let Isla pass through first.

An explosion. A puff of dust. A divot in the stone wall beside Arisa as she passed through the gate. She leapt from her horse, catching sight of Theodora reloading a hand cannon and aiming it at her, firing as the gate slammed shut.

'Isla!'

Sar was there, arms at the ready as Isla toppled from her saddle.

24

*T*akai paced the floor of his room. He'd been locked up for a full day with Noemi refusing to allow him any visitors, not even Sar. He'd demanded to see the King, but his cousin had scowled at his request, saying that 'traitors had no right to make any demands'. She had then left him under guard with orders that the King was not to be sent for either. But Takai had to get out. He had to go after Arisa.

Out of desperation, he'd convinced the serving boy delivering his supper to slip a note to Ambra. So when raised voices sounded outside his room within an hour of sending the message, Takai assumed it was the King's Counsel, when in fact it was the King himself.

'Uncle.' Takai met Laskar halfway across the room. 'You have to help me. I need to leave. Arisa and Isla are in trouble. I have to—'

King Laskar held up his hand to silence Takai, deep ridges carved into his brow. 'I'm sorry to find you here. I wasn't aware my daughter had placed you under arrest, not until Ambra told me just now.'

Takai grabbed his longbow and the bag he'd packed earlier. 'Hopefully Noemi's actions don't mean it's too late.' He made to stride past his uncle, but the King stopped him with a palm to the chest.

'You are free to leave this room, but not the city,' he said forcefully.

Takai shoved King Laskar's hand away. 'Surely you don't believe Arisa is a threat too?'

The King pressed his lips together. 'Whatever happened in Oisiri, I'm sure your Water Catcher had a reason, and when I meet her, she must explain that reason. But her motivations and character have no bearing on my decision. You cannot leave because it's too unsafe. We have received word that the Northemers are very close. We're about to close the city gate.'

'Close it! You can't, not before Arisa gets here—'

King Laskar gave a sympathetic sigh. 'If Arisa is everything she is said to be, she will be safe, as will Isla.' A half-smile came to his face. 'From the little I've seen of Arisa's cousin, the Northemers would be mad to take her on.'

Takai released a hollow laugh. 'Pity anyone who tries to go toe-to-toe with either of those women.'

The King raised both brows. 'The same must be said for Noemi. She is a fine warrior and leader,' he said proudly. 'She takes after her mother – if only she were still with us to see for herself.' He sniffed. 'My wife died of Lamorian fever not long after Noemi was born. She was one of the last Ivanians to die from the illness – a cure was brought to our country soon after.' He wiped a lone tear from his cheek. 'It is why I have indulged Noemi, overlooking her tendency to act rashly at times. She should never have arrested you.'

Takai clenched and unclenched his hands. He wasn't sure if he could forgive his cousin's behaviour, especially if something happened to Arisa. 'There seemed to be more at play than rashness. Noemi appears to hate me.'

'She doesn't hate *you*. She doesn't know you. She hates your...' King Laskar cringed as he searched for the right word. 'Your existence.'

Something between a scoff and a cry of disbelief erupted from Takai's mouth. 'Is that supposed to make me feel better?'

King Laskar waved his hands placatingly. 'That's not what I meant. You see, under Ivanian law, you are the heir to the throne.'

'That's ridiculous!'

'As ridiculous as it sounds, it is the law. A woman cannot inherit the throne − it is a custom that dates back many thousands of years.'

Takai remembered how his own mother, who was several years older than Laskar, had never laid claim to the throne. 'But I don't want your crown.'

The King shrugged. 'It doesn't matter whether you want it or not − under the current law, it will be yours.'

'Then the law must be changed.'

'I intend on doing that, but I need the Assembly's support, and many of them will not give it to me while they are at the mercy of the Discontented. And it is the last thing on anyone's minds now that the Northemers are here. Once this is all over, I will see that the law is changed, and I *will* leave Ivane to Noemi − assuming it is still mine to give…' Laskar's words trailed away in a whisper.

Takai's heart faltered. He knew Ivane's precarious position. 'Any word of my fleet and the Kengians?'

The King wrung his hands. 'I have had reports that the squalls at sea are settling, but it will be another day or so before they get here, assuming they've left Obira Port.'

'By then it will be too—'

Takai didn't finish his sentence, his words both unnecessary and drowned out by the ringing of alarm bells.

A guard burst through the doorway. 'They're here. The Northemers, approaching the city.' The King hurried from the room.

Takai rustled through his bag and retrieved his spyglass. He ran to the window and flung open the shutters, aiming his glass at the horizon beyond the city wall.

A cloud of dust. Dozens of horses. He turned the metal barrel, focusing it on the riders. In the lead, Malu, his brother Hafder on one side, Theodora on the other. They'd run out of time.

Please let her be safe. Please, he silently begged.

He lowered the device, but jerked it back to his eye after catching something else in the lower section of his view.

Another rider. Two. At full gallop just ahead of the Northemers. His fingers flew into action, focusing on the pair.

The first rider was slumped in the saddle, but her bright red hair was unmistakable. It was Isla. Takai's breath quickened as he focused on the other rider. He recognised her immediately.

The spyglass clattered to the floor. It lay abandoned as Takai raced to the city gate.

25

Sar lowered Isla's limp body into the back of a cart and leapt up to the driver's seat, taking the reins.

'I'm sorry,' Arisa murmured. 'It's my fault. If I hadn't insisted we go to Oisiri...'

Sar looked down at her. There was no room in his eyes for anger or blame, only fear. 'She'll be alright.' His voice broke. It was more a question than a statement.

'She has to be,' Arisa added in a whisper.

'I'll take you both to Ambra, a healer.' Sar held out his hand to help Arisa into the cart, but the vice-like grip of another hand on her injured arm pulled her back.

'You're not going anywhere but a prison cell.' An Ivanian girl, dressed as an officer, glared at Arisa with black-winged eyes. There was something familiar about her straight-backed posture and the way she held her chin.

'Let her go, Noemi,' Sar cried. 'She's the Water Catcher.'

Noemi. That was the name of Takai's cousin, the Ivanian Princess. Noemi appeared to have all of the stubbornness and high-handedness Takai had displayed when Arisa had first met him.

'I know exactly who she is,' Noemi sneered. Arisa had to

focus hard to catch her clipped Ivanian words. 'I'm arresting her for what she did in Oisiri.'

Arisa winced as the girl tightened her grasp.

'I'll face…punishment,' Arisa said in broken Ivanian, 'but first I make sure…my cousin is alright.' She nodded at Isla.

Noemi shook her head. The hard look she gave Arisa was uncompromising.

'Go, Sar,' Arisa said. 'Get Isla help. I'll come as soon as I can…' *If I can.*

Sar looked back and forth from Isla's prone form to Arisa.

'She needs help *now*,' Arisa argued.

Sar pointed an angry finger at Noemi. 'You're making a mistake.'

Noemi responded with an unblinking stare.

'Tell the healer Isla's been poisoned by the venom of the Ivanian desert asp,' Arisa pressed. Noemi's face twisted at the mention of the viper, but she remained silent.

'I'll get you help,' Sar promised Arisa before putting the cart in motion.

She watched as the cart headed into the city at a bone-rattling pace. Only then was she conscious of the chaos unfolding around her. The sound of hundreds of boots pounding up the stairs to the battlements. Shouted orders to archers. Volleys of arrows being fired at the Northemers on the other side of the city wall. Ivanians rushing for safety. Nadis was under attack, and the Ivanian Princess's biggest priority was arresting Arisa. Anger surged inside her.

'With all due respect, *Your Highness*,' she seethed, switching to Ettean, 'I should be the least of your worries right now. You have one of the most formidable armies ever known on your doorstep. It doesn't take a genius to identify the bigger threat.'

Noemi scowled. 'With all due respect, *Water Catcher*,' she responded in perfect Ettean, 'you haven't earned the right to an opinion.'

'Daughter! Let her go!' An authoritative voice.

Arisa and Noemi spun to face a stern-looking man –
presumably King Laskar. The King nodded at Arisa and she
returned the gesture.

'Father, she—' Noemi protested.

'There will be time for that later. Right now, we have a war
to fight.'

Noemi bowed her head.

'My cousin,' Arisa said. 'She's been taken to your healer.'

The King dismounted and headed toward the battlements,
his hand on his sword. 'Go to her,' he called over his shoulder,
taking the stairs two at a time. Noemi followed in his wake.

'Where is she…?' But Arisa's words were wasted on the
King and his daughter, who had disappeared from view.

'I'll take you to her.'

Arisa's breath hitched at the sound of Takai's voice. And
there he was. Seated on a sweat-lathered horse, his dark eyes
probing her, falling on her injured arm.

He dropped from the saddle. His hand hovered over her
bandage, too scared to touch. 'Are you alright?'

She nodded rapidly. 'I'm alright. But Isla…She's…I tried to
help her, but…' Her words disintegrated into sobs.

Takai took her in his arms. 'Everything will be alright,' he
murmured, and for a moment, cocooned in his embrace, Arisa
forgot everything that had passed between them, remembering
only how safe she felt with him. At that moment, she believed
him.

But then she forced herself back to reality and extricated
herself from his arms, ignoring the flickering pools of hurt in
Takai's eyes.

'Please,' she begged. 'Take me to her.'

Takai squared his shoulders and nodded.

ARISA CLUNG to Takai on the back of his horse, intent only on
reaching Isla. Nadis was a blur to her. In the palace itself,

Takai steered her through a series of courtyards and open corridors before finally coming to a stop outside an arched timber door.

'The healer's quarters,' he said.

Inside, Sar sat huddled over Isla, holding a blackened hand in his shaking palm. He didn't look up at their entry. A tall man dressed in Ivanian costume, with a striking resemblance to Lore, examined Isla's injured arm with a knitted brow. The only sign that Isla still lived was the painfully slow rise and fall of her chest.

'Ambra,' Takai addressed the Ivanian. 'I've brought Arisa, Isla's cousin.'

'I was there when Isla was—'

Ambra lifted his gaze to Arisa. The look he gave her sucked the air from her lungs and the words from her mouth. It was the same look she had seen on her late uncle's face too many times before, including the night he hadn't been able to save the Kengian boy, Hyando. And the night he'd thought he couldn't save Takai's life.

'No!' she cried. 'You have to be able to save her.'

Ambra approached her, speaking in rapid Ivanian, his words a jumble.

'Ettean,' Takai interrupted. 'She understands Ettean.'

Ambra nodded and spoke again in the Ettean tongue. 'I'm sorry, but there is no cure for the desert asp's venom.'

'But this is Nadis,' Arisa protested. 'The country's finest minds and healers are here. You must be able to do something.'

Ambra clasped his hands together until his knuckles were white. 'Perhaps if you'd got here sooner, but...'

Arisa clenched her jaw. 'No. Isla's not going to die,' she said with certainty. 'She didn't survive war and the Northemers once already only to die from a poison-laced staff. Even the untrained eye can see the fire that lives inside her. That fire won't be extinguished—'

Ambra's eyes widened. '*Fire*. And you – you're the Water

Catcher. *Three hearts – shared blood born of fire and water…*But there are only two of you. Still…'

He rushed out of the room. Takai and Arisa shared a perplexed look.

'Go with him,' Sar said, voice shaking with desperation. 'I'll stay and watch Isla.'

Takai and Arisa followed Ambra down the corridor. *'Shared blood of fire and water?'* Arisa said, racing to catch up. 'What do you mean?'

'The Ettean healer, Nima.' Ambra turned a corner swiftly, his long robe swirling around him. 'She brought Gwyn to the palace as a child, and when she was here she gave it to me.'

'Gave what to you?' Takai asked.

Ambra didn't respond. Instead he muttered to himself as he strode down a dimly lit hallway.

'She said she had seen it. A reckoning. That Ivane could only be saved by the three who shared blood of fire and water. It has to mean you – the Water Catcher – and Isla shares your blood…' Ambra took another sharp corner before coming to a stop outside a heavy oak door. He produced a set of keys from his pocket and unlocked the door.

The healer led them into a room lined floor to ceiling with shelves. On each shelf were precisely labelled jars and vials of potions and powders. Arisa was immediately taken back to her uncle's apothecary.

'But you said "three hearts",' Takai questioned. 'There are only two of them.'

One by one, pieces dropped into place in Arisa's mind. Nima, the Firemaster who'd saved Gywn's life so the Water Catcher prophecy could come to fruition. In her scrolls she had mentioned 'fire and water', as well as 'blood' and a 'reckoning'. Arisa had assumed she was referring to the original prophecy – but had Nima seen something else? Something that involved Arisa, Isla and…?

'There *are* three of us,' she said in a quiet voice. 'Rea – a

Firemaster, a firebird – she is Amund's daughter. Our cousin. Our blood.'

'What? How?' Takai asked.

'I'll explain later, but it's true.'

Ambra raced over to a carved mahogany cabinet in one corner. 'I've kept it, all this time,' he said as he tried one key after another in the lock. The last one on his ring of keys slipped into place, but when he tried to turn it, the door was stuck firm.

He tried the lock again, but it wouldn't budge. 'Damn!'

Takai crossed the room in three giant strides to stop by Ambra's side. He nodded at the healer to step aside and, with one swift yank, the cabinet door swung open.

Arisa's whole body immediately prickled, as if an army of ants had taken residence in her veins.

'Whoa!'

Takai stepped back to reveal the subject of his awe. The interior of the cabinet was awash with a silver glow. The source of the light was a vial of shimmering silver liquid with thousands of sparkling specks suspended within it.

'Alia Water,' Ambra explained. 'Made from crushed Alia crystals.'

The hairs on Arisa's arms stood on end. 'But I thought it was sacred?'

Ambra nodded. 'The Alia crystals in Oisiri are sacred, but this was from another source. Somewhere only known to the Ettean healer.' Arisa surmised that 'somewhere' must have been the Firemaster's cave in the mountains. 'Nima blessed the Alia Water, casting a spell for one purpose only.'

'For the shared blood born of fire and water?' Takai said. 'For the three cousins?'

Ambra smiled. 'I believe so.'

'Do you think it can heal Isla?' Takai asked.

'There's only one way to find out.' Ambra grabbed the vial and the trio hurried back through the palace to Sar and Isla.

With the briefest of explanations to Sar, Ambra pulled Isla's bandage aside to reveal the festering wound. He tipped some of the sparkling liquid onto the site. The exposed skin sizzled like it was on fire; the traces of yellow venom frothed and turned white.

'Is it working?' Sar asked.

Ambra compressed his lips in answer.

Arisa held her breath.

'Look!'

Takai pointed at the base of Isla's throat. Veins popped from her neck, a silver substance pumping through them like liquid mercury, spreading through her chest and down her other arm.

Arisa's hand went instinctively to the web of silver ribbons on Isla's face. Her cheeks were ice cold. She shifted her hand to the side of her cousin's throat. Isla's heartbeat was undetectable. She looked to Ambra, but his expression was painfully blank.

Sar caught their exchange and ran his fingers through his hair, saying, 'No, no, no,' over and over.

Then – something. A spike of energy underneath Arisa's hand. Cold giving way to heat. Isla's skin burning. Arisa was forced to pull away. Then thrashing. Isla's torso jerking, her back arching, her whole body twisting, then collapsing with a thud.

A gasp for air. Green eyes sprang open.

The silver veins were gone. Colour returned to Isla's cheeks and arm, the blackened flesh fading before their eyes amid their cries of joy.

'What are you all staring at?' she croaked.

26

Theodora threw her hand cannon across the tent that had been set up for Malu's war council, knocking an inkwell and bundle of maps from a table. The Northemers had chased Arisa and Isla – who, Theodora remembered, was the Water Catcher's Kengian cousin – all the way to the city gate, only for the pair to slip to safety. After a shower of arrows had rained down on them from the battlements, Malu had ordered their retreat. They had fallen back to a position further away on the plateau to set up camp.

At Theodora's outburst, Rayl jumped in her cage and Malu raised an amused brow. He dipped his head at the discarded weapon and addressed the snow leopard. 'I guess we should be thankful that it wasn't loaded.'

Theodora crossed her arms. She couldn't believe she had failed, again. Was she as inept as her father thought she was? She thought for a moment about Horace and whether he may still be alive. Something that may have been guilt squirmed in her stomach. But was it guilt over leaving her father to his death, or guilt that she had done it so easily? Was she as heartless as he was?

Theodora shook her head. She hadn't had a choice. As

Malu had taught her, sometimes cruelty was necessary to maintain and gain power. She had done what she had to do. She had to be rid of her father and his chains that bound her, just like she had to be rid of Arisa. She would never have peace or the power she deserved while the Water Catcher was still alive. All the things she had done to Arisa had been necessary for her own survival, and it was no different now.

'I can't believe she escaped, again, and right now is probably sitting back up there in the palace' – she waved a hand in the direction of Nadis's gate – 'laughing at us.' She kicked the sandy ground. 'Laughing at the great Northemers cowering on the edge of the desert.'

Malu's nostrils flared at the word 'cowering', but he composed himself before speaking.

'I know you're frustrated. Yes, you will have to wait a little longer for your revenge, but I promise that you shall have it.' He took her hands in his, thumbs stroking her calloused palms. 'You just need to have faith in me,' he said in hushed tones. 'You do have complete faith in me, don't you?'

Did she have *complete* faith in him? She searched his glacial blue eyes for the answer. Eyes simultaneously capable of intimidation and intimacy. Theodora had lost herself more than once in the white fissures like cracked ice running through his irises. She was drawn now into their mirrorlike depths, surrendering to their intoxicating call, needing to enter the inner sanctum of his soul, all while looking back at herself, seeing a reflection of herself in his eyes. Seeing everything she yearned to see. Devotion. Strength. Truth.

She lifted one of his hands to her mouth, brushing his fingers lightly with her lips. 'You never need to ask that of me. You and I are of one heart and mind.'

The fissures in his eyes blurred, a soft veil of clouds passing over the hardened icy terrain. The terrifying Northem leader disappeared in a blizzard of snow, leaving Malu, the man, the brother, the lover.

He scooped her into his arms and lay her down on the makeshift bed piled with fur blankets.

Malu kissed her softly on her cheek, her mouth, her neck, sending tingles through her whole body. As he kissed the cleft between her breasts, Theodora's heart drummed under his lips, threatening to explode from her chest. He raised his head to meet her eyes, his gaze as hungry as hers. She kissed him hard, her tongue probing his mouth, finding what she sought – the complete and undeniable knowledge that they were one.

FADING afternoon light filtered through the thinning canvas walls of the tent. Curled up in Malu's arms, Theodora shivered at the hint of chill in the air, typical of the Ivanian desert at night. He tucked a fur closer around her and brushed a stray curl from her forehead.

'It was unfair of me to ask for complete trust when I haven't shared all my plans with you,' he said.

'I trust you,' she said, meaning it.

'I know you do, but like everyone else, you're wondering why I ordered a retreat.'

Theodora propped herself up on one elbow. 'I suppose you are waiting for the rest of our party to arrive.'

'Which they now have. Yet I have made no orders to advance.'

Theodora frowned. Was he worried they wouldn't be able to penetrate the palace city's walls or gate?

Malu gave a knowing smile. 'I know what you're thinking. We can and will defeat Ivane. My plan is to draw out the Ivanians to fight outside the city walls, where our numbers will give us an advantage. I will torment them like your snow leopard friend taunts a mouse.'

A smirk formed on Theodora's face. She liked the idea of baiting the enemy and playing with them like toys.

A throaty, musical laugh escaped Malu's mouth. 'Yes, it will be quite the game, but that in itself is not enough to give us victory.'

Theodora tapped her chin in thought. 'Olix, the merchant. You said he has been working on something for you.'

Malu's eyes twinkled. 'For months now he has been visiting the Ivanian ports on my behalf. Secretly engaging suppliers and master craftspeople.'

'What for?'

Malu tapped the end of Theodora's nose lightly. 'Think about it, my love. What is it about those particular ports and cities that would be useful to us?'

Theodora thought back to the maps she'd seen showing the locations of the Northemer ships. Before her time with Malu, she had spent many of her years watching and listening to her father and the noblemen of the Lamorian court, so she understood both maps and military strategy.

'They are all major ports, but also...' She sat bolt upright, holding the fur to her chest. 'Mining cities. They're filled with quarries and forges.'

Malu sat up as well, a feverish grin on his face. 'Exactly! For some time they've been developing moulds and prototypes, but now – any minute, in fact – we should have everything we need to take Ivane and destroy your Water Catcher.'

Moulds? Prototypes? Was Malu referring to the plans Rea had made for him? He had to be. He must be referring to—

'Malu!'

It was Hafder's voice. He marched into the tent, his mouth curling in disapproval as he spotted Theodora in bed next to his brother.

'Yes?' Malu responded in a pleasant sing-song voice.

'You'll want to see this,' Hafder grunted, and stomped out of the tent.

Malu pulled on a tunic and followed his brother out. Theodora followed suit.

Outside, night had begun to fall. Northemers were

whooping in celebration, pointing to Nadis Port. Even from this distance and in fading light, Theodora could see a swarm of Northemer ships blocking the harbour entrance. It was the entire fleet that had been dispatched to Ivane's port cities.

Hafder handed his brother a spyglass to aim down the plateau toward the port. He slapped Malu on the back. 'I knew you wouldn't let us down, brother.'

Theodora rolled her eyes at Hafder's sudden show of support. Malu had the good grace to acknowledge his brother with a smile before handing the spyglass to Theodora.

She peered through the eyepiece, twisting the device, a smile of her own spreading across her face as the biggest reason for celebration came into focus.

Every ship's half-deck was outfitted with rows of firesky cannons.

Malu had never intended on strangling Ivane's supplies and trying to *outlast* them with siege tactics. He was going to *outblast* them. The ships had been sent to collect the weapons Olix had commissioned.

'Rea's plans. You had them all this time,' she said in wonder.

'And now you will have your revenge, my Queen,' Malu whispered, low and thick in her ear.

27

'Cowards,' Noemi declared, her stare fixed on the scrubby, sandy horizon. 'At the first sign of resistance they flee.'

As soon as Takai had been certain that Arisa was alright and Isla was in good hands, he'd headed back to the city wall, finding it eerily absent any battle noise. Instead, the battlements were flooded with the triumphant cheering and celebrations of the Ivanian soldiers, their weapons abandoned in favour of mugs of ale and cider.

King Laskar stood beside his daughter, tapping his fingers along the edge of the crenellated parapet. 'What do you think?' he asked Takai.

Gone was the time for diplomacy. His uncle had to know what they were dealing with.

'I think the retreat was all part of Malu's scheme,' Takai said with certainty. 'He is playing with us and will have something planned.'

'Something!' Noemi scoffed. 'That's a huge help.'

Takai took a deep breath. 'Yes, something. You need to put an end to those misplaced celebrations' – he jabbed a finger in the direction of the cavorting soldiers – 'and be prepared for anything.'

'What do you suggest?' King Laskar asked.

'My best guess is that they will try to breach the walls. Be prepared for scaling ladders, grappling hooks, ramming—'

'I say we go after them.' Noemi slammed a fist against the wall. 'Now! Did you see their numbers? We will see to them in no time.'

Takai shook his head. 'We know their numbers are far greater than the group we saw today. The others will be on their way, if they haven't already joined Malu.'

Noemi narrowed her gaze. 'I refuse to skulk here like a yellow-bellied Lamorian. Not when we can beat them before the war has even begun.'

Takai clenched his jaw. 'What you fail to understand,' he said through gritted teeth, 'is that ego and rashness have no place on the battlefield. Victory demands a clear head.'

Noemi's hand went to the hilt of her sabre, but King Laskar held up a hand to caution her. 'Takai is right. Going after the Northemers now would be a mistake. It will be dark soon and they will have every advantage. We are much safer here.'

Takai winced, but the King didn't notice. He excused himself to speak to Commander Letoi. Noemi, though, hadn't missed Takai's reaction.

'What is it now, *cousin*?' she growled. 'We have reinforced the city gate with the strongest Ivanian steel – there is none stronger – and our walls are solid. We're well supplied to outlast any siege.'

'Respectfully, Noemi, Nadis is more palace than fortress. You have a false sense of protection.'

Noemi's nostrils flared. 'Commander! When I'm wearing armour, you call me Commander.'

'For fight's sake,' he groaned. 'For just one moment, for the sake of your country, can you put aside your petty grievances?'

'There's nothing petty about them. I don't trust you.'

'This has nothing to do with trust. It has everything to do with the fact that you think I'll inherit the Ivanian throne.'

Noemi looked back out into the distance. 'Which you will. It is the law of this place.'

'Your father will change the law. As soon as the war is over.'

The Princess stood straight-backed and silent.

'In any case,' Takai went on, 'I would never accept the throne.'

Noemi rounded on him, her chest heaving. 'So you would let the Assembly members squabble over it?' She shook her head. 'As much as I hate to admit it, you are the better choice than one regional leader having more power than the others. That is how the Discontented rose in the first place and how Ivane got into this mess.'

'You agree, then, that Ivane isn't perfect?'

'Of course it's not perfect,' she snapped, 'but it's my home.' Her expression softened. 'It's the only home I've ever had, and it's my duty to protect it.'

'Then let me help you. Let's make a truce.'

Noemi's features hardened again. 'I'd sooner make a deal with a snake.'

Takai wished Sar were here. He would be able to get her to see sense, but he'd rightfully stayed to watch over Isla.

'I'm no snake,' was all Takai could manage. 'I'm half-Ivanian. This is my mother's homeland and I'm duty-bound to protect it, too.'

'You have shown where your loyalty lies, rushing off with the Water Catcher the moment the Northemers showed their faces,' Noemi said. 'And who is she to us, other than the person who tried to destroy Oisiri?'

'She was trying to protect herself and her cousin,' Takai cried. In reality, he didn't know exactly what had happened in Oisiri, but he knew Arisa wouldn't have caused the flood without good reason.

'She abused her powers. Powers that weren't even supposed to work here. Father should have let me lock her up.'

'What if her powers do work here? What if she can harness them again to help you? To help Ivane?'

Noemi screwed up her mouth. 'Is it possible?'

His voice flattened. 'I don't know.'

Noemi released a bitter laugh.

Takai pressed on. 'What I do know is that Arisa would do anything to protect this place. Her own mother grew up in the palace city. Ettean and Kengian blood runs through her veins. She grew up in Lamore. She is devoted to uniting the Kyprian nations. And she is the one of the prophecy.'

Noemi's mouth twitched, as if Takai were wearing away at her prickly exterior. Buoyed, he continued.

'The only people who died in Oisiri were Northemers.'

A *harrumph* from Noemi.

'And, like the Northemers, Arisa is someone I would never underestimate.'

Noemi tapped her hand on the hilt of her sword for several moments before speaking. '*If* what you suspect of Malu is true, that he has something else up his sleeve, and if your Lamorian and Kengian fleets don't arrive in time...I can see we may very well need the Water Catcher.'

Takai smiled. He had the truce he'd sought for himself, as well as one for Arisa.

THE AFTERNOON DRAGGED on into nothingness. Takai and Noemi watched the horizon for any sign of the enemy. Takai tried to pass the time by attempting to make conversation with his cousin. He wanted her to understand he wasn't the enemy. He wanted to understand *her* better, too.

'I remember the first time I picked up a sword,' he said casually. 'I was five years old and playing in my father's apartments.' A wistful smile came to his face. 'He was busy speaking to the

Chancellor about some business, and his broadsword was sitting in its sheath on a settee.'

Noemi shifted slightly, as if he had caught her interest, but didn't turn toward him. Takai continued anyway.

'The hilt was gold, with an intricate pattern carved along it. The way it caught the morning light drew me to it. I unsheathed it, carefully, quietly, knowing I was doing the wrong thing but unable to stop. The blade was taller than I was, and heavier than I expected. It took everything I had to hold it aloft, but when I did…' He shook his head and laughed. 'I felt invincible, like I could conquer the world…for all of the few seconds it took for my father to snatch it away from me.'

Something between a laugh and a grunt came from Noemi's direction. 'I was four when I snuck a sabre from Letoi's rooms,' she began after a pause, without looking at Takai. 'I used to watch him training our guards. Hours and hours of swordplay. I'd mimic their every move with an imaginary sword. But it was nothing like the real thing. Holding that blade in my hands…' She sighed. 'It was like I was born to it. Unfortunately, Letoi caught me unawares mid-swing, and I accidentally sliced an inch from his beard.'

'You did not!'

Noemi turned to him with a mad grin on her face. 'I did. I thought he would lose it, but he merely frowned and said if I insisted on playing with the real thing, he might as well show me how to do it properly.'

Takai raised his brows in surprise. 'You started your training at four years old?'

Noemi nodded. 'My training has been everything to me. I have known for as long as I can remember that I could never take the throne, so I would have to find another way to serve my country. To protect my people.' She gazed back out to the horizon, her gaze as steely as the tone of her voice. 'My sword lets me fulfil my duty to Ivane. I just wish it were enough…' Her voice rose. 'There's so much that could be done. *Should* be done.

I have watched from afar without being blinkered by power. While I don't condone it, I understand why some of our people have turned on us. Given the chance, I could put our regions right, ensure there is equity and prosperity for all. Then there would be no Discontented. I know I could help…' Her voice trailed away, heavy with the unspoken words: 'if only'.

Takai pondered not just Noemi's words, but the passion he heard behind them. He understood the duty that came with being born to a King. But it had never occurred to him how difficult it must be for Noemi, feeling the need to serve and lead her nation without the power to do so. If she were given the right to rule, he could only imagine how formidable his cousin would be.

'I'm sorry you have been denied what is rightfully yours,' he said quietly.

Noemi spun to face him. 'I don't need pity,' she spat. 'Least of all yours.' She leapt to her feet and stomped away.

It seemed their ceasefire was officially over.

As THE SUN began to set, Commander Letoi ordered a change of shift and they were relieved of duties. Takai's bed called to him, but he had to do something else first.

He found Arisa in a courtyard outside Ambra's rooms, where Isla rested. With arms folded and head tilted, she appeared to be intent on a fountain made from Ivanian moon-stone. At the centre of the fountain was a tree with water weeping from barbed, tentacle-like branches. The moonstone shimmered pearl, silver and purple, like the twilight sky over-head. The same hues were mirrored in Arisa's Kengian garb and her silver eyes, hidden from Takai. Her freshly washed hair, worn loose, shone bronze. A lump formed in his throat at the poignancy of the moment, of her beauty amid the ugliness of war.

'Majestic,' he said in a faraway voice.

Arisa spun to face him, stumbling in the process. Takai's quick hands stopped her from falling. She flinched at his touch and he hurriedly removed his hands.

'I'm sorry, I didn't mean—'

'No, it's fine...I mean...My arm.' She pointed to her bandaged limb. 'Theodora's snow leopard has quite the bite.'

'*Snow leopard?*'

Arisa nodded. 'There's a lot to catch you up on.'

'I'm sure, but first you should get your arm seen to. Get Ambra to use some of the Alia Water.'

Arisa compressed her lips. 'He offered, but I told him to hold on to it in case he needed more for Isla.'

'But I thought she was healed?'

Arisa shrugged. 'She's a lot better, but not out of the woods yet. She's still drifting in and out of consciousness. She keeps calling out for "Sir Sar" in her sleep.'

Takai laughed. 'He'd like that.'

Arisa smiled at him. A small smile, but a hint of how she used to look at him. Enough for his stomach to explode with butterflies. He opened his mouth to speak, to say the words he should have said a year before, but she turned back to the fountain.

'This tree. It reminds me a little of the sacred yew tree at Lochlen.'

Takai's heart lurched. He remembered Arisa's connection to the Kengian sacred site – and its keeper, the Custodian who'd fallen in love with her.

'How is Jaai?' Etched with envy, the words left his lips before he could stop them.

Arisa gave him a disappointed look. 'He's fine. He is courting a Scholar. He seems happy.'

Takai gave an unsure smile. Was Arisa disappointed that Jaai had moved on? Or was she disappointed by his own jealous enquiry? He told himself it didn't really matter, because while

Arisa was here before him, he had a chance to win her back...
albeit only a small one.

He indicated the fountain. 'It's modelled on Ivane's sacred
tree, the Batu-riek.'

Arisa nodded. 'Isla and I saw them on our travels. I'm
surprised my mother never mentioned them, though, given how
special they are to Ivanians. But I suppose the best way to
understand Ivane is to experience it for yourself.' She sighed and
returned her gaze to him. 'This place is remarkable.'

'It is. Assuming there will be something left after the Northemers are done with it.'

Arisa's face fell. 'Any news of the Kengian and Lamorian
fleets?'

'A day or so away, at best. And I'm afraid the Northemers
have something planned for us in the meantime.'

Arisa tilted her head in thought. 'It stands to reason they
would, given their past form. You know, they tried to recruit Rea.'

'They did?'

Arisa told him how she and Isla had tracked Rea to a cave in
the Ettean mountains, where they'd found Alia crystals and
letters from past Firemasters. Reading the letters, they'd discovered that Rea was Amund's daughter. Arisa explained how Rea
needed a Firemaster's spell and Alia crystals to heal herself, so
after the cave had collapsed, she had gone to Oisiri.

'That was where we ran into the Northemers and Theodora,' she finished.

'And her *snow leopard?*'

'Uh-huh. I haven't a clue how or why the cat was there, but
she ordered it to attack me. And there was someone else with
Theodora, an Ivanian girl...She was the one with the barbed
staff laced with asp venom. She also had a bow and arrow – its
head looked like a sharpened Alia crystal.'

Takai frowned. 'Black market weapons. But why?'

Arisa's brow furrowed, too. 'To kill Rea. She may have

succeeded if Theodora and I hadn't intervened. She chased after Rea like someone possessed.'

'But Rea escaped?'

Arisa nodded. 'I'm not sure where to, but she made it out of Oisiri alive.' Pain flickered across her face. 'Which is more than I can say for those who remained in the city.'

Takai reached for her uninjured arm. 'Don't punish yourself. The flood you created only took the lives of a few Northemers.'

She raised a brow. 'Everyone else got to safety?'

'They did. You must have had full control over your powers.'

Arisa shook her head. 'It didn't feel that way. I had no idea what I was doing, and I didn't set out to kill any Northemers. I didn't even know I could summon my powers here.'

'Do you think you could do it again?' he asked. 'Ivane could really use your help. My cousin is confident of victory, but the Northemers…'

'They're unpredictable.'

'Exactly.' Takai reached for her hand. 'Do you think you could harness your powers?'

Arisa looked down at her hand in his, but didn't pull away. 'I don't know,' she muttered. Words that bled sadness.

With his free hand, Takai lifted Arisa's chin so their eyes met. 'I believe in you…I always have.' A throaty whisper. 'Do you believe in us?'

Arisa closed her eyes and stepped out of his reach. Her next words were almost inaudible. 'I want to. But how can I when you can't forgive me for what I did?'

Takai blinked rapidly. '*Me* forgive *you?*'

She peered back at him with tear-filled eyes. 'But your father…I only did it to…'

Takai swallowed back the memory of his father's death. Arisa was part of that memory, of course, but not in the way she thought. He didn't blame her for anything.

'I know you did it to protect me, and that you had no choice,' he said gently. She sniffed back her tears. 'It is me who seeks your forgiveness. I didn't believe I had a right to ask you for it. Not until I had made amends to my people and Lamore. But I realised I can't do it…I can't do any of it without you. I need your forgiveness. I *need* you, Arisa.'

She wandered back to the fountain, as if collecting her thoughts.

'Please, Arisa,' he begged. 'Please say you can forgive me.'

Arisa turned back to him, her gaze steady. 'I understand now, Takai, why you did what you did. Why you thought you had to sacrifice your own happiness because of your duties to everyone else. But what about your duty to me?'

'I was wrong.' He held out his arms in supplication. 'Just give me a chance to earn your trust again. A chance – that is all I ask. I can't go to the battlefield without a glimmer of hope.'

A ghost of a smile tugged at the corner of Arisa's lips. 'There's always hope.'

In that moment he knew he had his chance, and he would take it. He made to close the distance between them—

An explosion cracked the air. Cries sounded from the battlements in the distance. Another explosion. Screams. A cloud of dust illuminated in the moonlit sky.

Takai and Arisa shared a look of horror.

It couldn't be true. How could they have done it without Rea or the Firemaster's book? It couldn't be possible. Yet the sound was unmistakable.

The Northemers had firesky weapons.

28

The pounding of cannons pierced the night. The sky was alight with the flare of the firesky weapons, orange embers and sparks preceding the ear-shattering blast of cannonballs, thick clouds of acrid smoke choking the air. While the Ivanians scrambled, Theodora revelled in the pandemonium. The archers on the battlements launched fire arrows at the Northemers, who were comfortably out of range, dancing, taunting the Ivanians from the darkness. The soldiers' screams split the night air with every explosion. And even if sleep had been possible, Theodora didn't desire it. She didn't want to miss a moment of her long-awaited triumph.

When dawn crept across the plateau, she clutched Malu's hand in anticipation, picturing piles of rubble where the palace city's walls had once been. Her heart sank when the outline of the wall and towers emerged in the morning light – they were practically unscathed. Here and there, crenellations were noticeably absent. Plate-sized divots peppered the outer wall, but nothing had fully penetrated it. One section along the top looked like a giant bite had been taken out of it. But the wall stood firm, as did the gate. The only sign of damage on the gate was a section of splintered and lifting wood, which exposed a thick layer of steel bars underneath.

Malu's hand tensed in Theodora's.

'I don't understand,' she said. 'The walls – they're made of earth. How can this be?'

Malu pulled away from her and lifted a spyglass to his eye. He shook his head.

Theodora took the spyglass from him, sweeping it across the boundary wall and city gate, stopping as it fell on a huddle of people near the main watchtower. A pair of Ivanians, and two others… Her breath quickened as she recognised them. Takai and Arisa.

Nearby, Hafder was deep in conversation with one of their Ivanian mercenaries, the merchant Olix translating for him. He finished up the discussion and stomped toward them.

'The rammed earth,' Hafder grumbled. 'It's been fashioned by master craftspeople. It is said to be a hundred times stronger than stone.'

Malu's mouth was set in a grim line. 'And the gate?'

'Reinforced with Ivanian steel. Its strength unmatched.'

Theodora could feel victory slipping through her fingers like the sand beneath her feet. 'The city is impenetrable?'

Malu stood up tall, his already imposing figure even more impressive and assured. 'Not impenetrable. We are making progress.' He waved his hand in the direction of the damaged parts of the wall. 'It will just take longer than we planned.'

'We can use some of the cannons on our ships,' Hafder suggested. 'Target the underside of the plateau from the sea and undermine the city from that side.'

Malu frowned. 'Making land from the sea boundary is a fool's errand.' He rubbed his beard, then his cunning smile appeared. 'But it will be a splendid distraction, drawing away some of their forces while we provoke the rest of them into meeting us on the battlefield.'

Hafder grinned maniacally. 'About time.' He patted the

handle of the axe tucked into his belt. 'My death-making friend here has missed the taste of blood.'

Malu put an arm around Hafder's shoulder. 'And blood you shall have.' He put his other arm around Theodora. 'You *both* shall have it. A sea of our enemies' blood for you, brother, and the Water Catcher's for you, my love.' Malu released his brother and hugged Theodora closer to him, his gaze earnest and determined. 'And after everyone's thirst is quenched, Ivane will be ours.'

Theodora gave a strained smile. Malu was promising everything she thought she wanted. Revenge on Arisa. Power over a land much grander in size, riches and warmth than Northem. Why, then, was her stomach churning so violently?

29

$\mathcal{T}$he horror of Ivane's situation unfolded in the soft dawn light. The two Ettean ships, along with Ivane's few vessels and Takai's, had been decimated by cannons during the night. Nothing remained of them except for rafts of flotsam. Shattered timber planks and barrels, remnants of sails and tangles of ropes littered the port. The palace city had fared better, with minimal damage to the boundary wall and gate — but the same couldn't be said for Takai's cousin.

Underneath a film of grime and blood was the face of a shattered young woman. Noemi wandered along the battlements in utter shock that her 'impervious' forces and country were crumbling before her eyes.

As soon as they'd heard the firesky cannons, Takai and Arisa had raced to the city gate, armed with longbows and swords. In all the panic, no one had questioned their presence, but it soon became apparent that the Northemers had set up just out of range of their inferior weapons, so they could do nothing in the darkness except hope and pray they survived the night.

Takai had begged Arisa to go back to the safety of the palace, saying they couldn't afford to lose the Water Catcher, meaning *he* couldn't afford to lose her. Of course, Arisa had refused, so they'd remained by each other's sides on the battlements throughout the night. Watching, waiting, wondering if they would be the next to fall under the cannon fire.

*Cannon fire…*It took a moment for Takai and the others to register that the firesky weapons had gone quiet.

'Why have they stopped firing? Have they run out of ammunition?' King Laskar asked.

Commander Letoi frowned. 'It's more likely they are planning something else.'

Takai nodded his agreement.

'Which is why they're watching us right now.' Arisa pointed toward the Northem front. A particularly tall Northemer stared back at them, a woman beside him. Takai didn't need a spyglass to know it was Malu and Theodora.

Noemi barrelled toward her father. 'This is our chance! We launch our attack on the ground now.'

Letoi gave a resounding shake of his head. 'No. We take this time to reinforce the gate, see to the wounded and dead, and relieve the night watch with fresh soldiers.'

'But—'

Noemi was stopped short by the raising of Laskar's hand. 'See to it,' the King ordered Letoi.

'Father,' Noemi cried. 'We can't sit here and do nothing. We have to fight!'

Laskar rested a hand on Noemi's shoulder. 'We're not doing nothing. We are leveraging our greatest asset – the strength and safety of our walls and gate.'

She slapped her father's hand away, thrusting a finger in the Northemers' direction. 'Our fortifications can't withstand those weapons forever.'

'But we only need to last long enough for the Lamorian and Kengian forces to arrive with their own firesky weapons,' Takai offered.

Noemi's head swivelled in Takai's direction. '*If* they arrive.'

'They'll arrive,' Arisa said with certainty.

'I believe *you*,' Noemi sneered, 'less than my faithless cousin.'

'I thought we had a truce?' Takai retorted.

King Laskar rubbed his temple. 'Enough. Go oversee the reinforcement of the gate,' he ordered his daughter.

She stormed away, but only after casting a death stare at Takai and Arisa.

The King gave them an apologetic look. 'It's been a long night. You two should go get some rest in your rooms.'

Takai and Arisa shook their heads in unison.

Laskar sighed. 'Will you at least take a rest in the watchtower?' He squinted up at the rising sun, already blazing. 'Shade, rest and water. My orders.'

'And you, Uncle?'

The King gave a wry smile. 'Sleep is for the damned and the dead.'

IN THE WATCHTOWER, Takai propped himself up against the wall, Arisa taking up a position next to him. They absorbed the news of how the Northemers had obtained the firesky weapons. The King had received hawk messages reporting that Malu's ships had all left the regional ports, seemingly never intending on blockading them. They had been there to load firesky weapons and ammunition forged in secret with the support of Ivane's greedy and Discontented. They had funded it with Ivanian gold – presumably the same gold offered to Malu to first leave Ette. Gold the Northemer had taken in bad faith, along with Lore's life.

Takai and Arisa discussed the extent of Malu's cunning and what he could possibly have planned next. They spoke of everything other than their relationship, talking until Arisa's eyelids fluttered to a close, her head resting on Takai's shoulder.

He put an arm around her to keep her steady, a sharp intake of his breath as the scent of rosewater perfume wafted from her hair. He was soothed by the steady rise and fall of her chest, a beacon of hope in the thick of war. His own eyelids grew heavy. Sleep was calling him. Just a few moments' rest, comfort in Arisa's closeness, was all he wanted right now. Just a few moments…

An explosion. Shouts in the distance. Another explosion, and another, reverberating through the air.

Takai and Arisa were on their feet. Guards ran along the battlements. Noemi raced up the watchtower stairs to meet them. King Laskar appeared in the doorway, spyglass in hand.

'The Northem fleet is attacking the palace city from the sea,' he addressed them all.

Noemi's brow knitted. 'Why there? They'll never make it up the cliffside.'

'A distraction,' Takai suggested.

The King's lips compressed into a thin line. 'It doesn't matter why. We have to meet their attack and make sure they don't succeed. Letoi and I will lead our defence at the sea boundary wall. Daughter, you hold our position here.'

Noemi's hand was on her sheathed sabre. 'Let us attack them on the ground here.'

'No,' the King said. 'We're safe here until reinforcements arrive.'

'With honour and courage,' Arisa said.

The King nodded. 'With honour and courage.'

Noemi watched her father and Letoi ride back into the city with a contingent of soldiers. Ridges of determination lined her forehead.

'It's a mistake,' she muttered. 'We should attack the Northemers now. We still have numbers on our side.'

'But not weapons,' Takai argued.

'Takai's right,' Arisa said. 'I've seen in person what those hand cannons can do – rip a soldier apart with one shot.'

Noemi glared at them both. 'Ivanians are not scared of death. Yes, many of us will fall, but an ample number of us will get close enough to fight hand-to-hand, and that is where we will win this war.'

'That's what we thought, too,' Arisa pressed. 'But the Northemers…' Her face twisted at the memory of fighting them.

'They're formidable,' Takai declared.

Noemi's mouth twitched indecisively.

'Commander!' a guard shouted from the watchtower window, pointing to the Northem frontline.

They raced to see what had captured the guard's attention. A small group approached, Malu and Theodora at its lead. There was something odd about the way they were moving. At least two of the party were stumbling, struggling to stay upright. Takai reached for his spyglass and focused it on the group. Half a dozen Northemers. Two other men, their hands bound, were being jerked back and forth via rope tied to their wrists.

'He's almost in range,' the guard said.

'Archers!' Noemi shouted. 'Fire at my command.'

The Northemers drew closer. Takai could make out one of the bound men. Kappu – the Ettean Commander they'd thought had gone down with the ships.

'Hold your fire!' Takai ordered. 'They have prisoners!'

Noemi snatched the spyglass from him and looked through it. 'Blast!' She threw the device back at Takai. 'They have the High Sheriff of the port. I won't negotiate with them.'

Arisa bit her lip.

'What is it?' Takai asked.

'Negotiation isn't Malu's style.'

'You're right,' Takai agreed. 'Another distraction.'

'If you're the expert,' Noemi said, stabbing a finger in Takai's chest, 'what do you suggest we do?'

He bowed his head. 'I don't know.' And he didn't. How could he know what the great trickster had planned?

By now Malu and his party had come within shouting distance.

Noemi gritted her teeth. 'What do you want?' she yelled down at them in Ivanian.

'For you to come out and play.' It was Theodora who responded, her characteristic smirk clearly visible.

Play? Noemi mouthed at the rest of them. Takai and Arisa shrugged. But they didn't have to wait long for an answer to Noemi's question.

With a tilt of his head and a blood-curdling laugh, Malu produced a long knife and ran it across Kappu's throat.

There was a collective gasp in the watchtower. Takai's hands curled into fists as the Ettean Commander's limp body dropped to the ground.

Noemi's hand was back on her sword hilt. 'If they want to play, I'll play with them.'

Takai blocked the doorway so his cousin couldn't leave. 'That's exactly what they want.'

'Look!' Arisa beckoned them back to the window.

Malu now had the High Sheriff. He held out his bloodied knife and grinned as he cut the man's throat.

'*No-o-o!*' Noemi screeched, grabbing a crossbow from the guard. She fired directly at Malu, but the Northemers were already putting a shield wall in place.

A Northem archer slipped from behind the shields and fired an arrow back toward the watchtower. Noemi, Takai, Arisa and the guard ducked to take cover, but it soon became apparent the arrow that lay nearby on the stone floor wasn't intended to injure them. It contained a message. A small coloured bundle – an Ivanian flag – was tied to the arrow.

Noemi told the guard to check it. He kicked the bundle open with his boot and the unmistakable stench of human excrement filled the tower.

The guard, Takai and Arisa recoiled, but Noemi was already halfway out the door.

'No!' Takai called after her.

'If they want war, they've got it,' she threw over her shoulder. 'Forces, assemble!'

Hundreds of bootsteps thundered on the ground below, rushing into formation.

Takai chased his cousin down the stairs. 'It's a trick. This is what he wants. We know this from experience. You have to listen to me.'

Noemi spun back to face him, her dark eyes wild with anger. 'I'm done listening to you and my father. The truce is over.' She unsheathed her sabre and marched over to the gatehouse. 'Open the gate!'

30

There was no time to find or mount horses. No time to formulate strategy. The decision had been made – they would fight the Northemers in hand-to-hand combat, on the ground where the enemy was at its most deadly.

Since arriving in Nadis, Arisa had looked for any sign of her powers, wishing she could summon the same magic she had manifested at Oisiri. She'd experienced a prickle of energy when Ambra had produced the Alia Water to save Isla, but it was a mere echo of what she was used to and needed to harness her full Water Catcher abilities. So Arisa did the only thing she could: she reached for her Kengian swords and raced to join Takai as he followed his cousin through the city gate.

On spotting her, Takai's face contorted. 'Get to safety!' he shouted, amid the roar of the Ivanian army and the Northem battle cries and drums. He cast a troubled gaze around him. 'This is a death mission.' A round of hand cannon fire punctuated Takai's point.

The Northem frontline was approaching rapidly, too fast and too close to deploy the Ivanian archers. Within seconds the Ivanians and Northemers would be clinched in battle, making it impossible to isolate and target the enemy. Longbows were being fired from the battlements at the Northern cavalry, but they would do little to dampen the attack. The first of the Ivanians were already being trampled underfoot.

They were at a significant disadvantage. If Arisa joined Takai, there was a reasonable chance neither of them would survive, yet the choice was simple. It didn't matter what had passed between them. The very real prospect that she may lose Takai forever made Arisa realise that they couldn't be apart. She had fought her feelings for too long, when listening to her heart had never failed her before. By each other's sides they had conquered every obstacle, and of those there had been many. The world had been pitched against them from day one. They had fought and overcome prejudice, distance and duty, finding understanding and comfort in each other among the turmoil and the chaos. They shared a knowledge that they were stronger together, were meant to be together in this life…and beyond, if that was their destiny.

She took his hand in hers. 'If you fight, I fight. We are one.'

Crinkles formed around Takai's eyes and he exhaled, a thousand heart-stilling moments in a single puff of air. Arisa willed her touch to convey hope and forgiveness. In Takai's shining gaze, she saw a vow that if they survived this day, he would never let her go again.

'We are one,' he affirmed, and lifted her chin with his free hand.

Arisa leant toward him, starved of the sensation of his lips on hers. His kiss didn't disappoint. At first tentative, then confident, then familiar. In that moment it was hard to imagine there had ever been a time that they were parted.

Then, all too soon, it was over. War was calling on them to put aside their own happiness for a while longer.

Arisa stroked Takai's cheek. 'Be careful,' she said in a soft voice – an inside joke. A reference to the many times he and Amund had said the same to her.

A shadow of a laugh. 'Aren't I always?' he teased, exactly as she would reply.

A final squeeze of hands and a release. Then they sprinted as fast as they could across the sandy flat, swords raised, *'With honour and courage'* on their lips, their hearts full.

31

In a daze, Theodora watched the battle unfold before her. Malu had instructed that she stay at the rear of their forces. Half a dozen Northemers were ordered to guard her, with a horse at the ready for her escape if needed. At first she had argued, but after the gruesome scene where Malu had slit the men's throats, she'd come to the sobering conclusion that she may not be ready to take another person's life.

The metallic smell of the fallen men's blood still infiltrated her nostrils. The image of them clutching their necks in a futile attempt to stem the scarlet flow was still fresh in her mind. The final thrashing of limbs before life faded from their eyes was burned into her memory. Being so close to death had unleashed something in her, a fear she hadn't expected.

Of course she knew that death was inevitable in war. Of course she knew what Malu was capable of. But it wasn't death or Malu she feared. She was terrified that she was as useless as the Northemers believed her to be.

She had prided herself on her strength, on a belief that she was capable and deserving of leading Malu's people. She had believed a crown was owed to her. She had believed that power and Ivane should be hers and had dismissed her father's criticisms, putting them down to jealousy. But she'd been wrong. She could see it now in the accusatory stares of her protectors, brave Northemer warriors who belonged on the battlefield, fighting alongside their countrymen and women, not guarding her.

While Theodora flinched at the sight of an Ivanian soldier's head being severed from his neck in a single swing of an axe, blood spraying through the air and painting the victor's face, her Northemer guards craved it, yearning to play their part. The leather armour she wore, the staff tucked behind her back, the hand cannon slung over her shoulder, mocked her. Decorative trinkets that would never fulfil their purpose.

Sensing Theodora's discomfort, Rayl, on a leash beside her, nudged her hand. She patted the snow leopard's head, wondering if the animal, an adept killer, coveted blood too – or was it a necessary evil, something she only did for survival?

Theodora remembered, then. The single truth about herself and Rayl that couldn't be disputed. They were survivors. They had the resilience and courage to go on despite what was thrown at them. By nature of being a survivor, Theodora was strong... and she would prove it.

She released Rayl from her leash, whispering, 'You are free to make your own choice.' And before the Northem guards realised, Theodora had mounted her horse and was charging headfirst into the battle.

It took everything she had to stay in her saddle. Her senses were overwhelmed by the screams of pain, the crack of hand cannon fire, the sight of hundreds of bodies splayed on the ground. Her horse baulked when an Ivanian soldier blocked their path, his sword pointed at the mare's chest. Theodora fought for breath as she reached for her hand cannon, despite knowing she couldn't load and fire it in time to save herself. Then the Ivanian's eyes widened. A gurgled cry. He fell to the ground, an axe embedded in his back. Oxygen returned to Theodora's lungs in sharp bursts as Hafder appeared to retrieve his axe.

'Go,' he growled, pointing the weapon back to where she'd come from.

Sweat sprung from Theodora's palms. Her shaking hands struggled to grip the reins, but she managed a small nod. Hafder grunted and returned to battle.

She was about to turn back when a familiar figure emerged from the smoke-filled air in the distance.

Theodora dug her heels into the mare's belly and headed straight for Arisa.

Tunnel-visioned, she plunged into battle, sweeping her staff through the air as she went. Everything Jade had taught her was flooding back. With deadly accuracy, she struck every attacker who came within reach, one eye never leaving Arisa. Underneath the Kengian's blood-splattered armour and face, Theodora could see her determination. One arm bandaged, she still moved with practised ease, wielding her Kengian swords like they were part of her. She had all the appearance of an experienced warrior – but she wasn't invincible. Here, away from Oisiri, away from home, she wasn't the Water Catcher. Arisa was no different to Theodora – except right now Theodora had the upper hand.

She stopped her horse about fifty yards from Arisa and loaded her hand cannon. She took aim, waiting for Arisa to stand still. The Kengian stabbed a Northemer in his belly with her short sword and dispatched another with the longsword in her other hand.

She looked up and cocked her head, as if sensing something in the air, her silver eyes falling on Theodora.

Theodora lit her weapon's fuse, a smirk forming at the sizzling of the wick. Arisa jutted out her chin and Theodora made to depress the trigger—

A visceral scream. An animal in pain. Theodora's horse reared. The mare's hind legs gave out, a spear sticking from her torso. Then Theodora was falling, tumbling from her saddle. Somehow she managed to manoeuvre herself so she wouldn't be trapped under the horse, but she hit the ground hard. She pushed herself to her feet, wobbling. Her hand went to her forehead. Her fingers met something warm and sticky. She forced herself to focus on her surroundings. Her hand cannon was pinned under her horse. The animal's eyes rolled back in its head.

'Die, Northemer filth!' An Ivanian soldier was running at Theodora, lance poised.

Theodora reached for her staff behind her back, but it was gone. She spotted it several feet away, lying next to a pile of Ivanian bodies. She raced to get to it, but the Ivanian was bearing down on her. Stretching out with one hand to reach her weapon, she watched in horror as the metallic flash of a lance head speared toward her.

Across the battlefield, Malu caught sight of her. He shouted her name and started running toward her, but another Ivanian warrior – a girl, the one who'd fired a crossbow at Malu from the watchtower – cut him down, slicing a sword across the Northem King's stomach.

Theodora closed her eyes, willing death to come swiftly. What was the point in living when they had lost – when *she* had lost everything?

32

Takai was determined to never lose sight of Arisa in battle, to never be more than a sword's length from her, but it was an impossible task. The Northemers were every bit as formidable as the previous times he'd faced them. Their thirst for blood was equally matched by their skills with axe and blade. Their firesky weapons outmatched anything that could be thrown at them. Takai saw more than one Ivanian cut down by hand cannon, mangled entrails spilling from ruptured bellies, skulls obliterated in a spray of blood, bone and brains.

He fought like a man possessed, but for every enemy he dispatched, another two appeared. His ears rang from the cannon fire, his throat and eyes raw from the smoke. He fought fatigue and the sickening knowledge that they were only delaying the inevitable – the Northemers would prevail. The only question was whether he and the woman he loved would survive to witness it.

The answer he feared appeared in the form of Theodora, armed with a hand cannon.

Takai's heart shuddered to a stop as he spotted her target – and then watched Arisa drop to the ground. A searing pain ripped through his chest, as if he were the one who'd been shot.

Then he was running, sprinting, his blade cleaving through anyone who stood in his way. His lungs screamed for air, Arisa his only focus. *Please don't let her be dead. If anyone should die, it should be me. Not Arisa, never her…*

He collapsed by Arisa's side, scanning her for injury, desperately trying to distinguish between her blood and that of the enemy. Her face and body appeared free of entry wounds. He inspected her limbs. A twitch of movement from her bandaged arm, the linen slathered with fresh blood. There was a chunk of material missing, but otherwise her arm was intact. Had the lead shot only grazed her? Could Arisa be so lucky? Could he? He stroked her face, calling her name over and over.

A groan.

A release of Takai's breath, gale-force relief.

Arisa's eyes sprang open and she sat bolt upright.

'Theodora!' Her head swivelled, searching the battlefield.

'Don't worry about her,' Takai said, helping her to her feet. 'We have to get your arm looked at.'

Her hand went instinctively to her injured arm and she flinched. 'I'm fine,' she said in a way that didn't invite an argument.

'You're not fine. Let me help you.'

Arisa retrieved her longsword from the ground, injured arm hanging limp by her side. She jutted out her chin. 'I don't need your help.'

Then, over her shoulder, Takai spotted a Northemer advancing, axe raised.

In one fluid movement, he pulled an Ivanian spear from a dead body on the ground and launched it at the rapidly approaching warrior.

Arisa spun to face the Northemer, who stared down at the spear embedded in his torso. The man appeared to do a double take before locking eyes with Takai, then Arisa. He pulled the weapon from his body, roaring as much with glee as with pain.

Only half a dozen steps away now, he rushed at Arisa. In

desperation, Takai made to jump between them – but Arisa was quicker. A flash of metal, Arisa lunging. One second her longsword was in the Northemer's chest, then it was back by her side.

The man's eyes widened. He stumbled a few steps, then swayed on his feet. He was dead before his body hit the ground.

'See, I'm fine,' Arisa said, her voice shaking. Rivulets of blood gushed down her injured arm.

Takai held out his hand to steady her. 'You need to get to safety,' he pressed.

Arisa winced. 'What about all of them?' She indicated their forces with a wobbly hand. 'The Northemers are winning. We have to retreat. You have to convince your cousin.'

Takai clenched his jaw. 'I'm not leaving you.'

'I'll take care of her.' A familiar voice beside them.

'Sar!' Arisa cried.

Takai's best friend beamed confidently back at him, as if they were meeting each other at a grand ball and not in the middle of a battlefield.

'What are you doing here?' Takai asked.

'You didn't think you could have a war without me, did you? I *am*, after all, the finest Knight in all of Kypria.'

To prove his point, he threw two Ettean knives in quick succession. They whistled past Takai's ear, striking one approaching Northemer in the neck and another in the chest.

'You nearly got me,' Takai protested.

'But I didn't.' Sar winked. 'Not bad, considering I only picked them up for the first time last week. Now go talk some sense into that cousin of yours.'

Takai glanced to Arisa, and she rested a palm on his arm. 'I'm fine. Go.'

He looked at her for one final moment, drinking in the determination in her steely eyes as Sar wrapped a clean bandage around her wound. He would get Noemi to retreat. He had to, for Arisa's sake. For all of their sakes.

TAKAI FOUND his cousin a few hundred feet away, surrounded by three Northem warriors. 'I'm coming!' he shouted as he ran to help her. Noemi threw her head back and laughed. Then, lightning fast, she leapt from a defensive stance, her feet gliding in a perfectly choreographed dance, her sabre thrusting, stabbing, striking. One. Two. Three. The Northemers fell like wheat beneath a scythe.

She gave him a triumphant smile. 'Do *you* need help?'

The embers of anger he had kept suppressed over his cousin's misplaced sense of superiority suddenly flared. How could she be so cavalier while her people were dying around her?

'You may be fine…for now,' he spat. 'But what about your people?' He waved his hand across the battlefield. Ivanian bodies lay thick on the ground. Those still alive were severely outnumbered.

Noemi's eyes narrowed. 'We have them,' she hissed. 'I cut their leader down myself.'

'Malu? Dead?'

'I expect so.'

'It doesn't matter. They will fight on without him. Perhaps even harder.'

'We are winning.'

How could he get her to snap out of her delusion?

'Commander.' An Ivanian soldier, Noemi's second-in-charge, ran up to them, the whites of his eyes stark against his blood-covered face. 'We have to fall back. They're gaining too much ground.'

'We are Ivanians,' she thundered. 'We fight on!'

An explosion. Blood showering over them. The soldier before them, suddenly faceless, falling to the ground.

Takai spun to face the hand cannoneer, who was now charging at them, a blade attached to the end of his weapon's barrel. Takai sidestepped and turned to plunge his sword into the man's back. The Northemer fell face-first, the tip of his blade landing at Noemi's feet.

His cousin didn't budge. She stood stock-still, save for the quivering of her sword. Her expressionless face was painted with her soldier's blood.

Takai put a hand on her shoulder. 'It's time,' he said gently. 'Order the retreat.'

At first she gave no sign of hearing him, but then, slowly, she nodded. 'Retreat,' she whispered through chattering teeth.

'Louder,' he urged.

Noemi wiped her mouth and blinked rapidly at the blood on her hands. No words were forthcoming.

'Retreat!' Takai shouted across the plain. 'Your Commander orders a retreat!'

33

A guttural growl reverberated in Theodora's head. And a scream. A scream that didn't come from her mouth.

Her eyes flung open to see Rayl standing on the Ivanian soldier's chest. Her jaws were locked around the dying man's throat.

She'd cheated death. Again. For what? Malu had fallen in her quest for revenge.

*Revenge...*Had she got it, finally?

Theodora looked back to where Arisa had been. The Kengian wasn't lying dead on the ground as she'd expected. Arisa was alive, albeit injured. Sar was with her, tending to a wound on her arm.

A caustic laugh escaped Theodora's mouth. She staggered back to her dead mare and made to pull her hand cannon free. She would have her revenge. She *must* have it – for Malu as much as for herself.

And she may very well have had it, if Malu's men hadn't followed orders.

Just as she grabbed her weapon, one of the guards tasked with protecting Theodora galloped toward her and scooped her up, carrying her away from the battle.

34

*T*akai redressed Arisa's wound, managing to stem most of the blood flow, but she cried out with pain as he worked. Theodora's hand cannon shot had shredded the flesh of her already injured limb. Takai begged her to use some of the Alia Water on it, but she refused. She argued that Isla was still drifting in and out of consciousness and may still need it. Arisa also made it clear she didn't want to be treated any differently to the hundreds of Ivanians who needed medical care – many of whom were in a worse state than she was.

She waited in the watchtower for her turn, dozing with her head against Takai's shoulder throughout the night that followed. Proper sleep was impossible, though, due to the pounding of the cannon fire, the shaking of the city wall and Takai's constant worry about her injury.

In the early hours of the morning, Ambra arrived with his medical kit and gave Arisa a tonic for her pain. Takai lost count of the sutures the healer used to close the wound. Eventually, Ambra announced that he was finished and that there hadn't been any nerve damage, but Arisa would have a sizeable scar for the rest of her life.

'Scars are the least of my worries,' she said dismissively. 'As long as I can still wield a sword.' She reached for her pair of Kengian blades, groaning as she tried to grip her short sword with her injured hand.

'You should rest,' Takai argued. 'And you can. We won't be going back out there until reinforcements arrive…We're safe here.' He didn't add, *for now*, but he knew that was what they were both thinking.

'Wasn't that the plan right before your cousin led us on a death mission?' Arisa spat.

Takai glanced over at Noemi, slumped against a nearby parapet. Her dark eyes were forlorn beneath a mask of dried blood. 'I don't think she'll make that mistake again,' he said. 'I was there when my uncle came and saw her. He was furious that his orders had been disobeyed, but he took one look at how crushed she was and left her to lick her wounds.'

A fire ignited in Arisa's eyes. 'Lick *her* wounds! What about all of her people who've died? What about them?'

Takai frowned. 'You remember what it was like to be in battle for the first time?' he said softly.

Arisa's anger appeared to dissipate, replaced, no doubt, by her memories of the battle on Kengia's Ambay Coast. The many lives she had taken when she'd summoned the sea against the Lamorian–Northem forces. Takai remembered how it had rocked her and regretted reminding her of it. An image flickered before Takai's eyes. The firewater and wreath, laid just weeks ago as part of a ceremony to remember all those lives.

'No one lives through war without regrets,' he said quietly. 'Even when they only did what was needed.'

'You're right,' she said. 'Let me talk to Noemi.'

He rested a hand on her shoulder. 'No. It should be me.'

Takai approached his cousin's hunched figure on the battlement and sat down beside her. Noemi gave no indication she was aware of his presence. He wondered what he should say – then it came to him. The words he had used to help Arisa at Ambay.

'I believe in you,' he said.

Noemi turned slowly toward Takai, looking at him as if he had lost his mind.

'I believe in you,' he repeated.

She looked away and stared at the opposite wall. 'I think you must be suffering from some form of head injury.'

Takai shook his head. 'I know what I'm saying, and I mean it. I saw you out there on the battlefield. You are one of the finest warriors I've ever seen. You have the heart of a leader.'

'A leader?' Noemi scoffed. 'I sent my people to their deaths.'

'You did what was asked of you.' Something else Takai had said to Arisa in Kengia.

'Are you mad?' Noemi jumped to her feet. 'I was specifically told *not* to go to battle.'

Takai stood up as well. 'You have been asked to be the Commander of your people, and as the Commander, you must make hard decisions. Decisions based on the best information you have at the time. Decisions that must be made in an instant. And you must own those decisions, whether they are good or bad. That is your job: to make decisions. And that is what you did.'

A single tear slipped from Noemi's eye, carving a trail through her blood-covered cheek. 'I do own my decision,' she said in a faraway voice. 'It is why I can never forgive myself. My people deserve better.'

At that moment, Takai didn't see Noemi before him. He saw himself. The guilt and the burden of responsibility.

'Your people deserve *you*,' he said firmly. 'You are their Commander and you must lead them. If you abandon them now, you will regret it forever.'

Noemi wiped the back of her hand across her face, taking her tear with it. A bitter smile came to her lips. 'Speaking from experience?'

Takai shrugged. 'Speaking as someone who believes in you.'

Noemi turned her back on him. 'If only your opinion mattered to me.'

Takai's hands balled into fists, but he wouldn't give up. He advanced on his cousin, but Arisa's hand on his arm stopped him.

'Tell her to prepare the city's defences.' Her grip tightened. Takai winced at the intense heat coming from her fingers. 'Something more is coming.'

'Something more?'

Arisa looked away. 'A reckoning.'

35

$\mathcal{W}$hen Theodora first learnt that Malu lived, she couldn't believe her fortune. But her thoughts turned to fresh fears when she saw the state of her King.

Malu had been carried unconscious from the battlefield, blood pouring from the gaping wound that traversed his stomach. Barely breathing, he'd been presented for surgery, and the Northemer medic had set to work suturing the wound with a curved needle and catgut thread, amid dire warnings that the King had 'lost too much blood'. Mopping his sweat-soaked brow, the surgeon had left Theodora and Hafder with instructions to pray for the best.

Theodora had never known Malu as anything but a giant of a man. Magnificent in stature and presence. Everyone who encountered him was equally in awe of him as they were afraid of him. That image now seemed distant, impossible, even, as she stared at the stranger in the Northem King's bed. A cadaverous form of sickly pale flesh that bore little resemblance to the man she loved. There was no indication of life within his body except for the occasional rise and fall of his chest. Theodora counted up to ten petrifying beats between the rattle of each of his breaths.

She clutched Malu's cold, limp hand and prayed to his spirit gods and his ancestors, begging them to spare his life. She bargained with them, promising she would forgo all of her selfish desires in favour of Malu's life. She'd abandon her quest for power and revenge on Arisa. She'd go with Malu to the ends of the known world, leaving everything she knew behind.

'Please, don't die,' she begged the unseeing, unhearing King.

'It will be you to blame if he does.' Hafder's gruff voice from the other side of Malu's bed. 'He wouldn't have been injured if he wasn't distracted by you on the battlefield. Somewhere you weren't supposed to be.'

Hafder's words stung like the tears in Theodora's eyes, because they were true. She had no defence – at least, none that would excuse the fact that Malu lay close to death before them. So she gave no response, gulping back the salty lump in her throat, but Hafder would not be silenced.

He leapt from his seat, jabbing a meaty finger at her. '*You* have made my brother weak. You have made *Northem* weak!'

Spittle flew from his mouth. Rayl snarled at him from her cage.

'We were winning.' Hafder held his hands up, snapping them into fists. 'We had them in our grasp. But we lost our edge when Malu went after you.'

Theodora's tears evaporated in an eruption of fury. She accepted that it was her fault Malu was injured, but that was where her responsibility ended.

She released Malu's hand and got slowly to her feet. She planted her palms on the bed and met Hafder's cold gaze, speaking in clipped tones.

'You know as well as I that the Ivanians chose to retreat before we could have our victory. And right now they sit safe behind their city wall and gate, recuperating, rebuilding, reinforcing their fortifications, and instead of doing something about it, *you*—' She screwed her mouth up in distaste. 'You, the leader of your people in Malu's absence, are standing here bellowing like a wounded bull.'

Hafder snorted, as bull-like as she'd described him.

Theodora gave a hollow laugh. 'Yes, here you are wasting precious time and energy, bellowing at someone you've always maintained is insignificant and unworthy of your notice.'

'Your foolish actions have forced me to take notice,' he growled.

Theodora's eyes went back to Malu's ashen face. A sigh escaped her mouth. 'I could no more force you to do anything than I could make Malu do anything he didn't wish to do.' She looked back at Hafder through pools of tears. 'Abusing me can't make me feel any more guilty than I already do. And if it's punishment you seek – seeing Malu here like this, believing I might lose him, is punishment enough.' Theodora took a deep breath. 'But right now, the best thing we can do is see this battle out and do your brother proud.'

Hafder looked down at his brother, and his expression softened. 'I still can't stomach this woman of yours,' he addressed Malu, 'but she has a point. I'll win this war for Northem. For you.' With a final grunt, he strode to the tent's doorway.

'What are you going to do?' she called after him.

He turned back to face her, his visible eye narrowed. 'We focus all our efforts on breaching that gate. We aim every cannon we have at it.'

Theodora was confused by Hafder's hunched shoulders and resigned tone. 'You do think we can destroy the gate and take the city before the Lamorian and Kengian fleets arrive?'

Hafder shifted his gaze to look out over their camp. 'It will take a miracle. I expect we'll be out of cannon shot by morning. We could recall ammunition from our ships, but we will need it if the battle moves to sea. Besides, by the time we moved it here, it would be too late.'

Theodora's blood ran cold. 'So you *don't* think we'll win?'

He returned his attention to her. 'If we don't win, we'll die trying,' he said matter-of-factly. 'We'll honour my brother in death. It is the Northemer way, and perhaps the best we can hope for.' He turned his back on her and walked away.

Theodora slumped back into her chair, absorbing what Hafder had said. Before now it hadn't occurred to her what would happen if they failed to take Ivane. If she had given it a passing thought, it had been that they would merely retreat to Northem as they'd done before – a cheerless outcome, but at least they would be alive. But under Hafder's leadership, the only way they'd live was if they won. Hafder was intent on steering his people toward 'honourable' deaths – retreat wouldn't be an option.

This wasn't what Malu wanted. He wanted security and prosperity for Northem. That was what he'd fought for his whole life. That was what he may die for.

She laid her head on Malu's chest, holding her breath until the next rattle sounded. 'You can't die for nothing. You can't,' she whispered.

'My lady.'

Theodora sat upright to face Olix, standing in the doorway with his hat in his hands.

'I'm sorry about Malu. We're all praying for him.'

'Thank you,' she mumbled, expecting the merchant to leave now that he'd paid his respects, but he didn't. 'Was there something else?'

'Something?' He shrugged. 'Perhaps nothing.'

'If it's about the ammunition, Hafder knows we are almost out.'

Olix cringed. 'Yes, but it's not that. It's news for you.'

Theodora sat up straighter. 'For me?'

'I have it from the port – word of a girl with Northemer tattoos seeking passage out of Ivane.'

'A deserter?'

Olix shook his head. 'She has silver eyes.'

Rea. It could be no other.

Here was her chance to bring Malu's beloved Kengian back to the fold. Here was their means of victory. This was how they could truly honour the Northern King.

Theodora was on her feet. She released Rayl from her cage and fixed a lead around her neck.

'Take me to her,' she ordered the merchant.

THEODORA DIDN'T TELL Hafder or anyone else where she was going. This was something only she could do.

As the air shook with cannon fire on the plateau, Olix led her to the port city and through the winding streets to the waterfront. Of the few people they encountered in the city, no one questioned or made to approach the riders who had come from the Northemer camp with a snow leopard running alongside. The city's residents scurried like frightened rats, rushing for shelter among the stone buildings that still stood. In its bid to destroy the enemy's ships, the Northemer fleet's cannon fire had gone beyond the water, leaving its devastating mark on the once-thriving metropolis. Stores and marketplaces were reduced to rubble. Shop windows shattered. Bloated bodies lay unclaimed in blood-streaked streets. Theodora pinched her nostrils to shut out the smell of death.

Two Northemer warriors emerged from a well-appointed building sporting jewels and gold. It wasn't unusual for the Northemers to pillage the territories they invaded, but they would never have done it in the middle of a battle under Malu's watch.

'Halt!' she shouted.

The pair stopped mid-step. On recognising Theodora, they exchanged cocky smiles.

She mustered up as much authority as she could manage. 'Get back to the camp at once. Every Northemer is needed for our assault on the city gate.'

'We don't take orders from you,' one of them sneered.

The other spat on the ground. 'Lamorian scum.'

Was this what lay ahead for her if Malu died? Theodora lifted her chin, hoping the quivering of her jaw wasn't visible to them.

'You shall not speak to your King's lady in such a manner,' Olix chastised.

'Doesn't matter if our King is dead,' the spitting Northemer retorted.

'Come on,' the other said to his companion. 'There's plenty more *spoils* to be had elsewhere.'

The Northemer grinned. 'Starting with women who know their place.'

'You bring dishonour on Malu and yourselves!' Theodora yelled after the pair as they strutted away, laughing.

'It will be alright, my lady,' Olix offered. He sounded as unconvinced as she felt.

'Nothing will be alright if Malu doesn't live,' she said to the smoke-filled air. 'Or if I don't succeed in this task.'

Olix led her to the docks. There, he pointed out a boarding house: 'The place the girl was last seen.'

He made an enquiry within and returned quickly.

'She is staying there, but is currently out. Apparently she has been speaking to every fishing boat and trading vessel captain she can find to seek passage out of Ivane. She may be at the tavern.' He pointed to an establishment further along the dock.

Theodora nodded. 'You go look for her there. I'll wait here.'

'Are you sure you'll be sa—?'

Rayl growled in response.

'Never mind. I'll be back soon.'

The merchant had not even been gone five minutes when the figure of a girl in a hooded cloak slipped from an alleyway onto the dock and headed toward the boarding house.

Rayl mewed, as if asking, *Is that her?*

Theodora tilted her head. The figure had none of Rea's usual confident gait, but that wasn't surprising, given what she had been through. Under the shadow of the girl's hood, Theodora gleaned a flash of chestnut hair, but couldn't make out any other details.

Then the figure stopped, turning her head slowly as if sensing something amiss. She raised a hand to shield her eyes from the sun, her cloak falling away from her wrist to reveal a red-and-gold feather tattoo. It was a symbol of a phoenix and the most powerful Kengian magic – the magic of the Firemasters. Yet when Malu had designed it to honour his prodigy's magic and heritage, no one had known the extent of her powers.

'Rea!' Theodora called out, running toward her.

Rea's eyes darted, seeking an escape.

'Don't,' Theodora warned, indicating that she would release the snow leopard.

Rea scowled at her, but didn't run. 'You know I could kill your little cat with a click of my fingers.'

'So your powers do work away from the Alia?'

Rea crossed her arms. 'What do you want?'

'I wanted to make sure you were alright,' Theodora said earnestly, noting that Rea looked as healthy and strong as when she'd first met her. The only difference was that her once-shining silver eyes were dull, tarnished with a layer of pain.

Rea made a *harrumph* sound. 'I'm heartened that you're so concerned about my welfare. I suppose Malu is too.'

Theodora winced. 'He was very worried about you. Losing you was like losing his sister all over again.'

Rea pursed her lips. 'If he's so worried, why isn't he here to tell me himself?'

'Because right now...he's...near death.' Each word slashed Theodora's throat, as if she had swallowed a barbed Batu-riek branch.

Something flickered in Rea's eyes, but her unforgiving pretence remained in place. 'Again. What do you want?'

Anger flared in Theodora. Rea couldn't be that heartless. It had to be an act. Theodora had to appeal to her conscience.

'I'm here to ask you to honour your debt to Malu. The debt you owe him for saving your life.'

'I already served that debt by creating his firesky weapons.' She waved a hand up to the palace city currently under fire from their cannons. 'The same ones you're using to try to destroy Ivane right now.'

'Yes, but you abandoned him in Lamore. Losing that war was devastating to him, but it was a mere shadow of the loss he felt when you left.'

Rea looked away at that. Theodora was hitting her mark.

'It's not too late to atone for hurting him. You can honour your debt while he still lives.'

Rea looked at Theodora again, her features perfectly composed. 'What exactly do you want from me?'

A smile itched at the corner of Theodora's mouth. 'It's simple. I want you to destroy the palace city gate.'

Rea laughed. 'Impossible. It's reinforced with Ivanian steel. There's nothing I can do to make your firesky weapons able to penetrate it. It's impervious.'

Theodora grinned. 'Perhaps not.'

Rea raised a quizzical brow.

'Fire could destroy it. *Phoenix* fire.'

Rea shook her head vehemently. 'I want nothing to do with this. All I want to do is leave this place. I have to get far away from here, where no one wants anything from me.' Her face contorted. 'Where I can't hurt anyone.'

Theodora placed a palm on Rea's arm. 'I understand. We don't want to hurt anyone either.'

'Ha!' Rea flung Theodora's hand away. 'I suppose killing hundreds, possibly *thousands* of innocent people isn't the same as hurting them.'

Theodora was losing her. She would need to tread carefully. 'I meant that we don't want people to die unnecessarily. All we want is what Malu has always wanted. To secure land and resources for his people. You know what it's like in Northem. It's only a matter of time before they have another great famine like the one that took Malu's family.'

Rea frowned. 'You should ask for Ivane's *help* instead of trying to take the country by force.'

'Help is for countries that have something to give in return. What does Northem have to give, other than mountains of dried fish?'

Rea shuddered, seemingly remembering the Northemer diet. Theodora was making headway.

'I can see you understand what it is to be a Northemer. It is why you must honour your debt to Malu. It is the Northemer way.'

Rea compressed her lips. 'I am not a Northemer.'

'Honour is also the Kengian way.'

'I am Kengian only by blood,' Rea said through clenched teeth.

Theodora softened her voice. 'I understand what it's like to be nationless. I am no longer Lamorian, and I am not a Northemer, no matter how hard I try. But this doesn't change who we are. And you, Rea, are someone who understands honour. You know you still owe Malu, and you won't be able to live with yourself if he dies before you honour that debt.'

Rea closed her eyes and took a deep breath. She opened them again, her face devoid of any emotion.

'If I help you destroy the gate, my debt will be paid?'

Theodora nodded.

'I have already caused too many deaths.' Rea peered down at her hands. 'I never asked for these powers, and I have no wish to use them ever again.'

'Will you help us?'

'I don't know. But if I do...I never want to see or speak to you or Malu again – assuming he survives.'

Theodora's heart registered a pang of hurt. 'But I'm your friend.'

Rea gave her a sympathetic look. 'I'm not sure you understand friendship.' Her gaze went to Rayl. 'Even that animal of yours is part of a symbiotic relationship with you – a relationship that is based on codependence, not friendship. You feed it. It protects you. You are using it and it is using you for survival. You use people the same way.'

'I don't!' Theodora protested, but Rea's words cut deep. Theodora didn't have friends; she had people who could help her. There had been Selina, who had fed her ego at the Lamorian court. Jade, who had helped her find Rea. But Rea…That was different…Wasn't it?

'I can see what you're thinking, but we are not friends, Theodora. We never have been.'

It was too much for Theodora to accept. 'What do you know of friendship?' she hissed. 'The only friend you ever had left you for dead when you were a child.'

'Arisa didn't have a choice,' Rea said in a quiet voice.

'How do you know? She speaks nothing but lies. Even now, she claims you're family. And what kind of family abandons its members?'

Rea's hand went under her cloak, presumably to an unseen weapon. 'Get out of here!'

'We may not be friends, but Malu and I are all you've got. You owe this to him.'

'*Go!*' Rea screeched.

BACK AT THE CAMP, Theodora returned to her tent, not knowing if she had convinced Rea to honour her debt to Malu. She crawled into the bed she shared with the Northern King, curling up beside him. His skin was cool against hers, which was permanently covered in a film of sweat courtesy of Ivane's sweltering daytime temperatures. But she could derive no comfort from it.

Cold skin meant life was seeping from him – and hers along with it.

She fought her body's demand for sleep, determined to watch Malu throughout the night. She clung to every one of his laboured breaths as a sign of hope. That and the relentless sound of the firesky cannons should have been enough to keep her awake, but eventually sleep found her.

THEODORA WAS WOKEN BY A NOISE – a voice.

'Good...morning,' someone croaked beside her.

She sat up and blinked rapidly, trying to adjust her eyes to the rays of early morning light piercing the tent. Malu slowly came into focus.

Eyes open. Colour in his face. Alive!

Her hand went to her mouth and a tidal wave of relief flooded her body. 'You're alive,' she sobbed. 'You're alive.'

Malu propped himself up on a pillow, groaning as he did so. 'Despite the Ivanians' best efforts.' He flinched as he made to give a dismissive wave.

'My love!' Theodora exclaimed, throwing her arms around him.

'Easy does it,' he said, holding a hand to his stomach. 'And how do you fare? Last I saw, you were surrounded by enemy soldiers...in the middle of the battlefield.' He cocked his head. 'Precisely the opposite of where I left you.'

She bit her lip. 'I couldn't stand by and watch everyone put their lives on the line while I did nothing.'

'Mmm.' Malu tucked a dark wave of hair behind her ear. 'I can't be angry with you for giving in to the lion's heart I know you possess, but if something were to happen to you...I don't know what I'd do.'

She leant forward and kissed him on the lips. 'I feel the same.' A bright smile spread across her face. 'My foray into battle wasn't a complete waste. I managed to shoot Arisa.'

Malu raised both his brows. 'Huzzah, my girl.'

Theodora shrugged. 'Didn't kill her. She is injured, though…Badly, I hope.'

His blue eyes twinkled. 'My Queen has tasted her first blood. We will celebrate – but first, tell me what I've missed.'

Theodora filled him in on the Ivanians' retreat and how Hafder had ordered the Northemers to concentrate all of their cannon fire on the city gate.

Malu trained his ear to the air, which was still punctuated by regular cannon fire – but the intensity had noticeably decreased, and there were longer gaps between each round.

'A sensible strategy,' he affirmed, 'but by the sounds of it, our ammunition is low.'

Theodora nodded.

A twinge of pain flickered in his eyes – physically or mentally induced, or perhaps both. He bowed his head. 'I'm sorry, my love, but I may not be able to give you Ivane. We must be prepared to retreat if we can't break down the gate before reinforcements arrive.'

Theodora didn't mention her meeting with Rea, in case it amounted to nothing. Instead she reached out to cup his chin. 'I don't need Ivane. I only need you.' Malu's chest lifted with a deep, life-affirming breath. 'But your brother appears to have other ideas.'

Malu sighed and swung his legs slowly over the side of the bed. 'That is the problem with my brother. He is so single-minded, focused on the next battle – he can never unite Northem.'

'But I thought Northemers relished battle?'

'We do…when it's necessary. While all Northemers are warriors at heart, we are human first.' He spoke in a measured tone, his back to Theodora, as if he were explaining himself to the world and not her alone. 'Many of us, if given the choice, would choose our own lives or those of our families over death. Some, of course, are like Hafder – they are true soldiers, born with an axe in their hand. But they lack the ability to see beyond the battlefield, to be prepared to make the hard decisions and put their own needs behind those of our country.'

Listening to Malu, Theodora thought she finally understood what it meant to be a Northemer, or at least a great leader. 'So there can be honour in retreat?' she said hesitantly. 'Because you're saving lives, preserving some future for your people?'

He turned to face her, peacefulness in his features. 'Exactly. It is why you must lead Northem if anything happens to me.'

'No, no, no.' She jumped up from the bed. 'Nothing's going to happen to you.'

Malu got to his feet, a tentative hand on his belly. 'But it might. And it must be you who takes my place.'

She shook her head. 'They'd never accept me.'

'They will.' He took her hands in his. 'If you're my wife.'

'But I'm not...'

Her words trailed away, because Malu was already gone, ordering a surprised guard to bring Hafder and Olix to him.

'No, Malu.' She went after him. 'Not now. Not for this reason.'

Malu returned and met her halfway across the tent, a face-splitting smile plastered across his face. 'This is not the reason. It is a sign that you must be my Queen in every sense.'

Hafder arrived at the tent, out of breath. 'Brother! I'm so glad...It's a miracle.' He embraced Malu.

'A miracle indeed,' Malu declared as he stepped out of Hafder's arms. 'We have much to discuss.'

Hafder grunted his acknowledgement. 'Our ammunition on land is nearly gone – the hand cannon shot is all gone – but we are making progress with the cannons. With luck we will breach the gate before our supplies run out.'

'And if we don't?' Malu asked.

'We fight,' Hafder said, thumping a fist to his chest. 'We fight the Ivanians, we fight the Lamorians, we fight the Kengians...and we prevail or die in our attempts.'

Malu's face was unmoving. 'Fortunately that is no longer a decision for you to make, now that I'm alive, and all that.'

Hafder's jaw tensed, but he said nothing.

'In any case, I have asked you here for something else.'

'Your Majesty!' Olix appeared at the tent doorway. 'You're alive!'

'I am,' Malu said. 'Is it not true, Olix, that you are also a ship's captain?'

Olix gave him a perplexed look. 'Yes, that is true.'

'And as a ship's captain, you can conduct a marriage ceremony, recognised in the eyes of the law.'

Olix looked from Malu to Theodora and back again with a growing smile. 'That is also true.'

Hafder muttered a string of inaudible Northem words under his breath.

Malu clapped his hands together. 'Splendid!'

THE MARRIAGE CEREMONY that followed was a simplified one, based on a Northemer handfasting custom. A ribbon was found among Theodora's belongings; a drop of her blood and Malu's was pressed on either end. Malu crossed his hands, taking Theodora's right one in his right, and her left one in his left. Olix bound their entwined hands with the ribbon, asking them to repeat vows as he wrapped.

'We are bonded as one in heart, mind and spirit,' they said, each word carrying Theodora away from their troubles and Hafder's disapproving stare. Under Malu's steady gaze, she went to a place of complete acceptance and unconditional love. Nothing had ever felt so natural. 'We are one in life, sharing our every joy, our every pleasure, and facing every challenge as one, stronger together.'

Theodora's heartbeat slowed to match Malu's weakened pulse beating against her palm.

'We are one until the end, bonded until death and beyond.'

They were more than words. They were more than a promise. This was their destiny. Nothing else was meant to be; nothing else could have been.

Olix nodded at Hafder. 'As has been witnessed, you are now man and wife.'

Then Malu's lips were on hers. His kiss gentle, loving. She returned in kind, laughing as Olix unwrapped their hands and gave her the ribbon. Rayl mewed her approval from her cage.

Malu slapped his brother on the back. 'Do I have your congratulations?'

'Congratulations,' he mumbled, giving Theodora the tiniest of nods.

Malu's smile vanished. A dangerous glint came to his eyes. 'Congratulations, Your Majesty,' he corrected. 'Theodora is now your Queen.'

'It's alright,' Theodora said, not wishing to further alienate Hafder.

'It's not alright. You will give Theodora the respect she is owed.'

'Congratulations, Your Majesty,' Hafder said through gritted teeth, giving a half-hearted bow.

'Thank you.'

Hafder spun on his heels and marched out of the tent.

'He hates me,' she said.

Malu waved his hand. 'He hates that you are closer to me, and the crown, than he is.'

'Your Majesty,' Olix addressed Malu, reaching inside his coat. 'The gift you asked for.' He handed over a brown paper parcel.

Malu thanked the merchant, who bowed and left.

'Now, don't get too excited – this is more of a gift for your friend' – Malu indicated Rayl – 'than you.' He handed the parcel to Theodora. 'I have spent all our gold on this campaign, but as soon as it is over, I will get you your own gift.'

Theodora opened the parcel to reveal a fine black leather

collar. A line of pyramid-shaped spikes made of silver ran the length of it.

'It's beautiful,' she gushed, letting the cat out of the cage and fastening the collar around her neck.

'A collar worthy of a royal companion,' Malu asserted.

'Thank you, *husband.*'

'You are welcome, *wife.*' He grinned wickedly and took her in his arms.

Just as their lips met, a screeching sound split the air.

'What was that?' Malu asked.

The screech sounded again overhead. There was great shouting and screams in the distance.

A knowing smile came to Theodora's face.

'It's *my* gift to you,' she said.

36

*T*he reckoning arrived in the form of the firebird, attacking the city.

'Fire!' Noemi commanded her archers on the boundary wall, as the phoenix swooped low toward the city gate for a third time. Each time the firebird neared the gate, she opened her beak and blasted silver fire against the timber and steel, scorching the timber façade, stripping it away layer by layer. The heat from the flames shimmered in the air – suffocating in its intensity.

A hundred more arrows were fired at the phoenix, disintegrating on contact with the creature's body. She launched herself back into the sky, circling, readying for another assault. Arisa spotted Sar standing among the Ivanian soldiers, six rows deep on the ground, watching with horror as the steel in the city gate glowed red, then began creaking and buckling under the power of the Firemaster's flames.

Arisa's head whirled. She couldn't believe her friend was attacking the palace city. For a moment in Oisiri, she'd thought she had connected with Rea – kin to kin. It made no sense, what Rea was doing...unless Theodora had got to her.

Arisa looked across the plateau in the direction of the

Northemer camp. The enemy was racing into formation, preparing to advance. Malu, who still lived, was at their head.

On the phoenix's next descent, Arisa tried to catch the creature's eye.

Why are you doing this? She planted the thought in Rea's mind.

The firebird's head swivelled toward her. She stopped in the air in front of Arisa. The phoenix hovered, flapping her fiery wings to stay in place, scrutinising Arisa with unyielding silver eyes.

'Reload!' Noemi ordered. The archers scrambled to fire again. Next to Arisa, Takai loaded his longbow.

The phoenix opened her beak and cawed fire. The word *honour* seemed to crackle among the flames that licked the parapet.

Don't do this, Arisa pleaded.

Another caw. *I must. I will not kill unless I have to, but I must repay my debt.*

'She's doing this for Malu,' Arisa muttered to herself. 'Repaying her debt to him.' She grabbed Takai's arm, preventing him from firing his arrow. 'Don't.'

Takai's brow furrowed in confusion. 'We have to stop her before she kills us all.'

'No. She doesn't want to hurt us.'

'She just spat fire at you. It's too late to save her. She's a killer!'

The firebird threw back her head and screeched as if she were mortally wounded by Takai's words, leaving Arisa in no doubt. There was nothing she could do to stop Rea.

The phoenix plunged back down toward the gate and roared fire, the timber now well alight and the steel rapidly bending into submission.

'No, this is different. Deliberate. She's focusing her efforts on the gate and the gate only. She hasn't hurt anyone.'

Takai cast his gaze across the battlements and the ground below, seeing what Arisa knew to be true. No one was injured.

'And firing arrows at her,' Arisa continued, 'is a waste of ammunition. Ammunition that we're going to need.'

Takai clenched his jaw, his eyes now on the Northemer forces, which were rapidly approaching.

'Noemi,' he called out to his cousin, nodding to the Northemers.

The Ivanian Commander took one look across the plain and reached for her sword. 'Get to safety,' she ordered Takai.

'We have to put up a fight,' Takai argued. 'We have to take a stand here.'

Noemi's face hardened. 'I'll do what I can to slow them down, but you must take all of the units but one, and get my father back to the palace – defend him with your life.' For the first time since Arisa had met the girl, there was no sign of arrogance, just a familiar steeliness. The same formidable determination as Noemi's aunt, Sofia, and Arisa's mother, Gwyn – they too were great warriors, forged within these city walls.

Takai looked to the Northemers and back at Noemi. 'I'm not leaving.'

'Damn you!' Noemi said. 'I have to give my people a chance. I have to do what is asked of me, but I can't do it if my father is in danger. If he dies, everything is lost.'

Arisa placed her hand on Takai's arm. 'This is what she must do. You believe in her, don't you?'

Takai's muscles tensed under her palm, but slowly, he nodded.

Noemi exhaled. 'Good. And if you can't hold the palace, you must make sure he escapes.'

'Escapes?'

'There is a set of secret tunnels – my father and Ambra know where they are. Take the tunnels from the palace down to a cave by the sea. There you will find a sloop. Small but fast. Take my father to safety.'

Takai nodded gravely. 'We won't need to escape. I do believe in you, Noemi.'

She gave a wry smile. 'At least somebody does.'

The stone floor beneath their feet shuddered, the sound of creaking metal intensifying to a scream. *Snap. Snap. Snap.*

The bulging steel bars of the gate had given way at their centre, leaving a gaping hole.

'Go!' Noemi yelled.

37

*T*he Northemers lowered the shield wall that protected Theodora after the last of the archers on the boundary wall fell. She watched with glee as the city gate finally collapsed and Hafder led a charge toward the remaining soldiers on the ground. The Northemers' battle cries sang in her ears as their blades hacked out a path for their victory march into Nadis. The terror in the eyes of the enemy was palpable, feeding her thirst for revenge.

Her bargaining when she'd thought Malu was dying was disregarded now. Her vow to forgo vengeance and Ivane if he survived was overshadowed by the promise of power – so close now she could feel it coursing through her veins. They would take the palace and Ivane. Malu had said he wanted to win this for his people, and for her, but from the glint in his eyes and the way he squeezed her hand, she knew he too couldn't resist the power on offer. Perhaps he'd just forgotten the exhilaration of being unstoppable.

'It's happening,' Malu said in wonder, his glacial blue eyes reflecting the silver flames that rose from what was left of the city gate. 'Once we have the palace and their King, we're invincible. Thanks to Rea.'

He peered up into the sky, smiling at Rea in her phoenix form like a proud father, then he looked back to Theodora.

'And thanks to you, my love.' He stroked the ribbon wrapped around her forearm, the same one that had been used for their handfasting ceremony. Her pulse quickened at his touch. 'My love, my wife, my Queen.' He lifted her hand to his mouth and kissed it. 'And now Rea has come back to us, we can be a family together.' Rayl mewed behind Theodora's back, and Malu laughed. 'You too, kitty cat.'

Theodora didn't want to be the one to tell him it could never happen. She didn't want to be responsible for breaking Malu's heart, but she had to tell him. She pulled her hand away.

A wave of concern washed over his face. 'What is it?'

'Rea only agreed to help us destroy the gate on one condition.' She paused to take a breath. 'That she would be freed of her debt to you.'

Malu closed his eyes. 'So she will leave me again?'

'She will.'

When he opened his eyes they were awash with tears. 'I asked too much of her.'

'Don't blame yourself. You saved her. She could very well have chosen Arisa over you, but she didn't. She chose you.'

'Out of honour?'

Theodora nodded.

'That I understand,' he said, the sound of his heart breaking present in each syllable.

A screech above. The phoenix inclined her head at them and, with a flap of her fiery wings, flew up and away over the palace city.

Hafder stomped toward them, dragging a crumpled figure in an Ivanian uniform along the ground behind him. 'I've got a gift for you,' he told Malu.

On the ground lay a girl, no older than Rea. One of her eyes was swollen shut. Underneath a layer of sand, blood ran from her nose and mouth, and gushed from her torso where her leather chest armour was slashed.

'She's one of their Commanders.'

'Is she alive?' Theodora asked.

Hafder kicked the girl and she groaned.

'It's the one who nearly killed you, brother.'

Malu squatted and tilted his head, scrutinising her face. 'She's just a girl.' He stood up, holding a hand to his belly where the girl had sliced him open.

'A troublesome one at that,' Hafder grunted. 'A dozen of our warriors had her cornered, but she wouldn't go down without a fight. Killed half of them.' He kicked her in the gut.

The girl's eyes flew open. 'Don't touch me, filthy pig!' she shouted in Ivanian, pushing herself up to her knees.

Hafder bent down and held a knife to the girl's throat. 'Should you kill her or should I?'

Malu shook his head. 'Leave her be. Let her watch as we take her city.'

Hafder's lip curled in disgust. He tightened his grip around the knife.

'Leave her be!'

Hafder dropped the knife on the ground and strode away.

Malu's face twisted in pain and Theodora's hand went instinctively to his arm. 'It's alright,' she said, knowing he couldn't take the girl's life so soon after losing Rea forever.

No one noticed the Ivanian girl springing to her feet with Hafder's abandoned knife in her hand. No one other than Rayl.

The snow leopard pounced on the girl as she lunged at Malu's back. A growl, a spray of blood, a whimper. The girl was back on the ground. One hand clutched her neck, futilely trying to stem the bleeding.

Theodora stood over the girl, hating her as much as she admired the defiance in her dark eyes.

'Give up now,' Theodora said in Ivanian. 'It's over.'

The girl laughed, spluttering blood onto Theodora's boots. 'For me...perhaps...but Ivane will live on.'

Malu tugged at Theodora's arm and gestured toward the city. The enemy was in full retreat. 'It's time.'

38

*F*lanked by Takai, Letoi, Sar and Arisa, King Laskar rode back to the palace, watching in bewilderment as his beloved city fell around him.

Laskar had initially refused the plan to take him to the palace and mount their final defence there. On learning that Noemi had stayed at the city gate, he'd wrestled against Letoi, trying to get to his horse so he could join his daughter. It had taken all of their combined strength and reasoning to get him to capitulate. Noemi had done what was needed to protect the future of their nation, but there would be no Ivane without their King.

Arisa could understand why the King was crushed and confused. The fact that his magnificent palace city had fallen defied his belief; his great Ivane that had defeated its oppressors, the Lamorians, more than once in battle. But that was before – before the time of firesky weapons. If only Arisa had her powers...But it was a wasted wish. Even if she could harness her Water Catcher magic, she knew she was no match for Rea – the daughter of a Firemaster and Kengia's greatest Scholar.

So they raced past overturned stalls, across ground strewn with smashed goods. The remains of shattered fountains teetered like broken teeth while Nadis's residents scattered in every direction, desperately seeking shelter. The heart-wrenching screams of those who came face-to-face with the invading Northemers cleaved the air. Black smoke rose in the sky like poisonous mushrooms, signalling the destruction of centuries-old buildings and the city gate.

They reached the palace unscathed and dismounted along-side the elongated pool that marked the entrance. The pool, with its thousands of glittering, star-shaped gold tiles, shim-mered in all its spectacular glory, oblivious to the ugliness around them.

Ambra came running out to meet them with the palace guards.

'Take the King to his rooms,' Letoi instructed them. 'Guard him with your lives.'

'The tunnels,' Takai addressed Ambra. 'If the palace falls, you must take him there.'

'Yes, to the sloop,' Letoi added. 'Make for Ette.'

Ambra nodded, but King Laskar stood fixed to the ground. He unsheathed his sabre. 'I cannot run from battle. My people need me.'

Takai placed a hand on his uncle's shoulder. 'Your people need you alive. When this is all over, they will need your leader-ship. You must leave the fighting to us.'

It occurred to Arisa that Lamore needed its King too. It needed Takai. *She* needed Takai. But this was the man she had fallen in love with. A man who'd give anything for those he cared about, even if it meant sacrificing his own happiness, or his life.

A sad smile tugged at the corner of Laskar's mouth. 'There is no doubt: you are your mother's son. A true Ivanian.'

'We must go,' Ambra urged the King.

'With honour,' Laskar said, nodding at Letoi and Takai, then at Arisa. 'And courage.'

'With honour and courage,' they responded. The King lifted his chin and strode back into the palace.

'Barricade all the entrances and guard everyone inside,' Letoi ordered the soldiers who had come with them, leaving just himself, Arisa, Takai and Sar as the last barrier between the Northemers and the palace.

The screams intensified in the distance. They were coming from the city gate. The sound of battle drums hammered toward them.

'They've done it,' Takai said, loading his bow and arrow. 'They've defeated our forces at the gate.'

Sar patted down his chest armour and boots, checking his knives and swords were in place. 'Malu will be on his way.'

Arisa reached for her long and short swords, ignoring the throbbing in her injured arm. 'As well as Theodora and her snow leopard.'

A protracted screech perforated the air. All eyes went to the phoenix in the sky, approaching their position and heading toward the sea.

'Shoot it!' Letoi shouted at Takai.

'No!' Arisa cried. 'She doesn't want to hurt anyone.'

'Not *hurt* anyone?' Letoi stabbed his sword into the air, as if he were stabbing the firebird. 'She made sure our city was penetrated. She is responsible for every Ivanian death on this day!'

'But she had no choice,' Arisa objected.

'How would you know what the creature thinks?' Letoi yelled.

'Because she told me. We're connected. We're family.' She added the last part in a quiet voice.

'Family?' Letoi looked to Takai and Sar for confirmation, but didn't wait for an answer. Instead he grabbed Takai's longbow and, amid their protests, fired at the phoenix.

It was a fine shot, but as expected, the arrow crumbled into a shower of ash as soon as it made contact with the firebird.

Takai snatched his weapon back off the Ivanian. 'We must save our ammunition for the Northemers.'

A collective roar rang out in the streets below. The enemy was closing in on them.

Arisa looked back to the sky, hoping to catch Rea's eye for one last time. Hoping she could send her friend a final message. That she understood why Rea had done it. And that she was sorry. Sorry she had ever left her on that Lamorian ship. Sorry Rea had had to go through life without knowing her father. Sorry it had ever come to this.

Her gaze went to the phoenix now directly above them, but something else caught her attention.

A hundred yards from them, an Ivanian girl with wild black hair – the girl Arisa had seen with Theodora in Oisiri – had loaded a bow and was training her arrow on Rea. It was no ordinary arrow. Bile rose in Arisa's throat as she recognised the Alia arrowhead and the shaft made of unusual wood.

'*Rea*,' Arisa said breathlessly as the girl released the arrow.

The Alia projectile arced swift and true, piercing the firebird's fiery form.

A visceral scream erupted from the phoenix's beak. Arisa's own scream and gasps of surprise from her companions followed.

The firebird's wings staggered to a stop – and then the creature fell. But it was not the creature anymore. It was Rea in her human form, plummeting to the ground. Arisa looked helplessly at her hands, cursing them for their lack of magic. She closed her eyes, registering Rea's landing from a splash and a sickening thud.

Arisa's eyes sprang open. Rea had landed in the pool. It was only knee-deep, but it would have gone some way toward breaking her fall.

She raced to the pool. A cloud of red was spreading rapidly from Rea's face-down body.

Arisa called for Takai's help as she jumped into the water.

Together, they turned the limp body over. The arrow stuck out from Rea's chest.

'I don't understand,' Sar said. 'I thought our weapons wouldn't—'

'The arrowhead was made of Alia crystal,' Arisa explained, leaning over to check whether Rea was still breathing. There was nothing.

Letoi's eyes widened. 'The shaft is made from a Batu-riek tree. That's how it survived the phoenix's fire.' His face hardened. 'Who dared to defile our most sacred items?' He looked in the direction of the Ivanian girl, but she was gone.

'Is she...?' Takai didn't need to finish the question. Arisa knew what he was asking.

She checked for a heartbeat, her ear against Rea's sodden chest. 'Come on, Rea. Come on.'

At first Arisa heard nothing above the sound of battle – but then...a *ba-dum*. Muffled and weak, but still a beat. She counted inwardly: one, two, three, four, five...*Ba-dum*.

'She's alive...just,' Arisa announced. 'We have to save her.'

Letoi shook his head. 'Let the witch die.'

Arisa stood up tall. She was at least a foot shorter than Letoi, but she would not be intimidated. She looked the Ivanian squarely in the eye. 'She is no witch. She is my family. And we will save her.'

'We shall not!'

'If we save her, she may help us.'

Letoi didn't look convinced.

Arisa softened her tone. 'Please, you must trust me.'

Letoi crossed his arms and said nothing.

'Let me ask you,' Takai addressed him. 'Do you trust me?'

Letoi screwed up his mouth. 'If you had asked me that question a week ago, I would have said no. But I have seen you fight. I have seen you put yourself on the line for my country and agree with my King. You are Ivanian. So...yes...I trust you.'

Takai visibly exhaled. 'Then you must trust Arisa. She has never failed me.'

Letoi's shoulders heaved as he took two deep breaths. Then he sheathed his sword. 'What do you need?'

'The Alia Water,' Arisa said. 'Ambra has it.'

Letoi nodded, then raced for the palace door.

Sar cocked his head as if listening for something in particular among the cacophony of battle noise.

'What is it?' Takai asked.

Sar reached for his broadsword. 'Horses, coming this way. Near.'

Takai leapt from the pool with his own sword at the ready. The pair stood close together, shielding Arisa while she held her dying friend in her arms.

It was mere moments before the riders appeared. Malu, Hafder and Theodora, her snow leopard running beside her. A few dozen Northem warriors trailed on foot behind.

The Northem leader's eyes went straight to Rea.

'What have you done to her?' he howled. He dismounted and ran toward them, but Takai and Sar blocked his path.

Theodora hurried to Malu's side. Her sharp eyes took in the scene and the arrow still protruding from Rea's chest.

'*Jade*,' she whispered.

'Let us be, so I can help her,' Arisa pleaded.

Hafder threw back his head in laughter. 'Let you be. I'll let you be *dead*.' He held up his axe and took three steps forward, so he was only a few feet from Sar.

Malu held out a hand to calm his brother. 'Can you save her?' he asked Arisa.

'Perhaps. I have sent for medicine.'

He nodded. 'Save her.'

Hafder's visible eye rolled. 'Then we kill them?'

'Then we kill them,' Theodora said. Malu didn't contradict her. 'Starting with her.' She pointed at Arisa.

'Why can't *we* just kill *them*...now?' Sar quipped.

'You could try,' Hafder snarled back at him.

'No one is *trying* anything,' a female voice warned across the courtyard.

They all turned to see Isla marching, albeit a little clumsily, toward them. The vial of Alia Water in one hand, a sword in the other.

'Isla!' Arisa and Sar cried in unison.

Isla wobbled up to the pool, letting Sar support her by the arm. 'Well, you didn't think you could have a war without me, did you?'

'That's what I said!' Sar replied. 'I knew we were meant for each other.'

'Enough!' Malu screamed. Arisa had never seen the Northem leader so rattled. He waved a sword in Rea's direction. 'Get on with it.'

Arisa took the half-full vial from Isla. She hoped it would be enough. 'I need you to remove the arrow,' she told Takai.

Letoi, who'd returned with Isla, joined Sar to keep watch on the Northemers as Takai helped Arisa.

He grasped the arrow's shaft and looked at her, his gaze steady and believing. 'Are you ready?'

No, she wasn't ready, but she had to be. She took the stopper from the vial with shaking hands and nodded. Everyone around her was silent. 'I'm ready.'

With one smooth movement, Takai pulled the arrow out of Rea's chest. Arisa rushed to pour the Alia Water onto the wound as blood gushed from it. The pool turned a rich shade of claret.

Arisa put her head to Rea's chest. There was no *ba-dum*. 'It's not working.'

Malu and Hafder exchanged a dangerous glance.

Theodora glared at Arisa, but then she narrowed her eyes, staring at the pool. 'Look!'

Arisa followed her gaze. An orb of silver light had formed around Rea's body. The glow slowly ballooned, consuming the blood in the water, until both Rea and Arisa were completely surrounded by light. Arisa's whole body buzzed with energy, as it had done in Oisiri.

Rea's eyes flew open and she sat up, taking a sharply drawn breath.

Arisa made a sound that was half laugh, half sob. 'You're alive!'

Rea's eyes darted around as she sucked in giant mouthfuls of air. 'I didn't want to...' she said between gasps. 'It was for...honour.'

Arisa smiled at her friend. 'I know.'

Rea turned to look at Malu. 'Say...I'm released...from my debt.'

'You're released,' he said slowly, his cold eyes swimming with tears.

Sar held a finger to his mouth. 'Did you hear that?'

Isla tilted her head. 'Kengian horn calls.'

Sar grinned. 'And Lamorian bugles.'

Everyone trained their ears to the air. They, too, could hear it.

Takai's face lit up. 'The reinforcements.'

Theodora shot a desperate look at Malu, but his eyes were still on Rea. 'Come back to us,' he said earnestly. 'It is where you belong.'

Rea jutted out her chin. 'I don't belong anywhere.'

Arisa reached for her cousin's hand. 'You belong everywhere. You are Kengian. You are Ettean. You have lived in Lamore. You have been healed by Ivane's sacred river. You belong to all of Kypria, but most of all you belong with us.' Arisa indicated herself and Isla. 'With family.' Isla nodded her confirmation.

'Don't listen to her!' Theodora yelled. 'She lies.'

Arisa shook her head vehemently. 'Look inside yourself and you will see. We are the ones who are born of fire and water. We are sisters in blood.'

Rea stared into Arisa's eyes. Silver meeting silver. Her pupils flared.

She could see it.

A series of cannon-fire blasts echoed from the sea. The Lamorian and Kengian ships were attacking the Northemer fleet.

'Choose now, Rea,' Malu snapped. 'Come with us and live, or stay here and die.'

But Rea ignored him. *Did you feel it?* she planted in Arisa's mind. *The magic in the water?*

I did, Arisa replied. *The power of fire and water, together.*

Rea raised both brows in challenge, and Arisa nodded.

'How about a third choice?' Rea threw back at Malu.

'Remember Oisiri?' Arisa said in a low voice to Isla, who grasped her meaning and prompted Takai, Sar and Letoi to fall back. Malu, Hafder and Theodora looked at each other in puzzlement.

Arisa stood up in the pool. Tendrils of silver light snaked their way into her body, awakening a familiar warmth inside her. The magic she had come to master in Kengia sparked to life, a sense of *kira* filling her being. She focused on the water and raised her hands, but nothing happened. Her muscles tensed. Tendons strained, popping from her forearms and hands, as she visualised the water moving.

She thought back to everything she had done in previous battles, how her power and the water were hers to command. She drew on the belief others had in her. How Amund had believed in her. How her parents, aunt and grandmother believed in her. How Takai believed in her. She drew on their love and her love for them. She drew on her connection to Rea, through blood, fire and water. And she drew a lungful of air.

Then, slowly at first, the water rose.

Arisa raised her hands higher, lifting all the water until it hovered over her head. Rea raised her own hands, fire springing from her palms as she murmured a Kengian spell.

In perfect synchronisation, Arisa launched the water at the Northemers and Rea threw fireballs at it. With a mighty *whoosh*, the water caught alight, forming a barrier of firewater between themselves and the Northemers. Silver fire and water weaved through each other in a perfectly choreographed dance. Fingers of translucent flame spat from an undulating wall, equally beautiful and terrifying.

'*No!*' Theodora screeched. Her snow leopard swatted at the firewater, but recoiled as it scorched its paw. Hafder stared defiantly at them through the flames as if he could conquer them.

Malu closed his eyes for a moment, and when he reopened them, it was Theodora he looked to first. A look of apology. After a protracted pause, Theodora bowed her head in acceptance.

'Retreat,' Malu said to his brother. He turned his back on all of them and called out to his forces. 'Retreat!'

39

*A*nger coursed through Theodora's veins as she fled with the Northemers from the palace city. No, it was much more than anger. It was *fury* – that once again they had been outplayed by Arisa. Not only had the Kengian found some way to conjure up her Water Catcher powers, but she had taken Rea from them.

Theodora had been filled with grief when she'd seen Rea lying near-dead in the pool. Her thoughts had immediately gone to how she would hunt down Jade and kill her, but then Arisa had saved Rea, and hope had sprung in Theodora. She had been sure that if Rea was alive, she could bring her back into the fold. She could do that for Malu and for the Northemers – she could secure their victory, even over the reinforced enemy.

But Rea had chosen Arisa, and now Theodora wished her former friend was dead – at least that way they would only have had to fight one lot of Kengian magic. Instead, because of Theodora's failure, they would be lucky to make it out of Nadis alive.

They rode into the port city, ignoring the jeers from the celebrating residents, who threw all manner of objects at them. A rotten tomato struck Theodora in the face, the stench of decaying fruit clinging to her nostrils well after she wiped it away.

'Our cause isn't dead yet!' Malu shouted to his ranks. His assurances were lost on their Ivanian mercenaries, who surreptitiously slipped away into the city's alleyways.

'We'll take our longships from port and take the fight to sea,' Malu told Olix, who rode ahead to make the arrangements. Hafder rallied the Northemers, and they roared their blood-curdling battle cries in the Ivanians' faces. But they were confronted with the full extent of their plight when they arrived at the docks.

The edge of the harbour, where a line of Northemer long-ships should have been, was blocked by a dozen Lamorian and Kengian warships. In the distance, dozens more were engaged, fighting what was left of the Northem fleet – a score of much smaller ships, though faster and more manoeuvrable than the enemy's. Both sides were armed with firesky weapons and alternating cannon fire bounced across the waves.

'Where are the rest of our ships?' Malu asked Olix.

'Destroyed,' he said simply.

Theodora could see the cogs in Malu's mind turning, calculating whether they could prevail with the number of vessels they still had.

'Can we still win?' she said in a low voice only Malu could hear.

He took her by the arm and steered her away so they couldn't be overheard. 'Perhaps. But only if—'

'—the Water Catcher and Rea don't join the fight,' she finished for him.

Malu rubbed his beard. 'Alia. They need Alia to use their powers to enough effect. You saw the water in the pool – it turned silver. Whatever Arisa poured on Rea's wound must have come from Alia.' His fingers stilled. 'And she used all she had in that bottle.'

'You don't think she has more?'

'If they did, they would have used it before now.' A twinkle came to his eye. 'In any case, I'm willing to take the risk if you are.' He took both her hands in his. 'We've come this far...'

He looked to Theodora for approval. Approval she couldn't deny him. He wanted Ivane for Northem. He wanted it for her.

'I trust you, husband,' she said.

'And I love you, my Queen,' he said softly, and kissed her – gently at first, then hungrily. Hungry for her. Hungry for victory. Finally he released her, leaving the sweet taste of power dancing on her lips.

'All we need to do is get ourselves a ship to get out there,' he said hopefully.

'Brother!' Hafder cried, pointing at an approaching Lamorian galleon, and Theodora's last hope of winning vanished.

'Arm yourselves!' Malu ordered his warriors. 'Archers, take aim.'

The Northemers scrambled into formation, all praying the enemy warship didn't open fire on them. Inexplicably, though, the Lamorian crew on the ship's decks made no move to light their cannons.

The explanation appeared in the form of Theodora's father, standing tall on the foredeck.

A smirk was visible underneath Horace's mask of red, blistered and peeling skin as the ship pulled up in front of them. Rayl bared her teeth and snarled. Confused murmurs rose among the Northemers as they recognised Horace. Theodora heard someone say, 'Isn't he supposed to be dead?'

'I don't understand,' she muttered, then called up to her father, 'How did you—?'

'Survive being left for dead in the desert?' His gaze hardened. 'You can thank some kind-hearted Ivanian farmers for taking pity on an *innocent victim* of the wicked Northemers.'

Theodora rolled her eyes. 'I should have known he'd survive,' she murmured to Malu. 'Cockroaches are indestructible.'

Malu merely smiled and raised his gaze to Horace. 'Ahoy there, sailor. Don't suppose you could give passage to' – he flung his hand to his chest – 'some poor defenceless souls.'

'Of course.' Horace sounded benevolent, but Theodora could see in the way he looked down his nose at Malu that he was revelling in the power shift. 'If you agree to one thing.'

'Whatever it is,' Hafder growled, 'say no.'

Malu's smile only broadened. 'Anything for my beloved father-in-law.'

Horace raised a questioning brow at Theodora.

'It is true,' she confirmed. 'We are married.'

Something that may have been admiration flickered across Horace's face – being Queen was a much different prospect to being Malu's lover, and no doubt Horace was considering how his own power would be boosted by her position. He turned back to Malu.

'You must make me your adviser – your Chief Adviser.'

'Ha!' Hafder cried in disbelief.

But Malu looked Horace straight in the eye and said, 'Done.'

Horace held a hand to his ear. 'Sorry, I'm not sure everyone heard you.'

Malu gave a strained smile and turned to face his people. 'As of this moment,' he said in a loud, clear voice, 'my father-in-law, Horace, is my Chief Adviser, and I expect you all to respect that.'

There was more mumbling and murmuring, but no objections, apart from the death stare Hafder had fixed on Theodora's father.

'Do we have a deal?' Malu asked Horace, and he nodded to his crew to extend the gangplank.

Horace greeted his daughter on the ship with a triumphant smile. 'So, here we are.'

'Here we are,' she muttered, glancing at the crew members, some of whom she recognised as having served under her brother, Guthrie. 'Is that how you did it?' she accused her father. 'You recruited my brother's pathetic, hangdog followers to help you?'

Horace clicked his jaw. 'Unlike *some*,' he hissed, 'loyalty means something to these men.' He waved his hand around the deck.

Theodora shook her head. 'No. You couldn't have done this alone. You couldn't have just happened to find the right ship and get a message to them, all the while keeping yourself from being caught.'

'You're right.' A female voice behind her. 'He couldn't have done it alone.'

Theodora spun to face Jade.

'*You?*' Her voice shook. 'I thought you hated my father.'

Jade shrugged. 'What do they say about my enemy's enemy...?'

Theodora squared her shoulders. 'What did he promise you?'

'Only to take me away from this...' She cast her eyes over Nadis and screwed up her mouth and nose. 'This vile cesspit of a place, where only the greedy and rich survive.'

'They're the only ones who survive anywhere,' Theodora said under her breath.

Jade narrowed her eyes. 'What was that?'

Theodora gave her a sickly sweet smile. 'I was just saying how pleased you would be to hear that Rea – the phoenix...She survived.'

Jade appeared to do a double take, then shook her head. 'Lies!'

'It's true,' Theodora chimed. 'The Water Catcher cured her with Alia Water, and she chose to stay with them. So we both failed.'

Jade ran to disembark the ship, but it was already pulling away from the dock.

Horace placed a fatherly hand on the girl's shoulder. 'Bide

your time. You shall have your revenge. Stick with me now that I have Malu's ear, and you will have everything you dream of.'

Theodora rolled her eyes. She was acutely familiar with Horace's special brand of empty promises.

'How do we get out of here?' Malu demanded, appearing in front of Horace. 'Blast our way through them?' He pointed at the blockade.

Horace nodded at Jade. 'The girl has delivered on that front as well.' He indicated a canal off to the side of the port. 'It will take us into a cove where we can swing around behind the enemy and take them by surprise.'

'Splendid!' Malu slapped Horace on his back so hard that he stumbled.

A genuine smile came to Theodora's lips. Malu was right. Their cause wasn't dead yet.

40

*A*risa and Rea released their power over the water as the Northern forces retreated. Arisa threw her arms around her cousin.

'We did it!' she cried. 'We made firewater. How did you know the spell?'

Rea extricated herself from Arisa's embrace, her lips set in a thin line. 'I know many spells. They just never worked before I knew I was a Firemaster.' She glanced down at the pool, where only a hint of silver glow remained. 'You had Alia Water. How?'

'It came from your grandmother—'

Rea's eyes widened. 'Grandmother?'

Arisa gave her a kind smile. 'Nima was your grandmother.'

Rea shook her head. 'No. She saved me from the Capital.' She paced the length of the pool. 'She cared for me all that time. If she was my grandmother, she would have said something.'

'It's true. It is how you are a Firemaster and have the powers you have. I have all the letters to show you. But you know it, don't you? Deep down inside, you know it.'

Rea froze mid-step. 'She should have said something.' She

spoke in the quietest of voices, and Arisa's heart lurched for her cousin, who'd been denied so much.

'Nima spoke of a reckoning,' Arisa continued. 'She claimed Ivane could only be saved by the three who shared blood of fire and water. She gifted the Alia Water to the healer here many years ago, casting a spell on it so it could only be used by those three born of the same blood.'

'Three?'

'You, me and our cousin.' She indicated Isla, who was beside Sar, Takai and Letoi, looking out to sea and following the battle. 'She must have seen all this. She must have known you would need help.'

Rea slumped to the ground, her head in her hands. 'I don't deserve to be saved. Not after everything I've done. Too many lives have been lost because of me.'

Arisa crouched down next to her and placed a hand on her back. 'And you have saved just as many.'

Rea looked up at her with tear-filled eyes. 'How can I make amends for what I've done?'

'You can start by helping finish this war, once and for all.' Isla stood before them with folded arms, flanked by Sar and Takai.

'But I thought our reinforcements...?' Arisa began, confused.

'They destroyed the Northemer blockade at port,' Takai said, 'and are fighting what is left of the Northemer fleet.'

'But the Northemers' ships are well armed,' Sar added. 'And they're smaller and swifter than our warships.'

Rea wiped the tears from her eyes and stood up. 'What do you want us to do?'

Sar, Isla and Takai shared a look, as if they had already determined exactly what was needed.

Arisa stood up as well. She had a fair idea what they may be thinking. 'Get us close enough to the enemy fleet and we'll see what we can do.'

Takai grinned. 'It's just as well I know exactly how to get you close.'

TAKAI EXPLAINED to Letoi and the King what they were planning to do. Laskar gave his blessing, saying he and Letoi would stay behind to maintain hold over the palace city – the Ivanians had finally learned not to underestimate the Northemers.

'I will go to the city gate,' Laskar said, wringing his hands. 'Do you think…Is it possible…?' His voice broke. No explanation was needed; he was going to look for Noemi.

Takai rested a hand on his uncle's shoulder. 'If anyone is strong enough to survive the Northemers, it's that single-minded cousin of mine.'

Laskar gave a ghost of a smile and wished them luck.

Sar gathered ten soldiers, who'd been part of the crew on the ship he and Takai had sailed on to Ivane. Ambra then showed them all through the secret tunnels, which originated from the King's rooms in the palace. By torchlight, they negotiated cobwebbed stone corridors that soon gave way to a sloping path and staircases covered in moss. The air hung damp and thick. Salt water dripped from the ceiling overhead. The sound of waves crashing on rocks intensified the further they descended. Eventually, they rounded a corner that opened up to reveal a cave tall enough to house Nadis's watchtower – or, in this case, a single-masted sloop.

'She's a fine ship, and fast,' Ambra said. 'Her shallow hull will get you over the reef with no trouble.'

Arisa watched Takai walk the length of the ship, inspecting it. 'She's in good condition.'

'Letoi made sure she was well looked after. She's been key to any escape plans ever since…'

'Ever since my father attacked,' Takai said matter-of-factly. 'And while I wish you'd never had to make such preparations, right now, I'm grateful you did. She'll do mighty fine, won't she, Sar?'

Sar's mouth twitched. 'I won't lie. I'd be more comfortable if she had a cannon or two.' He broke into a grin. 'But who needs cannons when you've got three Kengians who share blood of fire and water?'

THE CREW SET TO WORK, using oars to manoeuvre the sloop out of the cave. They emerged on the edge of the battle. The Lamorian and Kengian fleet was just ahead of them over the reef. A strong wind bit hard into their sails and they skipped across the waves, heading for the largest Lamorian warship, which bore Takai and Alik's flags.

Cannon fire roared around them like thunder in a deadly storm. A Kengian galleon on their starboard side took a direct hit, exploding in a shower of splintered timber and screams. There was another explosion and cannon shot flew over their heads, barely missing their mast. The cannon ball landed in the sea by their port side with a gargantuan splash. The resulting spout of water crashed down on them, flooding their deck.

'Any time you want to break out those powers of yours...' Sar shouted at Arisa and Rea from the ship's helm.

'Do you think you can harness your Water Catcher magic again?' Rea asked.

Arisa closed her eyes, trying to isolate the energy she'd felt in the pool. There was something, a buzz, but it was elusive. Each time she tried to tap into the energy, it petered out. She tried again and again, but if anything, the vibrations became weaker. Her eyes snapped open in frustration.

'I don't know...I don't think so.'

'You can do it,' Takai called out from beside Sar.

She shook her head miserably. 'I can't.'

Rea lifted her chin. 'It's alright. I can do this.' She stood up and aimed her hands at a Northemer longship that had its cannon trained on Lamore's lead ship. A silver glow filled her palms. Sparks burst from her fingertips; there was a hint of flame, but then it was gone. Rea stumbled backward, holding her hand to where the arrow had entered her chest and nearly killed her. She was still too weak.

'That's it!' Isla cried with excitement. She reached into her quiver and retrieved an arrow. Not just any arrow – the Alia-head arrow. She held it out to Arisa and Rea.

'You took it?' Arisa said.

Isla shrugged. 'Thought it might come in handy. Besides, I didn't want anyone else to get their hands on it. Just hoping I haven't cursed—'

The rest of her sentence was swallowed up by Arisa's hug. Isla batted away her arms.

'Thank me after you've won this war for us.'

'I knew we had to save you for a reason,' Arisa teased.

'Hey!' Isla protested.

'Are you ready?' Rea asked Arisa, nodding to the Alia crystal.

'She'd better be,' Isla said in a faraway voice, her gaze fixed on something over Arisa's shoulder.

Arisa turned to see a rapidly approaching Lamorian warship coming up behind the rest of their fleet. 'But it's one of ours…'

'Then why are they pointing all their cannons at our lead ship?'

Takai must have seen the same thing, because he hurriedly raised a spyglass to his eye. 'I can't believe it,' he said as he looked through the device.

'What?' Arisa asked.

Takai lowered the spyglass, and a shiver ran up Arisa's spine at the terror in his eyes. 'Horace. On the foredeck.' Arisa's breath hitched in her throat. 'Malu and Theodora beside him.'

Arisa took the spyglass from Takai and swung it to face the lead Lamorian ship. There, she discovered exactly what she didn't want to find. On the deck of the ship, dressed in full battle armour, were Elos, Sofia, Gwyn and Alik.

A fire ignited deep in Arisa's belly. Fire born of water and the magical Kengian blood that ran through her veins.

Arisa and Rea exchanged a swift look and reached out in unison to clasp the arrowhead. Their fingers intertwined, and the Alia crystal flared to life.

41

*H*orace's requisitioned ship bore down on the enemy fleet. Under Malu's lead, readying their cannons for a surprise attack, they sped up behind the lead warship, which flew both the Kengian and Lamorian flags.

Theodora stood tall on the foredeck, the wind whipping her hair around her face, Rayl by her side. The salt air bit into her cheeks and the cannon fire around them threatened to rupture her eardrums, but she was savouring every moment. They were almost within firing range.

'Today is the day.' Theodora patted the snow leopard's head. 'Today I will finally get my revenge.'

Her father was on her other side, holding a spyglass to his eye, his smug smile spreading wide. 'Perhaps more revenge than you think.' He lowered the device and indicated that she should take a look at the lead ship.

Theodora did as he suggested. It only took a moment for her to identify the object of his comment. On the warship's deck stood the Dowager Queen Sofia and Gwyn, as well as a man in Kengian armour – King Alik.

Destroying the lead ship wouldn't just deal a deadly blow to the enemy as a whole. It would personally devastate Arisa –

both her parents killed in one fell swoop. Justice would also be served for Theodora. They would take the lives of the two women who'd treated her with so many years of disrespect at Lamore Castle.

Malu strode up next to her. 'The cannons are ready, my love.' He gave a dramatic wave of his hand. 'I have told them to fire on your signal.'

Horace visibly bristled at his daughter being given the honour.

Theodora flashed Malu a brilliant smile and marched over to the ship's rail to gain the best vantage point for her victory. She watched the enemy ship fire its own cannons at the Northemer fleet, oblivious that they were about to be attacked by one of their own vessels.

She took a deep breath and projected her voice so it was loud and clear. 'Fire!'

The cannons exploded to life, launching projectiles one by one at the ship before them. The first shot found its target, clipping the warship's main mast. The timber post toppled over, taking sails and rigging with it. The ship was practically immobilised. The sweet taste of triumph filled Theodora as the following cannonballs arced toward the ship. But a *whoosh* of light and heat forced her to shield her eyes.

Through the cracks between her fingers, she watched in disbelief as the cannon shot struck a wall of silver fire and crumbled to ash.

'*No!*' she screamed, as everyone on deck raced to the rails to see the firewater wall extending at each end to form a protective ring around the enemy fleet. The flames were twice the height of the tallest mast. 'Arisa,' Theodora hissed through gritted teeth, searching the scene for the Kengian.

'There!' Jade pointed to a sloop at a distance to their right. 'That is where the fire is most intense.' Her nostrils flared. 'That is where the witches must be.'

Theodora squinted at the tiny ship, willing her eyes to see

through the flames, and slowly a familiar image emerged like a rippling reflection in a pond. It was a figure with long bronze hair, arms outstretched, surrounded by a silver glow. The figure slowly turned toward her. Theodora didn't need a spyglass to know it was Arisa staring back at her, challenging her with those unnerving silver eyes.

'Fire at them!' Theodora shouted, throwing a hand toward the sloop.

'There's no point,' Horace said, clicking his jaw. 'Our cannons are useless against the fire. We should retreat now, while we still can. If we move quickly we can make it to Lamore and slip into Obira Port unchallenged.'

'They can't maintain this forever,' Theodora argued, unwilling to give up when victory had been so close just moments before. 'Their weapons can't penetrate the fire either. If they want to win, they'll have to lower their defences sooner rather than later. Then we will take them.'

But she had spoken too soon. Balls of flame suddenly burst through the wall, carving a fiery path through the sky and raining down on the Northemer fleet. Spot fires erupted every-where, igniting decks, hulls and sails. Cannons were abandoned so the crews could fight the fires.

One fireball must have hit the firesky powder supply on one of the longships, as there was an almighty explosion and a cacophony of screams. When the smoke finally cleared, nothing was left of the vessel except a scattering of timber planks, oars and bodies. They floated alongside what was left of the snarling serpent figurehead from the prow.

Sweat broke out on Theodora's forehead as a trio of fireballs flew toward them and landed on the aft deck. Hafder, Olix and the crew scrambled to extinguish each fire.

Horace turned his back on his daughter to appeal to Malu, who had been disturbingly silent. 'We must go. To Lamore, where I have allies. We can regroup there.'

Malu's steely gaze was on the sloop, but still he said nothing.

Theodora shook her head. 'We can't leave our fleet to their mercy.'

A smile tugged at the corner of Malu's mouth at her reference to the Northemer ships as 'our fleet'. Then his smile grew, transforming into a sly grin.

'My Queen is right,' he said with certainty. 'We do not abandon our campaign or our people while there is still a chance we'll prevail.'

'Prevail! You fool!' Horace scoffed. 'Can't you see what is happening out there?'

Malu took two menacing steps toward Horace, then stopped and took a deep breath. 'I can see exactly what is happening out there,' he said in clipped tones. 'I see that every time Rea launches fireballs, the wall wavers a moment. The height of the flames dips for an instant, as if her powers are temporarily weakened.'

Theodora spun back to look at the sloop. Sure enough, with the next round of fireballs, the wall faltered. 'If we time it just right, we can get a volley of arrows in there!'

Malu nodded. 'Unfortunately, the sloop is out of range of our archers.'

Theodora's heart sank. The sloop was tauntingly close enough now for them to discern Arisa and the others on the vessel, but remained beyond their reach. 'And the fire wall won't let us get any closer.'

'I could do it,' Jade declared. She had clearly understood the gist of their conversation, and was already reaching for her Ivanian longbow. Its range was much further than the smaller variety of Northem bow. 'I only need one shot.'

Theodora translated for Malu. 'One shot is all she may get before they turn all their efforts on us,' he said gravely.

Jade must have heard the doubt in his voice. She pushed her shoulders back. 'As I said, I only need one shot to get the firebird girl.'

'No,' Theodora said. 'Not Rea. You must shoot the other one – Arisa.'

Jade scowled, but Theodora pressed her case. 'Without water, the fire wall will have no fuel. And we can use our weapons again.'

'Without Rea's fire powers, there's no *fire*!' Jade retorted.

'You shoot at the Water Catcher,' Theodora ordered Jade, who clenched her jaw as if she would refuse, but the new Northem Queen gave a dangerously benevolent smile. 'And if you miss, you will be thrown overboard, and can take your chances with the sharks and the Kengian firewater.'

Jade compressed her lips, but nodded.

'On my word,' Theodora said, 'you fire.'

Theodora, Malu, Horace and Jade got in position along the rail and watched, waiting for their opportunity. Malu handed his spyglass to Theodora, who focused it on Rea, holding up her other hand.

'Get ready…*Now!*' she yelled, and dropped her hand.

Jade released her arrow just as the firewater wall dipped. The arrow sailed up into the air – the wall was rising again.

Quickly, Theodora thought. *Quick.*

The arrow made its way over the flames by a whisker and began its descent.

A single yelp of pain cut through the battle noise and the fire wall shuddered.

Clutching Malu's arm, Theodora exhaled with a laugh. She raised the spyglass again, searching for Arisa's prone body – but instead saw that the Kengian was only wounded. Jade's arrow protruded from her back, just below her shoulder blade. Takai and Isla hovered over her, but Arisa was waving them away.

'Damn!'

Isla's head swivelled in Theodora's direction, as if she had heard her cry.

'She's still alive!' Theodora screeched at Jade, who hurriedly began to reload her bow.

'I'll take another shot. As soon as the next fireballs are launched. I still can—'

Jade crumpled suddenly before them, an arrow sticking from her chest.

Theodora's mind reeled, trying to make sense of what she was seeing. She turned toward the sloop. On the deck, Isla looked back at her, Kengian longbow still in hand.

Theodora leant down to where Jade lay on the deck. Instinctively, she took the girl's hand in hers. Jade grasped the arrow shaft – one made from a Batu-riek tree.

'My destiny,' she gurgled through a blood-filled mouth.

It didn't matter what had passed between them – Theodora didn't want her to die. Jade had been driven by the same things as she had: a need to survive. A desire for revenge. Did this mean she deserved to die?

'It will be alright,' Theodora tried to reassure her, but the waning light in Jade's green eyes said otherwise.

'This is my curse.' Jade gave a bitter laugh.

'Shush. You're not cursed—'

'I am. But you…can still…escape yours.'

Her curse? Was Theodora cursed? Had her quest for power and revenge led her down the wrong path? A path lined with death? Did her true destiny lie elsewhere?

All of her questions faded away as Jade's eyes fluttered closed, and her hand went limp.

THE BATTLE WAS DECIDED in the minutes that followed. Every Northemer ship that remained afloat was on fire, beyond their King's help. The sea was an inferno of lost dreams and vanquished hope. The shattering realisation that Malu had led his people to death and defeat again was branded on his face.

Horace saw his opportunity and rushed to the King's side. 'Let's go now to Lamore. If we move fast, we can still—'

'We must retreat,' Malu said, his voice small and unrecognisable.

But Horace persisted. 'Lamore is our best hope. Their lead ship is damaged. They won't be able to catch us in time—'

'We head south and swing back around Ivane, staying at a distance from the coast. That way some of us might make it back home alive.'

Horace clicked his jaw furiously. 'You must heed my words. You promised I would be your Chief Adviser.'

'I didn't promise I would listen to you.' Malu turned his back on Horace and headed in Hafder's direction to convey his orders.

'I'm not going back to that place,' Horace muttered – and in one swift movement, he grabbed Jade's folded Batu-riek staff from her quiver, flicking the weapon so all the sections fell into place.

'*No!*' Theodora screamed as Horace made toward Malu. She reached for her own staff behind her back and blocked her father's path. She thought back to everything Jade had taught her. *Shoulders back. Stay balanced. Move like the staff is an extension of your arm.*

'Out of my way,' Horace snarled. 'I will have no qualms killing you if that's what it takes.'

'Nor I, Father,' she said through gritted teeth, and struck out at Horace with her staff, the sharpened blade at the end cutting his shirt open.

Horace advanced on her with a flurry of striking and stabbing motions. It took everything Theodora had to avoid contact with the Batu-riek barbs. Rayl circled the pair, trying to reach Horace, but the swift arcing motion of the poisoned staff kept her at bay.

'Shoot him!' Malu ordered a nearby hand cannoneer, but the man couldn't get a clear shot. The Northern King howled Theodora's name, terror etched in his voice as he raced toward her. It was all it took for Theodora to momentarily lose concentration – she stumbled over a loose decking board and fell to the ground.

Horace whacked her staff from her hands and stood over her with a malignant grin. 'I always win in the end,' he sneered.

The sound of metal hissed through the air as Malu's blade sliced toward Horace, but Theodora's father was ready for him. With a mighty grunt, he charged at Malu—

And pressed the staff deep into the wound in the Northern King's stomach.

The effect was immediate. Malu howled as the poison took hold in his bloodstream. Horace twisted the staff, so the thorns ripped through Malu's insides. Malu's face twisted in pain matching the agony that had taken up residence in Theodora's heart.

Rayl grasped her opportunity and pounced on Horace, her jaws latching around his neck, but by then the damage was done.

Malu collapsed, a pool of blood spreading around him. Theodora scrambled across the deck and fell to her knees beside her husband, tears streaming down her face. An out-of-breath Hafder stood on Malu's other side, gaping and running his hands through his hair.

Theodora grabbed Malu's limp hand. 'You can't leave me,' she sobbed. 'You can't.'

Malu looked up at her with glazed eyes, wincing as he tried to smile. 'I'm sorry, but I must.' He took three shallow breaths. 'Please do something for me.'

'Anything.'

'The pyramids. Never lose sight of the pyramids.' He shifted his gaze across the deck, where Rayl still held firm to a struggling Horace's throat and a handful of the Lamorian crew were trying to stop the Northemers from getting to Theodora's father to finish off the job. Behind the Northemers stood Olix, his head bowed.

The pyramids. Malu wanted her to go to the lands with the great stone pyramids, the lands Olix had described.

'I promise,' she said, almost choking on the salty tears falling rapidly into her mouth.

Malu turned his head toward Hafder. 'Theodora is my Queen. I give Northem to her to rule. You must honour it as my last wish.'

Theodora shook her head before Hafder could voice his protest. She couldn't understand why Malu would want her to rule Northem when he'd just made her promise she'd go to the new lands...Unless he wanted her to lead Northem to them. But – no. She didn't want Northem. She only wanted Malu.

'Northem should be Hafder's.'

Malu's hand began shaking, forcing Theodora to release it. 'Promise me...brother,' he croaked.

Hafder held his head in his hands. 'Yes. Yes. I promise.'

Malu's back arched. His whole body started to convulse. Then, just as quickly as it had begun, it was over. Malu's back hit the deck with a sickening thud.

'Malu,' Theodora said tentatively, searching his eyes for a sign that he lived. Desperately, she tried to reach into the fissures in his irises, the same fissures where she'd once seen into his very soul – but they were empty. Cold and lifeless, like the glaciers of his homeland.

Hafder must have seen what she saw, because he threw his fists into the air and screamed.

Theodora's tears froze on her cheeks. She had nothing else left to give. She got slowly to her feet and raised her chin. Then she strode purposefully across the deck toward her father.

'*Out of my way,*' she ordered the Lamorians trying to guard Horace. They looked at each other uncertainly, and the Northemers made their move, yanking them out of Theodora's path.

Horace glared up at her, streams of blood snaking their way down his neck, where Rayl's jaws were still latched. It reminded Theodora of seeing the snow leopard with a desert rat one day.

Rayl always wanted to play with her prey first. Chasing it and catching it, holding it in her jaws just tight enough to prevent escape, but not enough to end the game before she wanted. She'd released the rat, just so she could chase it all over again. But today was different. It was clear in the snow leopard's icy blue eyes: she had no intention of releasing her prey.

'You can still…atone…for failing me,' Horace said between laboured breaths.

'*Atone?*' An anger like nothing Theodora had ever experienced churned inside her, but she would not give her father that satisfaction. Instead she laughed, a musical tinkle of a laugh, reminiscent of Malu at his most threatening. 'But you are the one who killed my husband.'

'You would…kill…your own father?'

Theodora squatted so she was just inches from Horace's face. 'You are no father to me. You never have been.' She bent over and whispered in his ear. 'Besides. Rayl is going to be the one who kills you.'

She got back to her feet, relishing in the terrified darting of her father's eyes as he searched for salvation.

'This, Father dearest, is for taking Rayl's cub from her.' Theodora's mouth curled into a sneer. 'And for every time you said I was weak and unworthy.'

'Theodora, *please*,' Horace wailed.

Theodora nodded at Rayl. The snow leopard's jaw crunched around Horace's neck, and with a shake of her head, she tore out his throat, spraying blood all over Theodora.

Something strange happened, then. A lifting of a weight from her shoulders. An understanding that *this* was the revenge she had sought.

It had never been about the Water Catcher. It had always been about her father. He was the one who'd always taken from her. He was the one who'd taken *everything* from her.

Hafder came to stand beside Theodora, stopping first to spit on Horace's body.

'What do you say, my Queen?' he said without looking at her.

'You should lead your people,' she replied.

Hafder grunted. 'I made a promise. It is a matter of honour.'

Theodora looked out across the Northemers' faces: a mixture of shock, resignation and sadness. How could she serve them? The woman whose father had killed their beloved King?

'And out of honour to them...' She nodded at the Northemers. 'I can't be their leader.'

Hafder's hand drummed on the axe tucked into his belt, as if considering whether to stay and fight, to die a warrior's death, or retreat. He looked back out at their decimated fleet.

'Damn it,' he muttered under his breath, then addressed his people. 'We must live so we can fight another day. To Northem!'

A smile came to Theodora's lips. Perhaps Malu's influence over his brother was greater than they'd all thought.

If only Malu were here to witness it himself.

42

*T*he Alia crystal had given Arisa and Rea the power needed to create firewater on such a grand scale, but its effects were temporary. When the arrow struck her, Arisa could already feel her magic starting to fade, but she had to go on. And she did, with the arrow still sticking from her upper back. In any other circumstance, they may have been able to rely on Rea being able to transform into a phoenix, but Rea was still too weak from her own injury to take her other form.

She fired fireball after fireball at the Northemer fleet and the Lamorian warship with Malu and Theodora on board. The light in her eyes grew dimmer with every throw. They could have tried to boost their powers again with the Alia crystal, but they'd lost it when Isla had fired the Batu-riek arrow at the Ivanian girl who'd procured the black-market weapon in the first place. So they fought on, until every muscle in Arisa's body screamed for mercy and her aching, burning hands threatened to combust.

It was cheering from Takai, Sar and Isla that alerted Arisa to their victory. Cheers fanned out like wildfire among the Lamorian and Kengian fleets. Once Arisa spotted her parents and Queen Sofia celebrating on the deck of the lead ship, she and

Rea lowered their shaking hands and the firewater wall petered out. Side by side, they surveyed the battle scene.

The last Northemer longship sat in flames, low in the water. Behind them, the ship carrying Theodora and Malu retreated, leaving its longboat behind. Rowing the longboat were Lamorian soldiers, waving white flags. Presumably, they wanted to take their chances with their King rather than go with the Northemers.

Takai glanced back at Arisa from the helm and mouthed, *I knew you could do it.*

Arisa bowed her head in acknowledgement. Then she and Rea looked at each other in disbelief for a moment before each bursting into happy tears.

'We did it!' Rea cried.

'We did, didn't we?' Arisa said, blinking back her tears.

'Don't you mean *we* did it?' Isla stood in front of them, hands on hips. 'The three who share blood of fire and water.' Her green eyes danced, teasing them. 'After all, I did stop that girl from firing another arrow at you.'

'Speaking of which…' Arisa looked back over her shoulder.

'Right.' Isla hurried to inspect Arisa's injury. She jiggled the arrow shaft, forcing Arisa to put a hand over her mouth to stop herself from hollering in pain.

'It's pretty deep,' Isla said. 'I can take it out, but it will bleed like nothing else. Could use some of that Alia Water right about now.'

'I don't care, just take it out,' Arisa said through gritted teeth.

'We can always cauterise the wound,' Rea suggested.

'But how——?' Then Isla laughed, realising she knew the answer to her own question.

'You're not going to like it,' Rea warned.

'Not going to like what?' Takai had left Sar to command the sloop and now appeared in front of Arisa. Isla told him what they were planning on doing.

Takai frowned. 'She's right. I *don't* like it. We should get Ambra to look at it back at the palace.'

Arisa shook her head. 'It's got to be done, now, because I'm planning on going over there' – she nodded toward their lead ship – 'to greet my parents and your mother. And I'm not doing it with a damn arrow sticking out of my back.'

Takai sighed in resignation, but took her hands in his. 'On the count of three,' he told Isla and Rea. Arisa gripped Takai's hands tighter.

'One...*I love you*.' He whispered the last part to her, and kissed her hand. 'Two—'

Arisa yelped as pain ripped through her upper back. Isla had pulled the arrow out before 'three', the metal head tearing new flesh as it retracted. Arisa was acutely aware of her racing heartbeat and the sensation of gushing blood. Takai's face twisted violently as she squeezed his hand even harder. She howled again a moment later as Rea used her fire to close the wound. The smell of her own scorched flesh turned Arisa's stomach.

Takai gave her an encouraging nod. 'It's all over now.'

Arisa's heartbeat slowed as the pain in her back abated to a dull throb. She softened her grip on Takai's hands.

'Is it over, though?' Arisa asked. 'What's to stop Malu coming back again?'

A shadow fell over Rea's face. 'He won't be back,' she muttered. 'He's gone.'

'How do you know?' Isla asked.

'Despite everything...he and I were connected. He was a big brother to me, my protector.' A hint of nostalgia crept into Rea's voice. 'I'll always be grateful that he saved me, like I'm grateful to all of you.' She smiled at them. 'But I can no longer sense that connection, or his lifeforce. Which means he's gone – and the Northemers will never be one again without him. No one else is capable of uniting them like he did.'

Hope flared inside Arisa. No, something much stronger than hope – an undeniable knowledge that everything *would* be alright. A knowledge that lived in Takai's dark eyes, in the love that filled his gaze. He pulled her to him so she was close enough to hear the quickening of his breath.

'I was wrong. Everything's not over.' His voice was low and thick. 'Some things are just beginning.'

'Or beginning again?' she responded in a whisper.

Takai leant in to kiss her, stopping midway at the sound of Isla and Rea's *ooh*ing and *ahh*ing. He gave them both a dirty look and they excused themselves with a giggle.

'Now. Where were we?' Takai asked.

'We were about—'

Arisa's reply dissolved as their lips met.

In the three days since the final battle, Ivane had made great strides in rebuilding their nation. Physically, the palace city and port were thrumming with activity. Stonemasons, carpenters and metalworkers streamed into Nadis to assist with repairing and reconstructing the damaged infrastructure. The country of many regions and mindsets had come together, jubilant in their win over the Northemers. National pride was at an all-time high, with much slapping of backs over their military prowess. When pressed, some Ivanians recognised the Lamorians and Kengians – two Kengians in particular – for their part in defeating the enemy, but they would always come back to one among themselves. One who had demonstrated the true spirit of an Ivanian warrior. One whose bravery couldn't be denied.

Today's commendation ceremony was in honour of that person. Two dozen rows of chairs had been laid out in King Laskar's presence chambers for the Lamorian Assembly members and other officials. Arisa took her seat between Takai and her mother in a section set aside for family. The Dowager Queen Sofia sat on Takai's other side. Everyone was dressed in their finery.

Gwyn held her head high. 'Sofia and I have waited a long time for this day.'

'Of course,' Arisa said politely.

Gwyn turned to face her daughter with a furrowed brow. 'She'll be alright. Your father is with her.'

Arisa forced a smile. They were speaking of Rea, who'd left earlier that day with Alik. The Ivanian Assembly had discussed at length what to do with the girl who'd caused so much death and destruction in her phoenix form. They had also discussed Arisa's actions in Oisiri. Takai had urged Laskar to take into account what both of them had done for Ivane, and how their magic had secured victory. Ultimately, they had both been pardoned. Rea's pardon, though, came with a condition. She must leave and never return to Ivane or Ette.

Rea almost welcomed the banishment, saying she didn't deserve to live among people whose suffering she was responsible for. She'd insisted she wanted to leave all of Kypria behind, but Alik wouldn't have it. Rea was family. So it had been agreed: she would go to Kengia, where she would study under the Head Scholar and High Shaman, and devote herself to sharing her Firemaster knowledge for good.

Arisa had farewelled her cousin with a promise to see her again soon. She'd also given Rea the Firemaster's book and all the letters she'd found in the cave.

'I don't deserve any of this,' Rea had lamented.

'You didn't choose your path. All you have done is survived. There is no crime in that.'

Rea hadn't looked convinced.

'Then dedicate your life to making amends, if you must. You have a gift that can't be wasted. You must leave a legacy. That is what Amund would have wanted.'

Rea had flinched at the mention of Amund. Arisa understood: it must seem impossible to grieve a father she never knew she had.

Arisa had hugged her cousin tightly. 'You can do this, Rea.

You are a Firemaster. And as foretold, the Firemasters will rise again.'

Rea had nodded, hugging Arisa back just as tightly.

Arisa knew Rea would be safe and cared for in Kengia. And she could only hope that with time, her cousin could learn to forgive herself.

Gwyn patted Arisa's hand. 'Today, we celebrate.'

Her mother was right. Today's ceremony was a reason to rejoice. It was why Gwyn and Sofia had decided to stay on in Ivane for a while, so they could witness the country they grew up in forging a new future – a future they'd waited a lifetime for.

Trumpets signalled the arrival of the guest of honour. The crowd turned to see King Laskar in his maroon-and-gold ceremonial costume and crown, arm-in-arm with his daughter.

Princess Noemi wore a high-necked gold silk gown that covered the snow leopard's claw marks – three parallel lines, gouged into her throat. The wounds had taken more than a hundred sutures to close.

The girl had been found on the verge of death by one of her loyal soldiers. He'd taken her to the abandoned watchtower and applied a pressure bandage, then waited for the Northemers to come, but they never had. It was King Laskar who had found them, and Ambra who had ultimately saved her life.

Word soon spread of Ivane's heroic Commander, who'd been prepared to sacrifice her life, taking the last stand at the city gate. No one doubted her ability or worthiness to lead the Ivanian people, and the Assembly had made it their first order of official business to change their succession laws.

The commendation ceremony wasn't just to recognise Ivanian acts of bravery and the soldier who had saved Noemi's life. It would include the formal announcement of Noemi as King Laskar's heir, with Ivane's leaders and nobles pledging their allegiance and fealty to their future Queen.

Arisa made to peer past Takai to watch Noemi go by, but her attention was drawn to the Lamorian King. As Noemi walked by them, Takai's shoulders relaxed and a puff of air escaped his mouth.

'Are you alright?' she whispered.

'Perfectly,' he whispered back. 'My duties are fulfilled.' He turned to face her. 'Or at least, my duties to Ette and Ivane are, which just leaves—'

'Lamore,' she prompted.

He smiled. 'Well…yes…but I was thinking of my duty to you.' He grasped both of her hands in his. 'Come back to Lamore with me,' he said, voice rising with excitement. 'Come back and be my Queen.'

'Lamore? Your Queen?' Arisa's head whirled. What about Kengia? What about Rea?

Takai's face fell at her hesitation. He released her hands. 'I understand. You don't want to leave your family.'

Then it occurred to her – what Takai said about his duty being fulfilled. Arisa had done everything asked of her, too. She had fulfilled her responsibility as the Water Catcher.

As foretold in the prophecy, choices had been made to unite Kypria – hard choices by her and by Takai. And now Kypria *was* united.

This choice would be hers alone.

'You're right,' she said in the smallest of voices. 'I don't want to leave my family.' Takai clenched his jaw, but said nothing. 'But…'

He spun to face her fully. 'But?' he asked hopefully.

This time, Arisa took his hand in hers. 'But you are my family too, and I choose you.'

Takai cupped her chin with his free hand. 'And I could say I choose you too. But that's not true. You were chosen *for* me. You were chosen for all of us.'

43

Theodora had always scoffed at the idea that a person's heart could actually 'break'. She'd been raised to believe that such things were for the weak and sentimental, and she was neither. She had understood love as a concept, something one could play at to obtain other things – be it a crown, a position or power. She had seen people like Takai and Arisa 'fall' in love, letting it burrow its way into their souls like a parasite, blinkering them to all reason. At least, that was what she'd thought had happened...before Malu entered her life.

Meeting him had been like the coming together of two suns. A collision of unexpected proportions. A fulfilment of each other's purpose, potential and desires. So when Malu had died, Theodora had waited for the moment when her heart would shatter into a million pieces – but it never came.

It didn't mean she didn't feel pain. What she suffered was beyond words. If the pain of a broken bone was represented by a single star in the sky, a whole galaxy blazed inside her, so intense it numbed every nerve. But it didn't encroach on her heart. There, where the images of Malu's twinkling eyes and quicksilver smile had once shone brightly, was nothing but a black ball of grief. No amount of tears – and there were many –

could shift it. The same way she couldn't be shifted from her place beside Malu's body. Not even Rayl's strained mews could move her.

Day had merged into night and back to day again before Hafder was finally able to persuade her to let the Northem King be put to rest. He reminded her that Northemer custom dictated that Malu couldn't take his place among the spirit gods and his ancestors until the burial rites were complete. That until this happened, he would be stuck between worlds – something Theodora couldn't bear.

Malu was owed a proper funeral – unlike her treacherous father, whose body had been unceremoniously dumped into the sea. Jade's body had followed Horace's, the Batu-riek-and-Alia arrow still protruding from her chest. Jade may have deserved better, but now, Theodora couldn't see past what the girl had done. If Rea hadn't been shot down in the first place, she would never have joined Arisa and Ivane's cause…and maybe Malu would still be alive.

Theodora tore her handfasting ribbon in two, wrapping one section around her husband's lifeless hand. She kissed his cold forehead and whispered, 'Farewell, my King, my love.' She choked back sobs as Malu's body was placed in a longboat with his sword and offerings of food, copper plates and bronze goblets found in the galleon's kitchen. Hafder recited a traditional poem that spoke of a great warrior and leader, a living god who brought prosperity to his nation. At its end, the Northemers thumped their chests with their fists.

'Our King!' they shouted.

Hafder signalled for the longboat to be launched. An archer shot a single fire arrow into the sky. Theodora held her breath on its downward trajectory, looking away as it landed and ignited the boat.

She walked away then, her gaze drawn to the eastern horizon, where the sea sparkled in the morning sun like a prized Ivanian gemstone. The horizon glimmered with possibilities –

promises of new lands and adventures Malu would never experience. Rayl emitted a soft mew next to her, and Theodora smiled down at the snow leopard, the pyramid-shaped spikes on her collar catching in the light.

'*Never lose sight of the pyramids.*' Theodora said Malu's words to herself, her voice dreamlike. She gave a small laugh, imagining Malu's awe upon seeing the great stone buildings, and how his blue eyes would have danced at their magnificence. Flinching at the impossibility of it all, she turned instead to face the north, where her future waited. Soon they would arrive on the icy shores of Northem – a land that was certain to be even more brutal without Malu.

'Your Majesty.' Hafder appeared by her side, his voice absent any form of mockery.

'You don't need to call me that,' she said tonelessly.

Hafder followed her gaze to the north. 'You are Malu's wife. I must respect that, and the promise I made to my brother.'

She winced. 'I can't be Queen to your people.'

'They are *your* people too.' He turned to face her, his expression serious, but not unkind. 'I didn't see it before, but you have proven yourself to be Northemer, time and time again. You fought on the battlefield like a warrior. You devoted yourself to our King and his cause.'

A bitter laugh escaped Theodora's mouth. She had waited so long for acceptance from the Northemers, and finally she had it. Now, when she wasn't sure she needed or wanted it anymore.

Hafder cocked his head in confusion. 'It is true.' He tapped his fingers along the ship's rail. 'I have a proposition for you… Rule with me. Be my Queen – in name only. I don't expect you to be my wife.'

Theodora's eyes widened. Was she hearing Hafder correctly?

'You possess many of the qualities my brother had, and the ones I lack,' he continued. 'We will regroup as a nation, and together we will be unstoppable.' His mouth twitched with excitement. 'You will finally have all the power you have craved.'

Power. Was all this about power?

Was that what she really wanted?

She had sought the power of a crown to please her father and to feed her own ego. But the death of a loved one had a way of exposing her quest for power for what it was: a protective mechanism. A way of compensating for a lack of identity and self-confidence. But now Theodora knew exactly who she was. She was a strong, independent woman. Someone who could forge a new life for herself, on her own terms. Someone with choices. Someone who knew she had all the power she needed within her.

She had nothing to prove to anyone other than herself.

Rayl placed a paw on Theodora's hand, as if to say, *I see you. I see your power.*

A thread of guilt tugged inside her. She had seen the snow leopard and her power, too. It was why she had saved her – but she had also taken Rayl's choices from her, pushing her into servitude.

She bent down and unfastened the snow leopard's collar. Rayl bobbed her head, as if she understood.

'What are you doing?' Hafder asked.

'Freeing her from any obligation to me. Rayl is free to decide her path.'

Hafder shook his head in bewilderment. Theodora knew he would never understand what it meant to be a prisoner of someone else's whims. For the most part, he had always done what he wanted to do, regardless of the consequences. It was why she could never rule with him.

'I relinquish any claim to the crown to you,' she said.

Hafder stared at her for a moment, his brow creased. 'It's your loss,' he grumbled finally, and walked away.

Theodora glanced down at the collar in her hand, remembering the day Malu had presented it to her – their wedding day.

She had admired how finely crafted it was then, but something else now caught her eye. One of the pyramids was lifting at the edge. A hint of something bright glinted back at her from a hollow interior.

She raised the collar to her eye and peered closer. A single ray of light latched onto the mysterious object, illuminating it…

Theodora gasped. It was a diamond. Her breath caught in her throat as she looked for another loose spike. Three pyramids along, she found what she was looking for. Sapphire facets gleamed through the crack where silver met leather.

She had to bite her tongue to stop from screaming. This was what Malu had meant when he'd told her to keep her eye on the pyramids. He had hidden the last of his treasure – gemstones prised from the Ivanian casket more than a year before – in the collar. A safeguard for her if anything happened to him. Her passage to freedom.

'Hafder!'

The Northemer turned and came back. 'Changed your mind?'

She shook her head firmly. 'I will come back to Northem with you, to see that Rayl is released back to the mountains… but after that, can I have this ship? In return for giving up the crown.'

His brow furrowed in question. 'Why do you want a ship?'

'I want to go to the new lands.' Her voice rose in excitement. 'I want Olix to take me to all the places Malu wanted to visit.'

'Sure, if you want to end up dead,' he scoffed.

'Perhaps, but this is what I want – what Malu wanted.'

Sadness crept into Hafder's eyes. His mouth twitched with indecision. Eventually, he nodded.

'Thank you,' she said, and he grunted his acknowledgement.

Theodora would go to the land of the never-ending sun. She would take a path independent of Kypria and its confines. Independent of all confines.

And she would honour Malu's wish to create a better future

for his people. She would invite any Northemer who didn't subscribe to Hafder's 'fight to the death' philosophy to come with her. She would make Malu's purpose her own, and find the peace she hadn't found in power and revenge.

She had no doubt it would be hard, and that it would take all of her wits to survive. But her failures and successes would be her own. Her destiny would be decided by her and her alone – not by her father; not by great weapons, or magic, or victory on a bloody battlefield. It would be a destiny born of freedom and choice. And for the first time in Theodora's life, the choice was truly and completely hers.

CAN I ASK A FAVOUR?

Thank you for reading *The Ice Queen's Revenge*. I hope you enjoyed it and would appreciate if you could take a moment to leave a review. Reviews are the lifeblood of independent authors and key to others learning about our books.

You can **share your review** via your favourite online bookstore or Goodreads.

And did you know there is a Book 0 (A Prequel) in the Kyprian Prophecy Series – *The Earth King's Heir?*

THE EARTH KING'S HEIR: THE KYPRIAN PROPHECY BOOK 0 (A PREQUEL)

One Broken Empire. Two Headstrong Princesses. A Mercurial King. An Idealistic Prince. And a Jealous Adviser. Together they can unite and bring peace to all of their nations but only if they can overcome their prejudices and hate for each other.

Luckily there's a thin line between love and hate, but for some that line can never be crossed.

Jealousy, revenge and greed face off against magic and a powerful prophecy, leaving one undeniable truth – in Kypria, love always has deadly consequences.

The Earth King's Heir follows the journeys of Gwyn, Amund, Alik, Horace, Delrik and Sophia from childhood until the fateful night of the blood moon that precedes *The Firemaster's Legacy* (The Kyprian Prophecy Book 1). You can read *The Earth King's Heir* at any stage during the series.

Get your copy now!

You can find out more about release dates for other platforms and paperback editions, and purchase any of Kylie's books via **www.kyliefennell.com** or the below QR code.

ABOUT THE AUTHOR

Kylie Fennell has made a 25-year career out of wrangling words, working as a journalist, editor and content creator, and more recently an author of speculative fiction. If she wasn't a writer, she'd be a superhero librarian – conquering the Dewey Decimal System by day and saving the world one book at a time by night.

As an Australian writer of European and Aboriginal (Gumbayn-ggirr and Bundjalung) descent she likes to explore culture and identity through her writing, as well as magic…always magic!

Kylie lives in Brisbane (Yuggera and Turrbal Country) with her husband, son and too many pets.

To find out more or to purchase Kylie's books go to *www.kyliefennell.com*.

If you want to stay up-to-date with Kylie's writing **or be part of her book review team** you can sign up to her mailing list via her website. All subscribers receive a **free book** – *Seeds from the Story Tree* – a collection of award-winning speculative fiction stories and other short works, exclusive to Kylie's subscribers.

You can also connect with Kylie on social media.

facebook.com/kyliefennellauthor

twitter.com/kylie_fennell

instagram.com/kylie_fennell

bookbub.com/profile/kylie-fennell

goodreads.com/Kylie_Fennell

pinterest.com/kyliefennell

tiktok.com/@kyliefennellauthor

patreon.com/KylieFennell

BEGINNINGS: THE KYPRIAN PROPHECY – AN ORIGINS NOVELLA

Get it now for free!

No Email Address Required

"Only a fool can't understand that there cannot be light without the darkness, and that power lies in harnessing the very thing people are scared of."

As a silver-eyes Laha has an extraordinary ability to harness the power within nature. She is also a royal companion to the Kengian Princess Mary, and with all of Kypria finally at peace Laha should be content…but she is far from it.

Laha has lost her powers and a darkness claws away inside her. She doesn't fit in at the Lamorian court, nor does she want to. She yearns for a life of excitement and adventure, but most of all she yearns to regain her powers and understand her dark urges.

The answer arrives in the form of a mysterious fortune teller whose prophecy and presence threaten to destroy everyone Laha cares about including the Lamorian Prince Emberto. Despite this she is drawn to the fortune teller and the woman's offer to help her realise the full potential of her powers...if she's willing to embrace her darkness.

Laha's choices lead to discoveries about her own identity and her friends being caught up in a deadly showdown between the most powerful of all Kengians – the Firemasters.

Beginnings is a stand alone novella that also sets the scene for the Kyprian Prophecy series and Book 1 – *The Firemaster's Legacy*.

Beginnings is **available for FREE** on all major online book retail sites including Amazon Kindle, Apple, Google Play, Kobo and Nook. No email address required!

LEIA TALON

DRAGONS
IN THE
WEAVING

BOOK TWO OF ROOTS AND STARS
THE WORLD TREE CHRONICLES

RHIANNON
PUBLISHING

This is a work of fiction. Names, characters, places, and incidents
are a product of the author's imagination. Locales and public names are
sometimes used for atmospheric purposes. Any resemblance to actual
people, living or dead, or to businesses, companies, events,
institutions, or locales is entirely coincidental.

Published by Rhiannon Publishing, 2022
British Columbia, Canada

www.LeiaTalon.com

Cover Design by Lara Wynter / Leia Talon
Pegasus by Glazkova Irina ~ Nutriaaa/depositphotos.com
Book Layout by Rhiannon Publishing

Dragons in the Weaving / Leia Talon ~ First Edition
ISBN: 9780987992376